JACK CHERRY

ELYSIA.

31 "Can you bind the chains of the Pleiades
or loose the cords of Orion?
32 Can you lead forth the Mazzaroth in their season,
or can you guide the Bear with its children?
33 Do you know the ordinances of the heavens?
Can you establish their rule on the earth?

Job 38:31-33

ESV

Table of Contents

Prologue

In life, only three things are guaranteed: death, taxes, and bullies. A humid summer air blanketed everything, dozens of humans scattered about, each of them sticky with regret, bound in jeans and coats. It was supposed to be much colder today. The setting sun lit the sky on fire and danced across the lake, illuminating the dozens of bugs that hovered over the cool water. In the distance the thump and drum of old music, and I mean really old music, echoed off the trees and over a field of ancient vehicles: cars. Hardly anybody drove to this event, except for the locals. The smell of warm grass and trees was left tainted by the odor of oil and beer, a smell only earthlings could consider good.

I never cared for the people, only the cars. They were primitive, invented nearly six hundred years ago. They were little more than toys these days, things that once dazzled and impressed millions now a thing of the past. Technology, as it always does, evolved. Suddenly we realized that the stars are far more exciting to explore than any backwater roads. Times changed just like that, humans were used to it. Old things always fascinated me. The rudimentary mechanisms, the irrelevant fuel techniques, the flimsy and dangerous design. I was firstly amazed by the fact anyone had the audacity to drive one, secondly shocked when I survived my first ride in one.

It was then that I learned a car would give me far less black eyes in my lifetime than other things, most notable of those being the earthlings. Water engulfed me as sharp rocks dug into my legs and hands. My nose burned as I gasped for air and struggled for footing in my wet sneakers. My eye ached with pain, the swelling dampened by the cold water, but that would have to wait. My hair stuck to my forehead, reaching down the bridge of my nose and over my eyes.

"What did I tell you last time, halfbreed?" His voice cracked on the word 'half breed.' "Looks like the smurf didn't learn his lesson."

His words didn't sting as much as the flat rock he threw at my head, thudding against my temple and showing me a thousand stars. I stumbled backwards, the water rising up to my waist as I attempted to escape my pursuers.

"How cute, he thinks he can swim!" The second scoffed while searching for more rocks.

The first snorted a laugh. "Let's hope not, he's just as important at the bottom of that lake as he is on the ground."

Anger bubbled inside me, like it might boil the lake around me and set the trees on fire. I pushed my blue hair out of my face, locking eyes with the two. The taller boy was the one who pushed me in, blond hair and bright eyes looking down at me. The second was a scrawnier kid, dark hair and dark eyes with a sharp nose. I seethed through the water that ran down my face, both of them laughing as I dragged myself through the water towards them. The second threw the flat stone between bursts of sharp, squeaky laughter, smacking against my forearm as I protected my face. My hands shot out for the first, grabbing him by the shoulders and dragging him in with me. He shouted in anger and took a handful of my hair, dragging me under with him. He slammed my face against his knee before letting go. A sharp breath drew water into my lungs before I could resurface, sending me into a coughing fit the moment I broke into the open air. Blood and lake water stained the arm of my jacket as I struggled to breathe and protect myself from more rocks.

"You are dead, Space Boy." The taller boy was absolutely livid, trudging through the water towards me. He threw a fist that crashed into the corner of my jaw, sending me to my hands and knees in the water. Before I could get up again, he planted one foot against my back, pushing me underwater and holding me there. I could hear his scratchy laughter as I thrashed for air. My lungs burned as I held the shallow breath in my lungs, desperation overcoming sense.

I could hear something, yelling from somewhere. The world began going black as the pressure on my back disappeared. I broke the water once more, drawing in a sharp breath and scrambling away. Flopping to my back, I could see Wendy, my savior once more. She held the boy by his collar, dropping two more explosive punches across his face. Red stained her hand as the boy's grunts of pain turned to what was almost a sob. Nobody would ever believe me if I told them Charlie Baker was crying after a girl wailed on him, not that people listened to me at all. Wendy dropped him into the water, stomping on his ankle and twisting her foot.

"You could have killed him, slaghead!" Wendy screamed sharply.

"You're still siding with the freak?" The scrawny boy on shore shouted, wiping the blood from his nose.

"He's my brother, moron! And he's more human than either of you monsters are!"

The boy in the water shot to his feet, grabbing Wendy by the shirt and tackling her backward. She shoved him off sideways, regaining her footing with ease. The boy threw two wild punches, Wendy bobbing out of their range easily. She threw a sharp uppercut, his head snapping backwards with the clack of his teeth. He wobbled for a moment on his feet, then splashed into the water. Wendy jabbed a bloody finger at the boy on shore.

"If you don't want him to drown, you'd best drag him out." Her voice was sharp, and had an edge like a knife. The world obeyed her every command; she was older and taller than us after all. The boy trembled there for a moment, listening to the bubbles slipping from Charlie's lips. He splashed into the water and grabbed him under his arms, dragging him across the rocks onto the shore. Charlie slapped him away the moment they reached the shore, both of them scrambling to escape. Wendy watched them until they disappeared into the trees before turning to me.

I coughed hard. "They're gonna complain to their parents, again. You're gonna get in trouble again, big time."

"I don't care. What did we talk about?" She held a hand out to me, concern and compassion gracing her face.

"Stop blocking with my face?" I teased, smacking my hand into hers as she pulled me out of the water.

"I'm being serious, Apollo. Does this look like my joking face to you?" She gave a frown, one so overdramatic I thought it was a joke.

"I don't think anyone can tell when you're joking," I mumbled.

"Come on now, I'm not that intimidating." She slipped her only barely damp jacket around my shoulders, the puffy sleeves wrapping around me in a toasty hug.

"I didn't say anything, I even kept all my jokes and... what do you call them?"

"Smart ass comments?"

"Yeah, those."

Wendy let out a sigh, wiping the blood off her knuckles onto her t-shirt. "You know I can't always be there for you, right? You gotta learn to stand up for yourself, without making them more upset."

"I'm all brains, you know that."

"Yeah you're smart alright, but you lack common sense." She tapped me on the forehead with a wet finger.

"Common sense is boring, I prefer uncommon sense." I tilted my nose up in the air indignantly.

"Like I said, smart ass." She ruffled my damp hair before brushing her curly, orange hair to the side.

We hiked back through the woods, up and over a grassy knoll that looked down at the rows of old cars below. We stood there for a second before Wendy dropped down into the grass, rolling her shoulders with cracks and pops. I plopped down next to her, near immediately making mud in a puddle around me.

"I'm important, right?" I raised an eyebrow.

"What kind of question is that? Of course you are, why would you think differently?" Wendy looked at me with slight shock.

I sighed. "One of those boys said I was just as important at the bottom of the lake as on the ground."

"Well they're wrong, dead wrong. You're just as important as me or Dad or Mom."

"That's a low bar." I rolled my eyes jokingly.

Wendy punched me on the shoulder playfully. "Laugh it up, you know what I mean. You're important on this planet and the next. Wherever you go, wherever you are, you will always be important to me. You got that?"

I nodded. "I got it."

"Good, now put it in that hard drive and never forget it."
She tapped the side of my damp head with her finger.

"But why? Why am I important? I'm just a... halfbreed."

"You think you're the only Half-Martian out there? There are
dozens and dozens of people just like you scattered throughout
all the systems, all searching for someone like them. You gotta be
there for them, understand? They need you, Apollo, they need
someone like them. Someone who is... different, in the best
way."

I picked at the dandelions around me, blowing fuzz into the
air before dropping my hands into my lap. "How will I ever find
them if I'm stuck on this stupid planet?"

"You're not stuck, nobody ever truly is. If you wanted to
leave, you could, and you will. One day you'll take off in your
own ship and see the cosmos for yourself. So will I." Wendy
smiled at me with a truly joyful grin.

"I can't wait to see it." I looked up at the first stars appearing
in the rapidly darkening sky.

"Don't be too impatient, there's still beauty to see here too."
She looked around and took a deep breath. "This planet is just as
much a part of the adventure as any other."

"Apollo! Wendy! Time to roll!" Dad's voice called from the
field below.

"Coming!" Wendy called, shooting up and waving down to
him. "Alright, let's go. You need a shower, you smell like a lake."

She crouched down with a smirk gesturing towards her back. I climbed onto her shoulders and held on for dear life as she romped down the hill, pretending to be some beast destroying a city, with the screams of pretend victims and all. I liked it, it made me feel big and scary. She did this all the time to cheer me up, and it never failed.

"How do you know all this stuff?" I asked as we reached the bottom of the hill.

Wendy made one more explosion sound before responding.

"Because I'm so old and wise. Don't worry, I have seven years on you. When you're old and decrepit like me, you'll know all the wonders of the universe."

I raised an eyebrow again. "You're only seventeen."

She shrugged. "Like I said, old and decrepit."

↳ 1 ↢

Zion

"Sir, I'm receiving an SOS signal from a nearby planet."

The words shot me to my feet, my head spinning as I rushed to the deck and dropped into my seat. Familiar lights, buttons, switches, and levers surrounded me, the only place that truly felt like home. The cosmos flickered just on the other side of the glass, light glowing behind the frost growing across the window

"Any bounty yet?" I asked, impatiently crawling across the dash to wipe the frost away with the puffy sleeve of my coat. The defrosters in this ship never did work well.

"It has yet to go public."

"What planet?"

"Proxima Centauri B, also known as Zion."

"Any incident reports?"

"Thirty five injured and three dead in recent years, twenty ships disabled and eleven abandoned."

"Death trap, just how we like it, right Thirteen?"

"I do warn you, the red dwarf star this planet orbits is well overdue for a solar flare. Being on that planet when it occurs may add us to the incident reports."

"We'll be fast, in and out. Set course for Proxima Centauri and fire up the hypercore."

"As you command."

The ship rattled as the wings unfolded into position, energy coursing through everything as the purr of the hypercore shook the walls. I slipped into the harness of my seat and buckled down tightly as a hiss filled the compartment. The pressure in the cabin rose slowly, my ears crackling painfully as I flicked on the floodlights. The usual white glow faded as a blaring red filled the room, the whir and whine of the engine rising in pitch.

"Prepare for light jump."

The world went silent, nothing to be seen outside the cabin but black, empty space. The ship slowly faded from sight, darkness creeping in from the windows like a living shadow consuming everything. With my eyes open, I saw nothing. My chest felt empty, my body shifting in its seat as I went weightless. A fog wreathed around my mind. It felt like a dream, and it never got old.

The ship snapped back into reality, snapping my head forward as light filled my eyes once more. Everything buzzed and hummed with energy as a metallic taste filled my mouth, energy washing over everything. The light in the cabin flickered on once more, a new world coming into view.

"Proxima Centauri B: a terrestrial exoplanet, home to three satellite colonies, the IEO's next candidate for terraforming."

It was remarkable, a brown red marble pockmarked with blue lakes and oceans. The smears of blue and brown felt just like Earth, but the terrain here could change on a dime. Lines were drawn all over the planet, appearing to be cracked and held together by ash gray glue.

"Show me the SOS signal." I flicked a switch next to me as a blue projection covered the glass before me, pointing out major terrestrial features and highlighting dangerous areas in yellow. A red dot popped up on part of the planet, just next to a large ocean and smack in the center of the most dangerous area of the planet. "Just our luck. Run the auto landing sequence, I'll need to suit up for this one."

⤙ ⤙ ⤙

My hand smacked onto the hydraulics above me as we dropped to the ground. Thirteen was always smooth as butter in his landings, leaving me only slightly concerned as to what awaited me. The ramp dropped down with a hiss as I made my way onto this new planet. Of all the systems I had visited, I had never visited here, and it was clear why.

A rocky landscape surrounded us on all sides. We had landed on a tall plateau, the closest clear landing site to the signal. It was a half a mile repel down and a two mile hike over rocky terrain, easy for somebody better prepared than I, but a poor engineer blames his calculator.

"Lock down the ship. I don't expect trouble but keep your radar online." I glanced down at my wrist, my watch slipped over my suit. It flickered for a moment before projecting a small hologram of the nearby terrain, a red arrow pointing me towards my next paycheck. I ran a hand over the hologram, it flickering out.

My suit clunked as I walked, dragging me down to the ground as I latched onto a large boulder and threw my line down the sheer face of the cliff. I gazed down the steep rock, my breath fogging the glass of my helmet for a moment.

"Your heart rate is rising rapidly, is there a problem?" Thirteen's voice echoed in my helmet and rattled my skull.

"Nope. No problem here." I lied through gritted teeth.

The rope snapped into place on my belt with ease, holding me tight as I leaned out over the cliff. Much to my dismay, I looked down. Fool's error. A mechanism on my belt hummed as it slowly but surely lowered me down the cliff, my feet guiding myself downwards. I examined the brownish red sky, looking for anything to distract me from the certain death below.

"That is the red dwarf star that is threatening to kill us. It's more than overdue for a solar flare, it could happen at any minute-"

"Thirteen, you've said all that before and if you don't shut up right now I am going to replace you with a toaster." My eyes squeezed shut, struggling to keep my cool.

"As you wish."

Before long, but not soon enough, I touched down on the ground. I buried the prospect of climbing this sheer rock and stowed my fear, turning towards the signal and starting my ruck.

The terrain was sharp, mostly sand and gravel with long pads of stone the size of football fields. I slid down a long hill, my suit turning a bluish gray as I covered myself in sand. In the distance, I could see a smattering of metal like a scar on the planet. A wave of relatively warm air washed over my suit. The air of this planet was freezing, the slightest hint of heat felt like a blast of fire. A flicker of light caught my eye, then an even more beautiful sight. Rippling waves of light danced across the permanently sundown sky, waving ribbons of blue and green contrasting an ever red and orange sky. Aurora. The sight drew my breath away, then sucked every ounce of confidence from my body.

"Solar flare." I gasped.

"Sir, I'm detecting an increased presence of electromagnetic radiation." Thirteen's voice was fuzzy now, the waves tearing at the signal between us.

"I can see that Thirteen, stay on this channel and keep the engines warm, I'll be back ASAP."

My heels pounded at the sand and rock as I dashed across the valley between me and my money. I ran past the parts and pieces of the odd ship, a model I didn't recognize, still smoldering on this frigid planet. My boots slammed into a large metal sheet as I ran up a long ramp of metal, what I believed to be the wing of a very large ship. I scanned the area, looking desperately for any survivors or a black box for the ship.

"Hello? Anybody out there?" My voice rasped as my heart threatened to drum right through my chest. Finally, my eyes locked onto a small pod, half buried in sand but intact. I slid down the ramp and scrambled across the sand, skidding to a stop next to the oddly ornate tin can. The door was bent, unable to open with a gap in the seal of the ship.

"Nonono please don't be dead. They don't pay me for dead bodies."

I rushed to the other side of the ship, finding a large circle of glass at the front of the pod. My gloves stuck to the dirt on the glass as I brushed it away. It was dark inside, the reflection of the aurora making it near impossible to see. My hands cupped over my visor as I got closer, the vague shape of a person bubbling up from the pool of shadows. I scanned for anything heavy or sharp enough to break through the inch thick glass, but nothing presented itself. The pockets of my suit jingled as I dug around, finding a spark plug for my bike in my pocket.

I sighed, "What a waste."

I dropped the spark plug into the sand, stamping my boot onto it regretfully. I grabbed a handful of the ceramics, being careful not to let them cut my suit. A deep breath filled my lungs, then I reared my arm back and snapped it forwards. The ceramics crashed into the glass, exploding it into a million circular pieces.

"I've always wanted to do that." My lips curled into a devious smile.

The pod rocked as I jumped inside, barely catching my balance on a nearby chair. It was nearly empty, only one person inside. She was tall, very tall. Her skin was ghostly pale like a Martian, but her wavy hair was pinkish purple like a Jovian. Her hair framed the gentle curve of her face, her stature fair and gentle even in a lack of consciousness. She was pretty, beautiful even, wearing a loose white shirt and pants that were smudged with grease and ash. This would pay well. I could see a hearty dinner and a round of drinks already.

"Hey! Hey! Wake up!" I grabbed her by the shoulders, shaking her violently. Her hair frizzed and her head drooped downwards. I shook her again, grabbing her face and opening one eye. "Come on now, you're not even wounded!"

Her eyes were gray, silver moonlight washing over a black sand shore. Her pupil dilated but had no focus. If nothing else, she was alive.

"Come on now! Wake up already!" I patted the side of her face only slightly gently as the temperature slowly rose around me. I groaned and pulled a spare tank of oxygen from my belt, slipping the mask over her face and tying the tank to her waist. My arms slipped under her arms and legs, her limbs firm with muscles under the white clothes she wore. Despite this, she felt strangely light.

"They better pay me extra." I grumbled as I dropped down from the pod.

The wind was picking up as a shift in temperature coated the planet. The aurora was getting brighter, the ribbons whipping in the wind like flags. The soft sand under me threatened to give way as my feet carried me up the steep hill out of the valley.

We reached the shear wall in far too much time, the rope snapping into my belt once more. I tied on the woman next, also attaching her to my belt. The mechanism roared to life, struggling to drag both of us up the rock. The weight in my arms shifted, a groan coming from the woman as her eyes slid open. Perfect timing. She shouted in fear, holding onto me with a constricting grip.

"Calm down! I'm here to save you!"

"Save me? This does not look like saving me!" She shouted, her voice muffled by the oxygen mask. She had an odd accent, her words swooping and diving at every vowel. It was like nothing I had ever heard before. Admittedly, it sparked curiosity in me.

"The atmosphere here is mostly oxygen and carbon dioxide, that mask is the only thing keeping you conscious. Now hang on tight. If we don't get out of here soon, we're cooked, literally."

Impossibly, her face went even more pale. Her arms tightened around my neck as another strong wind pressed us against the wall of rock. The rope groaned under both of our weight, fraying at the edge against the rock. The mechanism stuttered to a stop, holding us halfway up the rope.

"Is that supposed to happen?"

"Totally!" I beamed, giving the contraption a few firm whacks. The wind roared again, swinging us back and forth against the wall.

"Thirteen, requesting emergency evac! Thirteen? Come in, Thirteen?" I shouted into my comms with no reply but static. Of course an electromagnetic storm would cut my comms, just my luck. I wrapped the rope around my hand and tried to pull us up further, to no avail. A low rumble filled the air, the wall of rock crumbling and cracking at the roar of thruster exhaust beating against soft stone. A boulder cracked off the shear wall, falling down towards us. My boots dug into the rock as I pushed us to the side, swinging out of the way just in the nick of time. The Thirteen hovered over and down the edge of the cliff, the back door open and facing us.

I ran along the wall of the cliff once more, pulling my utility knife from the sheathe. With all my strength, I jumped from the wall and cut the rope. The rope snapped from the mechanism as we soared through the air, crashing into the hard metal of the ship. Thirteen tilted forward, rolling us into the cargo bay and snapping the door shut. For a moment, we laid on the ground breathless, then alarms rang off throughout the ship.

"Sir, the solar flare."

"I nearly forgot." I untied the woman from my belt and shot to my feet. "You stay here, and maybe hold onto something."

"Wait!" Her voice faltered through the blaring noise, failing to break through the hum of the engines. I slipped into the cockpit and dropped into my chair, taking manual control immediately. The joystick vibrated in my hand as I pushed the throttle forward, taking course away from the star. We pushed through the atmosphere, then broke out into open space. The ship slowed to a halt, the gravity fading as our speed decreased.

"Problem solved." I sighed, leaning back into my chair.

"Afraid not, the radiation appears to have knocked our communications and orienteering systems offline."

"I noticed. Luckily, we can fix that."

"It has also compromised the stability of our thrusters, which are rising in temperature rapidly."

"Okay, less good."

"Lastly, we're on reserve life support systems."

"You could've started with that!" I rubbed my eyes with an exasperated sigh. "Are any of the satellite colonies nearby?"

"Yes, a spaceport is headed our way in its orbit now."

"Good, use the reserve thrusters to guide us into its trajectory, we'll land there for repairs. I'm on life support duty, you fly."

"What do we do about our guest?"

"I told her to stay put, just make sure she doesn't break anything."

"Sir, she's behind you."

The ship went silent for a moment, my chair squeaking as I spun around. She was floating in the doorway, holding the frame with a white knuckle grip, the reserve thrusters sputtering intermittently. She looked frightened, deeply frightened.

"I demand to know what's going on here." She furrowed her brow, her lip wobbling.

"You... sent out an SOS signal? I saved you, you're welcome." I gave her a grin. She was lucky to have someone as good at my job as I was nearby.

"I did no such thing." Her forehead scrunched further, gray eyes not daring to lose sight of me, as if I was a rabid animal waiting to make another senseless move.

"Must have been automated, we received the signal four hours ago. You're lucky I picked you up instead of someone more...eccentric."

"I don't understand...where am I?"

"Welcome aboard The Thirteen, finest cruiser in the cosmos." I threw out my arms, leaning back in my chair.

"This can't be real, none of this is real." The woman grabbed at her head, then snapped her hands back to the wall as she began to float backwards.

"Ooookay then, Thirteen, how close to the spaceport are we? The sooner we get her out of here the sooner we can get back to Mars."

"Still ten minutes out, sir."

"What was that?" The woman gasped. Astonished by the voice in the walls.

I rubbed my eyes, exasperated. "It's the AI of the ship."

"AI? Spaceport? Mars? What is going on?" Panic was quickly rising in her voice.

I leaned forward in my chair, showing my hands plainly trying to be less threatening. She stared at me suspiciously. "Calm down, the life support systems can't handle a panic attack right now. You might be having temporal amnesia, after your ship crashed I can't blame you."

"Temporal amnesia?"

"Do you know anything? Okay, let's start with this. What is your name?" I spoke slowly and clearly, and just a little condescendingly.

"Melinoe."

"Melinoe?"

"You don't believe me?"

"No, no. So, Melinoe–can I call you Mel?"

"No." She frowned.

"Okay Mel, where are you right now?"

"Space."

"In?"

"A ship."

"Alright, good enough for me. If you want gravity you'll have to wear a jumpsuit, there's a few in the closet. Take a seat somewhere, we'll be on a spaceport before long and you can fly off to wherever you belong and I can get paid." I stood from my chair and walked past Mel.

"I still don't know what that is!" She followed me down the hallway and into the cargo bay. I stopped by the wall and stomped on the ground twice, a small hatch popping up from the flooring. The hinges groaned as I swung open the door, steam pouring out from the hatch. I waved the steam from my face and looked around.

"It's a place where you can take a transport anywhere you need to go, they'll take you wherever you need." My suit dropped over my shoulders as I slipped out of the heavy cloth. I tied it around my waist tightly, trading the top half for my jacket and pulling my toolbox from a shelf. I tossed her an extra jumpsuit. She caught it haphazardly and sent herself slowly spinning in the air. She squealed nervously.

"I don't...know where I need to go. Am I supposed to know?" Her voice wavered again as she struggled to slip the jumpsuit over her tarnished clothes. I stopped in my tracks to stare at her for a moment, taking account of her once more. Skin like a Martian, hair like a Jovian, ears like a human, and taller than me, significantly taller.

"Go to where you're from." I shrugged.

"Where I'm from?" A light sewn into the collar of the jumpsuit flickered on as she slowly floated down to the ground, gravity coming back to her.

"Like, whatever planet you were born on." The toolbox clunked onto the ground as I dropped into the hatch, pipes and panels surrounding me. I pulled open one panel, an array of buttons, sliders, and lights presenting itself. It was a simple fix, the radiation had imbalanced the atmosphere of the ship.

"I don't know where I'm...from." Her voice echoed off the metal around me, even the pipes seemed to go silent at the words. I shook my head, leaning against the panel.

"Look lady, I can't tell you where you should go or what you should do, and I certainly can't fix your amnesia. I'll take you to the spaceport, you can ask someone to run your name on public records, and they'll point you to where you should head until you get your memories back fully."

I heard no response, just a quiet, muffled sniffling sound. My conscience begged me to go comfort her, to do something, but my brain reminded me of the task at hand. You can't cry if you can't breathe, better sobbing than dead. The valve squeaked as I turned it with all my strength, letting more oxygen flow into the ship. Using the panel, I regulated the ratio of oxygen to nitrogen, seventy eight point one to twenty one point nine. My trusty duct tape helped seal a leaky pipe that I had yet to afford replacing. I pulled myself out of the hatch and looked around, the woman nowhere to be found. Somewhere in the ship, I could hear Thirteen's voice. He was making sure I didn't hear. The audacity.

"Thirteen?" No response. "Thirteen!"

I tossed my toolbox back on its shelf, stomping back towards the bridge. An invisible rope pulled me to a halt before I entered, waiting and listening for a moment.

"You're not alive?"

"Not exactly. I am only a program designed by Apollo."

"But you can speak?"

"Indeed. Consider me the brain of this ship, and the ship my body. I can feel and see the world through the parts of the ship, I compartmentalize all of the data and relay it to Apollo in an efficient manner."

"I don't understand."

"I find it's best not to understand everything."

I rounded the corner and with a huff of breath. "So, you two best friends now?"

The girl was sitting in the captain's seat, examining the buttons and levers all around her. She turned back to me with fear in her eyes, terrified of what I might do.

"Merely making our guest at home, sir."

"Well don't, she's just like every other passenger Thirteen. Don't get attached."

"As you wish."

I jerked my thumb over my shoulder. "Out of my seat."

Without a word, she jumped out of the seat and into the passenger's chair. I rolled my eyes and plopped down into my chair, reading a screen to my right. I flicked a switch and the HUD flickered on, the projection showing the rapidly approaching station. Radio static fuzzed in the speakers around me as I twisted a dial next to me.

"Thirteen, did you fix the comms?" I raised an eyebrow.

"Yes sir, I believe it may be user error."

"Very funny. Give me a hand here." I bit my lip as I twisted and turned the dial, struggling to find the proper frequency. A gentle pressure guided the dial to the left, voices pushing through the static. I was glad I invested in haptic control on these.

"This is Apollo Harrison, captain of The Thirteen, requesting docking." My voice relayed back through the speakers, fuzzy and muted but audible.

"Registration Code?"

"114106."

Silence for a moment, only the clack of computer keys. "Code accepted, you're clear for docking at Bay Five. Manual docking only."

I bunched my brow. "Is there a reason for that?"

"Suspicious personnel reported at other spaceports. I'd bet it's nothing but the LCCE is sticking their nose in our business."

I scoffed. "When aren't they?"

"Amen to that."

The Lawful Cosmic Conduct Enforcement, or as I like to call them, the galactic snitches. Originally meant to prevent and protect explorers from pirates and thieves, but after an amendment was passed to permit the installation of armaments on civilian craft for the sake of self defense, they quickly got bored and became the cosmic meter maids. Speeding infractions, parking infractions, non-regulatory modification infractions, not a person alive who can fly a ship who likes them. They would much rather inconvenience honest trade-folk than stop real terrorists like Angel Lights.

The comms snapped silent. I took hold of the controls as a green light flickered on at the side of the satellite. It was a tall, long spire, a long ring like a roulette wheel wrapped around the center, ships stuck to the outside of the ring. We pulled in between two large freighters, latching onto the ring with a loud clunk and a hiss.

"This is our stop. Thirteen, keep an eye on the ship while I'm gone. I won't be long." I stood from my chair and gestured for Mel to follow me.

"Yes sir."

We walked down the hallway to a small door. I tapped a nearby screen, the door slid open and revealed a long white hallway. My suit adjusted to the new environment as I climbed through the door, Mel's light footsteps following me. A man in an orange jumpsuit stood at the end of the walkway, a clipboard in hand.

"Need anything for your ship?" He asked.

"Recharge the life support, radiation got into my nitrogen supply."

"Understood." The man nodded, pressing a few buttons on his clipboard.

We stepped past him and into the ring. We followed the circle until we found another corridor, this one with a moving sidewalk that carried us into the spire. Mel seemed terrified and fascinated by everything, worry began bubbling in me. A tourist this far out was a recipe for disaster, and she knew nothing. I shook the thoughts away and focused on my money. We stepped off the moving sidewalk and into the main spire. A glass elevator in the center took people up and down to different facilities in the satellite. This main hub consisted of many benches for people resting and waiting for their ship to be fueled or repaired. Several windows were scattered along the walls, exhausted looking employees behind all of them. A sign above one read 'CTA', exactly what I needed.

The CTA, or Cosmic Trade Assembly, was originally a small group of tradesfolk seeking to create fair conditions around the cosmos, giving everyone a fair shot at wealth. As most organizations do, they eventually became corrupt. They sought to seek wealth and riches by any means necessary, "for the good of all people". What actually happened was work conditions became so hazardous that many blue collar workers risked their lives daily to make a dime.

To become wealthy is to exploit the needy, and the entry-level-hell of careers in the galaxy are often the most self-destructive; even I barely survived working under their rule for a time. In their eyes, debt made slaves, and those who tried to run were hunted by bounty hunters paid by them. If you were caught, the cost of paying the bounty hunter was added to your debt. Amongst other services, the CTA pays these bounty hunters or "Sharks" top dollar for dangerous work. Whether you bring them back alive or not, their lives are ruined by these hunters.

We strolled up to the window, the aged woman sitting behind the glass eying me and rolling her eyes as she saw the smug look I held proudly. I leaned against the window and slid my card through a small gap. Without a word, she took the card, slotted it into her computer, and examined what popped up. She glanced at me again, then back to the computer.

"A little young to be a Shark are we?" She scoffed.

"It's a part time job."

"Clearly. What can I do for you, Mr. Harrison?"

"I picked up Mel here on Zion after her ship sent out a default SOS signal. I'm here to collect the rescue fare."

"Uh huh, well it appears the signal you detected originated from a ship not registered with IEO or CTA records." She pursed her lips and gave me a smug smile now. "Tough luck kid."

The IEO, those damn tyrants. Even the acronym made me gag. The Interstellar Exploration Organization held an iron fist over all scientific advancement, they held every discovery, every data point, and every piece of knowledge with a vice grip. The only way to access this knowledge is to pay ridiculous sums to attend university, a boot camp to create loyal explorers to sell their discoveries to IEO. I'd seen too many explorers fade into obscurity under their demand, and after twelve of their finest went missing after expressing desire to separate from their organization, I knew it was rotten to the core. Knowledge is power, and they held their cards close to their chest. They sought to perfect human knowledge, but swept their dirt under the rug whenever it forced them to call themselves wrong. CTA, IEO, LCCE; role models for a kingdom of manipulating monsters, proof that money really is the root of all evil.

I gave an exhausted laugh. "You're hilarious, just give me my money."

"You don't have any money to collect, there's no bounty on this signal, understand?"

"It must be an error, check again."

She rolled her eyes again, typing on her computer once more. "Still nothing, obviously."

I rolled my head back and blew an exasperated sigh into the air. "Then check missing persons."

"Name?"

"Melinoe...what's your last name?" I looked back to Mel.

"My last name...my last name is-" She looked down at her hands for a moment, brow furrowed as she struggled to think. "I don't know."

"You don't know your own last name?" My teeth gritted, fear rising up in my gut. My money was falling through my fingers like grains of sand, all this for nothing. "What about identification? Do you have your card?"

"Card?" Mel raised an eyebrow.

The woman laughed to herself and leaned back in her chair. "Better luck next time."

↵ 2 ↩

Spaceport

My fingers ached as I sat there, biting my nails as my leg bounced quickly. I looked around, the entire hub felt like it was looking at me, I checked my watch again. The ship wouldn't be ready for another fifteen minutes, and every minute I spent here felt like an eternity. Quiet music played through the worn speakers of the room, the squeaky horns creating a dissonant sound that put me ever more on edge. I thought I would go crazy if I had to sit and listen to those wailing trumpets for a second longer.

"Apollo, I-"

I put a hand between her face and mine, looking away. My knee didn't stop bouncing for a moment, I didn't know what to do. Without that money, I couldn't afford to eat. It would take everything I had left just to get back to Mars, if I didn't starve before then. Payments were coming up, and I had no money. I could feel the Sharks breathing down my neck already. The predator was becoming the prey.

"I'm sorry, okay? Is that what you want to hear?" Mel sighed.

"No, I don't want to hear anything from you right now."

"You'd rather sit there bouncing your knee and biting your nails anxiously?"

I glanced at her with daggers. "I'm thinking."

Nothing but an exhausted huff could be heard. I looked down at my watch again, only a minute had passed. I stood up, pacing back and forth to shake out my nerves. Mel traced me with her eyes, staring at me through her lashes with a frown. I scoffed. "Don't look at me like that."

"You were gonna ditch me here for money, how else should I look at you?"

"It's my job! Now I spent all that gas and sustained all those damages for not even a cent!"

"Well I'm sorry for crashing on a planet with no memories and no money! If I had known it would inconvenience you so much I wouldn't have done that!" She scoffed sarcastically.

A few people nearby glared at us, watching intently. I turned away from Mel and pinched the bridge of my nose. "I can't stand you and I don't even know you."

"Now you know how I feel! I've only known you for thirty minutes and you're already the most insufferable, selfish, and rude person I've ever met."

"You don't even remember anyone else!" I threw my hands in the air.

"Exactly! The bar was very low and you still managed to crawl under it." Her voice had a sharp edge to it as she also stood from her seat. "I'm done with you. I'll find someone else to help me, anyone other than you."

She walked past me with a sharp elbow in my side. A sharp laugh escaped me as I sat down once more. "Good luck with that! Have fun being kidnapped or murdered!"

"Screw you!" She screamed as she sat down on the other side of the hub, arms folded. I folded my arms as well, looking down at the ground with a grumble. Minutes passed, the hub tense with the fire between us. My eyes stayed glued to the ground as I heard the whispers of others around me.

"Those kids couldn't shut up soon enough."

"Lovers' quarrel maybe?"

"About what I expected from a halfbreed."

The last word made my head snap to whoever had said it, a skinny man with glasses and a briefcase. Nobody would care if some snobby businessman never left the outer rim, would they? My senses caught up to me and I snapped my head forward again. I spared one glance at her, then watched intently. Two broad shouldered men sat down next to her on either side, a shorter one with a bald head and a taller one with a long beard and thin hair.

"Rough pilot?" The bearded one asked.

"That's an understatement." She glared up at me, forcing me to look away for only a moment.

"Happens to the best of us, can't trust nobody these days." The bald one grinned.

"You know what, it's your lucky day. I happen to own a transport business and I'm willing to take you wherever you need to recover from your amnesia. It's not fair to treat someone like that, especially someone who's going through what you are, and I'm feeling generous."

"I'm not sure...where to go." Mel mumbled.

"We're headed to Mars next, to the capitol city actually. It's a good place, you'll be safe there." The bearded man put a hand on her shoulder, his sleeve slipping down to reveal a tattoo on his wrist; a circle with a plus in it. My stomach dropped, a deep rooted fear bubbling back up into my system. I stood up slowly, but my feet were cemented to the ground with deep rooted terror.

"I think I would like that." Mel nodded.

"Don't." My throat croaked, barely a sound at all.

Mel looked up at me with disgust, standing from her seat. "I'd like to leave now, if that's alright."

"Certainly." The bearded man stood and looked at me as well.

I took a deep breath, a memory welling up in my mind. Wendy, teaching me to fight. Her hands were gentle on mine as she taught me how to form a fist. I blinked hard and let out a deep breath. My legs were stiff, but I walked. "Get away from her."

The second man stood up now, stepping between Mel and me. "You've done more than enough, pal. I suggest you walk."

"Mel, listen to me, these guys are not your friends." I looked past the man and locked eye contact. "I'm sorry for what I said and did but you need to trust me on this."

She glared at me. "I don't need you to tell me what to do."

"Walk, kid." The short man declared, shoving me backwards. The dissonant music wailed louder, I could hear my pulse in my ear. My breath picked up and I swallowed hard.

I took one sharp step forward, slamming my fist across his face. He stumbled, dazed and confused as I rushed forward and kicked him in the sternum. He tripped over the bench and fell backwards, thudding into the metal flooring. The bearded man stepped forward, towering over me. He threw two punches, I dodged the first and pushed the second away. I raised my fist into his gut, but he didn't flinch. Fear boiled my blood as I did it again, then once more. He looked at me with a smirk, elbowing me in the side of the head. He shoved me backwards, against the glass of the elevator. I raised my hands, barely blocking the two more blows he dropped down on me. His hands were like metal clamps as they locked down on my forearms. My arms didn't budge as I attempted to pull away, his grip felt like it crushed the bones in my wrist. He threw me to the side, pulling his knee up into my gut. The ground welcomed me as the air was sucked from my lungs, the world spinning. I failed to block a harsh kick to the ribs, pain throbbing my heart.

"That's enough," Mel said.

I rolled away from a hard stomp that barely missed my head. My hands tried to pull me away as I scratched at the metal floor. His hand clamped around my leg and dragged me backwards, twisting my ankle sharply. I flopped over on my front, kicking at the man's hands. He shouted in pain and let go as my boot made contact with his knuckles with a crunch. I sat up and scrambled backwards, the man stomping down on my leg and twisting his heel. I shouted in pain, my hands helplessly latching onto his boot.

"That is quite enough." A cool, flat voice declared. An electric buzz filled the air, the man seizing with bunched shoulders. He flopped to the ground, body twitching with pain. Above him stood a tall woman in a dark uniform, her face calm and collected. Her skin was dark brown, pairing well with her deep purple hair and eyes. The tight curls of her hair were bunched up in a low ponytail running down her back like a river of amethyst. She held a long stun stick loosely at her side, eying the man and me.

"Officer Sintara." My voice wobbled with pain and fear of who stood in front of me. The second man swayed on his feet just behind her, a thin blade held at his side. He rushed towards her, knife poised to strike. She sidestepped the swipe swiftly, cracking the metal stun stick over his ribs. He pivoted and slashed at her again, the knife dropping from his hand as she smacked the metal over his wrist. She twisted the handle and jabbed the end into his neck, electricity burning into his skin as he fell to the side as well. She turned back to me.

"Nice to see you again, Apollo." Her voice was flat, devoid of emotion. It didn't take a threatening voice for her to scare somebody. She slid the stun stick back into a holster at her side and held a hand out to me. I carefully grabbed her hand, limping as she pulled me to her feet.

"I didn't think I'd ever say this, but nice to see you too." I dusted myself off and took a deep breath.

"Tell me, for who exactly are you causing all this racket?" Officer Sintara folded her arms and turned to Mel, who stood with terror on her pale face.

↩ ↩ ↩

The plates clanked onto the table as a delicious aroma filled the air, making my mouth water. The plates were lined with eggs and sausage, three fluffy pancakes stacked high smeared with jam and topped with strawberries. The real thing too, not the freeze dried and resaturated stuff. Warm mugs of coffee were set down next to us, the sweet smell reminding me of home. I eyed the food hungrily, then realization dropped onto my shoulders.

"I can't afford this." I squinted at Officer Sintara. Sintara looked at me over the edge of her mug, taking a long sip of her coffee. She didn't even put any sugar or cream in it, that monster.

"Dig in, my treat." She spoke into her cup. I glanced at Mel who already dug into the food as if she'd never eaten before. The fork was heavy in my hand as I took a stab at the sausage. "It's not poison, I promise." Sinatra rolled her eyes. I took a bite and, surprisingly, didn't die.

"You know Apollo?" Mel asked curiously.

"We know each other." Sintara took a bite of the eggs scattered on her plate. Mel looked at me with curiosity and confusion, to which I shrugged with a half-hearted laugh.

"So, you're not...mad?" I asked cautiously.

She swallowed down her bite and stared through my soul. "Me? Mad? Why would I ever be so? Please do inform us."

Mel's eyes dug deeper, trying to scrape the information out of me with her eyes alone. I sighed and looked down at my lap like a child with their hand in the cookie jar. "I disabled your warp core."

"And?"

"Left you on Titan for two weeks."

"What else?"

"That was it!"

"What else did you do, Apollo?"

I sighed. "I stole your chain code to slip through LCCE barricades."

"Now that we're all caught up on what happened." Sintara folded her hands in front of her. "No, I'm not mad."

"Really?" I reached out for the mug in front of me and took a long sip, she remembered how I like my coffee; overflowing with sugar.

"The past is the past. I saw you were in trouble, so I helped. Now I need your help."

I cleared my throat. I wasn't sure I believed her. "How so?"

"We'll talk business later. For now, I'd like to meet your new friend."

Mel's hands slapped onto the table, the cutlery jumping in the air. "He is not my friend."

Sintara raised her eyebrows, her voice with only the smallest hint of sarcasm. "Really? I've yet to hear of anyone who could resist Apollo's charisma."

"He may have rescued me from that planet but I am not required to like him." Mel frowned.

Sintara nodded slowly. "True words. Tell me about yourself then."

"I...My name is Melinoe. I crashed on that planet and..." Mel stopped, slouching back into her seat.

"I'm still listening."

"I don't know. I don't know anything more than that. I don't know my last name or where I'm from or anything. I don't know what Spaceports are or 'cards' or chain codes or AI or hyper cores are, I don't know anything about anything!" Mel's voice quivered with tears once more as she poked at her food. "I don't even know what's on this plate."

"It's a classic American breakfast, right Apollo?" Sintara glanced at me, seeming completely indifferent to the conversation.

My voice fell flat, just like her own. "Now is not the time for jokes, Sintara. This is serious."

She sighed. "Sounds like a nasty case of temporal amnesia. I'm sure you're scared, or more than scared, but I promise you things will get better. Apollo here is a master of temporal amnesia, he knows more about it than anyone I know. And based on the display back there, he seems to have just enough fight to protect you. I'd say you're in the safest hands possible with him."

"Safe, maybe, but not happy."

"Give him some time, you'll warm up to him, I promise. Apollo, take her to the university on Mars, I'll send word of your situation and they'll find someone to help you. If not, you'll just have to wait out the amnesia until you get your memories back."

The university? For a brief moment, I was convinced Sintara had fallen into hysteria. I was most certainly not welcome there, not anymore anyways. Beyond that, what would any professor or scientist do for us that a doctor couldn't? I was at a loss for words, Mel spoke instead.

"Respectfully ma'am, I'm not certain I can survive another minute with...him."

"Well, I need to go examine the crash site on Zion, so unless you own and can pilot a ship, he's your only chance off this satellite." Sintara finished off her plate and slid it forwards. "You think it's just a coincidence I ended up here out of the blue? Finish your food, we'll talk more at my ship."

↪ ↪ ↪

The narrow cruiser stood over me, painted matte black with tinted windows. The Wasp crouched in the large hangar, contrasting the white of the walls. Its main thruster was like a long stinger, ready to chase down any prey it spotted. I climbed up into the rear landing gear, opening up a panel and crawling into a small room.

"And I thought I had it bad." My voice echoed off the cocoon of metal around me, a sprawl of pipes and wires hanging in the center. It was the heart of the ship, metaphorically and literally.

"Can you fix it?" Sintara's voice bouncing through the crawlspace.

"Yeah, I can fix it."

The hypercore was the most simple, complex machine ever designed. It was a generator for infinite energy, the energy that made space travel possible. It was first designed hundreds of years ago, developed and expanded over time. The idea was easy to explain but hard to understand. In my first year at the university, the professor set a power strip on his desk. He plugged its own cord into one of its outlets and set it before us.

"This is a hypercore."

A hypercore was a system of energy, powering itself and other parts of the ship simultaneously. It does this by using what scientists call a pseudo-temporal rift, but us engineers just call it the The Eye. The Eye is a nearly impossibly narrow tube that fires hot plasma, at a couple thousand kelvin, so fast with so much pressure it transfers through space and time backwards. Keeping up? No? Good, I'm not either.

They taught us loosely how they work but more importantly how to fix them. If the interval of energy is off, meaning the energy being sent to the past is not equal to the amount of energy needed to send the energy into the past, it cannot produce excess power to fuel the rest of the ship. If these two things become desynchronized beyond a point of repair, the hypercore can collapse and kill everyone within a light year or so. At least that was the estimate. I wasn't convinced.

I could fix this, it was a simple fix even, but my head already began to hurt just trying to comprehend it. I surrendered my understanding to the whims of the universe and got to business. No amount of knowledge without action ever put food on a man's plate or air in his ship. At least, I presumed I was getting paid for this. I suppose I was undoing what I had done, and free labor was better than prison bars.

"Let me go grab my toolbox and I'll get down to-"

My tool box slid in from the small opening, clattering and clanking as the latch barely held, like always. I popped open the metal box and got down to business. Fifteen minutes faded into thirty, then thirty into an hour. My mind stayed sharp on the job, keeping my edge and letting the world fade around me. By the time I was done, I couldn't remember what I'd done at the start, a sign I'd done a good job. The temperature had been rising steadily as I worked until my skin was slick with sweat. I wiped my brow with my sleeve and crawled my way out of the ship. The hypercore was humming, radiating blue light as it came back to full power. I sealed the panel behind me and dropped to the ground with a rattle, dropping the toolbox next to me.

"Alright, done." My hands were stained with gray and black smears. The cool air of the hangar filled my lungs, a true breath of relief.

"That was fast." Sintara set down a hand of cards on a large crate, standing up from her seat. On the other side of the crate, Mel was staring intently at her hand, trying to make sense of a game of cards.

I scoffed. "You know full well it was all too short."

"Don't we both?"

"What are you talking about?" Mel's accent seemed even thicker at this moment.

I pointed at my head with a smudged hand. "Temporal amnesia, it happens to the best of us. Now we have one thing in common."

"What did you...forget?" Mel asked curiously.

"Nothing much, just the past hour of work or so." I shrugged. It was true, the last thing I remember of sound mind and body was calling for my toolbox, everything past that was a blur. "Not my first rodeo, means I've done my job well."

"How do you know you've fixed it if you can't remember doing it?"

"I trust in my skills. Like I said, if I've done my job correctly I won't remember. The moment I leave it be, I'm back to my full mind. Anything up until then was fair game."

"Curious." Mel eyed her game once more, then climbed off the crate she was perched on and stepped cautiously over to us.

Sintara tapped at the screen woven into her suit on her forearm, examining a series of percentiles and statuses. She continued tapping away without so much as an appreciative glance at me. "Looks like we're back to normal, better last this time."

"I can promise you I did a better job than any other technician you'll find."

She gave a short laugh at this, a genuine one. "For your sake, I wouldn't suggest making any promises, considering everything you are."

"Hurtful, but probably wise."

Sintara walked between the landing gear of her ship, sliding open a door with a small cabin inside. She climbed up into the ship and looked around, glad to see everything back to full power. No dimmed or flickering lights, no sputtering or lurching machinery, just a well oiled machine. "You did well Apollo, keep it up and maybe next time I won't arrest you."

"You mean to say I burned my one pass on this?"

"I trust you'll do something arrest worthy before I see you next, you've always had a knack for finding trouble."

"Officer Sintara! Wait!" Mel ran to the ship holding a small box of cards in her hand.

"Keep it, and take this." She handed Mel a small communicator. It was a small device, roughly the size of a thumb drive. It had a sleek aluminum casing, a single button on one side of it. "If you ever need me, give that button a press. Emergencies only."

"Are you certain I can't come with you?"

"More than certain. I promise he means well, he couldn't hurt a fly anyways." A flicker of humor glanced behind her eyes as Sintara glanced at me, a ghost of a smirk gracing her face.

"Also hurtful," I mumbled.

"Thank you for everything, Officer Sintara." Mel stepped up and pulled Sintara into a tight hug. She may be the only person brave enough, or dumb enough, to do that. An inkling of respect filled my mind.

"May you have safe travels and a quick recovery." Sintara hugged her back for a moment before Mel climbed down from the ship. "One last thing, Apollo, check your card."

My heart fluttered as my eyes snapped to my watch, a small pop up filling the screen. A transfer, ten thousand dollars from an anonymous sender. Hope washed over me. Maybe I'd—we'd make it back to Mars after all, and even eat along the way. Sintara closed the door of her ship and climbed onto the bridge of her ship. She nodded down at me before the ship hummed to life, taking off from the hangar with a roar. Mel waved with a somber smile as the ship flew off into the cosmos.

The hangar was still as we lingered there, soaking in the silence. I cleared my throat and dusted off my pants. "Listen I uh...I think we got off on the wrong foot."

"You don't say."

"I'm...sorry, for what I said and did. I shouldn't have done any of that, it was selfish and rude of me."

"You're only saying that because we're stuck with each other until Mars." She frowned and folded her arms.

"Maybe a little, but I do mean it."

She sighed, unfolding her posture before drawing in her next breath. "Why did you and Sintara attack those men? They didn't hurt me."

The question stopped me in my tracks for a moment. More and more it dawned on me just how little she knew. "Those men were a part of a cult called The Angel Lights. They're dedicated to the preservation of humans, Earthly humans to be specific. They don't think humans born on other planets are real humans, and they especially don't like people of...mixed lineages, like you and me. They could've kidnapped you, or worse."

Mel's face twisted in confusion. "You were protecting me?"

"Somebody I once knew got twisted up in their business, they killed him. I won't let that happen to you." I picked up my toolbox and turned for the door. "About time we head for Mars, we'll need help if we want to crack this mystery, and I know just who to ask."

Mel followed close behind me. "What mystery?"

"You."

⤹ 3 ⤸

Mars

A clunk echoed through the ship as we detached from the satellite. The familiar sense of freedom filled my heart once more as we took off, roaring up to our full speed. In the reflection of the glass, Mel's face was peeking through the doorway. I pressed a button and a small chair popped free from the wall, sliding into place next to me. I didn't have to use that often, flying solo has been my usual.

"Care to join me?" The console lit up, all systems nominal. They'd done a surprisingly good job of repairing my ship, and I was even able to pay them.

"How far away is Mars?" Mel asked curiously while dropping down into the seat.

"Pick your measurement; miles, light years, or parsecs?"

Mel simply looked at me like I was crazy.

"For us, about twenty five trillion miles, four point two light years, or one point three parsecs away." I explained.

"Is that a lot?"

"It'll take us about twenty five minutes, but we won't remember a second."

"I'm going to forget more? I don't even remember anything! What else do I have to lose!" Her voice was thick with panic, nearly leaping out of her seat.

"No, no, not like that. The hypercore affects short term memory. By the time we get there, you won't even realize any time has passed, but you'll remember everything before and after."

"Are you sure?"

"I promise, now hang on. Thirteen, prepare to jump."

"As you wish, charging hypercore now."

The cabin hissed once again as the white lights were replaced with a bright red. My ears cracked with low pressure and the raspy breathing of Mel. She was holding onto her harness with a powerful grip, breathing sharply and shallowly. The ship began to rattle and she pressed her eyes shut in fear. I put a reassuring hand on her shoulder, her eyes creeping open only to spare me a glance.

"Just breathe," I practically shouted over the engine. The seemingly living shadows begin to creep into the cabin, running over the console and up Mel's legs. I could see her struggling to watch as the shadow crept over herself and me. The world went black, then, light again. The red, white, and blue marble stood before us in all its majesty, taking the breath out of both of our lungs.

It was carved with oceans and spotted with masses of clouds, a dull orange filling the gaps. Satellites filled the distant atmosphere around it, light flickering in sync. The hexagonal shape of a city sat just near the coast of the largest ocean, tucked between two large bays. We soared closer and closer, past satellites and freight ships alike.

"Welcome to Mars, the fourth planet of the Solar System." A proud smile pulled at the corners of my mouth despite my best efforts to fight it.

"It's beautiful," Mel said listlessly.

As we broke through the atmosphere, fire broke out over the glass of the ship. The flames fought against the heat resistant panels on the ship, making us glow bright red. Mel's breath sped up again as panic filled the cabin thicker than the heat.

"Don't panic, we'll be okay. This is normal." I did my best to reassure her.

"Normal?!" Her eyes examined my insanity once more.

"Normal doesn't mean 'not crazy.'" I shrugged.

The fire died away and the ship quickly cooled. The freezing air built water on the edges of the ship as we glided through the winter air. The city crept closer and closer, built almost like a pyramid. The outer edges of the city were primarily residential and industrial space, the buildings in each ring closer to the center getting higher and higher. We soared around the west side of the city, over the orange beaches of the shore. Mel was out of her seat now, pressed against the glass and looking out over the snow dusted city. It was the early winter months now. I had always preferred the six winter months compared to the six months of summer. The days were short, but sweet. The city always looked better at night anyways.

"Thirteen, take us home."

"Right away, sir."

"Welcome to Arcadia." A helpless smile spread across my face, wide enough that even Mel couldn't resist smiling with me.

We hovered over a small district of warehouses, all with flat roofs suited for landing small craft on. A few ships were scattered about, sitting like birds in their nests. We touched down on one with a clunk, the ship humming quieter as the engines cooled and slowed. I didn't own this warehouse, but it used to belong to an old friend of mine. I looked after it since he'd passed, and the city hadn't come to stop me yet. I stood up from my chair and glanced at Mel.

"Come on, it's time you meet somebody important."

⤙ ⤙ ⤙

I glanced down at my watch, then back up to the tall apartment building standing over us. This was the place, at least I hoped. There aren't exactly many places to move on Mars, but one could never truly know. Maybe she'd flown off to Jupiter or Pluto, or one of the outer colonies. Perhaps she'd taken a job on one of the other settlements on Mars...as if. You couldn't pay her to stay in the wilds of Mars, nobody wanted to live out there. There was a reason why so many blue-haired folk settled in Arcadia, it held sixty percent of the population of Mars. It was nice to be here, in a place I blended in. A few Martians walked past us, their gray eyes giving us half a glance as they continued about their day, blue hair dusted with snow.

"Didn't Sintara say to go to the university?" Mel inquired. "This doesn't look very...scholarly."

"Trust me, we'll get better help here than there. This is the place, I know it." My finger scanned the rows of buttons on a small screen beside the door, tapping on one that read 'Wendy Harrison.' A small chime occurred, then played several times over. The tone stopped abruptly as a voice buzzed out from the screen.

"Yeah?"

"Hey, Wendy. It's uh...me. Apollo."

There was no response for a moment, then the door to the apartment swung open. Mel watched me carefully as I stepped through the threshold, embracing the wave of heat that washed over us. It looked like any old apartment building from Earth: rows of doors and a staircase leading upwards. The carpet was matted down and stained orange from the dust, deep green wallpaper threatening to peel at any moment. It contrasted the dark wood of the banister in a way I quite liked for such a dingy place. For someone who wanted to forget Earth, she was doing a lousy job of it as far as her place of residence goes.

I brushed the snow off my jacket and began up the stairs, Mel following as she swiped the snowflakes from her flowing hair. We climbed one flight, then two. I counted the lines of doors and stopped at one that bore the number '303.' My shaky hand reached out to knock, but the door swung open violently. Standing in the doorway was my sister, Wendy. She wore dirty overalls smeared with paint both dry and still wet. Her hair was up in a sloppy bun, falling apart from the hard work. She wiped her hands on a towel as she eyed me up and down. "After all these years, look who the cat dragged in." She scoffed.

"Wendy, I'm sorry, I me-"

She pulled me into a tight hug, pressing her face into my shoulder with something between a laugh and a sob. Her arms were tight around me, and like that I was a little kid again, watching Wendy face down my bullies and thanking her relentlessly for it. For a moment, we were back on Earth, just kids again.

"I missed you, bro," she mumbled into my jacket.

I sighed and leaned into her. "I missed you too."

She grabbed me by the shoulders and held me an arm's length away. "You've gotten so big, has your ego grown with it?"

"It's...outpaced it. Look, I am here to see you, but I also came to ask for your help."

Wendy's eyes trailed to Mel, scanning her up and down. "I think I see why. Come inside, I'll put on some tea."

We followed Wendy through the door, down a short hallway, and into a small living room. A clear tarp had been laid over the floor in one corner, an easel with an unfinished painting atop it. The painting was of a sunset, the clouds dark and turbulent but glowing pink and red over a tumbling ocean. Tubes of paint had been scattered all over the floor, as well as brushes and paint knives. A small couch, only large enough for two, sat under a large window showing a beautiful skyline. A small coffee table stood before it, and a TV was attached to the wall on the opposite side of the room.

Before we even sat down, Wendy placed two steaming cups of tea onto the table. A floral aroma filled the air with a hint of cinnamon. The two small mugs held images of buildings on Mars; more things I knew that Mel didn't.

"And on my day off too, you're lucky I'm even home right now." Wendy pulled a stool hidden behind the easel closer to us and sat down. She held out a hand toward Mel. "I'm Wendy, Apollo's sister."

Mel glared at her hand, unsure of what to do. I made a small gesture, shaking the hand of an invisible person. Mel took a gentle hold of Wendy's hand and bobbed it up and down several times.

"I'm Melinoe, but you can call me Mel."

I frowned. The double standards. Mel gave me a smug look.

"Nice to meet you, Mel." She stared at their hands for a moment, Mel still not letting go. I cleared my throat, which made Mel jump in her seat. She let go and nodded. A smirk spread across Wendy's face. "You're an odd one, aren't you? That means we have something in common. I like your accent."

"Thank you. You and Apollo talk like robots," Mel said bluntly.

Wendy barked out a laugh. "Yep, the Pacific Northwest will do that to you."

Mel raised an eyebrow. "The Pacific Northwest?"

"Long story," I interjected. "Listen, I found Mel in a crashed ship on Zion. She has no memory of her home or how she ended up on Zion, and she has no card or any other form of ID. She doesn't even remember her own last name. Sinatra said to take her to the university, but we both know she trusts them far too much. We need to find her home, and help her restore her memory."

"Tall task, but you came to the right gal." Wendy leaned back on the stool, nearly tipping the thing backwards. She took a deep breath and closed her eyes.

"What's she doing?" Mel whispered.

"I'm thinking, just give me a moment," Wendy declared. She hummed to herself for a moment, then snapped forward again. "I got it. An old partner is working on a story about the dangerous work conditions of hypercore engineers and their bouts with temporal amnesia-"

A scoff escaped my lungs at the words. "Trying to pin the CTA for dangerous work conditions is like punishing a fish for swimming." I leaned back into the couch. My right arm tingled with pain as those dark memories bubbled up in my stomach, tying a knot of nausea in my gut. I shook out my nerves and took a hold of the mug of tea, taking a long sip.

"Listen, I hate them just as much as you do, so consider this your chance at revenge. The IEO has been studying temporal amnesia for years but never released any progress reports. Trying to find that research online is near impossible, believe me I have tried. You think the greatest minds of our generation can't figure out something that simple?" Wendy stood up and disappeared down the hallway for a moment, reappearing with a yellow folder in hand. She dropped the folder onto the table, a label across the front reading 'Apollo's thesis.'

"Look familiar?" Wendy asked as I grabbed the folder. My hands shook as I flipped it open, a wave of shock rolling over me. "Don't look so surprised, I have ears everywhere. When I heard my little brother had dishonorably graduated from university, I had to know why. That's why, isn't it?"

My senior year thesis, the last project needed to graduate. Of all the things I could've written, I chose the one thing that went against the rules. My teacher sat me down after I turned it in, giving me a stern warning and one chance to write a new one. After all my time and effort, I wasn't restarting. Wendy pulled the folder from my hand and began reading.

"Your thesis was about an alteration to the generic hypercore design to solve temporal amnesia, but they refused to accept it as an official discovery. You refused to resign from your findings, steadfast in your hope to change the world. As not to cause a scene, they let you graduate silently, locking you into your debt forever. Am I wrong?" Wendy dropped the folder onto the table again. "This wasn't even your degree, you did this of your own free will and choice. You were smarter than every other student in your class, you should have been teaching the dang class, but you chose this. Why?"

"I..." The words were caught in my throat.

"The IEO didn't want you solving the problem of temporal amnesia, they like it. It's not a design flaw, it's a feature. It's a safeguard, it keeps their employees' testimonies unreliable. You can't complain about work conditions when you can't remember your work. They use humans as living machines, expendable and silent. You tried to fix it, but they wouldn't let you. All for money."

"How did you get this?"

"It's an incomplete copy. I only have about a third of it, I'm piecing together the rest."

"You don't know what they can do." I was out of my seat, standing on wobbling legs.

"I know everything, it's my job. You know there's a way to cure it, don't you? And you know that they know." Wendy's inquisitive eyes dug into my soul, scraping my mind for everything I knew.

"It's purely hypothetical..."

"But they know."

"We could never get in! I'm banned from university grounds."

"Leave that to me."

"It'll never work."

"Have a little faith."

The air was silent between us, the smell of tea and paint the only thing keeping me in this time and place. After everything I'd been through, I couldn't imagine going back to that place. The weight of the past felt unbearable, so much so that I had buried it for years. I glanced at Mel, her eyes wide as she watched the conversation. She was curious, but she didn't understand half of what we said. A sigh escaped my lungs. I wished I could've simply stayed here, reunited with Wendy and enjoyed her company, found my parents again and said I was sorry, but Mel didn't have any of that. She had no past, no family to run to, nowhere she felt safe.

"Fine. But if it gets sketchy, we leave. Nobody is getting hurt on my watch." I conceded.

Wendy smirked. "You scared?"

"Of course not." My bunched shoulders and tense jaw spoke to that lie. "I've been through worse."

"Good, keep it that way. Now go get yourself cleaned up, space travel has done nothing for your complexion." Wendy's face stood somewhere between joyful and mischievous as she held out a hand to Mel. "Come on, you deserve some clothes nicer than a dingy jumpsuit."

She pulled Mel out of her seat and they disappeared through a door down the hallway, leaving me standing alone in the living room. My heart tried to call out to Thirteen, my only friend for a long time. He could do nothing here, he would be of no service to me. He didn't feel emotions, and yet he always managed to cheer me up. It was quiet without him, too quiet for my liking.

The hall closed in around me as I explored the apartment. I found a half open door to a bathroom and stepped inside, glaring at myself in the mirror. My face was smeared with grease and dirt, deep blue hair frizzy and uncared for, dark bags under my stormy blue eyes and skin paler than a ghost. For a moment, I couldn't remember the last time I slept. Not since before I found Mel, going on forty eight hours ago. I had gotten used to long periods without sleep, such is so when there's no sun to make you sleep and wake. The realization dropped the weight of exhaustion onto my shoulders, but the cold water woke me up quickly.

Hunched over the sink, I scrubbed the grease off my face and arms, hair stuck to my forehead and over my eyes. My mind flickered with the memory of that day, the day Wendy saved me from near certain death. I wiped away the memories and water with a nearby towel, running my fingers through my hair to its desired style. It didn't hardly make a difference, but I acted like it did. The lines of my face made it seem as if I was perpetually sad or frustrated, maybe I truly was.

I floated back out into the hallway, stopping by the closed door to my left. Voices could be heard just beyond it. They were joking and laughing, truly enjoying each other's company. It was the first time I'd heard Mel sound so happy. In reality, it was the first time I heard Mel laugh at all. Maybe she was better off with Wendy, maybe Sintara was wrong. A thousand thoughts rushed through my head, I brushed them away.

"I can't stand him, his AI is kinder than he is." Mel's voice fought through the doorway.

"That makes two of us, he can be a real pain," Wendy replied.

"You two seem so different, it's hard to believe you're related."

"He used to be a lot more like me, and I used to be a lot more like he is now. Always trying to be tough, constantly at odds with someone, thinking I'm smarter, stronger, and better than everyone else."

"What changed?"

"I grew up, and so did he."

"Even though he's such a jerk now?"

Wendy sighed. "You wouldn't believe what he's been through, if you did you might just understand."

"Can't you just tell me?"

"Not my place to tell, you've got to ask him."

"Even though you've been spying on him?"

"Well, I wouldn't call it...okay, kind of. But I was worried for him, he's the one who's been dodging my calls and texts all this time."

The rest of the words faded away as I sighed. Had I grown up or had I become even more of a child? Flying around in a ship taking whatever job comes my way isn't exactly responsible, neither is ghosting your family. After everything, I still felt like a scared kid with bullies he couldn't fight on his own. The world snapped back into reality as the door swung open. Mel was standing in the doorway, hair tied up in a wavy ponytail behind her head. She was wearing a red flannel loosely around her shoulders and a white shirt under it. She had ditched the jumpsuit for jeans and sneakers, she looked just like the half-Martian half-Jovian I expected, but something in me thought it still looked wrong.

"Were you eavesdropping on us?" Mel raised an eyebrow.

"No...okay, kind of." I laughed nervously. "You look great."

"Correction, she looks spectacular, thank you very much. You however look like Space Trash, there's some clothes in a box in the closet, change. Nobody wears jumpsuits around here." Wendy declared indignantly.

"Why do you have men's clothing?" I raised an eyebrow.

"Old boyfriend never cared to pick them up and I never cared to give them back. Now go change, once we eat we're leaving."

"Harrison! How are we looking?"

"Better than best, sir!" Grease was smudged up to my elbows, my fingers tingling underneath my sticky gloves. Sweat dripped off my chin as I ran my sleeve over my brow.

"Glad to hear it, now heave your slag and get out of there, we're jumping soon."

"On it!" I slammed my tools back into their box and took hold of the ladder out of the hypercore bay. A heavy hand grabbed at my arm and pulled me up as I neared the top, my feet landing on the catwalk. The beating heart of the ship pulsed ten feet below our feet, four times bigger and eight times more powerful than a commercial hypercore.

Above me towered a seven foot tall Saturnian man, a flat cap tight over his thinning white hair at all times. His face was grizzly and fierce, a patchy white beard contrasting his bushy and broad mustache and brows. Sometimes I couldn't see his eyes under the mess, he swore it kept the sweat out of his eyes. His broad shoulders and back made him nearly bigger than the doorway, making him more than suitable to handle the tougher jobs. He wasn't the greatest hypercore engineer ever, but that was only because I existed.

"Not a half bad job." He nodded.

"I told you, better than best, Cratus."

"Reel it in, Harrison. You'll be humbled before you know it. You're only two shot plasma vents and a broken ratchet away from being sacked."

"You say that every time."

"I mean it every time."

We strolled down the catwalk as the lights flickered out, a deep red filling the room. A pang of panic poked at my heart, barely resisting the urge to break into a full sprint down the catwalk. Mr. Cratus simply raised his pace. We reached the door at the end of the catwalk with time to spare.

The door slid open, revealing the sight of a small room full of tools and machines designed to make our job easier. There were four seats built into the wall, harnesses only slightly worn out. We trusted they wouldn't give out, most of the time. I rushed to my seat, failing to purge the anxiety in my gut. Mr. Cratus casually sat down and fastened his harness.

"I don't know if I'll ever get used to this," I said breathlessly.

"I've done this for twenty years son, trust me, you do," Mr. Cratus said with a sigh. He stretched out his arms and back, sinking deeper into his chair. He changed the subject to ease my nerves. "My wife keeps asking when I'm bringing you by for family dinner next."

"You always say that too."

He smiled. "And I mean it, every time. You remind her of our son."

"Hyperjump commencing in ten, nine, eight, seven," a fuzzy voice buzzed over the radio, one I would never get used to. "See you on the other side." Cratus gave a deep sigh, looking ready for a light nap.

A blinding blue light poured through the cracks of the door, slowly overtaken by shadow that filled the room and crawled up my legs. I held my breath and squeezed my eyes shut. The world went black, a peaceful, quiet black. But something wasn't right. The room flickered into view, then disappeared. Then again, then again. We were stuttering between beyond light speed and below light speed, something was desperately wrong.

"Kid?" His voice the only thing consistent between the flickering.

"What's happening?" I gasped, unable to calm my panic now.

The room flashed back into sight again, the speed near unbearable, dragging us down to the floor like half a ton of weight had been dropped onto our backs. My teeth gritted at the pain as a voice flooded the room.

"Hypercore synchronization at seventy percent."

"That can't be, I triple checked it!"

"We must've flown through a solar flare." His voice was strained, pain thick in his voice. His harness clicked as he fell out of his seat, barely staying on his knees. He heaved himself to his feet, struggling as he pulled his toolbox off a shelf.

"I'm coming with you!" I shouted.

"No, you stay. I got this." The door groaned open under the speed of the ship, Cratus stumbling through. Something shouted inside me, begging me to help. I couldn't let him do it alone, he couldn't do it alone.

My harness snapped off as I slipped from my seat, falling to the ground despite my best efforts. My arms pushed against the floor with everything they had, like doing push ups with the weight of a star on your back. I grabbed a nearby ratchet and crawled through the doorway, unable to make it to my feet. My hand smacked onto the railing of the catwalk, pulling myself onto the metal as my feet struggled not to give way. Cratus was halfway down the ladder, the hypercore beneath him spluttering and spewing energy through the room.

"Hypercore synchronization at sixty percent." The voice warned.

Cratus dropped to the floor with an impossibly loud boom, his feet shaking the walls harder than the hypercore. He pushed up his sleeves and took out a long wrench, jamming the end into the hot metal covering of a panel. It popped off with a searing heat washing over him, burns arcing over the flesh on his arms as he protected his face. I was wasting time.

I slid along the railing of the catwalk, rushing to the far side where a wall held a large screen. My arms pulled me across the harsh metal, my body threatening to give way. My arms heaved against the ratchet as I tore the bolts out of a panel beneath the screen. The metal fell away, revealing an array of buttons and levers attached to a bright blue pipe. It radiated heat, like an oven door opening to the core of a star. Fear gripped my throat, my sense screaming for me to turn and run, but the sound of Cratus screaming in pain was louder, a sound that burned like the flesh of my arm as I reached into the panel.

The edges of my jumpsuit caught fire as I took hold of a hefty lever. The flesh of my hand burned as I pulled, lightning arcing off the pipe as the excess power was cut off.

A shrill scream escaped me as an overwhelming strength I didn't know I had rushed through me, just enough for the lever to reach its lowest position. A last pulse of power arced off the pipe, seizing my hand and running up the flesh of my arm as electricity coursed through my system. My muscles convulsed on their own as my body seized, the cold metal of the catwalk icing my burning flesh as I fell to my back. The world spun as we slowed, my body feeling weightless as we neared a halt. Gravity disappeared, only the magnets of the catwalk holding me to the floor. My head fell to the side, my blurry eyes only just making out the horrific burns that covered my arm. Another panicked scream tore at my throat as I felt the pain and passed out.

The world came in flickers, moments between consciousness and unconsciousness. Pain gripped my body as I was moved onto a stretcher, men wearing white jumpsuits examining me with wide eyes. I screamed again before they stabbed something into my neck. The world went blurry as I was carried away, and in passing, saw a body bag being zipped over Cratus.

When I faded in next, I could see myself. A clone of me. A corpse, really. Emotionless, still, pale skin and blue lips, only the faint curl of a frown proving it was indeed human. It was dead, laying on a cold metal slab just beside the operating table I lay on. Another scream escaped me as my head fell to the side once more to see my right arm missing.

"We got a screamer." A man wearing a white jumpsuit and mask stood over me, pulling latex gloves over his hands. The world faded once more.

When I awoke next, into true consciousness for the first time in seventy two hours, my arm itched like a swarm of ants had made their home under my skin, even the feeling of hospital sheets too coarse against my skin. It was limp, only the dull tingle of pin and needles proving it was indeed attached to me. I pulled at the collar of my shirt, seeing a fine seam where the old arm ended and the new began.

A clipboard clattered onto the table next to my hospital bed.

"Eight hundred thousand," the nurse deadpanned, barely glancing at me before turning for the door. I reached for the clipboard with my left hand, my right arm proving useless. My fingers grasped onto the cold metal, shaking in my hand as I read it. Eight hundred thousand units for a flash clone arm transplant, a million and two hundred thousand in dollars. The CTA refused to pay for damages for 'reckless and/or intentional self harm.' I was laid off. No money, no ship, a right arm that barely worked, trapped in a hospital on a satellite near Pluto, and one million units in debt.

↪ 4 ↩

University

The sight was familiar, in the worst ways possible. As I dragged myself through the iron gates, the world felt like a dream. The clouds opened, pouring buckets of snow over us. Wendy and Mel walked under an umbrella, I let the snow soak through my hair and stick to my face.

Central Arcadia University. It was not a place I had ever intended to come back to, and it was not a place I was welcome. The University was one of the many hells that kept its chain around my ankle. I had been a slave to this place, and I still was. To them, I'm just a walking debt, money waiting to be made.

The red brick of the courtyard was slick with snow, not a soul left to enjoy the purple sunset reflecting off the white powder. Everyone had gone home for the holidays, a time part of me despised. Being back in the house with my parents had felt like a death sentence back then, being coddled and babied for three weeks straight. My old room never changed, it was always the same as it had been when I left. Old band posters on the wall, a cruddy flat screen I bought from a vintage store with some old gaming consoles scattered about in one corner, a desk covered in notebooks and papers.

I missed those days, I took them for granted. Times were simpler then. Now, I was back, and it was like I had never left. A tall building stood over us, staring down with its tall windows, stone pillars, and brick walls. The office was a place I did my best to stay out of, but my best hadn't been enough to keep me from trouble. Too often was I dragged here for a slap on the wrist, a firm warning, and a threat. If curiosity killed the cat, I was standing six feet above where I should be.

Wendy hopped up the steps with more excitement and positivity than anyone should be able to muster. She rapped on the door firmly and stepped back. We waited for what felt like a century before a woman peeped through the door, opening it only enough to see us.

"Can I help you?" She jeered.

"Hi, I'm Wendy Harrison with Arcadia Today. I'm here for a blind interview about the reduction of paid time off for teachers and staff in local schools. I called earlier today and spoke with Mrs. Jefferson?" Wendy's voice was level, cool, and friendly. The badge around her neck shimmered like a free pass into anything. She was fluent in the retail voice and her years of acting put a more than convincing smile on her face. The strain in Mel and I's face did nothing to help, but Wendy did enough for all of us.

"Oh yes, yes! So you're the young lady I spoke to, please do come in, weather is nasty out there." The door swung open fully, heat washing over us as we gratefully stepped inside. Well, everyone was grateful except for me. The door closed behind us like the maw of a beast snapping shut around its prey. It was a simple little room, high vaulted ceilings of carved, faux wood with equally fake trim. The wallpaper was a deep blue with a white print on it, daring not to peel under threat of replacement. About a dozen wooden chairs sat against the same wall as the door, a large desk across from it. On our left and right, long hallways extended into the building, doors evenly spaced along them.

The woman hobbled behind the desk swiftly, I couldn't tell if it was a past injury or age which caused her limp. She had thin hair in tight curls that hugged her head, wisps of blue amongst the grays and whites. She wore a knit cardigan that she held tight around her, the sleeves running over her hands to keep her warm. I couldn't tell how she'd get anything done like that. Her face was gentle with a kind smile, wrinkles from a long, well lived life showing on the corners of her eyes and face. She was so ghastly white you would think she was already a ghost, as was true for all elderly Martians. Thick glasses with thicker rims sat on her nose, beaded strings hanging from them and connecting behind her neck to keep them from falling. I remembered her, she'd worked here for fifteen years, but she never could remember my name. I wasn't worried about being recognized.

"Thank you for your hospitality on such short notice, these winter beats are brutal on all of us journalists." Wendy walked up to the desk and leaned against it, examining the surface.

"I think I can imagine, these work weeks have me run ragged. Now, what shall we do to start?"

"Well, as I said this is a blind interview, meaning you may be quoted but purely anonymously. Is there a quiet room where we can chat?" Wendy asked with an overabundance of politeness that exhausted me. If I wasn't already throwing up in my mouth out of fear, that would do it for me.

"Yes yes, a good idea, but if you don't mind my asking, what exactly are they here to do?" Mrs. Jefferson gestured vaguely at Mel and I.

"Oh, yes yes, they're just here to grab some b-roll for the holo-airing. They won't wander far, just looking for something to put on our viewers' screens. Is that okay with you?" Wendy raised an eyebrow, half wary of her request.

"Yes, yes. They seem harmless, and they won't be able to get into anywhere they shouldn't. But to fulfill safety precautions I will have to dispatch a security guard to keep an eye on them."

Wendy nodded. "Of course, we are happy to accommodate for that."

The woman mumbled into her watch and before long a tall, broad man stomped down the hallway towards us. He was an Earthling, a large mustache below his equally large nose. His hair was thinning below his cap that read 'security' and a stun stick hung at his side. I pulled my hat down onto my forehead, glancing down at my shoes and fiddling with the camera at my side.

Mr. Barker was not on my list of favorite people, and I was not on his. His frequent stops to my lab when something caught fire or exploded always led to less than friendly conversations. Shockingly, my irresistible charm and wit proved worthless against him. He frequently spent time busting my chops over safe lab use and damage to university property, usually unimpressed with my excuse of the progression of science. He was more often than not the reason I ended up here, and I can only assume he was more than overjoyed when I was dispatched from the university permanently.

"Ah, Mr. Barker! If you would be so kind as to follow our visitors as they roam for some footage I would be very appreciative. Ms. Harrison and I will be in the conference room, if there are any problems just buzz me." Mrs. Jefferson raised her hand and gestured to her watch. She led Wendy down the hall to the left, making friendly chit chat as they went. Wendy glanced back at me once before she stepped through a door, giving me a nod as she went.

I gave a sideways glance to Mel, who stared at the security guard with more anxiety than I knew one could display on their face. I nudged her with my elbow as I held the camera up to my eye, examining the hallway through the viewfinder. The camera zoomed as I looked just over Mr. Barker's shoulder, reading a sign on the wall. I cleared my throat and held my voice low, hoping for him to not recognize me. "I'm thinking we start down there, get a long shot of the hallway."

"Oh, um, yes, I think that would be an excellent idea." Mel nodded vigorously.

We stepped past the man, his heavy footsteps following us down the hall. I reached the end and spun around, kneeling down with the camera in front of my face. Mr. Barker had his arms folded, looking suspicious of us. "Hey buddy, stay out of the shot will ya?"

He rolled his eyes and stepped away as I let the camera roll for a moment. I grumbled, acting unsatisfied with the shot. "I'm thinking we use a jump cut for this, could you fetch the tripod from your backpack?"

Mel pulled off the backpack Wendy gave her and set it on the floor, unzipping it and rummaging through it. She mumbled to herself in a low voice. "Tripod, tripod, tripod."

"Don't tell me you forgot what a tripod is." I scoffed, kneeling down next to her. Her face was flush with embarrassment as I stuck my hand in the bag and pulled out the metal stand. I began extending out the legs one by one. "Perfect, this'll do nicely."

My hands clamped around the bottom of the heavy metal, swinging it into the jaw of Mr. Barker. His head snapped sideways as he fell against the wall, dazed. I jabbed the end into his gut as Mel pulled his stun stick from his belt, twisting the handle as electricity arced from it. She stuck the shocking end into his neck, his body seizing and convulsing as he fell to the ground. His body lay still, on the ground as I dropped the now bent tripod.

I nodded slowly. "Not bad."

"Sintara taught me, said I should practice on you." Mel said with a small grin. "What was that for though?"

My hands rummaged through his pockets, finding a ring of keys in his left pocket. Along with it, I nabbed the card hanging from the collar of his shirt. A metal door sat beside us, just next to a sign that read 'basement.' I held the card up to a small screen on the door, a beep echoing down the hall as the deadbolt slid free. I pushed the door open to find a staircase leading downwards into a large room. The lights above hummed as I stepped carefully deeper into the belly of the beast. A sound made my ears twitch, a dragging sound, followed by a series of thumps. My feet flew out from under me as a heavy object slid under my feet and knocked me over, Mr. Barker sliding down the steps and falling still at the bottom. I smacked against the sharp stairs, holding my side with a groan.

Mel rushed down the stairs and grabbed me by the arm, helping me up. "I'm so sorry! My hands slipped!"

"Obviously! What the hell are you doing?" I hissed in what was barely a whisper.

"We couldn't just leave him in the hallway!"

Mr. Barker was still unconscious, just at the bottom of the steps. I groaned, knowing she was right. "Fine, help me tie him up."

We slid the belt free from his pants and tied his hands around his back, pulling the laces from his shoes to tie his ankles. An old friend taught me that, and I hated having to use it. I heaved him to the side, leaning him against the wall and dusting off my hands. Clearly I was not built for espionage. We stepped onward and examined the large room at the bottom of the stairs. It was a file room, and an ancient one at that. Dozens of shelves stood on rails with cranks allowing them to move. There were two large sections of shelves on either side of the room, the random and sporadic gaps in them making it feel like a maze with moving walls. They were all labeled alphabetically, all stocked to the brim with files. The shelves had been left open to a row labeled 'E.' My curiosity was piqued, but time kept me focused. I followed the letters down to 'T' and took hold of the crank. It spun loosely, moving a mere inch with each rotation. When we finally got it open, I slipped inside and ran my finger along the rows and rows of files.

In a world entirely connected by the internet, the only way to keep secrets was to never upload them. The web was useful, but it was far from secure. Too many cyber attacks had taken place in the past decades, anyone with half a brain knew not to trust a firewall with their deepest secrets. Paper couldn't be hacked or leaked without an able person taking it, and no sweaty hacker in their mother's basement was tough enough to slip past security for the sake of credit card numbers.

My finger stopped on a file that read 'temporal amnesia', a file I took eagerly. I flipped it open, reading the words swiftly as Melinoe came to my side. The file had been redacted, half of the paper I held was black ink. Only a few words were left.

'Temporal Amnesia is a phenomenon that occurs when hypercore engineers are exposed to high doses of electromagnetic waves. A similar phenomenon has been observed in ancient forms of cancer treatment. The IEO has deemed the phenomenon safe unless other complications in patients prove otherwise.' The rest was redacted.

"Nonono, this can't be." I shoved the file back into place and rushed to shelf H. I cranked the wheel with all my might until it was just wide enough to fit in. The creaking, grinding sound of spinning wheeling only added to my anxiety. My eyes scanned the files in a panic, grabbing another file so quickly I thought I had ripped it. This one was labeled, 'hypercore technology.'

'The hypercore is an infinite energy loop created through a form of pseudo time travel, first hypothesized by Jonathan Clarkson in 2122. The first functional hypercore was created in 2135 and functioned to power the minor satellite Cyclo 11. The hypercore failed after a solar flare occurred, desynchronizing the power loop and causing a catastrophic functional collapse. The implosion killed all eleven crew members and rained harmful radiation over the southern hemisphere of Earth.

The disaster is believed to have been a main cause of the following nuclear pandemic, causing a large portion of the southern hemisphere to become uninhabitable and the following nuclear winter which significantly dropped the global temperature. However, the blame of this disaster has been redirected to the solar flare that occurred on the same day.

The hypercore was perfected in 2178 and connected the solar system to the following three star systems: Proxima Centauri, Wolf 359, and Sirius. The hypercore has become pivotal in the life of humans.'

Everything else was nothing but black lines.

"Please, please don't tell me." The file dropped from my hands as I rushed to the next one, a shelf labeled S.

"Apollo, what's going on?" Mel asked in a panic as I cranked the wheel aggressively. Unintentionally, I ignored her as I rushed to the final group of files. Almost the entire shelf was labeled as 'students' as I searched. I hopped up and pulled a file with my name on it. My hands tensed as I pulled it open, flipping past pages and pages of incident reports, missing assignment reports, and tardy slips. I tore out the sheets and threw them to the floor, searching for something that was never there. My thesis was missing, burned from the record. The file slipped from my hands, the empty folder falling amongst the scraps of paper. Mel took hold of my shoulders, shaking me so hard it made my head rattle.

"Apollo, what is happening?" Her face was stern, but concerned. Worry had taken hold of her as terror had gripped me.

"It's gone. They burned it from their records. There's only one clue left and we walked right past it."

We looked down at the mess of paper as realization dawned on Mel.

"Wendy's apartment." We said in synchronization.

"We need to tell Wendy," Mel said.

"Immediately." I nodded.

My shoes slipped on the papers as we ran from the room. We hopped over the slowly waking body of Mr. Barker, dashing up the steps and bursting through the metal door. Our shoes squeaked as we sprinted down the long hallway, skidding to a stop as the door to the conference room swung open. Wendy and Mrs. Jefferson were laughing as they stepped through the door, but stopped suddenly as they took in the sight. Our breath was the only thing filling the air for a moment before Mrs. Jefferson broke the silence.

"What is that?" She pointed down to my shoe.

I looked down at the paper stuck to the sole of my sneaker. A scan of my Student ID. I picked it up and looked at it, laughing awkwardly as I examined it.

"Apollo?" Mrs. Jefferson gasped.

"Y'know what, when you look at it from this angle you can kinda see the resemblance." I held out the paper away from my face, nervously laughing as I did so. "We need to leave, now."

"I'm sorry, what is going on?" Mrs. Jefferson shouted now.

A thud echoed down the hall as I turned around. Mr. Barker lay on the floor, flopping out of the doorway and shouting expletives at us as he struggled to stand. I dropped the paper and grabbed Wendy's wrist, dragging her out of the building with Mel in tow. We burst through the door and down the slick steps, gasping our way through the courtyard as the snow came down in droves. The dusty snow clung to our shoes, making me slip as we made a turn.

"What is happening?" Wendy shouted angrily.

"I'll explain later!" I held my watch up to my mouth. "Thirteen! Do you copy?"

"Yes sir, I copy."

"We need an emergency exfil, asap!"

"On it sir."

My lungs burned as the courtyard flashed by, then the iron gates. We skidded out onto a busy sidewalk. We pushed past the mass of blue haired martians, going against the flow. The sidewalk was slick, threatening to steal my balance at any second. In the distance, I could hear the roaring thrusters of Thirteen. We stopped at the corner of an intersection, a space just large enough for Thirteen to land.

The thrusters burned as it soared down to the concrete, cars slamming on their brakes as a starcraft landed before them. Horns blared as we ran out onto the wet asphalt and up the cargo door, coming to rest in the bay as the thrusters roared to life again, lifting us off the street and into the sky.

"Thirteen, we need to get to Wendy's apartment immediately!" I shouted as I rushed to the bridge.

"Sir, you may want to see this first." A screen popped up on the display the moment I dropped into my seat. It wasn't just a news broadcasting; it was Channel 6, The Bounty Hub.

Plastered across the screen in broad lettering read, 'hot new bounties for you!' There was a picture of Mel and I. My name was plastered across the bottom:

Apollo Harrison, wanted for harboring a dangerous fugitive. The girl is needed alive, but lethal force is permitted against Mr. Harrison, given such precautions are provoked.

The bounty was listed as one million units, roughly one and a half million dollars. I was a wanted man, and Mel was a dangerous fugitive. With a number like that, every bounty hunter alive would be after me. I hadn't done anything, at least, nothing that warranted all this. My irritation with Mel's arrogance now faded into fear for who she was. A dangerous fugitive? Who was this girl?

"Apollo..." Wendy choked on her words as she read the screen. Only the hum of the ship filled the tense air. My hand eased down on the throttle, slowing us to a hover. I looked down at my lap, thinking hard.

"Apollo, what does this...mean?" Mel asked.

I drew in a deep breath. I wanted to yell in her face, demand answers, but she was just as scared as I was, just as confused. "It means...it means we're in deep trouble."

"But, we can fix it, right?"

"Yeah...yeah, we'll fix it. Thirteen, redirect for the docks."

"As you wish sir." He buzzed.

"Apollo, how can I-" I cut Wendy off.

"We'll drop you off at the bus stop by the docks. You'll have to stay at Mom and Dad's for a few days while things cool down. You can't go back to your apartment until we're long gone."

"But what about...my memories?" Mel asked.

"We'll find another way. It won't matter what you remember if we're both dead, we need to survive first, remember later."

Wendy put a hand on my shoulder. "Apollo, I'm not going to leave you when you have a cosmos wide bounty on your head. You need my help."

"Wendy, you can't get caught up in this, I'm sorry. I'll...we'll talk to Sintara, we'll figure something out. I'll contact you when I know we're safe. Until then, we need to take every precaution."

"I'm not afraid of a bounty, you think I've never gotten in hot water before? You're my brother and I am not leaving you!" Wendy shouted.

I slammed my fist against the arm of my chair. "It's not a fight! It's a hunt. He is out there, he's been waiting for this opportunity."

Wendy's anger morphed into fear, horrified by the edge of my voice. "Who is out there? Who is hunting you?"

Thirteen interrupted. "Sir, you have an incoming transmission. It's labeled 'from an old friend.'"

Silence so thick you could hear a pin drop filled the cabin. We were over the docks as I eased off the throttle, slowing us to a hover over the sea. My hand hovered over the screen on my right, the signal waiting to be accepted.

I glanced at Wendy and Mel. "Don't say a word, understood?"

They nodded. My finger brushed against the screen, a beep filling the cabin so loud it made me jump. White noise filled the cabin, morphing into a clear signal. I could hear the roar of thrusters on the other side, part of me wished I didn't know who was on the other end.

"If it isn't Blue Moon himself, how've you been? I missed you, y'know. I know you're good at getting into trouble, but a bounty like that? I expected less from you, Star Man." His accent was thick, something from the outer systems, he never did tell me where.

"Let me guess, you see the news? I thought it was a rookie mistake to trust the media."

"Do you really think so lowly of me? I've known for a while now."

I held down a button on the screen, my microphone cutting out. "Thirteen, find the origin of this transmission."

"Let me guess, you're searching for my location? No need, I'll tell you. I'm on Mars, landed early this morning."

"You..." My throat burned as my voice hitched.

"I've known since you stopped at that spaceport and got tangled up with those Angel Lights. CTA came straight to me with an offer, a quarter million unit bonus if I brought you in before this got out of hand."

"Did they tell you I was on Mars?"

"Of course not, I already knew."

"Why are they hunting me?"

"You don't know? That makes two of us. I don't ask questions, I just get my hands dirty. Shoot first, ask questions later."

"What do you want, Zivko?"

"My money."

A roar tore through the air just over the ship. The air split as a sleek, sharp, shape broke from the clouds. It soared towards us at an impossible speed before stopping just before us, hovering. It was narrow, two sleek wings held tight to the body of the ship. Two long guns hung below the wings, locked onto us. The tinted glass reflected the sun, nearly blinding me. Along the black body of the ship, bold words were painted in white. 'Dark Matter.'

"You have two choices: you can hand over the girl or I can hunt you down and take her by force."

"You'll never find me."

He laughed at that, genuine amusement from my weak words. "Won't I? Even if I couldn't, which I absolutely can, I don't need to find you. I'll just find one of your dear old family and...I think you know the rest. Maybe I'll start with that reporter sister of yours, or your dear old parents, maybe I'll even find Officer Sintara, or maybe that old coworker of yours...what's his name? I remember best when they're on tombstones, but he never did get a proper burial, did he?"

Anger coursed through me as I glanced at Wendy, gulping down the fear that rose in my throat. Her face held a deep frown, but fear flickered behind her eyes. He was trying to get under my skin, and it was working. "This is between you and me, Zivko, no one else."

"Is it? The CTA doesn't pay such a pretty penny for worthless heads, especially not yours. Whatever she's done, whoever she is, it makes her dangerous, and that makes you dangerous."

I glanced at Mel now, who looked utterly terrified. "She hasn't done anything."

"Look, Apollo, as your best friend and the person with a finger on the trigger, I'm going to make a suggestion. Hand her over now and we can be done with this. What does she matter to you anyways? She's just a nobody, she doesn't mean anything."

"Clearly that's not true."

"Don't say I didn't warn you. But since I'm feeling generous, I've chosen to give you a head start, for old times' sake. You have fifteen minutes, starting right...now." A blip popped up on my screen, a timer, counting down. "Best not waste a second."

The transmission cut out with a beep, all three of us jumping. I took hold of the throttle and slammed it forward, soaring just past the Dark Matter and over the docks. My heart pounded as the city flew by us, pulling me back in my chair.

"Who was that??" Wendy shouted in my ear.

"He's…a bounty hunter, someone I used to know. He's the best there is, and he will do anything to claim his prize. If the CTA is working with him directly, then he means business."

"What do we do?" Mel's voice was thick with fear.

"I…I don't know. Wendy, I'm dropping you off at the warehouse, catch a bus home and stay inside for a few days."

"I already told you I'm not leaving!"

"I'm not asking!" I threw my hands in the air, Thirteen taking control. We locked eyes, anger crackling in the air between us. "This is final, you are leaving. Your half brother is a dangerous criminal, harboring a fugitive. If people see you trying to help me, you could lose everything. Your career, your status, even your citizenship."

"None of that matters to me if you're dead! I just got you back, I am not losing you again!"

"You won't. You won't, okay? We'll figure it out, we'll fix this. I'll be back, I just need a few days to smooth things over." I looked at Mel and drew in a deep breath. "I've survived this long, I'll do it again."

"You don't have to do this alone."

"I'm not alone, I have her." *Whoever she is,* I thought to myself.

Wendy's jaw hung for a moment, trying to formulate another rebuttal. She sighed, dropping her head and staring at her shoes. "You're such a pain sometimes."

"Thanks, I try."

"You get three days, if things don't smooth over by then I will come find you, okay? Just...stay safe, and be careful."

We sat down on the roof of the warehouse, a clunk echoing through the ship. I rose from my chair, my legs weak with fear but determined to fix the problem. It was what I did, it was what I had always done. People would give me broken things and I would fix them, and if I couldn't fix them, I would use those broken pieces to make something better. This was just like anything else, only with a whole lot more guns pointed my way.

"I'll fix it, like I always do."

"I know you will." Wendy pulled me into a tight hug. "Remember, fear is a choice—"

"And not a choice to let others make for you." It was our old saying. "Now get out of here, we only have ten minutes left."

Wendy stepped back and hugged Mel next. "Be safe."

"We will." Mel nodded.

Anxiously, Wendy disembarked out into the cold winter air. We stood for a moment, watching her from the bridge as I mumbled a prayer to whoever may be listening to protect her. I dropped into my chair, taking hold of the controls. Mel took a seat next to me, determination coating her face.

"Are you ready?" I asked.

"As I'll ever be." She nodded.

"Thirteen, how fast can we get into a light jump?"

"To get out of the atmosphere and up to full speed, twelve minutes."

"Then we'll do it in eight."

⇀ 5 ⇀

Earth

The city roared past us, but our eyes stayed glued to the timer. Four minutes left, our speed agonizingly slow. My hands quaked, floating over the throttle and desperate to be outside city limits. A green light popped up on my monitor and I slammed the accelerator forward. We were pulled back into our chairs as the thrusters burned hotter. Mel's face fell low, despondent if not dreadful as the city faded behind us. I swallowed my guilt and stuck my eyes to the console, brain rushing with calculations.

"Three minutes left, looks like someone's not gonna make it." Zivko's voice buzzed through the ship.

I shook my head. "We'll make it."

Mel leaned forward in her chair. "What if we don't?"

"Then we'll fight our way out." I tapped and swiped on a screen to my left, a hum rising under us.

Thirteen confirmed what I knew. "Preparing defensive measures."

We burned through the atmosphere, the roar of the ship lessening as the air pressure dropped. We broke out into the vacuum of space, the cosmos welcoming us with open arms. Two minutes now. No ordinary ship could get to light jump speeds that fast, but this was no ordinary ship.

"Thirteen, increase power output to engines to one hundred and ten percent."

"Sir, are you certain?"

"Demagnetize the ship and focus life support only on the cabin.

After a moment of hesitation, he responded. "As you wish."

The door to the cabin slid shut and hissed as the pressure throughout the rest of the ship dropped. Though it had little effect on us, the magnets built into the floor powered off, letting go of the magnets sewn into the jumpsuits. Our street ware did little to keep us on the floor as the harnesses over our chests worked overtime to keep us in our chairs.

Our backs pressed deeper into our seats as the hull of the ship was pushed to the brink of failure under the sudden increase of speed. The temperature inside the thrusters was climbing steadily, we couldn't keep this up for long before we bent the chassis of the ship or melted an engine from the inside out.

"Uh oh, time's up! Ready or not, here I come." His voice taunted, signal fuzzy as the distance between us grew.

"Warm up the hypercore."

"Sir, I'd recommend-"

"Just do it!"

The ship slowed as the engines sputtered, whirring low as the temperature dropped rapidly. My head snapped forward as our speed decreased, something was slowing us farther and farther from jump speeds. The joystick in my hand vibrated so violently my hand ached and my fingers cramped under the white knuckle grip I held onto the throttle.

"Not so fast, old friend."

I swore under my breath. "Thirteen, bring up the rear and side cameras."

Just behind the Thirteen, staring into the cameras, was the Dark Matter. A metal cable was clamped to the rear of the ship, the boosters on the Dark Matter pulling back with all their strength. The Thirteen was built for distance, but Dark Matter was a creation of pure speed. There had been no faster ship ever designed, and it was all thanks to me.

"Where are you going? This reunion isn't over." Zivko barked a laugh into his microphone, the speakers crackling.

"You're right, we're just getting started."

Mel took hold of the joystick to her right, a screen before her displaying exactly what the guns saw. They spun around in a blur, opening fire against the hull of Dark Matter. The bullets pounded against Zivko, the rhythmic pounding of the turrets like music to my ears just beneath us. The cable snapped loose and retracted as Zivko went on the defense. He veered upwards, out of sight of the guns.

"I can't get a shot on him!" Mel shouted.

"Hang on tight." The stick snapped left as we flipped upside down, Mel taking fire on him once again. We followed him as he rotated left, the bullets running wide and unable to keep up with his speed. He went on the offense now, his guns taking fire against us. We broke right, a few bullets pounding against the wings of the ship. He leveled out just behind us as a high tone filled the cabin. Flashing red text filled the HUD, 'missiles locked.'

"We can do this the easy way or we can do this the hard way, your choice." He was serious now, we'd rattled him.

"Apollo, do something!" Mel shouted.

"I'm not exactly a master pilot, Mel!" My teeth were gritted under the stress in my jaw and my mind raced faster than either ship. I took a deep breath and narrowed my eyes. "Alright…I saw this in a really old movie one time."

The joystick nearly snapped as I pulled back on it, the ship pointing upwards as I pulled back on the throttle. The Dark Matter flew right under us as we leveled out. Our nose chased his tail as we picked up speed, he was leading us on. I hesitated, slowing for a moment, the moment he was waiting for. He broke left and spun around, a skilled maneuver. A smattering of bullets ran up the side of the ship, everything rocking as we followed him left.

Thirteen's voice was fuzzier than usual. "Sir, we've taken critical damage to major systems."

"Get the hypercore online." I spoke through gritted teeth.

We pulled ahead, the Dark Matter following close behind. Another spray of bullets slammed against us, then another. Everything rattled as darkness leaked into the cabin. It pooled at our feet as we struggled to reach speed. I blinked hard and sent another prayer into the cosmos. When I opened my eyes, the darkness was at my neck.

The last thing I heard was Zivko, speaking calmly through his communicator. "Not bad, luck was on your side this time. How long can you live on luck, Star Man?"

The next thing I knew, Earth snapped into view, dangerously close. I screamed a curse and pulled on the brake, thrown forward in my chair as we entered the atmosphere. Blue fire roared over the hull as we slowed, the air making quick work of our speed. The joystick snapped back and forth in my hand, threatening to break from my grip and lose control. My fingers were sticky with blood as my fingers were rubbed raw, tearing the skin on my palm.

"Mayday! Mayday! We've taken critical damage! We are going down!" It was rare to hear Thirteen so urgent, but I had no time to revel in it as a yellow sanded beach appeared beneath us.

We leveled out and glided over the water, skipping off the surface once before crashing into the waves. Pain shot through my neck as we were whipped forward, the water putting out the fire that had broken out over the wings. The sea wrapped over us and pulled us under, battering against the hull as we landed on a crop of rocks just under the surface.

We teetered on the edge, staring down at an underwater ravine. My breath hitched and I wondered if it may be my last, eyes wide as the abyss below beckoned us. Water filled the back of the ship, weighing us down and settling us nicely on the cliff side. Only the bubbling of water around us and our breath left us company, our panic slowing and the pain of the crash growing.

"Thirteen? Thirteen?" My voice was raw from the screaming I hadn't realized I had done in the crash. There was no response, only the tap of a curious fish bouncing against the window. My neck protested as I craned to see Mel looking equally terrified and fascinated. "You okay?"

She nodded. "I think so."

The lights flickered out, only the emergency systems left online. I cursed as I unbuckled my seat and slipped out, knees wobbling on the uneven floor. I knelt down next to Mel and popped open a small compartment full of emergency supplies. My fingers closed around a small electric lantern, the light flickering on as I opened it.

"Here." I handed it to Mel who looked more than happy with having light other than what little had reached us this far down.

"Where are we?" Mel asked as I set a first aid kit and a bundle of emergency blankets on the console.

"Earth, in the Pacific Ocean." A grunt of pain escaped me as my palm burned with pain as blood dripped from my clenched fist. I pulled a roll of bandages from the first aid kit and fumbled with it for a moment.

Mel set the lantern on the console and gently took them from me. "Let me."

"I got it-"

"I won't be having you bleed all over our blankets, now give me your hand." Her brow furrowed as she held her free hand towards me. I sighed and placed my hand in hers, wincing as I opened my palm. "I'll be gentle, I promise."

She was true to her word as she dabbed the blood from my hand and tenderly applied a salve. The wrap was skilled, something so well practiced it must have been muscle memory. The pressure soothed the pain as the medicine tingled. I regretted flexing my fingers for a moment, but was surprised to find them no worse off.

"We're gonna be here a while," I sighed, still observing the bandages. I gently shook my head so as not to hurt my neck and knelt down next to the console, fingers failing to find a hold in the flush metal. I swore at the metal and gave it a smack, making no progress.

"Here, let me try." Mel knelt down next to me and pressed her fingers into the metal. The edge of the panel bent inwards, giving her just enough room to pry it open. The panel and my jaw swung open.

"You...that's solid steel," I gasped.

"Didn't seem all that solid to me." She brushed the hair out of her eyes and returned to her seat, pulling a deck of cards out of her pocket and fiddling with it.

I blinked hard before pulling a handful of wires out of the panel. I took hold of a knife from the emergency kit, a clean and sturdy multipurpose edge. I cut a few of the wires and scraped off the rubber coating, tapping them together and making sparks fly. The lights flickered for a moment, a low, warm light surrounding us. Though the air was bitterly cold, the light was close enough to heat for me.

The console powered on, though the screen was admittedly dark. My fingers danced across the screens as I assessed the damage. Almost every critical system had been struck, including the AI systems. Thirteen was listening, but he was mute. Despite the fact that he was a simple program, one of my own design, it still hurt me to see him wounded. Thirteen was my only friend for a long time, the only thing to keep me sane on long trips across galaxies. Zivko had hurt my friend, and I intended to hurt him back.

Though there was one thing I could thank Zivko for: his love for talking. The communications were perfectly intact, only powered down. I filtered the reserve power through the comms, fuzzy as it fought through the water but good enough for a short range SOS signal. I set a signal on repeat and stepped away, all I could do for now finished. I never liked being underwater, or swimming at all for that matter. Water was only ever good for drinking and cooling my engines. Being surrounded by it, trapped down here, it suffocated me. The situation began to strike home in my mind, realizing that this small cabin could be our permanent residence for days.

My eyes squeezed shut as I took a deep breath. I glanced over at Mel who held the cards in her hands, eying them curiously. She held them close to her face, then far away, twisting them and holding them upside down.

"What's so interesting?" I asked, desperate for a distraction.

"Memories…" Her eyes went wide, then narrowed down again. "My parents, my mother and my father."

"Do you remember them?" My neck ached as I leaned to see the cards in her hands, the king and queen of hearts.

"She looks just like me, but I have his eyes."

My eyes danced over Mel's features, trying to picture how they would look. I found myself staring for far too long. I turned back to the console and continued addressing the damage.

I smiled. "They're very lucky to have you as a daughter."

"Do you think they miss me?"

"Dearly, wherever they may be."

She echoed my words. "Wherever they may be…"

"We'll find them."

"If we don't die here," she sighed, shuffling the cards haphazardly. "What about your parents? It may not be my place to ask, but you and Wendy don't exactly…" She hesitated.

"Look alike? Same dad, different moms. Wendy's mom…passed when she was very young. She looks so much like her, from the pictures at least."

"And your mom?"

"Alive and well, though we haven't spoken in a while."

"Did something happen?" Mel glanced at me.

A pang of sadness pushed me into my chair, crushing me like the sea above. "No, we just...drifted apart. It was my fault really."

"Do you still love them?"

"Of course I do, and I'm sure they love me. I just...I'm not the same person I was. Maybe I'm just afraid they wouldn't like who I've become." My hand had wandered to my shoulder, fingers running over the seams of my jacket like the scars on my skin. I shook my head and looked to Mel who was still glued to my cards. "Are you even listening?"

"Scarcely, these are just so captivating." She squinted deeply at them, glancing at me once again. "I'm joking, I'm not that mean."

"I think I'm a bad influence on you," I mumbled. I leaned over the edge of my seat and took hold of something to my right. A small table unfolded next to me, its flat surface glimmering with the reflection of water. "I see Sintara taught you poker, but how about I teach you a real game?"

Mel laughed gently, setting the cards on the table. "Like what?"

I was laughing at my own joke before I ever said it. "Go Fish."

↜ ↜ ↜

There was no time to debate what was more terrifying, the way the ship scraped against the rocks or the rumble of thunder that echoed into the depths like a growling beast. Mel shot up from a deep nap at the first lurch, gasping as we leaned over the edge of the cliff. The waves turned, slamming us back down against the rocks and pulling us away from the edge.

"Seatbelt on!" I shouted.

The ship turned sideways, the wings folding under the weight of the storm. The glass scraped against the sharp rocks as we rolled over onto our back, landing on our side against a sandbar. The blood rushed to my head as I looked to the console, the panel of wires clattering against itself as the lights flickered on and off. My shoulder ached as I reached for the wires, unable to take hold. I took hold of my chair and pressed the button on my harness, the restraints snapping away as I dangled from the chair. I pulled myself up and stood on the side of the chair, reaching out for the wires when the ship rocked again. I caught myself against the console, taking hold of the wires.

"Come on, old friend." I tapped two of the wires together, the thrusters whirring as they fought for life. Sparks flew from the wires as the engines groaned to life, struggling to spin in the frothy water. The ship lurched against the sandbar, digging its nose into the sand. "Mel, the throttle!"

The thrusters roared as we scraped up the hill of sand. Rain battered the glass as we broke the surface, the waves trying to draw us back under. A heavy wave slammed against our rear, pushing us further onto the shore. The engines sputtered as the rain battered against them, giving us just enough push to plant us on the sand. I could hear the water purging from the ship, pouring over the sand and returning to the sea. Lightning cracked across the sky, revealing a rocky coast and a tree line in the distance.

I lay against the cold metal, wires still bundled in my hands. The sound of rain was nostalgic at best, a rhythmic drumming against the roof of the ship. A laugh escaped me, eager to escape the ship but not willing to run headlong into a thunderstorm. Cards were scattered across the floor, the supplies tucked in another corner. My back ached as I leaned against the console.

"We didn't die!" I exclaimed.

Mel still clung to her chair, clearly rattled. "Is the bar that low?"

↦ ↤ ↤

The ship was a wreck. The walls were still damp, water dripping from between the cracks in the ceiling. Seaweed was scattered across the floor, water pooled in puddles all around us. Every storage unit along the walls of the hallway smelled of saltwater, all of their contents soaked through. The cargo hold was the worst of all. The wall had been torn open, a slash in the metal like a wound, water bleeding from the gash. It pained me to see my finest creation like this. Broken, bleeding, wounded.

I pressed my hand into the cushions of the small couch in the corner, water squelching from the foam. I scoffed. "So much for a flotation device."

"Apollo, I..." Mel hesitated.

"Don't even think about blaming yourself. I wasn't going to hand you over to those psychos. I'm not that self absorbed." I reached up towards the ceiling, taking hold of a slick handle. The long compartment unfolded from the roof, relief washing over me as I found the inside dry. The narrow bike was fitted tightly in a frame that allowed me to store it in the roof, safe from loose cargo or wandering passengers. Its frame consisted of orange pipes I had bolted and welded together, the engine and battery just under the seat. Long shocks and broad wheels were fitted to it, a truly all terrain electric bike to be easily charged by the hypercore. One of my finest inventions, though my old professor would argue minor modifications to a previous concept does not qualify as a new invention.

"Does it work?" Mel ran her hand over the seat, examining it with curiosity. I hooked my arms under the handlebars and heaved the front wheel off the frame. Mel grabbed the back of the seat and lifted it off with a single hand.

"Let's hope so," I mumbled. I was still unable to comprehend her strength. We wheeled it out onto the still-damp sand, the tide far out from the ship. The air still tasted of rain and the gray remnants of the storm filled the sky above us.

The Thirteen looked like a corpse strewn over the beach, its side pecked open by a hungry bird. A sigh escaped me, my breath like fog in the cold morning air. I hated seeing it this way, I didn't know if it'd ever be air worthy again. It wouldn't be long before Zivko was after us, but Lady Luck was on our side. With the ship underwater, our sensors never reached far from the surface. It was unlikely, if not impossible, to know where we were. But that wouldn't last.

"We'll be back soon, Thirteen." I whispered. The flood lights flickered on for a moment, Thirteen's voice echoing in my head as nothing but my imagination. "Be safe, sir."

I swung my leg over the seat of the bike, the engine whirring to life under me. A low hum shook the sand, nearly inaudible. Mel hopped on the back, wrapping her arms tight around my stomach. My breath hitched, but I refused to let anything distract me.

"Something wrong?" You could hear the smirk on her voice.

I cleared my throat. "Of course not, let's get moving."

Sunlight had broken out over the golden sands, light cascading over everything and soaking the world in warmth. Fog had settled low on the beach like a blanket of gray mist clinging to our shoes. The waves lapped up further onto the beach as the tide rose. The wind sent chills down our spines and whipped our hair in wild bundles as we slowed before a break in the tree line, which appeared almost like a road.

"Where are we going anyways?" Mel asked through the rushing air.

"To find help. We need supplies, and I need material to fix the ship. We can't stay here, we'll freeze to death before Zivko ever finds us."

"Will people help us? I mean, we're being hunted, aren't we?"

It made me uneasy to know she was right. Our wheels spun on the loose sand of the hill before we broke out onto the soft dirt. It was dark under the cover of trees, so dark I needed the headlight to be sure I didn't hit any rocks or roots. It was quiet as the sounds of the waves faded out and the chirp of birds and the buzz of bugs faded in. The trees stretched over the road like a tunnel, a generous protection from the morning sun.

Mel gasped. "I didn't know Earth was so beautiful."

"With air you can breathe and water you can drink and plants you can eat...I don't know how anyone could take this place for granted." I sighed.

The trees disappeared from around us as we broke out onto a road, a real road, pavement and all. The lines were faded and sand and dirt had dug itself in the cracks of the asphalt, but it was most certainly a road. I pulled to a stop, hopping off the bike and straining to see which way to go.

"Down there, I can see lights." Mel pointing south, holding a hand to her face to block the sun.

I squinted, eyes aching from the light. "I don't see anything."

"How can you not? You can clearly see the lights on the hill!" She exclaimed, clearly convinced I was pulling her leg.

"My eyes have never been the best...alright, fine. I'm trusting you on this one." I stretched my back before swinging back onto the bike.

"You need to get your eyes checked," she scoffed.

We followed the road for at least thirty minutes, slowly curving further and further inland. I quickly learned how uncomfortable the seat was and made a mental note to upgrade it as soon as possible. The terrain around us consisted of hills with scattered trees over the tall green grass. With every hill we drove over, another spark of hope filled us as we reached the top, then faded as we found nothing but more fields.

We rolled to a stop, staring down a metal fence with a sign on it reading 'private property, do not enter.' Beyond it, I could see a long gravel road leading further into the countryside. The gate was locked by a sturdy padlock and chain. Nervously, but slightly joyously, we left the bike behind and hopped the fence. The air got quieter with every step down the loose road as the sun still sat low in the early sky.

"Are you sure this is a good idea?" Mel asked halfway down the road.

"Absolutely not," I replied. "But who else is gonna help us all the way out here? We'll just ask for directions towards a town and be on our merry way."

An old, rusted truck sat on deflated wheels just off the side of the road. Just as we passed by it, I caught a glimpse of a small cabin sitting amongst the trees. It was an A-Frame cabin with tall front windows. The wood had been stained like the trees around it, a simple camouflage to trick the common eye. In a flash of light, the gravel just before my feet exploded into a hot blaze, molten rock exploding into the air. By pure instinct, I grabbed Mel by the collar and dove behind the truck. Another blast tore through the air, this one glancing off the bumper of the vehicle and melting the metal of the grill.

A voice echoed over the distance between us and the cabin, as gravely as the rocks which dug into my knees. "Private property, get lost."

"We don't mean any harm!" I shouted.

"I'm sick of your Angel Light propaganda, this is your final warning to leave." He didn't shout, but he spoke with such authority it shook the air.

"We're not Angel Lights! We're just travelers!" I raised my hands over the edge of the truck, revealing both wrists clean of tattoos. "Hell, we're exactly what the Angel Lights hate!"

A long silence coated the field. My hands shook as I slowly raised to my feet, showing my face to the invisible assailant.

"See! Blue hair and tan skin!"

"I gathered that." The voice replied. A stick snapped. From behind a tree, across the field and near the cabin, a man stepped out from the shadows, as if he appeared from thin air. He slung a long white rifle over his shoulder and hiked towards me, eyes tracking up and down at me. "You're damn lucky I ain't nobody else."

"Same to you," I scoffed, scanning him back. He was tall and broad. His shoulders were like shelves and his arms like beams of iron. A short, brown beard clung to his face, matching the wavy hair on his head and the hair on his arms. Two eyes, cold and dark, bore into my soul and etched fear on my heart. A worn out pilot's jacket was wrapped around his shoulders, the rolled up sleeves coated in patches and embroidery.

"Never seen an Earthling before?"

"I am an Earthling, probably more human than you are, bear."

"You're hilarious, I can't wait to get to know you." His voice was overflowing with sarcasm.

"Apollo, can I come out now?" Mel whispered. I sighed and held a hand down to her, pulling her up to her feet.

"Well, I'll be…" He gasped.

"Do you know me?" Mel asked.

"That's a…complicated question. Come inside and we'll talk." He turned back to the house, trudging through the field and gesturing for us to follow. I glanced at Mel, her shimmering eyes scrutinizing him.

"This guy seems crazy," she whispered.

"Agreed…your call."

"I'll hear him out. Besides, I'm freezing and my butt hurts."

I sighed. "Also agreed."

↳ 6 ↲

Oregon

It was a small little cabin. Some would call it quaint, I'd call it cramped. We carefully lowered onto a stiff threadbare couch and examined the room closely. There were photos on the wall, the man with his family. A beautiful wife, two lovely daughters, clearly long gone. There were diplomas on the wall; a PhD in Biology and astro-chemistry, as well as a minor in exo-planetary theory. But of all the things in the room my eyes never strayed far from the rifle he left leaning against the door.

"Can I get you two anything?" The man lifted a kettle off the stove of a small kitchenette in the corner. "I can't say I have much, but I have tea."

"No thank you," I mumbled. I glanced at Mel, she shook her head.

The man shrugged, "Suit yourself."

He poured a boiling stream of water into a small cup and dropped a tea bag into it. His feet dragged on the floor as he shuffled over to us and dropped into a lounger opposite of the small coffee table between us. He leaned back in his chair and cradled the mug, the hot water clearly having little effect on his rough hands.

"You probably think I'm just some senile old man." His voice was gravely and harsh, breath raspy as he sighed. "There I was devoting my life to my studies and the answer decides to trespass on my property."

"What do you mean?" Mel leaned forward.

"Tell me, how many planets are in the solar system?" He looked out the window as he spoke, far out of the window. Not to the trees, not to the distant waves, not to the horizon, but past it all. Past the horizon, past the atmosphere, far into deep space. He had eyes like mine, the kind that always saw the whole of the galaxy. The man smiled dryly.

"Officially eight, but I think Pluto still counts." I folded my arms with a groan. "Do you have something to give us that's more important than a pop quiz?"

"You're right, I'm getting ahead of myself. Firstly, introductions." He held a hand out to Mel and I. "Henry Day."

Mel shook his hand confidently. "Melinoe Ouranos."

My ears perked at that.

He raised an eyebrow curiously. "Unique name."

"Call me Mel."

"And you, sir?" The man held a hand to me.

I took his hand and shook it firmly. "Apollo Harrison, now get on with it. We don't have all day."

"I understand why, I've seen you on the news." The man took a long sip of his drink, letting the anxiety sit with me. "Not that I care."

I scoffed. "One and a half million dollars sitting on your couch and you don't care? I'm not convinced."

The man laughed. "Money only matters so much when you get to be as old as I am."

"Looks good on a will." I frowned.

Mel smacked me on the arm and blew an exasperated breath through her teeth. "Do us all a favor and shut up for once, let him talk!"

The man truly laughed at that. "You remind me of my granddaughter. Bold, proud, and strong. Where are you from?"

"I don't...remember where I am from. I was in a wreck, I lost my memories." Melinoe eyed a family portrait on the wall, her eyes full of melancholy with a smile. "You look like a wonderful family."

Family was never a simple thing for me. Wendy and I got along, but we had our differences. I loved my parents, but some dark and twisted part of me never forgave them for making me who I am. All the bullying, all the pain, all the hate, simply over my bloodline. After I left for university, I got so distracted with myself that I just faded away from them. Then after I became a bounty hunter, I knew for certain they wouldn't want anything to do with me. I couldn't put them in danger because of my means of making money, and my conscience was too heavy to ignore the guilt.

Henry gave a smile, and a sigh. "We were, before I let my work come before them. Nine planets, there are nine planets in this solar system. That was my thesis at least. The math checked out. Trans-Neptunian objects moving in unnatural ways, only explainable by a mass gravitational force orbiting our sun. One seemingly invisible to humans, always there but never seen."

"I read about this in middle school, it was proposed all the way back in 2016." I leaned forward on my knees, suddenly given a reason to care about the conversation.

"Purely hypothetical, but curiosity was a burden I carried. I was tasked with using my mastery in biology to create a model of what a being on said planet may look like. My team and I studied it for years, we poured our hearts and souls into our research. After many calculations and hundreds of hours of research, we were able to develop a model of the planet, and its hypothetical inhabitants." His chair squeaked as he leaned forward, placing a small tablet on the table, sliding it towards me. It displayed the image of a male humanoid with a smattering of information to the right of it.

He was tall, broad shouldered. His hair was somewhere between a light red and shade of pink, skin a ghostly white and eyes a shade of gray. The information listed the hypothetical average weight and height, roughly 200 to 300 pounds and 6' 7" to 7' 1".

"Their bones would be incredibly dense and their muscle mass off the charts, yet still lean. A larger thyroid makes them able to resist high levels of radiation and have an increased immune system due to the conditions of their planet." He made a gesture to swipe on the screen. I flicked a finger across and the truth became abundantly clear. It moved to a female model of this possible species.

"It looks just like her." I mumbled.

Mel took hold of the screen and held it close to her face. She was almost identical to the depiction, matching the description as well.

"Now, I know it sounds crazy but…" Intrigue filled his eyes as he eyed her up and down. "Mel, if you wouldn't mind me running just a few quick tests-"

"She's not your lab rat," I growled. Always hated biologists, I've seen what they can get away with. Of all the lives ruined by poor experiments, she wouldn't be one of them.

"Simple tests, think of it like a medical checkup. We both have her best interest in mind." The man sat forward in his chair. "Listen, I'm not saying that you're some…alien, but I just want to consider this coincidence as providence. And understand me when I say that if you are not entirely human, exposure to humanoid bacteria could cause serious complications to your livelihood."

"What happens if I am…an alien?" Fear was thick in her voice and faint tears filled the corners of her eyes.

"Then you will be the most important person alive," Henry smiled contently. He was genuine, and it unnerved me.

Mel looked to me, eyes pleading for permission. I sighed and waved a dismissive hand. "I'm not your dad, do as you please."

A soft smile graced her face. She nodded to Henry. "Let's do it."

They rose and shuffled through a nearby door, chattering with excitement and anxiety. The couch was itchy against my neck as I fell into the cushion. I closed my eyes for a moment, letting everything that had happened in the past days replay. I met Mel, saved her from a cult, reunited with Sintara and Wendy, raided my old college, got in a dog fight with an old friend, became the most wanted man alive, and crash landed on Earth. To think last week all I did was eat ramen and program an AI as a freelance gig. This much action was foreign to me, and it was exhausting.

The tablet on the table buzzed; Henry must have left it behind. My eyes bounced around the room like a kid about to steal from the cookie jar. I gently took the tech into my hand and clicked it on. A notification was displayed on the home screen but stayed locked behind a password. A huff of frustration escaped me as I looked around, eyes landing on the family portrait in the corner.

"It couldn't be that easy, right?" I whispered to myself as I tip-toed over to the picture. My fingers took hold of the edge, pulling it off the nail in the wall. Marked on the back of the painting was a date, "10/15/2285."

A smile crept onto my face as I tapped the date into the tablet, the screen opening with a click. I tapped on the notification, pulling open a news application. The top headline was clear, plastered across the top of the screen in bold text.

Intersystem Wide Bounty On Apollo Harrison Raised To Two Million Units, Fugitive Still At Large.

Three million dollars, more than enough to change someone's life. Anxiety bubbled in my stomach. Suddenly losing my intrigue, I set the tablet back down and leaned back, bouncing my knee up and down. The weight of the situation dropped onto my shoulders in an instant. Thirteen was almost beyond repair, the most dangerous bounty hunter in the galaxy was after us, as well as every other bounty hunter this side of the Milky Way, and Mel was making little progress on her memories. We were diving headfirst into the shallow end of a pool of acid. Every move was a mistake, every action a fool's error.

No ship, no money, no plan, no allies. The galaxy called for action, I had no response. I had no idea what to do, I needed help, but there was nobody left to help us. We were on our own now.

I dug deeper into the article, relieved to find no mention of Wendy or my parents, though I was shocked to my core when I stumbled upon a photo of Sintara. The article read, "Officer Sintara, seasoned officer of the LCCE, is rumored to have had previous connections to Harrison. Despite the rumors, Sintara is actively leading a search squadron on the convict. Other persons included in the search consist of several anonymous members of the Bounty Hunter's Guild. One known member of this guild is a bounty hunter known as Zivko, pilot of the fastest ship logged in current record. Despite previous rumors between Officer Sintara and Zivko, they appear to have teamed up as an unlikely duo to lead this squadron."

Those traitors. My knuckles turned white as I dropped the tablet back onto the table. My fists hung stiffly at my sides as I paced the room. Zivko or Sintara I had a chance against separately, but not together. It made no sense, Sintara and Zivko always hated each other, especially through their mutual distaste of the other's occupation.

A yelp came from the other room. A shiver ran down my spine. What was I thinking? I was so caught up in my own head I let emotion overrule logic. I left Mel alone with a complete stranger to run 'tests'. My feet carried me before my mind could come up with a plan of action, mentally jabbing myself for the fool's error. My shoulder slammed into the hard wood as I burst through the door. Mel sat on a small chair in the corner whereas Henry sat on a tall stool beside a clean counter covered in computers and medical equipment. The room smelled of cleaning solution and was lit brightly by white lights. The walls were tile and the floor was laminate, completely different from the rest of the cabin.

"Is there a problem?" Henry's voice was thick with confusion as he looked up from a small computer.

"I-I heard…"

Mel eyed me with a frown.

"Ah, I had to do a simple finger prick to analyze her blood, it just surprised her, that's all." Henry adjusted the latex gloves on his hands.

Mel waved a hand at me and frowned, a small bandage over the tip of her index finger. "Quit being so protective."

"Right, sorry." I nodded, backing from the room.

"It's alright son, I understand your worry." Henry's smile was genuine and warm, yet still difficult to believe. "Come, sit down. The result will be ready any moment."

Henry gestured for a small chair near Mel. I obliged hesitantly as a small ding came from a machine about the size of a toaster. A long slip of paper stuttered from the machine, Henry ripping it off and reading it curiously.

"Temperature is an even one hundred degrees, pulse is sixty three to the minute, roughly ten respirations per minute, and your blood pressure is ninety over sixty. Not too far off from the average human. On all levels except genetic, you're close to average." Henry nodded with a smile.

I leaned forward on my knees. "What exactly do you mean by 'all levels except genetic'?"

"Well, to explain it would be…incredibly complex." Henry cleared his throat before gesturing to himself and I. "Our bodies are similar in many ways, despite our minor differences. At our core, we are humans, yet we are different based on the conditions we experience as we develop. The way our bodies react to threat, injury, and disease is a slow process. However, her body is...far more effective."

Mel raised a hand. "I am...confused."

"See, in some ways the human body is inherently flawed. However, your very genetic makeup is near perfect. Your immune system is perfectly effective, your body heals wounds and injuries far faster than any human. The makeup of your bones and muscles are near perfectly effective, making you stronger and tougher. Instead of being damaged by excess sunlight, your body absorbs it and uses it in a way similar to photosynthesis. Your genes lack any of the flaws that cause cancer, and your body can destroy cancer cells that are caused by foreign effects." Henry stopped for a moment, mouth slightly slack and eyes glassy.

"You're making less and less sense here, man," I said.

He gestured to Mel. "See for yourself. Melinoe, if you'd please lift the bandage and look at your finger."

She peeled back the sticky cloth and pulled away a wad of cotton to reveal her finger completely healed, only the faintest white mark left behind that faded by the second. In the span of mere minutes, her body had healed an abrasion of the skin.

"How is that even..." I simply stopped, in awe.

He cleared his throat once more. "To put it very simply, you are the perfect human being, and yet you are not human."

"So I am...an alien?" Mel swallowed the fear in her throat.

"We're all alien to an environment we don't belong to. What good is there in calling yourself that? You are still a person, and an important one at that. We need to get you home." Henry set the long paper aside.

I was nearly out of my seat at this point. "You said you were tasked with researching it, so you must have an idea of where it is."

A hearty laugh escaped him. "If only it were so simple. Besides, I was only the biologist, you'll need to speak to the physicist on our team to get those answers. Luckily for you, she's my best friend. She lives in town, I'll take you to her."

"She knows where my home is?" Mel was out of her chair immediately. I couldn't read her emotions, some kind of mix. I don't know how I would react to news like that, but I understood the confusion.

"She may be able to point you in the right direction, I can make no promises on her behalf. Now please, give me a moment to fetch my coat. It'll be a bit of a drive into town, make yourselves appropriately ready." Henry shuffled out of the room, leaving us on our own.

It was quiet, painfully so. I cleared my throat to break the still air, speaking quietly. "So, how are you feeling?"

"How are you feeling? Knowing the person you've been traveling with is an alien," Mel mumbled.

"I really did think you were just like me. Evidently you're something…much better. Honestly, it doesn't bother me much.

As far as my entire world view, everything has been flipped upside down. Though, I always thought aliens would be a lot more frightening." I gave a shrug, really signaling to myself that I couldn't think on this any longer. It was like my mind still couldn't accept the truth, still considering it a joke to be ignored. "Definitely not the least exciting thing to happen to me since I met you."

Pain spiked through my neck as I rolled my shoulder. A harsh aching lurched along my collar bone with every movement of my neck. I pulled at the collar of my shirt and craned my neck to see, to no prevail.

"Oh my." Mel gasped.

"What? Is it bad?" My heart rose to a jog as her hands rose towards my neck.

"Your skin here is all blue and black." Her cool fingers danced across my shoulder as she examined it. "You're hurt."

"No kidding. Not everyone can heal from injuries as easily as you can." The back of her hand hit against my shoulder as she huffed. "I'm kidding, I think it's quite cool. You're like a superhero."

She raised an eyebrow, staring down at me and tilting her head back. "A superhero?"

"Someone who has incredible powers that they use to fight good. Usually people fear superheroes for their power, eventually the world turns against them." I rose from my chair and ran my hands down the seams of my jeans. "But eventually they save the world with their powers and everyone comes to love them again."

A giggle escaped Mel, one that made my heart flutter. I cursed internally, stuffing the feeling into a bottle and throwing it off a cliff. She rolled her eyes. "Surely these superheroes can't do it alone."

"Of course not, they always have sidekicks. Usually someone who stands to the side, causes trouble, cracks jokes."

She nodded with mock curiosity. "Sounds accurate to you, I'd say."

A smirk pulled at my lips. "What can I say? I ooze with charisma."

Mel laughed again, I beat down my heart. She rose from her chair and stretched her arms upwards. Her knuckles knocked against the ceiling, much to her surprise. "I need to use the bathroom, I'll be back."

She left swiftly, leaving me alone with my thoughts. I leaned against the counter and sighed. A feeling was creeping up on me like a sudden storm, as if clouds were rolling in and I had forgotten my umbrella. It was all too complicated. My mind refused to call it love. Love was for the young and sentimental. Love replaced reasoning and logic with emotion and instinct. Love clouded the judgment of the already foolish and led the blind off a cliff. It had no place here, not in my heart. Survival was the most important thing of all, above any emotion. Besides, she's an alien, right?

She only wanted to go home and I swore to protect her. For what reason? That I still didn't know. Once she was back home and safe, I'd figure out the rest. All problems had a solution, that much was a fact that was rooted deep in my mind. It was the driving force that urged me forward and allowed me to persist through all my hardships. It had been seven years since I graduated from the university at the ripe age of eighteen. All the challenges I had faced, all the choices I had made, it was what created who I am.

If I needed money, I caught bounties. If I needed a ship, I'd build one. If I needed friends, I'd make them. But at the end of the day, in this moment and time, I was standing in a stranger's home with no money, no ship, and no friends. The solutions to my problems never lasted long, they never had. All I ever did was postpone the inevitable.

The door swung open to reveal Henry wearing a heavy coat and large boots. His face was grim, but he masked it with another smile as he noticed me.

"Forgot my keys, and forgot how old I'm getting." He pulled open a drawer and pulled a keyring from it. He dropped the keys into his pocket and turned to me. "You look deep in thought."

I narrowed my eyes. "I'm always thinking, it's what keeps me alive."

"Right, of course…" His face fell despondent again. My fight or flight blared in my head as he pulled back his coat, a matte white pistol tucked between his belt and his jeans. He pulled it from its makeshift holster and held it out to me. "Take it."

Whatever game he was playing, I wasn't biting. "Why?"

"Do you have any other weaponry?"

"No."

"Then take it."

"I don't want it."

He sighed, squeezing his eyes shut for a moment. "The entire galaxy is hunting you. The most prolific bounty hunter and officer have teamed up to capture you. You are wanted dead or alive. You need to be able to defend yourself."

"I've made it this far, I intend to keep my streak going." I rolled back my shoulders and tilted my nose up.

"You can't rely on luck forever."

My voice raised in anger. "I don't kill people."

His voice was sharp, like a father disciplining his son. A truth bigger than both of us weighed in his voice, something I had yet to understand. "You want the honest truth? I couldn't care less if you survive. But right now that girl is the most important person in the galaxy. You think an alien species is going to welcome us with open arms? We need to bring her back unharmed to build trust with them. Nothing matters more than bringing her back." He pushed the grip of the gun into my sternum. "I don't care if you use it, as long as she gets back safely. Whether you or anyone else dies does not matter, only that she survives. Do you understand?"

"I-"

"That was a yes or no question, son." His brow bunched as he burned holes in my soul with his very eyes. He spoke evenly, clearly, and slowly. "Do you understand?"

He was getting to me. "Yes."

"I'm glad we understand each other." He placed the gun in the palm of my hand. "We're leaving in five."

He turned and left the room. The weapon in my hand was heavier than a thousand stars. The weight of the world dropped on my shoulders. If my problems felt like a storm before, I had become nothing more than a speck in a roaring ocean, and it was sink or swim.

⇀ ⇀ ⇀

The rusty old truck rattled down the road as the mid afternoon sun beat down on the coast. The roads were rough, as expected. The radio buzzed with a twangy tune, something I'd expect to hear on the West Coast, at least that's where I thought we were.

"Where are we anyways?" I leaned against the window and watched the world flash by.

"Central Oregon Territory. Are you familiar with it?" Henry's curiosity was genuine, without a hint of sarcasm.

I nodded nostalgically. "I grew up here, farther north."

"How far is farther north?"

"Almost to New Canada."

"No kidding," Henry mumbled. He leaned on the wheel of the truck and pursed his lips. "We're headed to a town called Monmouth, just southwest of Salem."

I sat up rigidly in my seat. "Salem? You're kidding me."

Henry sighed as a cool breeze ran through the cracked windows. "It has a bad reputation, but it really is a nice place."

"For people like you maybe."

Henry glanced at me. "The Angel Lights won't hurt you. They aren't immune to the law."

Mel leaned forward in her seat behind us, leaning against the backs of our chairs. "Someone mind filling me in?"

"Remember the Angel Lights? Yeah, the crazy cult that hates people like you and me. They started here, in Salem." I glanced over my shoulder at her clearly frightened face. "It wasn't my idea."

"We aren't even going into Salem, quit overreacting." Henry looked at Mel through the rear view mirror. "Besides, I'm with you both. I promise to protect you from any 'crazy cult'."

"I mean, he did almost glass you back at the farm," Mel mumbled while tapping me on the shoulder.

"He almost glassed both of us, thinking we were Angel Lights!" I gestured at myself in frustration.

"I live out in the middle of nowhere, I've had those Angel Lights come to my door trying to convince me to join them."

Henry drummed his fingers against the wheel. "I haven't, by the way. They're less than logical in many ways."

I rolled my eyes. "Glad to know you don't want to put me on a pike and burn me."

Henry pursed his lips. "I've got time to change my mind, if needed." Mel giggled, I rolled my eyes even harder.

The seat was surprisingly comfortable as I leaned heavily into it. My body ached from injury and my mind was exhausted from the lack of sleep. The sun flickered through the branches of the trees as we sped through the shadows cast over the roadway. The first of many buildings passed us, an old restaurant made of cracked brick and caked with moss. The next flashed by, a small bungalow tucked under a willow tree.

Before long, we were rolling through the heart of town. A university flashed by with dorm windows dimly lit by warm lights and a drove of students wandering towards a coffee shop pallidly. The red brick and white roofs felt welcoming compared to the ominous orange brick and black clay tile back on Mars.

Next to fly by us was City Hall, as well as a light blue church with black ceilings. Mel was pressed up against the glass in awe, zipping from window to window in the back seat to catch all the sights. She hardly fit in the small truck with her height. I couldn't help but smile at the hilarity of it.

"What's that?" Mel asked, pointing towards a drove of high schoolers that flooded from the church doors.

"Those would be teenagers, and a church. It's a place where people go to worship and give thanks to God." Henry sounded like a tour guide of Earth, I could hardly believe he could explain such a thing with a straight face.

I scoffed. "Don't tell me you're a believer. You just discovered the first truly alien life form ever, religion doesn't account for aliens."

Henry shrugged. "Who am I to judge the will of God?"

"It hardly makes an ounce of sense anyways."

"Doesn't it? When you've been around as long as I have, you start to realize just how hard it is to say all this was by accident." Henry gestured a hand towards everything and nothing.

"There is religion on my planet as well, though the details of such are escaping me," Mel added.

My curiosity was piqued. "Do you remember your planet?"

"Only that it is very different from yours." Mel sighed, leaning out the window as we turned onto a main street.

The sun was tucked behind the roof line of the tall brick buildings on either side of us as we followed a long road eastward. Before long, we pulled into a parking spot of faded white lines and Henry clicked off the car. Henry popped open the center console and pulled out two dingy hats, tossing one at me and handing the other to Mel.

"Genius disguise," I grumbled as I pulled the hat over my hair.

"It was the best I could do on short notice." Henry glanced at Mel up and down for a moment. "Not much I can do about the height though."

"I'm good at making myself small." Mel bundled her hair together and pulled the hat over it, mostly hidden by the cap.

We hopped out onto the dingy street and into the evening air. It was cold, but not nearly as cold as it was on Mars. By my guess, it was early spring, just shaking off the ice of winter.

Mel and I dared not fall far from Henry as he strolled casually down the street. A few people noticed him, one even saying hello in a voice I could tell was genuine. So much for a town full of cult members, these people were innocent.

I jogged up to Henry's side. "Where are we going again?"

He stopped and nodded at the drab brick building we stood under. A large neon sign was bolted just above the wooden door with a diamond shaped window cut in it, the sign reading "Angel's" in swooping lettering.

↪ 7 ↩

Angel's

The door groaned on its hinges as the foyer swallowed us whole. It was cleaner on the inside than on the outside, much to my surprise. The dented drywall was painted a dark blue and the floor was polished in a dark stain. The tables and chairs scattered about were clearly worn yet still held their shape. A long bar seemed to fill half the narrow room, metal stools lined up against it. It was a quieter day, yet about a dozen patrons still filled the bar.

"What day is it today?" I whispered to Henry.

"Sunday, this is their church," Henry whispered back.

A round man hunched over the bar glanced at us, cradling his beer like it was his child. He scanned Mel and I up and down and scoffed. "You kids old enough to be here?"

Part of me was genuinely offended. "I'm twenty five, dips-"

Henry backhanded across my arm. "Don't."

A door behind the bar swung open. An older woman with broad shoulders and curly dark brown hair pulled up in a high bun strolled out with a case of alcohol in her arms. A smile crept onto her face the moment she saw Henry. "I knew the cat was acting weird, she must've smelled you coming. From a mile away at that."

At the words, as if summoned, a short haired tabby cat with stripes across its forehead rubbed against my leg. It stared at me and meowed loudly. It's deep, copper colored eyes dug into my soul.

"Margarita likes you, it seems. She doesn't usually like new people." Henry knelt down and ran a hand down its back. "It's been a while, both of you."

"I see you've adopted some new students." She set the case down behind the bar and leaned against the hardwood.

"We both have a habit of picking up strays, it seems," Henry said jokingly. His smile dropped a moment later, revealing a face that screamed 'serious.' "We need to talk, it's important."

"It best be about her," the woman mumbled while scanning Mel up and down. She held a hand to her mouth, blasting a loud whistle through the room. A scrawny man younger than myself with dark skin and light pink hair appeared in the doorway with a crooked apron on. A Jovian, smaller than most. "Ajax, take the bar."

He straightened out the apron and ran his damp hands down the front. "On it, Kate."

Kate strolled around the bar and gestured for us to follow her to the corner booth, not nearly as private as I would have liked. Henry sat down and Mel followed him quickly. Begrudgingly, and with an ounce of salt directed at Mel, I sat down nervously next to the woman.

"Introduce me," Kate said to Henry.

"Right." He gestured to myself and Mel. "This is Apollo and Melinoe."

"Kate Angel." She shook my hand firmly, then Mel's, pausing for an awkwardly long time to examine her once more.

Henry cleared his throat. "I could hardly believe it either, but she is still a person, Kate."

Kate drew her hand back to herself. "I've heard all about you two on the news, though I assume it's all hog wash anyways. If you're with this senior citizen and you're here, that could only mean one thing."

"We need your help," I said.

"You need more than help. I can tell just how desperate you are." Kate folded her arms and leaned back in her seat. "Henry and I used to work on the same research team, I was the head astronomer and physicist. Lord knows why I agreed to track down a planet that only maybe existed, or why I let it consume my entire life."

I leaned forward. "Did you find it?"

"Mathematically? Yes." Kate nodded. "And yet we never did see it."

"You couldn't see it?" Mel piped up now.

"We knew we were looking exactly where it was, the math was perfect, and yet there was nothing, only empty space."

"Like a ghost," Henry added.

"Why didn't you send someone there?" I couldn't help but ask, despite it being a dumb question.

"We did, he never came back," Kate mumbled.

We all went silent for a moment. I could hear another patron mumbling on the phone, the cat meowing as it hopped up on Mel's lap, and Mel yelping in surprised at the unfamiliar creature. She ran a hand down its soft back, only after a moment of hesitation. Kate cleared her throat.

She turned to me now. "You got a ship, kid?"

"I have...a ship," I mumbled.

"It's a bit soggy at the moment, but I'm sure Apollo can fix it in no time." Mel hardly glanced away from the cat, smiling at it now.

My back stiffened. "It's in need of repair."

"Good enough for me. I'll give you all the data I have on Planet Nine, plug it into a starmap and it should take you to the right place."

"Should?"

"Like I said, the last guy never made it back."

"What makes our odds any different?"

Kate gestured to Mel. "You got her."

I frowned. "I appreciate the sentiment but I don't think that will give us any better chance at finding a planet that even you have never found."

Kate raised an eyebrow. "I mean it, just not like that. Whatever civilization is on that planet, they're clearly more advanced than us. If they've never been found it's because they didn't want to be found. They've managed to hide an entire planet for thousands of years on all levels except gravitational. She is the only thing to slip through the cracks."

"Why haven't they sent anyone to find her?" I leaned against the vaguely sticky table. "If they've been hiding all these years surely they'd wanna cover up their mistake. Besides, how did that ship crash? Why so far out in our systems?"

"All great questions to ask when you get there, for now you better go fix that ship. I'll dig up my old drives and get you that data as soon as I can. Until then, you two need to lay low." Kate became even more serious, if that was any possible.

Henry popped back into the conversation in his usual unusually cheery voice. "You can stay with me until then, I have a spare room."

The door to the bar creaked open, a sound I'll never forget so long as I live. Like it was warning us of the threat that strolled through the doors. Four men, all tall, all broad shouldered and barrel chested, all wearing white shirts and pants. One looked right at me, eyes digging into my soul as he mumbled to his friends. He unbuttoned the end of his sleeve and rolled it up, revealing a familiar tattoo.

Shock spiked through my system. "Angel Lights."

Kate's eyes went narrow. "Move kid, I'll handle this."

My knees felt like jelly as I slid from the booth and shuffled back against the wall of the bar. I swallowed the fear in my throat but it only further dared to burst from my chest in a sharp pain. I could see one of the patrons nod to the men before slipping out of the bar, the same man who insulted us as we walked in. Many less than family friendly words roared through my head. First Zivko, then Sintara, now this.

"You're in the wrong place if you think you're welcome here." Kate rose to her feet and folded her arms. Though she was shorter in height, she towered over them with a nose tipped to the sky. Mel came to my side as Henry rose to his feet as well.

"We'll be needing you to leave," Henry declared in a deep voice.

"They're wanted by law, protecting them makes you an accomplice." The man in the front of the group looked down at them.

"In case you haven't noticed, so long as you're in my establishment you're under my law. I'll say this once and once only, go tell the rotten coward you call a preacher that these people are under my protection, and any attempt on their life will result in the ass whooping of a lifetime." Kate's very presence was like a wall of force, an indomitable spirit that let nobody tell her otherwise.

The pistol tucked under my shirt felt heavier than ever. It was like fate itself was whispering in my ear, and I wouldn't let it tell me the time had already come. I refused, I wouldn't, and yet here I stood in the shadow of death. What I wouldn't do to be back on the Thirteen and flying away safely like I always did, like the coward I always was.

"Apollo, I'm scared," Mel whispered in my ear.

I wanted to say a thousand things back. I wanted to tell her I was afraid, that I was on the verge of tears in fear, that I wished Wendy was here because she always protected me from bullies. A deep part of me wished she wasn't even here, knowing she's the one who got me into this mess. But I didn't say any of that. My voice trembled, giving not even an ounce of confidence, and yet it was as if the words themselves had power. "It'll be okay, I'll protect you."

The first punch was thrown by Kate, a harsh crack against the leading man's jaw that would echo in my mind forever. His heels fell from under him as he fell back into his compatriots, pushing off them in a flurry of attacks. Kate met his attacks with a side step and shove over a nearby table, meanwhile Henry met two forwarding attackers with a chair that broke into a thousand pieces off one man's shoulder. He continued his attacks with two pieces of chair still left in his hands, but was shoulder checked into a table by the fourth man.

I jumped in without thinking, literally. My feet planted harshly against the fourth man and sent him flying as I hit the floor. A heavy boot slammed just short of my head as I rolled under a table. My breath hitched as a solid hand grabbed the collar of my shirt, threads snapping as I pushed against it. The grip pulled me to my feet and slammed me back down onto a nearby table. I grabbed onto a tall glass and smashed it over the man's face. He screamed and held his hands over his eyes.

I had no time to survey the damage as one man fell back from attacking Henry to go for me. He shoved me like a freight train, forcing me to land on my back and sucking all the air from my lungs. Mel pulled me out of the way of a chair and back to my feet. Mel raised a protective arm in defense as he swung again, the chair breaking like glass. Mel was left undaunted, looking intently at the strength even one arm held.

The man realized her strength in horror as Mel learned her power in awe. Boldly, she went on the offensive. She'd clearly never thrown a punch, at least not to her recollection, but she was a devastating force. After a few misses, she connected right to his temple. The man's eyes rolled back into his head as he folded to the ground. Her fear had completely vanished and was replaced by a giddy laugh full of awe.

Henry clocked in one last punch on the man he held against a table, bruised but far from out of the fight. Kate threw a man over the bar with a crash of glass and dusted her hands off. The only man left conscious was huddled in the corner, hands pressed against his face that bled profusely.

He squirmed and writhed in pain as Kate stepped up to him. "My eyes! You blinded me, damn you!"

Her hand closed around his collar and picked him off the ground. She threw him into a chair and pulled his hands away. He screamed and fought against her grasp but it had little effect. Kate scoffed. "Just a cut below your brow, the only thing in your eye is blood."

The man seethed in his chair, mumbling nondescript curses and slurs under his breath.

"Henry, use the phone behind the bar to call 911, Sheriff David will recognize the number. Melinoe, Apollo, help me gather up these clowns before they wake up," Kate demanded.

We obliged, helping Kate gather the unconscious men and sit them back to back before wrapping them up in duct tape. Kate also duct taped a rag over the eye of the bleeding man, only after complaints of feeling faint. Melinoe made it look like easy work, lifting the several hundred pound men with ease. Her physical strength couldn't be understated.

"Kate, the sheriff is on his way," Henry said from behind the bar.

"Good, you get these two back to your place as fast as possible. Don't open the door for anyone unless I call and say to open the door. Keep the blinds closed and stay indoors for at least twenty four hours." Kate's voice was stern and clear, a natural born leader.

"We can't sit around like that for that long, I need to get back to my ship and get it fixed," I objected.

"It'll have to wait, it is of utmost importance to protect you two from the Angel Lights." Kate was not arguing with me, it was her way or the highway.

Mel put a hand on my shoulder. "It'll be okay, just trust them."

I drew in a deep, exasperated breath and sighed, secretly okay with the idea of hiding from the Angel Lights. Like a child under the covers, it was cowardice which controlled me. "Fine. Twenty four hours, no more no less."

⊹ ⊹ ⊹

The truck ride back home was deafeningly quiet. The truck rattled on as we cruised back through town, listening to the sirens in the distance as they approached Angel's to pick up the assailants. My body ached from the brawl, previous injuries digging their claws deeper into my flesh. I leaned back in my seat and reached into the flap of my jacket. The three bottles tucked tightly into the pocket inside my coat threatened to slip loose and break as I pulled them from their concealment.

I held one bottle out to Henry. "You guys want a beer?"

"Where on Earth did you get that?" He raised an eyebrow.

"Behind the bar while I was helping Kate tie up one of those guys."

Henry pulled one of the bottles from my hand and glanced at it before shoving it back into my arms. "Of course not, I'm driving, and how exactly did you pay for that?"

I shrugged, popping the cap off one with another bottle. "Put it on your tab, and for the record I'm used to my transportation driving itself."

Henry rolled his eyes. "Do you get drunk every time you leave a planet's atmosphere?"

"Ain't much else to do up there," I mumbled while handing Mel an opened bottle.

She hesitantly took the bottle and drew in a long sip. Her face screwed up with disgust as she forced herself to swallow the concoction. She coughed harshly, trying to rid her mouth of the taste. "This tastes disgusting."

I took a long gulp and examined the bottle as well. "That's Earthlings for you."

The sun had gotten very low now, the sky painted vibrant colors of orange and pink. A cool breeze ran over my neck as I leaned out the window to take some deep, fresh breaths. By the time we got back to Henry's cabin I had downed the bottle and, to my surprise, so had Mel. She handed me the empty bottle as she climbed out of the truck.

"How's it feel?" I asked mockingly.

"Don't feel a thing," she shrugged. "You humans have weak alcohol."

Henry laughed with genuine hilarity as I stood in shock. He took the last full bottle from my hand and popped the cap off. He stopped on the first step up to the cabin, looking out at the colorful sky and the setting sun.

"You did good today kid, but don't let your guard down. This is only the beginning of your troubles," Henry said.

"I've been in trouble since I was eighteen. It never ends for me."

Henry thought about the question deeply for a moment, taking a long sip before sighing. "Everyone's troubles end eventually."

He turned for the door Mel left open, leaving me alone with the sunset and his words. I couldn't tell if his words were wise or something stupid wrapped in a nice bow. I stepped towards the cabin and pulled the door shut. A slow jog down the long dirt road leading to and from the cabin ended with me hopping over the gate and up to my electric bike. It still had a small canvas bag strapped to the handlebars, containing a few crucial pieces of tech I kicked myself for leaving out in the open for so long.

The knots were stubborn, but I pried the bag free of its straps and threw it over my shoulder, pain flaring again as I did so. The gate screeched open as I wheeled the bike through and up towards the cabin. I did not intend to waste twenty four hours, this would not be a setback but rather an ace in my sleeve.

The kickstand flicked out and caught the bike as I took one last look at the setting sun. I'd missed it, but not enough to come back. I was in the eye of the storm, every move had to be calculated and precise so as not to step back into the torrent that surrounded me. But calculated and precise was my middle name.

The door swung shut behind me, twisting the deadbolt into place before shuffling into the kitchenette and yanking open the freezer. I took the ice tray out and dropped it on the counter. Ravaging the drawers, I found a plastic bag and towel to make an ice pack for my shoulder.

"You better refill that ice tray," Henry declared from the other room.

"I see you Earthlings didn't learn your lesson about plastic," I shouted back, spilling half the water in the ice tray on the floor as I put it back in the freezer.

"You better not have spilled a drop of that on my floor," Henry added. I wiped it up, begrudgingly.

On my way towards the small lab Henry had set up, I saw Mel strewn over the living room floor looking up at a small TV. She seemed completely enamored by a cheesy romantic comedy that filled the screen. I rolled my eyes as I left the room, pushing down a grin that tugged at my lips. Henry leaned against one of the counters, phone up to his face with a voice buzzing in his ear. I dropped my bag down next to a stool beside him, dropping into the squeaky seat.

Henry gave me a sparing glance while continuing on with his phone call. "Right, gotcha. Well stay safe, you and I both know how important this is. If there's any more trouble, you call me first. Talk soon." The call blipped away as he set the phone down on the counter with a sigh.

"Everything alright?" I asked while pulling an assortment of items from the bag.

"Everything is fine," Henry replied. "What are you doing?"

"Damage assessment, mind if I use your computer?"

He hesitated. "Fine, but if I see a single rubber ducky downloaded on that laptop I'll have your head, is that clear?"

I almost forgot to respond as I had already begun to pull open the laptop. "Crystal clear."

"And would it kill you to rest?" Henry added as he began to leave the room.

"No rest for the wicked." I shrugged painfully. "You're not my dad."

"You don't seem like the type to listen to your parents anyways, maybe that's how you got tied up in this mess."

My hands slapped down on the table out of instinct. "Not a word about my parents."

Henry's eyebrows raised, watching intently as I slowed my breathing and dropped back into my seat. I didn't even realize I had stood up. The room was silent for a moment before Henry spoke again. "I didn't know it was a sensitive subject."

I pulled a small rectangular machine from the pack and plugged it into the computer. "It's not, I'm just tired."

Henry nodded slowly, listening to me clack away as I uploaded a direct connection to Thirteen.

"Let me know if you need anything," he said before leaving the room.

A blue light flickered from the small machine connected to the laptop, a projection flickering to life on the empty wall to my right. Lines of text started at the top and ran all down the projection before flickering to life with a schematic of Thirteen. I ran a command in the text box on the laptop, more lines of code running over the schematic while processing all damages sustained in the crash. The schematic updated, all the wear and tear of our harsh reunion with the Pacific Ocean included. I tucked the ice pack into my shirt just over the injury and pulled a long metal pen from my pack. A tap on the table made the tip of it flicker with blue light as well. Making gestures with the pen, I could spin or zoom In on the schematic, perfectly portable and efficient. I had become glad I spent the money needed on my emergency kit, it was quite the dent in my wallet when I invested in it.

"Alright Thirteen, it's airborne or bust. Let's get down to business."

I spent the entire night meticulously analyzing every system and examining every part. Not a single wire, pipe, or bolt that I had placed with my own two hands went unseen. Before long, or more aptly, three hours later, I had a list of every part in need of being replaced and every system in need of repair.

The damage had been mostly surface level, the gash in the wall creating a system-wide disconnect from the primary power. Luckily, the reserve power line had been built into the ceiling, meaning crucial systems had managed to stay online as we sat underwater. The wall could be repaired using scrap metal from another ship, the same way I built the ship in the first place. I'd need a scrap yard, one with a large freight ship, a freight ship with half a kilometer of wiring I could salvage.

Easier said than done, but not impossible, especially not to me. I opened a browser page and began scouring the local internet, bare bones as it may be. Whether it be a miracle or a stroke of unimaginable luck, there was a scrap yard north of us. It was an old slough that was once a wildlife refuge, now the permanent resting place of several gen three freighters, older variants than what I worked on but good enough. It was six miles away, the bike would never make it there and back. I decided Henry's truck was the only viable option.

The keys to Henry's truck rattled as I pulled open the drawer that contained them. I pat myself on the back for making the mental note of where he kept them as I folded up the laptop and shoved it into my bag. The door creaked as I pulled it open to see Mel asleep in front of the TV. My footsteps were hidden under the sound of romance tropes and cheesy dialogue. My icepack had gone to nothing but water, leaving a puddle of condensation on the counter I left it on.

Just as my hand closed around the handle of the door out of the cabin, an itch of anxiety crawled up my neck. Leaving Mel here alone felt dangerous, but staying on Earth for much longer was far more dangerous. If not cultists or bounty hunters chasing us down, the moderately toxic atmosphere was practically suffocating. I'd be quick, very quick.

I made a quick exit as not for the cold night air to wake Mel as I shuffled down the steps towards the truck. A few light smacks to the face shook off the fog of exhaustion that lingered over me. The door clicked open with a quick turn of the key before I hopped inside. It had been a while since I drove a car, but how hard could it be? Just like riding a bike. The electric engine whirred to life, leaving the headlights off as we rolled away from the cabin. After a brief interaction with the gate, I broke out onto the open road and began making my way north.

↤ 8 ↦

Scrapyard

Despite my efforts, most of the radio stations had gone dark. An ominous darkness had fallen over the land, not a single excess light or device left on, as to preserve electricity. Life hadn't been easy for Earthlings, especially not for myself when I lived here long ago. It was a messy, broken planet, one that science had done its best to heal, but the scars never left. Risen sea levels, a weakened and unbalanced atmosphere, and soil that fought against growth were all proof of that.

Martians had an endless land ready for terraforming, the Jovians had a vast system of satellites and spaceports, and the Saturnians had a connected ring of asteroids, but all Earth had was a planet broken by a past civilization. We all held appreciation for it, for it was where our distant forefathers had first dared their expansion into space, and yet we all held it with an open grasp of disgust. Its history was important to learn from, but most wouldn't grieve if it vanished in an instant.

My reminiscing vanished as the first edge of metal appeared through the trees that hung over the cracked road. It was taller than the landscape around it, the long freight ship nestled crookedly in a pocket of rolling hills. Portions of it were nothing but bare frame, massive panels ripped from the hull leaving the remnants of pipes and wires like sutures over a wound. It had enough parts to build a fleet of cruisers, and yet it sat as scrap. The Martians would've had a field day with it.

A chain fence approached quickly, broad signs of warning bolted to the wire. I rolled to a stop and hopped from the truck, leaving the headlights on and engine running. There was a small booth with just enough space for a security guard, but not a person to be found. Compared to the megastructure that loomed above, the security measures were not as grand. The gate wasn't even rigged with an alarm, only a simple lock with a mechanism for opening and closing.

Without hesitation, I pulled a long tool from my backpack and jammed it into the lock of the small booth. The door snapped open as the lock broke, and I gingerly tapped a button within the booth to open the gate. The tool retired to my belt as I knew I'd need it later, hopping back into the truck and rolling into the scrap yard. Sheet metal, pipes, and rusted wires had been stacked high in the piles all around a long ramp leading up to the cargo bay of the ship. Had the slightly corrosive rain not ripped the metal to shreds, my job would've been easy. The truck surged up the steep incline before falling level in a massive room, tilted only slightly askew. The area was lit by the headlights of the truck, a long and tall room leading far into the ship. Cracks of moonlight bled through holes in the walls and ceiling, sprinkling the dim room with a sparkling kaleidoscope of color. It was large enough to fit entire homes into the bay, and that's exactly what it was used for. I parked just next to a tall panel on the wall to my right.

The glass had been broken, leaving a metal frame encompassing a wide board of switches and plugs. I left the engine on again, this time for good reason. My bag slumped against the wall as I wasted no time getting to work. The hood to the engine popped open, presenting a whirring battery perfect for what I needed. I dragged two jumper cables from under the driver's seat and plugged them into the battery of the car. Sparks flew from the ends as I tapped them together. I missed the smell of sparks. The ends clamped onto two prongs jutting from the panel as sparks whirred through the air. Lights flickered dimly all throughout the room, a dull buzz filling the air around me.

"Now this is exciting," I mumbled while sliding a respirator over my mouth and a set of wide glasses over my eyes.

Time was of the essence, popping the laptop open and plugging it into several ports on the panel. I ran several commands, discovering a few systems still intact, the most useful of which being the satellite array and high altitude sensors. Connections to the power grid meant plenty of usable wire, and surface level at that. They couldn't have made my job tearing things apart any easier. I yanked a long metal pole off the ground and jammed it under the edge of a large square of sheet metal, working to pry it off and revealing dozens of wires and pipes. A smile pulled at my lips that I couldn't resist, our luck was turning around.

"Thirteen, you'll be back in action in no time."

I got to work quickly, cutting off power to the wires and pulling them out in long strings. One by one, I cut each wire and attached it to a small winch on the front of the truck, making instant spools of cable perfect for repairing the ship. It was monotonous, but before long I had managed to pull enough wire from the walls to repair Thirteen, plus some extra. I then pulled more sheet metal off the walls and threw them in the back of the truck with the wires. But curiosity got the best of me.

"What else might be around here..." I hunched over the laptop and typed away, comparing Thirteen's schematic to the freighter.

"Your hypercore is still running, suppose they didn't care to risk destroying this ash heap of a planet... Cratus always said to never let laziness overcome initiative." My fingers clacked away at the computer, cautiously clicking into the primary controls of the ship. I ran power from the hypercore to the panel next to me. In what seemed like an instant, the laptop became completely charged, as well as the truck.

A static fuzz filled the room with an electronic whine like a dying beast. The high pitched frequency buzzed as a transmission came into focus, coming through a speaker built into the panel.

"Incoming transmission, registration code 114106." A text-to-speech program buzzed from the panel. I thought I had shocked myself, a jolt of fear arcing through my body like rushing electricity. My fingers tingled and my knees felt weak, that was Thirteen's registration code. I accepted the transmission.

My voice trembled, much to my chagrin. "Thirteen?"

"S-Sir, Zivko's ship entered the u-upper atmosphere."

As if the fear before hadn't been enough. "When?"

"The Dark Matter b-breached the upper atmosphere three hours ago, he entered the sh-ship one hour ago," Thirteen's voice elaborated, the stuttering echo bouncing around the cargo bay.

A light projected from the panel and onto the floor just before my feet. I stepped back and observed the camera footage of Zivko wandering through my ship, picking at my lockers and fiddling with my controls. Rage overwhelmed fear, my feet crushing the projection as I leaned into the speaker.

"Where is he now?"

The question was answered in perfect timing. All around me, the specks and dots of sparkling moonlight disappeared. A low rumble bore at my ears as I craned my head to see it. In the perfect shape of the Dark Matter, Zivko hovered over me.

"Thirteen, can he-"

"The ship is equipped with thermal sensors, but the metal around you makes you almost invisible."

"Almost?"

"It senses the electricity."

The ship dropped down onto the frame of the ship above us, the metal creaking and groaning under the weight. I scrambled to pull my things back into my bag but I already heard the cargo bay door opening. A long rope dropped from the ceiling in a perfect line leading up to the ship, and it rattled with activity. I could hide a computer and some tools, but not an entire truck, and not one connected to the ship like this. Time ran out as I heard the rattle and whir of gear as Zivko repelled down from the rope. I slid behind the truck and pressed up against one of the tires. His feet hit the ground in a menacing thud. My ears rang as they struggled to hear the sound of his careful footsteps and quiet whistling over the buzz of the truck's engine.

His voice was cool like ice and smooth like glass, he'd done this a thousand times before. "End of the line, Star Man."

A light bulb flickered on in my mind. With a lack of witty response, I dug into my bag furiously and pulled out the small rectangular machine and plugged it into the control panel. The click of a gun was enough to make me freeze, the small metal box slipping from my hands and dangling from the panel.

"Turn around," Zivko demanded, I obliged.

He wore a black canvas jacket with a thick vest over top, dark pants to match. His arms cradled a long, black, metal assault rifle, it looked just like the kind they'd used a long time ago with less black powder involved. A black cloth had been placed over the lower half of his face, his coppery skin and white hair peeking over it with steel gray eyes. His Venusian side was showing, I could see the old friend I once knew.

"Hands above your head, now." The demands continued, and I obliged once more, with a long metal pen entwined in my fingers.

"We used to be friends, weren't we? You taught me everything I know about how to survive out here."

"Where is the girl?" He wasn't exactly asking, more so ordering I told him. My attempt at stalling was a certified failure. Worth a shot.

"Not here," I shrugged.

"Where." He raised the rifle level with his eye, glare sharp through the sight attached to the top rail.

"If I told you, I'd have to kill y-"

"This isn't a joke Apollo, she's coming with me whether I have to kill you or not. I don't want to do it, but I will. Now tell me where she is or quit wasting my time."

"Okay, okay, I'll tell you. She's that way." I swung my hand wide, pointing at nothing in particular. An electric whir filled the room as the magnets in the floor burst to life for the first time in years.

Zivko fought to keep the rifle in hand, but before long it had slipped from his grasp and stuck to the floor solidly. I whipped open my jacket and pulled my gun from my belt. The hard polymer rattled as I held it level at him. He paused. His eyes were tense on me, a look of what I could only call fear in his eyes. He believed I was going to kill him, and it scared me. But that moment was over, his eyes relaxed and his shoulders eased.

I was weak, he could see right through me. Too cold for hell, too fiery for heaven. He used to say that about me, maybe it was still true.

"Go on, do it."

I swallowed hard. "We both know how much I want to do this."

"But you won't. You've never killed, you won't start now. Especially not me." His hand rose, pulling down the mask and revealing his familiar face. His clever smile had once been a beacon of hope to me, he was once someone I could call a friend. "We were friends once, maybe we still could be. I mean, all this for some random girl? Since when did we let a bounty get between our friendship?"

"Those days are long over, we both know that."

"Are they? Don't you miss it? We fought together, worked together. Chipping away at your debt every day, living on our own terms. It was fun, wasn't it?" Zivko truly did think fondly of those days, back when I was easy to manipulate.

"You made me everything I am, and I made you everything you are."

Zivko gave a genuine laugh. "Glad to see you've kept your humor. It was all just business. You gave me a ship I couldn't lose in and I...well, I gave you a friend. The only one in the galaxy. If I wanted to thank you for giving me the fastest ship in the galaxy, I would've paid you. But I didn't, did I?"

A bang rang out, flying wide and thudding into the metal far behind Zivko. He seemed to expect it, slowing his laughter on his own time. "Let's be honest with ourselves, we all know you're just one big suck up with Oppositional Defiant Disorder who looks only for approval from others. Honestly, it's shameful to say you've run free for this long, it gives us real bounty hunters a bad name. It won't be long now though, they say it's good to make friends in high places."

"Sintara would never ally with the likes of you," I snarled.

"Of course she wouldn't, that's why it wasn't her decision. We all take orders from someone." Zivko shrugged.

"And you take orders from who exactly?"

"Myself."

Zivko lunged forward with near blinding speed. His palm slammed hard against my wrist, making a wild shot ring off before the gun dropped from my grip. He reached down for it but was met with a solid kick to the hand as I sent the gun across the room, raising my knee into his gut. He stepped back and recollected himself.

"You've heard the rumors, they say I bested Sintara in hand-to-hand combat in the past." Zivko bounced on his toes with hands raised and a grin.

"Only drunkards believe rumors." I never thought quoting him would sting so badly.

He was blindingly fast, each punch looking for quantity over quality. My arms struggled to block each blow to the head, taking one to the temple that nearly knocked me out. His shoulder bashed hard against my body, sending me into the control panel in the wall. He grabbed me by the collar and slammed me against the metal several times. My head spun.

"Tell me where the girl is and I'll leave you for Sintara to find." Zivko still smiled, like this was a friendly conversation.

"Go to hell."

My hands closed around the jumper cables plugged into the console and jammed them into Zivko's gut. His body seized from the shock with rattling pain before he fell hard against the metal floor. I dove for my gun and took hold of the hard plastic, rolling to my back ready to take a shot instantly. Zivko was out cold, two trails of smoke rising from charred marks on his vest. I rose to my feet, keeping the sight trained on his head. My finger pulled on the trigger, but I flinched. The bullet flew wide, harmlessly landing far behind him. I dropped the gun out of horror. I nearly killed him. I wasn't even thinking, just seeing red. I wasn't like him, I wouldn't be, and yet. In my mind's eye, I could see the blood pouring from his head, gray matter painting the cold metal. My knee hit the floor and I wretched against the wall of the ship. When I finished, I turned and ran.

I yanked the jumper cables out from the truck and slammed the hood down, sliding into the driver's seat and pulling a tight u-turn. The wheels spun on the slick metal as I tore through the night air, headed back to the cabin. My eyes strayed to the rear view countless times, imagining the horrifying shadow of the

Dark Matter chasing me. I beat the thought out of my head and locked my eyes on the road, focusing on the goal and not the obstacle.

"Twelve hours," I mumbled.

~ ~ ~

The engine clicked off in an instant as I twisted the keys from the ignition. My head thudded against the wheel as exhaustion began to overtake me. I couldn't recall the last time I got a full night of sleep, I could hardly remember the last time I was on a planet long enough to see both day and night. Years of space travel left my sleep schedule in shambles, though Thirteen tried his best to keep my circadian rhythm intact. The cold air chewed me to the bone as I shambled up the stairs and crept through the front door. Scattered across the room, wrapped up in the ratty old clothes Wendy gave her, Mel lay in a light sleep as the TV buzzed with more romantic comedies. I sighed, tip toeing across the room and over her to reach the TV and flicking it off.

"Hey, I was watching that." Mel's words slurred together through the fog of sleep as she failed to sit up and make a proper protest.

"Clearly. How can you even watch this garbage?" I scoffed.

"They're heartwarming and hilarious," Mel declared.

"Wrong." I flopped across the couch in an exhausted stupor. The room was silent for a bit, a while even. I snapped out of my sleep at the soft whisper of Mel's voice.

"Have you ever loved someone Apollo? Other than yourself, I mean."

My head rolled to the side to see Mel with her knees to her chest, staring at me from across the table. The cabin was almost completely dark, lit only by the light creeping through the edges of the curtains, yet it was still enough to see the gentle curve of her face and the glow of curiosity in her eyes.

"I love my parents, and my sister." I sighed.

"You know what I mean." Mel frowned.

"No, I've never loved someone like that."

"Why not?"

"I'm a busy man, that's why. I don't have time for being sentimental and sappy. Now will you please let me sleep?" My arms folded as I stared deep into the ceiling, forcing my eyes shut to block out the world. I surrendered to sleep once more, snapping awake again at more words.

"I think there's more to you than that, Apollo. Back at the bar, you told me it would be okay, but you didn't actually know if it would be okay. You lied...to make me feel hopeful."

"That's just what we humans do, tell ourselves and each other pretty little lies until the truth swallows us whole."

"But things did turn out okay."

"They don't always."

"And yet you would lie and risk your wellbeing to protect me. That sounds pretty heroic to me. You're more than just your anger."

"Yeah?" I yawned.

"I think you lie to yourself, Apollo."

"Thanks for the therapy session, now can I please sleep?"

Mel responded only with a quiet huff and the rustle of blankets, throwing one at me before wrapping up in one herself.

"Thank you, and good night," I said lethargically.

"Good night," Mel mumbled quietly.

It felt like I had merely blinked before the dull light of morning beamed through the edges of the curtains while my eyes ached. My mouth was completely dry and I had lost any sense of time completely. It could've been two hours or twelve, I didn't know the difference. The couch shook as Henry tapped on the armrest.

"Care explaining what is in the back of my truck?" Henry frowned.

"Important materials," I grumbled.

"From where?" Henry's voice raised in frustration.

"An old shipyard nearby, now leave me alone." I grabbed a nearby pillow and slammed it on my face. Henry yanked the pillow from my grasp and threw across the room.

"Up and at 'em, you have no daylight to burn and I can't get you out of my hair soon enough. At least one of you is pleasant to be around, and it's a good thing it's her and not you."

"Fine, fine." My body ached as I pushed myself out of the relentlessly uncomfortable couch and onto my feet.

"What happened there?" Henry gestured towards my arms. They were covered from wrist to elbow in bruises, all blue and purple. I restrained my surprise and shrugged, pushing my shoulder further into pain.

"Crash landings aren't meant to be easy." I ran a hand through my hair and felt dried blood coating my hair. Whether from our bar brawl or Zivko slamming me into the wall, I didn't want the evidence there any longer than needed. "Do you have a shower?"

The answer was yes, and it was cold, but it eased the swelling on my shoulder and up my arms. My curls were in such bad tangles it hurt to wash the blood out of my hair, and I regretted not bringing an extra change of clothes with me as I pulled on the same clothes again. I found myself caught in the mirror again, examining closely. The bags were still dark under my eyes, but with clean hair and a clean face I looked healthier than I had in a long time. Doing the right thing was a drag, but it seemed to do wonders for the complexion.

My hands fiddled with my messy hair as I shuffled back out into the living space, finding Henry sitting in his chair with a plate of food and Mel eating like she had never eaten before on the couch. Henry nodded towards a plate of eggs, bacon, and toast sitting on a counter by the kitchenette. The plate was hot on my hand, but as much as I hated saying it, I missed Earth food.

Real eggs were far better than the mostly fake kind they shipped out to Spaceports. I dropped down next to Mel, more entertained by how fast she ate than the cartoons plastered on the TV. We sat in mostly silence, scarce conversation popping up between bites. Henry sat a pot of coffee on the table once it had finished brewing, I took a cup of it and poured sugar into it. Then another cup. Then a third. I had drunk half the pot by the time breakfast was over, Henry was impressed.

Mel slipped off after she had finished her food and I ran to the truck to get my bag. I stood in the morning air for a moment, taking it all in. The wind ran through my hair and sent chills down my spine, the smell of fresh grass and sea salt filled my lungs, and the warmth of the sun beat down on my skin. There were many places one could live on Earth, and though it was dangerous to spend more than an hour unprotected in the sun, there was nowhere else you could feel the warmth of the sun on your face like you could on Earth.

"You ready to make some repairs?" Henry asked from the top step of the cabin.

I rolled my eyes. "Don't say it like you'll be any help."

"There's no I in teamwork, kid." Henry shuffled down the steps with Mel in tow. Her hair was darker than usual, still damp and stuck together in thick strands. Her face was slightly pink in the cold, rushing into the truck only to find it more cold inside. My hand clamped down around Henry's keys after their brief flight through the air.

"I'm driving?" I asked.

"Seems like you drove just fine yesterday, and I'm still sore from that fight back at Angel's." Henry groaned.

"I am an excellent pilot." I grinned.

Mel bobbed her head and Henry mouthed the words to the repetitive pop music that buzzed through the radio as we tore through the cold morning air.

"This music sucks," I mumbled.

Henry laughed. "It was my daughter's favorite, now my granddaughter's. You'll survive listening to it for a day, besides, it's kind of addicting."

It kept me awake at least. I was painfully tired, there wasn't enough sleep in a lifetime to cure this level of exhaustion. We came to a halt near the path we took off the beach. I squinted down the long tunnel of trees, unsure of whether or not we would fit.

"Do you know of another path?" I asked Henry.

"People didn't care much for tourism after the shoreline changed, there are very few real roads left. Go ahead, it'll be alright." Henry nodded, though clearly unsure.

The road was bumpy, rattling my skull and reminding me of the crash landing that put us on this planet. The rattling truck broke the serenity of the quiet forest, even a few birds peeking through the trees to see what all the commotion was. The wheels touched down on the soft sand and the trees faded behind us as our destination lay on the horizon.

"That's your ship?" Henry raised an eyebrow.

"What's with that tone?" I raised an eyebrow back.

"God help us all," he mumbled as we pulled up beside it.

My boots slammed down into the oddly firm sand around the ship, the recently receded waters leaving a packed pad of sand as hard as stone. I pulled a spool of cable from the bed of the truck, also finding my bike securely tied down.

"You brought it with you?" I asked Henry.

"I guessed you'd be in a rush out of here," Henry replied while pulling a panel of sheet metal out of the truck and dragging it across the sand. I took a spool of cable and threw it on my shoulder.

"I mean...obviously." My heart hurt. Nostalgia had taken over, maybe I did miss Earth after all. "Let's get to work already."

We started from the inside, finding the interior of the ship mostly dried out after a stretch of cold but dry weather. The waves lapped at the edge of the ship as we shuffled through. The main living space was dimly lit by what crept through the gash in the wall. I began by fixing the wires within, cables slowly stretched across the gap like stitches pulling a wound together. Using a small welding kit at a painfully slow pace, I welded a large panel over the gash that slowly sealed the light and left me in the dark inside the ship. I nearly jumped out of my skin to find Mel sitting in the captain's chair, fiddling with her deck of cards.

"What are you doing in here?" I asked after composing myself.

"Thinking. What are you doing?" Mel asked over my shoulder as I leaned on the console.

My fingers glided across the screens with perfect familiarity, I barely needed to look at it. "Running a diagnostic, the sooner we get Thirteen back online the faster we can get off this rock."

A bar popped up on the screen with a small label declaring that it was indeed running a diagnostic, though painfully slowly. I groaned and dropped into one of the seats. I watched Mel sloppily shuffle the cards, narrowly avoiding sending them into the air. I gave a small laugh at it, despite her proud face.

"I've been practicing, it's harder than it looks," she said indignantly.

"Riiight." I nodded sarcastically, slowly stopping and thinking deeper. "Sounds like you've been getting more memories back."

"Slowly, and vaguely. It's like trying to remember a dream." A few cards spilled from her hands as she spoke, one of which being the queen of diamonds. "It helps when I'm watching that box thing. It seems to…remind me of things."

"You have crappy romance on your planet too?"

"No, it's…everything here is so dreary and dark. Those shows and movies are so much more light and optimistic."

I laughed. "Like I said, us humans love our lies."

"It's only as much of a lie as you let it be." Mel frowned. "My home is...was also dreary. We worked hard to make it a paradise."

"Very deep, you should be a motivational speaker."

"I have to be, or else you'd have given up by now and I'd be...well I don't want to know what'd happen to me. So please don't give up, for my sake."

I gave a snort. "I dunno, I don't work this hard for free."

We sat in silence for a brief moment, a luxury I found less than common anymore. I soaked in the sounds of electricity flowing back into each piece of the ship, restoring the systems like blood delivering oxygen to each organ. A dead animal coming back to life, the Thirteen was slowly resurrected.

"Can I ask you a question, Apollo?"

"Must be something sensitive, you never ask if you can ask me questions." I sat up in my chair, readying my defenses.

"When this is all over, do you think you could bring one of those boxes back to my home planet?"

My sides burst in laughter, doubling over in my seat and putting my knees to my chest. "Really? That's your deep question?"

"It's an honest question!" Mel defended herself.

"Right, right, serious." I wiped a tear from my eye, getting the last laughs out of my system. "They're called TV's and I'm afraid the signal won't reach you that far out, but we do have recorded versions of most things."

"I don't wanna watch a bunch of old stuff, I only like brand new stuff," Mel grumbled.

"You'll have to start a broadcasted entertainment industry back home," I suggested. A planet without TV's, maybe these aliens were less intimidating than I thought. If their technology isn't advanced enough to make crappy romance movies, it'd be easy picking for the humans.

"I will do what I must," Mel said confidently. "By the way, you didn't have those bruises on you arms last night-"

Saved by the bell. A beep came from the console as the floodlights gave way to the familiar white light. I was on my feet in an instant, reading the console quickly. All systems were back online with minor damages left to repair.

"Tell me, do people on your planet believe in miracles?" I asked.

"To an extent, you?" Mel asked back.

A grin pulled at my lips. "I do now."

"Sir, can you hear me?" Thirteen's voice made its welcome return back to the cold halls of the ship.

The air was pulled from my lungs in utter relief, leaning against the console and seeing my efforts come to fruition. "Yes I can. Great to have you back, old friend."

"I am not programmed to feel extreme emotions, but I am theoretically glad to be back."

"Is that something you two did?" Henry called from the outside.

I rushed out of the ship and back onto the cold sand. The hydraulics unfolded the wing which had been forced by the waves. It had only taken a few hours of work, but the Thirteen was back. "We're back online, let's get these repairs finished up."

"Besides a new paint job, it's good as new out here." Henry wiped the oil from his hands with an old rag. He did an exceptional and quick job, not that I'd admit it. "It's a tough little ship, I'll give it that."

"No other ship I'd rather fly, and none like it. 'Cause I built it." I smirked, overwhelmingly proud of my achievement.

Henry's pocket buzzed. He pulled a small phone from his pocket and held it up to his ear. "Great to hear your voice. Yep. Send it. Thank you for everything, I'll repay you later." He rolled his eyes at a final comment before putting it back in his pocket.

"Sir, I've received an encrypted message from someone by the name of Kate Angel."

"Decrypt it, we're up and out in five." I turned to Henry and held out a hand. "I can't thank you enough, and I don't thank people often."

Henry laughed and took a firm hold of my hand. "Don't thank me, just get her home. That's all the thanks I need. The world is about to change, I expect to see the two of you leading the charge."

"We'll do our best." I looked back at the ship to see Mel stepping out from the ship. "There's an old saying on Jupiter, only help a man you're willing to help twice. Keep an ear out for us, we might need you."

A smile, somewhere between pride and melancholy, crossed Henry's face. He placed one hand on each of our shoulders and shook his head. "Between the two of you, you have everything you need."

"We'll miss you." Mel pulled us both into a tight hug, which would be hard to resist even at my full strength. Without another word, she let go and took a teary eyed step back.

Henry laughed. "It's a small galaxy we live in, I'm sure we'll see each other again."

"Take care of yourself," I said while following Mel back to the ship. I glanced back one final time as the cargo door slowly lifted. Henry gave one last wave before turning back to his truck. I called out one last time. "Thank Kate for us!"

"I will by paying for those beers!" He called back without turning.

The door sealed shut. The ship was quiet, messy, but functional. Every inch of the ship needed a deep clean, but there was no time for detailing. I stopped by one of the lockers built into the wall on the way to the bridge, pulling out two jumpsuits that had stayed mostly dry. I pulled one over my clothes and put my jacket over top of it, handing the second to Mel. "If you want some semblance of gravity–"

"I'm aware of why I want it. You couldn't make it any more stylish?" She teased.

A small laugh escaped me as I finally made it to the bridge, dropping down into my seat and flicking an array of levers and buttons. The ship truly came to life now, the engines roaring to life after a bit of resistance. The early morning condensation rattled off the ship as we lifted off the sand. I welcomed the sense of relief that arrived with the familiar feeling of being airborne. Mel held a look of despondence as we made our way higher and higher into the atmosphere. She craned her neck to look back down at the land below, struggling to catch a glimpse of the ground.

"Something wrong?" I asked.

"I'll miss this planet," she replied. "It was so quiet, so peaceful. For the first time since I met you, I felt...relaxed."

"Well, before long you'll be back on your home planet sipping margaritas...or whatever you drink there."

"But then you'll have to leave, won't you?"

"You gonna miss me?" I scoffed, assuming it was a joke. She went quiet, I realized the foolishness of my reply. "Oh–look I...I don't know what will happen after we get you home. It's near impossible to say what might happen next. But I'm sure you have plenty of people back home who miss you a lot. Believe me, you'll forget about me eventually, most people do..."

The cabin was quiet for a moment, Mel still straining to look down at Earth as it slowly faded away from us. "Apollo, what's that?"

"What's what?" My fingers moved faster than my brain, flicking a switch to reveal a live feed from cameras on the back of the ship. Just behind us, following at an impossibly close distance, the Dark Matter was on our tail. "You've gotta be kidding me."

"Sir, it appears the sensors failed to detect him due to his close proximity," Thirteen declared.

"I gathered that, Thirteen! This bounty brain has persistence, I'll give him that," I seethed. "He's had the chance to shoot us down but he hasn't. He must be waiting for us to reach the upper atmosphere."

"Why would he do that?" Mel asked in a fright.

"He has someone waiting up there. He wants us stuck between a rock and a traitor." My eyes narrowed on two blinking lights in the distance dead ahead of us. Two lights, blue and red, flickering in rhythm with each other. I could only assume it to be Sintara, though I refused to shoot them down regardless.

"Apollo, do you copy?" Sintara buzzed through my radio.

"Yeah, I hear you loud and clear, traitor."

"I deserve that, but I need you to understand that I don't want this anymore than you do," she added.

"I can tell by the fact that your lap dog is hot on my tail with guns hot and ready to turn me to stardust!" I shouted back.

"This is bigger than that, Apollo. You and I both know that." Her voice was remorseful, and scared. "They're dissecting the crash, they're decoding the coordinates as we speak."

My words choked me, hesitation gripping my heart. "I don't know what you're talking about."

"There's no time for playing coy, Apollo. Zivko reported who you found refuge with, it only reaffirms what the IEO already knows about her. They know, and we can't change that."

Henry was in danger, and it was my fault. "I have no clue what you're talking about!"

"Listen to me, Apollo. If they get those coordinates, it will be a war between her people and ours, and it's not a war we can win." Her voice broke in terror. "We need to stop them, and we can only do it together. For the sake of our civilization, I need you to trust me right now."

I looked at Mel, the look in her eyes hurt my soul. She was scared, more scared than I had ever seen her before. The idea that her people would crush us in an instant wasn't an over exaggeration, and her eyes showed that. The sound of the ship rattling had already been enough to frighten her, but this new realization was far more than enough. She nodded her head up and down. "We have to trust her, there's no other choice."

"I know," I conceded.

"If you're with me, set a course for Proxima Centauri. Jump as soon as you exit the atmosphere, we'll rendezvous in the atmosphere of Planet C. Use the planet for cover from solar flares."

"Why the hell should I listen to you?!" I shouted.

"No time to debate, the clock is ticking. Sintara out." The radio cut silent.

"I can't stand cops," I grumbled, setting course for Proxima Centauri.

The hypercore began to warm as the atmosphere began to melt away. A slow beep filled the room, a beep that raised in frequency quickly and rapidly. Zivko was locked onto us, ready to engage. In record time, the hypercore whirred to full capacity. Just as we broke the atmosphere, Sintara and I both launched into the stars, leaving Zivko alone and confused behind us

↵ 9 ↩

Return to Zion

Proxima Centauri blinked into view with a sickening feeling gripping my stomach. Zion could be seen orbiting it in the distance, a tiny speck paling in comparison to the size of the star. It wasn't nearly the largest star I had ever seen, barely a fraction of the Sun; but it was thirty-three times as dense. These factors created the closest star to the Solar System, as well as one of the most dangerous systems to explore. But the familiar star would have to wait, for Planet C was rapidly approaching.

Planet C, dubbed Acheron by the IEO; seven times the size of Earth and two hundred times colder. A band of asteroids curled around the huge icy blue marble, creating rings around the planet of ice and chaos. Few people had ventured onto it, fewer had made it out alive. It was deemed that the asteroid belt around made for a more habitable place, and as such a series of bases had been built on the largest of the asteroids. It was primarily inhabited by asteroid miners, and with their hulking beasts of machinery made to crush and refine asteroids on-site, our ships were nothing but tiny blips in a colony of mechanical miracles. Our signal was hidden amongst the radar pings of machine and rock. The ships found equilibrium in orbit around the planet and hovered as near to each other as possible, the port on the bottom of my ship connecting to the bottom of hers.

I lurched from my chair and stomped out into the hallway, pulling open a hatch in the middle of the floor that hissed as it swung open. At the other end of the long tube, Sintara locked eyes with me. Without thinking, I climbed into the tube and soared through the weightless tunnel, colliding with her and crashing to the floor of her ship. I got at least one good punch in before a sharp tool pressed into my side. My fist held its place above my head as I froze. Sintara had pressed the barrel of a revolver into my gut.

"What the hell, Sintara?! First I thought you were on our side, then you work with Zivko and hunt us down, then you have a change of heart and decide to help us? Do you ever make up your mind?" I spat the words like a bitter taste in my mouth, hoping she would ingest some inkling of the anger that coursed through me.

"I never wanted to work with him, but orders were orders, and if it meant finding you I would do it without a doubt," Sintara said calmly. "I let him lead the way because I knew he'd find you. He knows you better than I do."

I bit my tongue hard, choking back the insults and barrage that would only earn me a hole in my stomach. "How do they know about the coordinates, and what does the IEO know about Mel?"

"I'd be happy to answer if you'd be so kind as to get off of me. This isn't an interrogation, and if it was, you would be the one being interrogated." She poked the gun into my stomach harder.

With a scoff, I pushed myself off of her and smoothed out my jacket. My thumb ran along my jawline, finding a long bleeding scratch running over the corner of my jaw. She always was good at hand to hand combat. Mel pushed me to the side and helped Sintara back to her feet, though she needed no help at all.

"You always were too quick on the draw, I'll admit you're fast." Sintara nodded at me before giving Mel a close hug. "I'm glad to see you're safe. You haven't murdered one another yet, so I take it you two have been getting along?"

"To an extent." Mel glared at me, frustrated with my behavior.

With a scoff, I turned away from the two. The Wasp was a significantly smaller ship than the Thirteen. The narrow hallways gave only barely enough headroom for Sintara, Mel had to hunch over so as not to hit her head on the ceiling. I followed the sleek white hallway down and into a cargo hold, one that had room for criminals to be handcuffed to the walls and a thick metal panel that hid what could only be a stockpile of weapons. I made note of it, still unsure of Sintara's loyalties. The floor and ceiling here were made of the same sleek white material as the hallways, but the walls were made from a gray gunmetal material. It was a trick engineers used to make a room feel bigger, convincing the brain that it was in a wide open space and not in a tin can floating through a void that constantly wanted to kill you. A stack of crates stood in a staggered pile next to a small table connected to the wall. This was the common room of the ship after all, very welcoming.

The crate I dropped onto creaked as I took a seat, CTA stamps of authenticity streaking across the side of it. I fiddled with the locking mechanism of the small metal box I sat on. Sintara kicked the side of it, making me nearly jump out of my skin.

"Don't touch that."

"Clearly not that important." I scoffed as her fingers ran across a screen built into the forearm of her uniform. The panel I had made note of popped open, revealing what I expected to be there. Two rifles, one an assault rifle and one a long rifle, were strapped along the top and bottom of the stockpile, framing the array of weaponry in the center. Several pistols, even a few knives. She had a thing for guns.

"Half of that stuff is ancient you know, you're overdue for an upgrade," I pointed out. Boxes of ammunition were also stuck to the wall, containing bullets that had black powder in them instead of what I liked to call 'death batteries.'

Gunpowder was a thing of the past now, too expensive to import so far out. We'd found much more use in making batteries out of the material than burning it once, despite those very batteries having poisoned the oceans of Earth not long ago. Lithium ion batteries were good for flashlights and tools, lithium sulfur batteries were good for killing people. Cost efficient, greater energy storage, but less rechargeable. Some idiot thought taking the molten plasma used in the hypercore and strapping it to his arm would be a good idea, something I've always wanted to try but was never brave enough to do so. The idiocy created a new age of weapons, energy guns capable of melting a hole straight through even the thickest of metals.

Gunpowder became a collectors item, and the new age of energy weapons spawned more than just plasma-arms. Railguns became popular amongst bounty hunters and law enforcement. Instead of plasma, these weapons fired metal projectiles using powerful electromagnets. Some fired tiny pins, others sharp spinning discs, and they all hurt a hell of a lot more than plasma. Better than that, trackers could be implanted into the projectiles, and subsequently their targets. Lead was a thing of the past, now you'd be lucky to walk through an outer colony Spaceport without having a hole burned through your gut or your arm ripped off by flying blades. Suddenly, lead didn't seem so bad.

"I have a thing for classics." She pulled the long pistol one would call a revolver out of the holster at her hip and placed it inside, showing her empty hands to me. "I'm unarmed, your turn."

"You have electrodes built into the knuckles of your gloves, I've seen them up close and personal." I interrogated with a suspicious squint.

She rolled her eyes. "Just cough up the gun already."

Of course she'd notice, it was her job after all. The zipper of my jumpsuit snagged a few times as I revealed the clothes underneath it, along with the gun that was still tucked under my belt. The gun felt lighter in my hand after I pulled the long battery out of the handle and set it on the floor at my feet. "That's the best I can do."

"Where'd you get it anyways? You never carried a weapon on you before." Sintara stepped forward and kicked the battery across the room.

"Hey!" I stood up, looking up and locking eyes with her. Her glare dug into me, but I held my ground.

"No man carries a weapon without the desire, need, or expectation to kill or be killed."

I took a micro-step closer to her, close enough to feel her breath on my face. "Tough times for me, I never know what to expect anymore. Especially from people I thought I could trust."

Sintara sighed. "In another world, you and I could've been great partners. We make a good team when we aren't at each other's throats."

"Well this isn't that world, and we are at each other's throats. You should be used to it by now."

A look of genuine hurt graced her face. A rush of...excitement? Fear? Something coursed through my system. The kind of shock you feel as a kid when you get away with something bad, wondering if you could do worse, wondering what punishment was waiting. It wasn't a good feeling, but it was intoxicating, addicting. Sintara stepped away, showing Mel standing in the doorway with an awkward look and a nervous posture.

Sintara leaned heavily against a crate, looking down at her shoes and running fingers through her hair. "We were friends once, weren't we? After you and Zivko…I was the only person you had. I tried my best to keep you out of trouble, but I could only do so much."

Shame dropped onto my shoulders, crushing my lungs and pressing the life from my body. Guilt, my one weakness, the one thing I wasn't immune to. It was like making a fist with a handful of needles. All signs pointed to danger, to a mistake I needed to fix, and yet I decided to turn away. I knelt down and picked up the battery of my gun, putting it back into my gun and the gun back onto my belt.

Sintara continued, the weight crushing me harder. "I knew the risks, but it was a gamble I was willing to take. I'm all in now, and I know I made the right decision because you could've flown anywhere in the galaxy and you still followed me."

I nodded slowly, admitting to the foolishness of my actions. Henry would not be proud of me for following Sintara's orders to follow her here, but I did. "I made a promise to protect her, and if whatever is happening here may compromise her safety, then it's my job to put an end to it. I didn't come here because of friendship."

"Fine." Sintara stood up sharply. "Only business, I understand. Let's get on with it then, shall we?"

"Sintara, wait." Mel stepped forward. An inkling of confidence started to flicker off of her, like beams of light touching the ground through the branches of a tall tree. "We all know something big is happening here, something that could threaten the safety of everyone in this galaxy. We can't let our past transgressions get in the way of the protection of all the innocent people in this world, and we can't work together if we don't truly trust each other."

Silence for a moment, hope and uncertainty mixing in the air. The crushing weight of the world rested on all of our shoulders now, a burden that becomes lighter with teamwork. I'd experienced it before between Cratus and I, between Zivko and I, but I'd never have imagined this triad. If I was being honest, being out in the cold vacuum of space standing next to Sintara and Mel felt like an oasis and a prison. Somehow, the three of us together made the task feel possible, but I was still stuck doing it. But if I had to do it, I may as well not do it alone.

"She's right," I admitted. "If you wanted to kill or capture us, you would've done it by now. So for now, I trust you, Sintara. Now please, inform us why we're in this star system of all places?"

For a moment, I saw something in Sintara's eyes. Something soft, like if you could hug someone with just a look. She was so proud of Mel, and of me. I didn't want her to be, it meant I owed her. She snapped back to her regular self in an instant, I wondered if I had imagined her odd look. "The crash. They've started dissecting it after some...anomalies. You wouldn't believe me if I told you, but I have footage of it happening."

She brushed past me and tapped on the table, the white surface blinking into a screen that displayed video logs from the ships cameras, as well as videos from the cameras woven into Sintara's uniform.

Sintara turned on one video and stepped away, as if frightened to relieve the moment again. Few things were able to shake Sintara, which only added to the uncertainty that crept up my spine. "This happened twelve hours ago, I saw it with my own eyes."

The video began with Sintara trailing three other men in IEO regulation spacesuits, examining the wreckage with tools that scanned every piece and part by running a web of lasers over the environment. They were mumbling nonsense, trying to sound as smart as possible in front of an officer of the LCCE. Sintara turned to see a huge thruster laying in the rubble just below where it had once been attached to the ship. The camera rattled to a halt, lowering down as Sintara crouched to look at something. Her fingers reached out to grab a stone that rattled in place. It wobbled on its own for a moment before starting to roll uphill. Dust followed it, like a film ran backwards. The dust wrapped around Sintara in a cloud, rewinding back into place as dirt on the ground.

A rumble filled the microphone and the ground had begun to shake. She rose to her feet in shock; the massive thruster that lay buried in the sand had begun to spark and creak. Disbelief stirred in my heart as something out of a movie occurred. The thruster lifted off the ground, reattaching to the body of the ship as bolts and rivets rose from the dirt and twisted back in place. The scientists shouted in fear, the camera shook from what could only be astonishment and fear.

Sintara reached over and turned off the video, leaning against the table. Her face was devoid of emotion, refusing to feel the fear and shock she had felt before. "They're calling it time regression. Their guess is that it's the result of the hypercore of the ship failing."

My hand ran along my chin thoughtfully. "But the hypercore couldn't have failed, we would've noticed it. Every scanner in this system would've gone haywire."

"Because it hasn't happened yet," Sintara said quietly.

"For it to create this extreme of an effect on time would have an equally extreme effect on...space." The light bulb flickered on in my head. "Oh...oh no."

Mel raised a hand with her face screwed up in confusion. "Is anyone gonna tell me what this means?"

"The rapid transference of infinite energy into an explosion of equal size." I bit at my thumbnail, pondering the implications of such a disaster. The possibilities of consequences were endless. Very few hypercore explosions had ever occurred, most happening while exerting an excess of energy and dampening the force of the collapse. But the nature of this explosion meant something entirely different.

Other collapses caused a forceful lapse in space time, forcing a ship forward in time. One might not realize a hypercore collapse had even occurred for weeks, that is until whatever location that ship had been going was plastered with shrapnel like a blast from a shotgun. The amount of energy required to push what is left of a ship through space and time would eat up the brunt of the explosion, yet calamity still often followed. But an object being forced backwards was unheard of. For an explosion to launch a ship back in time was near inconceivable, and the implications of this were even more mind bending. Beyond all of this—

Mel clearly didn't understand, but Sintara and I exchanged a glance of realization. If the ship came from the future, it explained why none of Mel's people had come to find her; she hadn't left her planet. If our theories were correct, that means two versions of Melinoe must exist in the universe at this exact instant. My head throbbed. The IEO was already hiding everything they knew about her people, but their desire to claim Mel as not only a prisoner but a subject of experiment could have only multiplied tenfold. As many questions were raised as were answered. It made my head spin, so much so that I stumbled backwards into a crate.

"Sweet stars above," I mumbled.

"The implications of this are..." Sintara blew a breath through her teeth. "They've already raised the bounty to two million units, roughly three million dollars."

I waved a hand dismissively. "I assumed so. We're running out of time, we need to do this before they can get their hands on the coordinates. We need to be the only people who have them, and for now, they do not. It's only a matter of time though, assuming the black box of the ship is still intact."

"It is, they're attempting to decrypt it now but are running into some very particular troubles."

"That means?"

"The database is backwards," Sintara declared, accepting the words as pure fact and nothing less. It was foolish to rationalize between reality and myth anymore. I was standing next to an alien from the future, the horizon of possibility was endless now. "It's corrupting their softwares, it even killed an AI. They're attempting to develop something to solve the problem before everything goes bang."

"How long until then?"

"By their observation of how the ship is...reconstructing itself, about six hours."

I pulled up my sleeve and checked my watch. "We'll make do. Am I to presume you have a plan?"

Sintara smiled, the first smile she had manifested since we saw her at the Spaceport. "As a matter of fact, yes, yes I do."

The toes of my boots dug into the dust of Zion and my breath gently fogged the helmet of my suit. I shimmied up a tall dune and poked my head just over the crest, looking down at the crash site. Scrap had been scattered all across the planet, but this was the central hub of the remains. Several sleek white hubs had been built, triangular panels making up wide domes with climate controlled environments inside for scientists to do what they were told. Several of these hubs were set up over smaller parts of the ship, including the pod I had found Mel in only a few days prior. I swore under my breath, if only I hadn't left evidence, not that I knew any better at the time.

Sintara's ship ripped through the air over me, low enough to give me a well deserved scare. I huddled under the apex of the dune, hiding from possible onlookers who might desire to glance at the incoming ship. The ship touched down on the opposite side of the base, a well needed distraction for the plan Sintara had created. Slipping over the edge, I slid down the rocky dune for several feet before leaping to my feet and running down as fast as possible. The sand slipped from under my soles as I came to a halt behind the nearest hub. Air came back to my lungs through ragged breaths.

A wing stuck up from the sand like a monument to future mistakes to the left of the hub, tiny parts and pieces left in the sand with no time to be categorized or collected. It was most certainly a ship of foreign make, at least not one I had ever seen. It looked more similar to the ships in history books of man's first expeditions into space, and yet the sophisticated internals could be dated at least a thousand years later. Internally, I screamed in rage. There was a puzzle of the universe I'd begun building since I was a child, only now it was clear; I was missing half the pieces. I threw the half built image off the metaphorical table of my mind. Better to start from scratch than try to fit in this madness. A breath released all reason left in me, finally accepting this new reality. There was no more logic to be found, anything was possible at this point.

Rounding the edge of the hub revealed a hexagonal door leading into an airlock. It was hastily built, I'd be surprised if anyone inside had actually taken off their suit, much to my advantage. I ducked down as a figure emerged from the airlock with a backpack of tools dragging him down. The gravity here was heavier than that on Earth, meaning it was also heavier than that on Mars. A real Martian might crumple under the weight, an Earthling might hardly feel a difference, but changes in gravity were my specialty. My feet carried me through the airlock before it hissed shut, leaving me standing in a white void as some pressure came to the room. The next doors opened, revealing a room with at least six scientists looking at me. They all wore equally white suits of cheaper make, fitting the 'good enough' standard that all of the IEO and CTA held to the utmost degree. As expected, none dared to remove their helmet, though a few had removed their gloves for ease of work. They gave me a suspicious look due to my more "sophisticated" suit, though the rough patchwork around the elbows suspended some disbelief.

"Who are you?" One asked as the rest went back to their work.

"I'm uh, Ben. I'm an engineer from a nearby freighter, said they needed some extra work for a bonus." I lied excellently.

"Whatever," the woman mumbled, clearly jealous at my prospect of a bonus. She waved a hand haphazardly to the opposite wall. "Take your pack and get to work, they're breaking down these hubs in one hour."

I shambled over and heaved the heavy pack over my shoulders. It weighed more than it looked, but it had all the tools I would need to cut into the most crucial parts of the ship. In truth, they hadn't had time to call in any engineers, the CTA was too busy working them all to death on freighters or in Spaceports. A ship was a delicate piece of technology, one that we had trained day and night to understand the ins and outs of. No thirty minute debrief would give these researchers the necessary experience to see a ship the way I did. Like a doctor knows human anatomy, I knew a ship better than the back of my hand.

Exiting the hub proved to be a most eventful scene. Sparks lifted off the ground and into the wired innards of the remains, something I wouldn't believe seeing had I not observed Sintara's body cam footage. An odd hiss gave me a jump as I approached a door that had been pried open. A hose that lay splayed from the ship was sucked back into place, the pressure going with it. My helmet gave light to an already unfamiliar scene as I hopped aboard the ship. It felt as though the world around me had not been moving backwards but I had been moving backwards through it.

The ship whirled around me as I was flipped forward onto my back, my pack crunching as the danger of this environment revealed itself. The metal panel I had stepped over had lifted off the ground just as I had gone to step off of it, flipping me over my head. It rose into place on the wall with burning red hot edges. Starting at the bottom left corner, it burned brighter before cooling in an instant, melding flush with the wall before our very eyes. An arm helped me back onto my feet as a nearby engineer came to my aid.

"You alright man?" His voice was shaking, astonished at what was happening all around us. "That was...gnarly."

I groaned. "I'll be fine. Broken ribs don't pay my bills."

"Amen to that. Just watch your step," he warned, though far too late.

I brushed off the arms of my suit and continued through the ship. Counting panels as I walked guided me to what should be the heart of this ship, however, this ship had not been designed as I'd expected. Panels had been cut out of the walls already here, but no researchers were in sight, nor taking any interest in it. Through the gap, I could see a familiar spider web of pipes and wires connecting to a backwards beating heart. The hypercore lay in the same room as the ship's mainframe. Foolish design for a society we expected to be advanced. Glancing back and forth down the hallway to avoid being followed, I crawled through the gap and into more of the unexpected.

I had hoped to find the familiar blue glow illuminating the room, but no blue light was to be found here. The room was a burning red, despite the air being bitterly cold. Frost built up on the edges of my visor, and a buzz had started in the back of my head. I didn't have much time, if hardly any at all. Anxiety forced me to glance back at the panel I had entered through, only to see it lift and seal me inside the hellscape. With a rush of adrenaline I searched the room for an alternate exit, but I couldn't find any.

With the press of a button, the radio in my helmet buzzed to life. "Sintara, do you copy?"

"Excuse me for a moment please," Sintara said to someone other than me. "I'm here, where are you?"

"Inside the ship."

"Good, now look for-"

"No, I mean inside the ship. I'm sealed in, I don't see any other exit."

Sintara swore under her breath. "Don't panic, I'll figure something out." The fuzzy blare of ship thrusters came over the radio followed by a distorted thunk. Another curse from Sintara with one final message before the connection was cut abruptly. "Zivko is here."

If I could get any more anxious, those three words did it. In a desperate attempt to ignore the newfound hurdle, I began my work. A computer had been built into the wall, a simple screen and keyboard jutting from a panel. My mind continued to buzz as I powered it on, only to be greeted by dozens of symbols and signs completely unfamiliar to me.

A tap on my watch brought a live camera feed of my ship into the heads-up-display of my helmet, revealing Mel sitting and fiddling with her cards in the bridge. "Thirteen, access suit camera. I need a translation."

"Certainly sir," Thirteen declared as Mel shot up from her chair.

"And pull up the camera on bridge controls," I added.

"With pleasure," Thirteen continued. "My translator appears to be malfunctioning, unless we are lacking this language in my database."

"I've never seen anything like it," I mumbled. The lines consisted primarily of sharp lines with corners connecting in triangle and square patterns, connected at the bottom with a congruent line below all of the text with gaps for what I could only assume to be letters and numbers. "Mel, do you recognize this?"

"As a matter of fact, I do," she replied. "This is...our language. I can't remember what it all means but...I can try."

To rely on someone with an unsure memory was less than optimal, but I had no choice. "I'm looking for star maps, ship logs, set courses, anything."

"It's all backwards but…" Mel leaned into the screen and squinted hard. "You're looking at the details of the crash, you need to go backwards somehow."

Go backwards on a backwards moving computer, simple enough. Clacking across the keyboard, I tried a few things to no avail. Though I had no clue what any of the keys meant, I could understand the arrows that allowed me to select icons and words on the screen. "Mel, I need some kind of select or enter key."

"Uhh— Oh, third button to the top left."

With a press, I was pulled back to some sort of menu screen, backwards icons with labels lining the screen.

"Third row down says something about star maps."

I selected the third screen, pulling open a single star map. It was a planet. Scientists would categorize it as a super-earth, or a sub-neptune. It had a rocky surface and large oceans of ice. Its moons had been mostly developed and populated, though a few settlements and one massive city likely to be the capital rested upon volcanoes reaching out of the icy seas.

"Is this it?" I asked breathlessly.

"Yes, that's my home," Mel said with teary eyes. "Elysia."

"But there's no other planets on this star map. Not even the sun is charted here. To us, you're invisible. But to you, we don't even exist," I said, utterly bewildered. Questions and confusion would wait. "I'm taking it, the entire hard drive."

Wires and cables stretched from the wall as my hands tugged at the keyboard and ripped it free. The internals of the computer were messy, hastily wired and unsecured. This ship had been built in a hurry. Pulling a screwdriver from my belt, I dug away at excess parts and exposed a flat, rectangular piece of glossy black metal. It was heavier than it looked as I pulled off the arteries and nerves of wires that held it in place. Flipping it over in my hand, text exposed itself, laser engraved on and exposing the bluish gray of the unrefined internal layers of the metal.

An explosion shook the room and slammed against my chest like a mallet hitting a gong. With ears ringing, I pulled the pistol from my belt and scanned the room. Light poured from a harshly opened metal hole in the ceiling framed by sheer metal sticking out in jagged edges. A metallic ping filled the air before a metal tube dropped into the hole, ticking as it spun across the floor towards me.

"Holy sh-" My body moved before my brain as I dove out of the way of the explosion, this one a brutal wave of piercing sound and pressure. I writhed in pain as a figure dropped down through the hole. Dressed in a sleek, plated, black suit with a tinted, narrow lensed helmet was Zivko.

"Miss me?" I could hear the smile on his words.

"With that face only a mother could love? Absolutely not," I replied, distracting him with my words as I tucked the hard drive into a padded pocket on my belt.

"I always knew you were the jealous type." A kick to the ribs pushed me to the side, weight like an elephant crushing me, pressing into my sternum as the thick heel of his boot bore into my chest. "I admire your tenacity, but I have men taking your ship now. I'm sure you can hear it."

To my horror, he was right. The bridge's camera feed was displayed on my helmet's HUD. I could hear Mel shouting incoherently, the sound of a struggle, and two figures rushing into the cabin of the ship and taking her by force. She threw a harsh elbow into one's face, a crunch coming from him as blood poured from his face in an instant. She shoved the other back into the wall and kicked him hard into the chest. His breath vanished and he slumped to the side.

I smirked. "You underestimate her."

"Do I? I guess I'll have to hunt her down next. I'll have much more fun with her than I did with you."

I seethed. "You bastard—"

His weight came down heavier atop me. "I'm a man with orders, nothing more and nothing less. Don't think that traitorous deserter Sintara got off any easier. She and her ship have also been detained. I really didn't want to do this, but this is where this story comes to an end." Zivko pulled the revolver

Sintara had from his belt and held it towards my forehead. "See you in hell."

"Save me a place," I groaned.

A bang rang off, Zivko stumbling back as a blast of energy wrapped around his leg. His flesh cauterized instantaneously and his suit melted to his skin and held its seal. I raised the weapon and fired again, hitting only the hypercore as he ducked behind the metal heart at the center of the room. Up on my feet now, I followed him only to be slammed by a gut-wrenching hit to the stomach, a metal pipe curled in Zivko's hands. Another swing collided with the hypercore, giving me the opportunity to rush towards him, only to find the blunt of the pipe sending a crack across my helmet. I held my ground as he dropped it and pulled a knife from his belt. It shimmered in the red light, as if my blood was already on its edge.

"You shot me, you actually shot me. I'll be damned, looks like I lost a bet. I didn't think you had it in you." He took a limping step towards me. "Not to my worry of course, your bounty will pay it off nicely." He limped closer, feinting another rush only to throw the knife with blinding strength. A scream escaped me as the blade found a home in the flesh of my shoulder. Zivko leveled his gun again, limping closer to me as I fell back against the wall. "Too selfish to be a hero, too weak to be a villain, too stupid to be another innocent bystander. What does it all make you? A moron with no friends, no money, and no safety."

Blood soaked into my glove as I pressed against the wound. "They don't need me. They'll find a way, and Sintara will get her home."

"Always so optimistic. You and I could've made excellent partners, in another world." He took a shot into my gut, a second into my chest. The pressure in my suit dropped instantly, sucking the air from my punctured lungs only to leave me gagging on the blood that welled in my stomach. My throat burned as an unbelievable cold gripped me. My flesh was wreathed in burning and freezing. Was it the fire of hell that brought a strange warmth to my freezing body? The liquid in my eyes froze in an instant, the warm blood nothing but frost now. Blind and drowning in my own blood, I accepted my fate as another bang rang off.

In the blink of an eye, it was dark, quiet, still. My body didn't feel right, as I didn't exactly feel my body at all. I couldn't quite tell where I started and oblivion began. I urged my fingers to flex, only to grasp a sense of loneliness and emptiness that left me afraid. Then, a light. Not heaven's light, nor hell's fire. A blue light, a warmth and a chill. A thousand and a half memories flooded my mind. Summer nights spent in a tree house with Wendy. Saying goodbye to my parents before leaving for college. Getting in trouble with an old friend from university. Stories told by Cratus in the belly of a freighter. Drinks with Zivko after a successful bounty capture. The first time Sintara caught me in the act. The laughs Mel and I shared under the surface of the

Pacific Ocean. What I wouldn't give to hear that laugh one last time. I had nothing left to give, not even my soul.

I'm not sure which I felt first, the pain or the repair. Time ticked backwards, eyes unfroze and bullets were pulled from my body. Red light, then purple light, then blue light. Time became one again, and I became one with time. My fingers wrapped around my pistol again, no more loneliness and so much less than empty.

Zivko pulled the revolver Sintara had from his belt and held it towards my forehead. "You and I could've made excellent partn—wait."

I didn't hesitate, I didn't try to understand, and I didn't miss. Four shots bore into Zivko's chest, melting away his armor and exposing burned flesh. I could see the striations of his muscles through the burnt red, body shivering from a heartbeat slowing. He gasped as he fell back against the hypercore, now glowing a bright blue. His head fell back and eyed the cool glow. Through the tint of his helmet, I could see his warm eyes pondering that light. But it wasn't the light of the hypercore, it was another light, one from beyond. He bathed in that blue, the thing that had brought me back from the dead. It wouldn't do the same for him.

He choked out four final words before slumping to the side. "You actually did it."

The clatter of my gun on the floor made me jump. I hadn't realized how quiet it was when I saw his last breath leave him. I looked down at my shaking, quivering hands. "I...I didn't mean to...I thought you–why did you make me do this? You were going to–!" I gagged on my own words. It was him or me. I chose myself.

My gloves were stained blue with my own blood, I felt so cold. I turned to my side to wretch onto the ground, but nothing came. Only a wracked sob. Sinatra was gone, I had no idea where Mel was. I shivered and curled into a ball as darkness overwhelmed me.

"I'm sorry."

↪ 10 ↩

Hospital

Life came to me in fiery breaths, burning me from the inside out with teeth clenched and eyes running with tears. As easily as it came, the air was torn from my lungs in a fit of harsh coughing, the kind that uses every muscle in your body to squeeze any semblance of comfort from you. My hands failed to take grasp at my burning chest with tight wrappings around my wrists holding me to the bed I was strapped to. Cold hands held me down to my bed as a nonsensical voice gave its best attempt to comfort and soothe me. With a sandpaper tongue and desert dry throat, I took control of my body with a harsh gasp.

With eyes blurred from tears I took in my surroundings. It was a hospital room. Two chairs stood on either side of a narrow table on the wall across from my bed. Gleaming metal carts bearing medicine and tools sat on either side of my bed accompanied by a frazzled looking figure wearing purple scrubs. There was a window on the wall to my left presenting the distant red-orange sands of Mars past the familiar city skyline. I was back on Mars, in a hospital, strapped to a bed. With only brief entertainment of the idea that this was all a dream, I continued the deep, raspy breaths that slowly brought the strength back to me.

I reached across my chest to pull the IV out of my arm that burned like fire ants had crawled under my skin, only to be stopped by the bindings that held me down. A hand swatted at my attempt, a voice of contempt and exhaustion shouting their defiance.

"Absolutely not! I spent all night keeping you alive, I'm not letting you end it now. This takes a gentle touch."

"My arm," I groaned. "It burns."

"Your replacement arm was struggling to clot your blood properly, which is why you need to leave that in." The voice added. "Just give it a few minutes, I was just trying to take it out when you gave me a heart attack with that coughing fit."

My head turned to observe the voice coming from my right. She was older than myself, perhaps a bit older than Wendy. She wore purple scrubs that had been stained by medicine and fluids. Her hair was tied in a knot so tightly it gave me a headache just seeing it. She was a first generation Martian, born on Mars to two Earthling parents. Her blond hair held streaks of gentle blue and white. Her skin was pale undertones to a more tan surface. She had a gentle posture, her hands meeting together in front of her at seemingly all times. She felt comforting in a way I couldn't explain. Her eyes drooped with exhaustion but an optimistic and positive aura clung to her. All of it warmed my cold heart.

"Where am I? Who are you?"

"I'm Kara, you're on Mars at the New Galileo Medical Center. They brought you late last night in a real tizzy. We spent three hours resuscitating you before you would hold a regular heart rate." She had a subtle accent from the south of Earth's Old America. She might look Martian, but she still carried her Earthliness. "You're in good hands now."

"Who brought me in? Why am I tied up?" I asked in the kindest tone I could manage while trying to ignore the pain in my arm that faded at a brutally slow pace.

"A team of first responders hired by IEO brought you in. You were a real mess, said you were exposed to deep space. But it was more than just that, I could tell. Frankly, it's a miracle you lived. The Lord wanted you alive so here you are. Anyways, they said to keep you bound and that we weren't allowed to release you until they said. Didn't say why though." She ran a finger along the edge of her jaw curiously. "None of my business at least, my only job is to keep you alive and make sure your heart isn't beating backwards or something."

"Hilarious," I scoffed.

"I wish it was a joke," she mumbled.

"What did you just say?"

She moved swiftly to extract the IV from my arm safely before unbinding me slowly. "Lucky for you, someone's been waiting to speak with you. He showed up not long after IEO brought you in. He has patience, I'll give him that." She gestured to the small table across from me, calling attention to the stack of clothes that sat atop it. "Feel free to get changed while I retrieve him."

My hand shot out and grabbed her by the wrist. With best effort to keep my cool and ignore the alarm sirens that prattled off in my head, I spoke in a clear and serious tone. "Is he with the IEO? Who is he?"

"I don't know, some kind of reporter." She looked down at my hand with a match of tone and frustration on her face. "I have spent the last twelve hours of my life keeping you alive and you dare to lay your hands on me? Let go of me this instant."

"I...I'm sorry, I didn't mean–" My grip snapped free as I shook my head. I wasn't feeling like myself. Something was off, I just couldn't tell what. "You do understand the situation I am in with the IEO, correct?"

"Plenty aware. He's promised not to bring any harm to you, he only wants to talk," she continued. "Nobody knows you are here at this time, I told you, you're in good hands."

I massaged my wrists which had been rubbed raw by the bindings with a deep breath. "Alright, bring him in."

"Change quickly, he's been waiting all night for you." Kara snapped back into her cheery disposition in an instant as she went to exit the room only to pause at the doorway and turn back to me. "I only found one thing on you when they brought you in. I hid it under those clothes."

She finished exiting the room and sealed the door. My feet smacked hard against the cold flooring. I made swift steps over to the table while discarding the thin gown I wore. I pulled on the jeans and t-shirt which had been laid out. They weren't very comfortable, nor had they been very warm in the cold months of winter on Mars, but it was better than nothing.

Beneath the pile of clean clothes was a small device, one barely bigger than my index finger. It was a shiny, aluminum communicator; the same one Sintara gave Mel after their first meeting.

A knock against the door made me jump. I cleared my throat and ran a thumb across the small bead of blood the IV had left behind, the blue smear staining my pants as I rubbed it off. "Come in."

The door slid open to reveal a man in similarly generic clothing to me wearing a heavy jacket with an umbrella dangling from his arm. He was Martian, bright blue hair and matching eyes with ghostly white skin. He had an equally cheery disposition to Kara, but his positivity felt off. Like something was hidden beneath the surface, all just one big facade. "It's nice to meet you, Mr. Harrison."

As it stood now, there were only two types of people willing to talk to me like this. Those hoping to befriend me only to betray me for instant millions in their bank account, or those who knew me and truly desired to help me. With a lanyard that bore the clear symbol of the IEO and a smile that felt just as real as it was fake, this man was not likely the latter. All this to say, pushing through the fog of my mind, something about him did seem familiar. My mind was still foggy from my past day, my memories felt farther away than usual. It annoyed me deeply.

"Can I help you?" I asked him.

"Unfortunately not, but I am here to help you. Please, take a seat with me." He gestured for me to follow as he sat down in one of the chairs near the table. I refused, my fight or flight still firing. If I had to run, I would be ready to do so. "I see the clothes I fetched for you fit well."

Curiosity got the best of me as I gave into a small sense of comfort. "You brought me these?"

"Hard to assess what the exact damage had been to your clothes when we found you, though the generally catastrophic nature of the rubble we found you buried in made your survival truly a miracle." The man waved a hand dismissively. "I'm getting ahead of myself. My name is David Marshall, I'm a journalist with the IEO. I presume you're familiar?"

"Ha ha ha, hilarious." I mumbled sarcastically.

His smile didn't drop even the slightest. "A little lightheartedness is good for the soul."

My brow crumpled in curiosity. "Is there a point to your visit?"

"As a matter of fact, there is." He cleared his throat and pulled a notepad and pen from the fold of his jacket. "I'm here on behalf of IEO as a negotiator of sorts. Assuming all goes well, you'll be leaving this hospital as a new man."

"And if all doesn't go well?" I challenged him.

"Best not to tease that possibility." His voice stressed a reason for fear, yet his disposition didn't move an inch. "The IEO has proposed an offer. If you sign a simple NDA and promise never to speak of this… 'Elysia' again, they are willing to scratch your bounty and debt from the record. Under the condition that you enter the witness protection program and assume a new identity for your safety."

I frowned. "You mean the safety of your secrets."

"Not inaccurate." David slid a clipboard bearing a clutter of papers across the table towards me to read. It was a medical certificate ready to legally declare me as dead.

A scoff escaped me. "I take it the press doesn't know about this?"

"I am the press, Mr. Harrison. When the information of IEO is involved, I write the stories. As for you, I'm here to write the cover story for your new life. Presuming you accept our deal, from now on you will no longer be Apollo Harrison. Just another face in the crowds."

I slowly dropped into the seat across from him, leaning heavily on the table as if interrogating him. "And what exactly would have happened to Mr. Harrison?"

"Died in an equipment malfunction on Zion."

"And Officer Sintara?"

"Died a hero protecting innocent lives."

"And the girl?"

"What girl?"

He was lying, clearly he knew Mel, but he was saying the new truth; the truth he was weaving. We both knew that what he was saying wasn't real, but it would be real according to history. The question was what was factual in his tornado of fiction. His words molded reality, and it scared me. I needed to know where Mel and Sintara were, and it would not be easy information to get out of the gatekeeper of all of the skeletons in IEO's closet. I decided to try regardless, I didn't have anything to lose.

"Let's say I choose not to accept this deal, what happens then?"

"Then for every dollar of your debt you'll spend a night in a cell, most unfortunately."

A laugh escaped me now.

"Something funny?" His cheery expression was gone. He tapped the pen to his notepad in a rhythm that induced nothing but anxiety in me.

"I want to speak to a lawyer," I mumbled.

"With what money?" This was the most true thing he had said all day. Hurtful.

"I'm not accepting those terms. Do you really think you can hide the truth from the world for so long? Eventually they will find out, and the longer you wait the more public opinion will be turned against you. I'm not the only person who knows Elysia exists."

"You remind me so much of your sister. So much optimism and desire for truth, yet so little voice to spread that truth with."

The familiarity clicked in my mind. David Marshall, he and Wendy were once close friends, maybe even more. Then he turned his back on truth and retreated to a life that offered more money and less accountability. She had learned everything she knew about journalism from him, and after his betrayal, she questioned everything she knew. He had tried to lead her astray from the truth, but she held her path.

My chair clattered to the ground as I stood. "I'm leaving."

"I'm afraid you've yet to be officially discharged from this hospital, nor will you ever be." His pen glided across the clipboard, signing across the dotted line at the bottom. "You are dead after all."

"Like that will change anything." I made way for the door, pressing the pad next to it, only for it to stay sealed shut.

David rose from his chair and made a step towards me. "Bounty gone, debt erased, and a new start in life. What good is that girl or her people to you? She's not even human after all."

"She's more human than you know," I said sternly.

"Her people will be the death of all of us." David reminded me.

"The future is coming, you can't stop it," I stated. The door behind me slid open, a firm hand grabbing me by the elbow and pulling me out into the harsh fluorescent light of the hallway.

"You're a real piece of work, David." Wendy stepped up to him and shoved him back. "I told you to stay away from my family."

"Spirited as usual, glad to see you're doing well." David's smile was all the more aggravating.

"Apollo, we're leaving." Wendy grabbed me by the arm and dragged me down the hallway. I glanced over my shoulder as we pushed through the crowd, David was watching us with pen and paper in hand. Only trouble could come from this, but there were more pressing matters at hand.

⇀ ⇀ ⇀

The smell of rubber stung my nose as we wandered through a parking garage lined with electric vehicles. I could tell by the way her heels smacked the concrete that Wendy was upset, but that became all the more evident when she spun and yelled in my face.

"Three days, I told you three days to figure it out. Four days later, you dodge my calls all night and I see the news suggesting that you're dead? What the hell is going on with you Apollo?!"

"Look, I'm sorry, I thought I had figured this out but it's all gone downhill. You're right, we should have done this together, and I need you. You're all I got now." To my own chagrin, I stood wringing my hands like a child. "I'll explain everything, I promise, but we've got to find Mel as fast as possible."

Wendy nodded, pursing her lips in frustration. "You can explain in the car. We're going to Mom and Dad's."

A sigh of relief escaped me. I wanted a hug from Mom right now, and I needed Dad's wisdom not more than ever. "Thank you. Man, I owe you."

"You're damn right," she mumbled, pulling a keyring from her pocket. With a click, a car to her left unlocked with a flash of its lights. She popped open the driver side door, and swung herself inside. "Get in and start explaining."

As rain tapped across the windshield in a rhythmic dance, I explained everything; from the crash on Earth, my close encounter with Zivko, the argument with Sintara, and our plan to infiltrate the wreckage. As I came to it, it became hard to explain what happened as the hypercore collapsed. My descriptive skills came up short as Wendy only returned a frightened and confused glance.

"Did you hit your head or something?"

"I know what I saw—I think. I know it sounds crazy but…" I hesitated. My forehead pressed against the window as I leaned to the side, watching the lights of Mars flicker by. People lined the streets, people living average lives and believing the world was so simple you can understand it without even trying. Seas of blue haired folk not realizing the dangers of the world they lived in. Maybe I was crazy, maybe it all was in my head, but when your entire worldview begins to crumble, your understanding of the world becomes maddeningly flexible.

"You know when we were kids and we would watch a scary movie, and no matter how many times Dad reminded us it was just a movie and it was all fake, we still got scared?" I asked.

"Hard to forget, but I fail to see how this relates to the discussion."

"It feels like that, but also the opposite. You're afraid because you try to convince yourself it's fake, but you know it's real. But if this is real, then everything I know must be a lie."

Wendy scoffed. "That hardly makes everything a lie. Perspective changes all the time, though usually not on such an existential level."

I leaned back into my seat, looking up through the skylight in the ceiling and watching the splotches of dark gray sky slide by. The rain came down in buckets now, drumming the roof in a near deafening roar. I wondered who the world was crying for. Just as someone can smell the rain before it falls, brewing trouble was dripping bitterness on my tongue. Since when did I start seeing the world so poetically? I blinked the thought away.

"So after this light you saw, what happened?" Wendy continued the conversation.

"Memories, like my life flashing before my eyes, only I had already died," I replied.

"But you were still thinking, so you weren't fully dead." She flexed her fingers out and held the wheel with her palms, trying to grasp the situation.

"It's hard, if not impossible, to say. I was definitely dead, but I...was still thinking regardless. I remember being shot, I remember seeing those memories, and all the sudden I was back, only a few moments before I had passed."

"And then what?"

By breath hitched as I opened my mouth to reply. Perhaps I wanted to deny it, believing nobody would know if I said nothing, but if I had still been intact after the explosion then so had he. "I killed him."

Wendy didn't reply to that for a long while. We cruised down a suburban road and pulled into a spot on the side of the street. A house not much different from one you might see on Earth was just to our right, only a far more sophisticated array of materials had been used to construct it.

"Look, I can't say whether he deserved it or not, and I'm sure you didn't want to do it. What I do know is that it was either him or you, and I need you right now. So do Sintara and Mel. I don't think of you any less because of it, okay?"

Wendy placed a gentle hand on my shoulder and shook me, snapping me out of my head and prompting me to reply. "Okay."

"You were defending yourself. I'd have done the same. No matter how many times I call you a dork or an idiot or worse, you'll always be better off alive to me."

My face screwed up for a moment. "That seems like a backhanded compliment."

"It was, now get out, and do NOT bring up the fact that you're a murderer to Mom." Her tone was half joking, half not so. Par for the course where Wendy was concerned. She popped open the door and stepped out into the heavy rain, both of us rushing for the doorstep. We shook the rain off our clothes the best we could before Wendy went to knock, only for the door to swing open before she could.

Dad never seemed like any less of a dad. With a stone gray shirt and thick flannel, he didn't hesitate a moment to pull Wendy into a tight hug. A thin beard clung close to his face with hairline thinning and peppered with silvery gray hairs scattered amongst the dark brown. He turned to me now, grabbing me by the shoulders and taking a good look at me.

I couldn't say "I meant to call" or "I wanted to visit." I had no excuses. Nobody was to blame but me, but I don't think they could hold it to me, especially not now. All I could utter was a simple "hey Dad."

"You've grown," he said with tears in his eyes.

"I didn't want to put you all into trouble," I mumbled.

His arms wrapped around my neck. "Trouble be damned, I just want to see my son."

Mom came through the foyer next, hugging and welcoming Wendy before turning to me as well. Dad had yet to stop hugging me before she stepped forward. "You look tired, Apollo."

A small laugh escaped me. "You'd be right."

Dad stepped away and she pressed a hand to the side of my face, rubbing away a tear that dared to trickle down my cheek with her thumb. Crow's feet framed her tender look with a smile so soft it warmed your soul. "Have you been sleeping enough? Eating enough?"

"Best I can." Which was to say 'not very well.'

"I'll be sure to fix that all before you leave." She hugged me now, even tighter than Dad did. Her light blue hair was frizzy in the stormy weather, and her gray eyes matched the rain clouds above. My heart hurt with how much I missed her, and leaped with how glad I was to be home. Wendy and I both took after our mothers, only Wendy's mom had passed long before I was born. Being half-siblings barely broke our bond though, if anything it strengthened it. Life on Earth wasn't easy for either of us, but it was easier together, which is why it had hurt so bad when Wendy had left.

"Let's get you two inside, you look cold." Mom grabbed my hands for a moment before recoiling from the ice of my hands. "Especially you, no jacket? And…no shoes?"

"It's a long story," I said with a laugh.

As I took steps back into the home I had spent my most formative years in, I wondered if I had been the same person I was when I last walked through these doors.

↵ 11 ↪

Home

Laying on the edge of consciousness, I drifted in and out of sleep. Before long, despite personal expectations, I found myself slipping into a slumber, coming to life in a dream as unsolicited as it was horrifying, though the fiction of the dream was up for debate.

I was on the cold ground with dust stinging my eyes. I had curled in on myself in horror. My gun sat on the floor not far from my face, painted with blood and staring at me like a menacing reminder of my actions. My body refused to respond as I urged myself to get up, only to hear someone approaching. My arm reached for my weapon, only to find Mel crouching down beside me. She had no suit on, no helmet and no protection from the harsh vacuum of this world. Her hands hovered over me as she analyzed the damage. She glanced at Zivko, or rather, the slumped over, smoldering pile one could hardly recognize was Zivko. A spiderweb crack had formed on my helmet, and my breath was slowly escaping me. Mel rummaged through my tools and pulled out a roll of duct tape, tearing off a piece and smoothing it over the crack.

"You're gonna be okay, Apollo."

As my breath came back to me, I croaked half coherent words that prompted just as much confusion as I had felt.

"You're supposed to be with Thirteen. You shouldn't be here, it's dangerous."

"Plans changed. This is going to hurt." She scooped me off the ground and into her arms, carrying me without breaking a sweat. Amazement overwhelmed me as much as pain did, both increasing as her legs pushed off against the metal floor and lifted her through the hole that had been blown open in the ceiling. Her feet carried her with miraculous speed as she dashed across the ship that seemed only newly crashed. Fire broke out over the hull in front of us, Mel daring not to stop as she leaped through the flames, protecting me with her body.

We came to a landing in the sand, Mel landing on one knee with a grunt of pain. Her body was so cold from the vacuum of space, but I could still feel her heartbeat. My head turned to observe the dozens of soldiers surrounding us with weapons drawn and LCCE badges gleaming in the wavering light of the fires around us.

A commanding voice barked through the speakers built into the outside of their helmets. "Put him down and put your hands behind your head."

One of them whispered loudly. "She isn't wearing a suit."

Mel looked down at me, a look of determination and concern like that I had never seen framing her face in a light that one could only describe as heroic. The curls of her hair fell down around us, all I could see was her face. Her eyes sparkled in the fire around us, like a million stars were hidden within her gaze.

This was not the Mel I had come to know, something had changed.

"Let us pass peacefully, I command it."

The voice barked again. "Set him down and put your hands behind your head or we will shoot!"

Mel considered her options. With my blood spilled across her arms and weapons aimed at her, she had no choice. "He needs medical attention. I will turn myself over if you swear to retrieve help for him."

I tried to protest, but the commanding officer spoke into his radio before I could croak out any desperate cry. His voice declared hesitancy, but he obliged. "I need medical response on my location immediately, one injured and one being taken into custody."

I watched Mel place me gingerly onto a stretcher. She took hold of my gloved hand and leaned closed to me, whispering some words I couldn't hear through my helmet. A cool weight lay in my grasp as she turned away and placed a set of cuffs on herself. The men led her away as I urged myself to move. I shot up from the stretcher, awaking to a far more familiar sight.

A cold sweat had broken over my body, dampening the edges of my clothes. It was surreal to wake to my childhood bedroom for the first time in years. I felt like a kid again. Scared, alone, desperate. My throat itched from the dryness and my head ached from the fog of sleep. Mel's shouts bounced around my head like a virus I couldn't shake. It was all in my head, yet something about it left a bitter taste in my mouth. I always did care for her, but more so, I missed her. I had only met her a few days ago, but I felt so alone without her.

My voice was barely more than a croak, speaking to no one in particular. "I have to save her."

"How sweet," Wendy declared while stepping into the room with a cup of foggy liquid and a handful of nondescript pills. I swung my legs over the edge of the bed as she placed them in my hands. "Just a little magic potion for you. Calcium, iron, zinc, magnesium, protein, all the vitamins in the alphabet. Everything you deprive yourself of in your excursions through space."

Grateful for any liquid, I gulped down half the cup in an instant, fighting the strong urge to gag at the bitter, grainy taste. "This tastes like motor oil," I sputtered.

"You would know that, wouldn't you?" She was joking, but motor oil was more spicy. "I caught wind of something. Lots of IEO ships have been spending time around Zion. They recruited a nearby freighter to help them drag several ships to Callisto. The shipping manifest details the detour, but it also details a large presence of LCCE personnel accompanying the shipment for unknown reasons."

"Meaning my ship is on Callisto?"

"More than that, Callisto is also home to the largest prisons in our solar system. If I were betting on anything, I'd bet that Mel and Sintara are there."

Callisto, the prison planet as we called it. I had made an excursion there once, not by my own choice of course. It was a miserable place, it twisted my gut to think Mel was stuck on that rock. I gulped down the handful of pills and polished off the bitter tasting water, shaking my head in disgust before replying again. "That's great and all, but how do we get in?"

Wendy shrugged. "You tell me, you're the wanted man."

"You want me to turn myself in?"

"You said it, not me." She shrugged. "We'll figure out the details on the way. In the meantime, we need to get ourselves to Jupiter."

My hand ran along the scruffs of hair at the corner of my jaw. "Easier said than done, it's not exactly a vacation destination. There's no shuttles between Callisto and the Jovian colonies."

"I can get us a ride, you just need to get us in. You've done plenty of bounties, surely you've been able to get into your fair share of secure institutions?"

I patted my hands down on the knees of my jeans. I stood abruptly, much to my own chagrin as the world spun around me for a moment. "I might have an idea. Jovian colonies it is. But as soon as we get Sintara free, she's taking you straight back here."

"I can handle myself," Wendy said sternly.

I shook my head. "I'm not taking any chances."

We both made our way downstairs and enjoyed dinner with our parents. It was delicious, my favorite from my childhood, made of the real stuff too. I drank half a pitcher of water while we talked about my excursions in space. I told them all the exciting parts, left out the criminal parts. They asked me about Mel, I said she was a friend who needed help. They could tell I was holding back from them, and it hurt to do so, but I needed them to be uninformed. It was for their own safety that they didn't know about Mel and her home, and I couldn't explain it in a way that made it hurt any less. They loved me regardless, and I would make it up to them once all this was said and done.

Mom and Dad weren't happy to see us go so soon, or at all. Mom reminded me a dozen and a half times of all the things mothers said. Remember to eat well, take your medicine, and get plenty of sleep. I smiled and nodded all the way, assuring her I would take care of myself despite knowing I'd have no time to do so.

Dad accompanied me to the doorstep, offering me an old jacket and sneakers that didn't fit him anymore. I might have assured him I didn't need it if I hadn't been bitten to the core by wind chill. Pulling on the beaten faux leather, he cleared his throat to begin one of his speeches.

"Look, I know I…I know I wasn't always the best father–"

"Dad, you're amazing, you know that. It's not your fault you got such a sucky son."

He shook his head and laughed. "One that can't help interrupting me too. Your mother and I will always love you, never forget that. I always knew you'd come back eventually, I just didn't think...well, I didn't think you'd be caught up in this much of a mess."

"I didn't try, I promise."

"I know you didn't, Wendy told us everything. That girl is counting on you, don't let her down, you hear? She needs you, be there for her. I know being a hero wasn't always your style." He brushed off my shoulders and smoothed the sleeves of the jacket down my arm. His finger ran over one of the patches on the left arm, from his time in the military. He'd saved so many lives, I always thought of him like a superhero. "Being a hero looks good on you, son. It doesn't pay to be good, but it costs more to be bad. Don't forget that your mother and I are always here for you."

A nod gave him the answer he desired. "I know, Dad."

"Once you get all this figured out, come visit for longer next time, okay? And bring that girl with you." He gave me a teasing smirk.

"I will, promise." Assuming I got out of this alive, I meant it.

⇥ ⇥ ⇥

The docks of Mars are many things, the name itself a double entendre. Though the docks were, in their traditional sense, a place for boats to come to rest off the not-so turbulent sea which had not always been there, this place had also been a place for ships to dock, setting down after long travel through space. This all being said, the docks were not a nice place. The average person doesn't go to the docks, plainly they have no need to. It was a grimy, dirty place that stinks of fuel and makes your hair stand on end from the sheer amount of energy condensed into one place. It surely was not healthy to be here too long, and I had spent more than my fair share of time here in my first years out of university as an intern.

The hike from the car to the docks was paved with anxiety, making the mile between the parking lot and the dock a tense walk through city streets. The status of my bounty was dubious at best, and I wasn't eager to discover whether or not my head still spelled a new future for any poor schmuck. Without a hood to hide my face, I simply kept my eyes on the ground, tracing Wendy's heels as she led the way.

"You're not a criminal, don't act like one," Wendy mumbled as a ship roared overhead.

"Aren't I?" I replied.

"Not to me you aren't."

I scoffed. "I've done horrible things."

"Far worse has been done to you."

That silenced me.

We crossed the street and stepped onto the first of the metal panels that the docks consisted of. The area was swarmed with large trucks moving palettes that seemed to hover off the ground like an air hockey puck. The burly, grimy men and women inhabiting this place of hard work dwarfed Wendy and I. If Mel had been here, she'd put them in their place. I shook my head as three dangerous words floated in my head. I miss her. Instead of brushing them away, I grabbed onto them. I'd need motivation for this plan to succeed.

We made our way across the docks and onto a platform labeled "Dock 3223." A beefy looking ship sat on the large platform that we climbed a short set of steps onto. It was a tough little thing, scrap metal held together by meaty bolts with jagged edges and sharp angles. It sat taller than it was wide on crouched gear like mighty legs holding its weight. A spray-painted icon and label was splattered across the panels near the thrusters, a cartoon of a green amphibian with the label "The Toad." An accurate name, I thought.

A loud voice echoed across the docks, making me cringe at his volume and want to shrink into my jacket. "Ms. Harrison, in the flesh. I always enjoy seeing stories from you!"

I noticed the opposite side of the ship was open with a large ramp leading down from it, facing the ocean. A large man with broad shoulders and a pot stomach hobbled around the ship with a wide grin and a bush of facial hair clinging to his face. His arms were like logs, his legs like trees. I suspected the man had built the ship with his bare hands, bending the metal into shape.

"Neeson, do control your volume, this is a public space. Besides, I know you understand the situation."

"Apologies, I've been unlucky to not see you around lately."

"I've been busy." Wendy gestured to me, smacking my shoulder to get my attention as I scanned the dock for people suspicious of our words. "This is my brother, Apollo."

The man held a hand out to me. "Ahh, a famous man. I know much about you."

"I assumed so," I mumbled, shaking his hand only for my own to feel crushed under the vice of his grip. "I take it you're a trucker."

"You're a bounty hunter, aren't you? I suppose both our professions have been turned on their heads." He let go and took a mighty step back. "The name is Neeson, captain of The Toad."

"How certain are you of your ability to get us to Callisto?"

"I'll do my best, I pulled a few favors for this, you know. Come aboard and make yourselves at home, it's too cold out here." He waved us onto this ship as a light rain began to trickle from the sky and drum across the surface of the ship.

Wendy led the charge once more, scaling the steep ramp into the bottom half of the ship. It was a cargo bay that reeked of fresh polymer and rubber, a scent some find pleasant until they smell it for hours on end. A balcony was set along the walls above us with catwalks leading to what had to be the helm and a bunk in the back of the ship.

"You might want to put these on," Neeson declared while handing us two pairs of metal rings surrounded in plastic. These were the most expensive variety of artificial gravity on ships like this. Where the jumpsuits on my ship had metal sewn into them that held you to the magnets under the floor, these small but powerful magnets held you to the metal of the ship. I'd used them to scale walls before, it was quite the core workout.

"Fancier than your ratty jumpsuits," Wendy mentioned while snapping them onto her ankles.

A small laugh escaped me. "Probably pulled them out of one of his shipments. Hear anything about missing mag-gravs, Ms. Reporter?"

"I think you'll find my business to be fully within the law." Neeson continued as he climbed up the narrow ladder and onto the catwalk above us. "Can't say the same for either of you, however."

"Well you know what they say, can't make an omelet without breaking a few eggs," Wendy declared while sitting down on a crate and pulling her phone out of her pocket.

"It will take us a while to get there, this isn't the fastest ship in the world. Make yourselves comfortable!" The door to the helm hissed shut, the hydraulics whistling in unison with the large ramp that rose and sealed the main entrance and exit of the ship. I settled down near a small box as an overwhelming roar filled the room. The familiar feeling of liftoff returned to me. I missed Thirteen as well.

It was quiet after we broke the atmosphere. The sound was significantly lessened in the vacuum of space, but the vibrations in the ship were no less powerful as we picked up speed, nearing warp speed. In a ship this size and with this much weight, it would take longer for the ship to get up to speed than it would take for it to make the jump, but the alternative was a couple years journey even at its fastest speeds.

My back decompressed in the lack of gravity, my crossed feet holding me to the floor in a comfortable and secure way. Wendy on the other hand struggled to find comfort, her feet sticking but her body desiring to float in any other direction. She glared at me as I watched her struggle, snickering at her fight against the mag-gravs.

"Still missing my jumpsuits?" I asked.

She grumbled, unable to reach me in a manner fast enough for a swat across the shoulder to deem worth it. "Zip it. You're the one who practically lives in space, you're used to all this."

I took a deep breath, letting myself, for a brief moment, relax. For this moment, the world could feel small without collapsing. Traveling was always so simple. The journey between point A and point B was the simplest part of it all for me. Knowing the time it would take to arrive but the lack of memory of most of it gave me a sense of peace. I would not take this moment to relax for granted. I let each muscle slowly loosen, each joint relaxing. I took a moment to inspect my body, feeling the many injuries I had sustained healing slowly and draining me of energy. Sleep was a fickle master in space, but it was not helped by the nature of recovering from injuries. The body needs rest after being injured. There was only so much rest to be found in space. I found my eyes closed in this instance, a welcome sense of darkness, though visions hid in the shadows. Sintara, Mel, Zivko. Too much to handle, I pushed it all out of my mind.

"You seem oddly self reflective."

"I'm relaxing," I mumbled without opening my eyes.

"Usually you'd be pulling something apart and putting it back together or worrying about a way to make more cash." I opened one eye to glare at Wendy for this, staring down at her with my chin tilted up. She shrugged. "Am I wrong?"

I didn't have the energy to quip back. I wanted to rest, to have all this taken from my mind, to find some peace. Instead I simply let out a deep, painful breath. "I'm just tired."

A few minutes passed, the rattling of the ship the only sound to be heard. I heard a sniffle, something one could assume as a simple running nose and offer a tissue without even blinking, but once a second came I was concerned. Wendy had dreary eyes. She wasn't crying. She didn't want to cry. Her eyes trickled all the same.

"Are you okay?" I asked, body tensing as I reconsidered my choices of words and searching for where I had gone wrong.

"Either you've gotten too old or you've seen too much." She smiled, pushing away the tears with her sleeve. "Sometimes I wish you were still the small boy I had to pull out of the lake when he refused to stand up for himself."

A laugh escaped me at this, one full of self pity. "More so a lack of ability to stand up for myself."

"You never stood up for yourself because you believed them."

She had me there. All those things they said stuck with me, and I did believe them. It was my motivation, and my burden to bear. I wanted to prove them wrong, but with every step I only proved them right, proved myself right.

"But you don't need me to protect you anymore. You're strong enough on your own now."

"That doesn't mean I want to do it alone."

"You wanted me to stay on Mars."

"I still do, but I want you to be with me more."

Wendy laughed at this, something between sadness and joy. "Do you know what the meaning of your name is?"

A random thought, on par for Wendy. "I was named after the mission to Earth's moon, but the name...doesn't it mean 'destroyer'?"

Wendy shrugged "It does mean that, but it also means 'a sheepfold.'"

"A sheepfold?" I laughed.

"It means you're a protector, Apollo. You protect people, even at your own expense. A star gives off its light by burning itself. In the process, it changes, in many different ways. A star can never see the brilliance of the light it gives off, only the darkness of space around it."

"I appreciate the sentiment but-"

"You are not the same person I once knew. You've changed, and you alone are blind to it."

The cargo hold was then flooded with red light. The familiar startup of a hypercore filled my ears, I was likely sitting right atop it. Something was different though. My body felt light, and my mind felt clear, more clear than it had ever been. Like the sun breaking out on a rainy day or the surface of water falling smooth after ripples and waves, my mind felt as clear as glass. The hypercore was affecting me in a different way, or rather, my body was reacting to this familiar sensation differently.

The inching flood of darkness began to permeate the walls, pouring down their surfaces like water flooding a submarine. I could see the fog overwhelm Wendy. Her eyes were unfocused and her jaw hung lightly slack. She blinked hard several times, staring nervously at the shadows that crawled up her legs. She was not nearly as familiar with this sensation as I was, yet this sensation was equally different to me at this moment than ever.

"Wendy?" I asked after the darkness had climbed over my neck and left me in the dark.

"Huh?" She mumbled back.

"Can you hear me?" I asked again.

"Can I...what?" She replied listlessly.

This was truly bizarre. I was awake, clear minded. I could feel my body just as I ever had. The buzz of my toes curled within my shoes, the ache in my back as I sat hunched, the bruises running along my spine and across my side. Above all, I could feel my arm, as alien as always. It buzzed and twitched and burned as it always did. The pins and needles that had always covered its skin were unwelcome in this instance. My body felt in tune, all but this one piece of me.

For the five minutes we spent traveling between Mars and Jupiter, I sat with a clear mind. It felt illegal to exist in a place nobody remembers. All people who travel beyond light speed experience that five minutes just the same, only they can never recall it by memory. Some kind of side effect the hypercore has on the human mind that they never seemed to truly understand. Some were affected more deeply, an experience we call Temporal Amnesia, but to my knowledge nobody has ever been immune to these effects. The now ancient theory of relativity stated that time moved slowly the closer an object moved to the speed of light, but our understanding is more complex now.

We now know that time moves faster, equal to how much faster one moves beyond the speed of light. Back then, we believed that nothing could move faster than the speed of light, that is until we discovered how the universe expands faster than the speed of light. Our universe is not homogeneous, the laws of physics are not equal everywhere. We were appalled at first, but now we use it to our advantage. Many consider it dangerous to play with the nature of our world. Some suggested that we could cause the mass extinction events predicted, such as the Big Rip or the Big Crunch. Danger never stopped human expansion of course. If anything, they were fueled by spite.

We came to a slow pace as the hyperengine winded down. As light flooded the room, I watched the light come back into Wendy's mind. She couldn't have known what I just experienced. If anything, she likely assumed we had equal experiences. I decided against telling her. It was all too complicated to explain.

"I only want the best for you, you do know that?" Wendy asked.

I took a deep breath, nodding and blinking hard to shake off the peculiarity of the scenario. "Yes, I know."

"And I also want the best for Mel, and her best is for all of our safety. So tell me you have a plan cooked up in that big brain of yours."

I couldn't help a tiny smile. "As a matter of fact, I do."

⇾ 12 ⇽

Prison

I didn't know how to convey believable anger in any way other than screaming profanities at the highest volume I could muster. Wendy shoved me through a narrow porthole and into a barely less narrow hallway. Guards were positioned at the far end, uniforms similar to Sintara's lining their figures. Their hands rested on their guns as they came closer, watching me stumble over the lip of the entryway.

"Ma'am, this is a restricted area, who gave you permission to land here?" One guard asked. He was a Jovian, taller and broader than his Martian counterpart.

"The flight deck, obviously. I brought you a gift, someone you should have taken when you had the chance." Wendy shoved me forward to the ground in front of the guards. In an instant, the Martian pulled me back to my feet and held me by my hands, which were haphazardly bound behind my back with wire that dug into my wrists. Wendy said it was more believable that way, I think she just wanted to be mean to me.

The Jovian raised an eyebrow at Wendy before pulling a small device from his belt. A series of lasers blinded me as he held it to my face. I struggled to thrash my head back and forth as the Martian took a tight hold of my collar. The Jovian looked at the device. "Your name, young lady?"

"I think you know." She narrowed her eyes. "Wendy Harrison."

"This is your brother, is he not?"

"Half brother."

Both guards scoffed at this. "Makes me feel a bit better about my family," the Martian jeered.

"Betrayed by your own blood, tough luck kid." The Jovian waved the Martian on as he shoved me down the hallway. I craned my neck to look back at Wendy, mustering a furious glare to mask the fear I felt.

"He has a bounty, I want it now."

"You must understand, a transaction of that size isn't so simple."

"I'm not leaving this moon until I see those funds transferred to my account immediately-"

The Martian shoved me around a corner and through a heavy blast door. "Move along."

The walls of this room rattled with a not-so distant sound. It was a sound of loud speaking, heavy footsteps, cheering and shouting. It had to have been just on the other side of a wall somewhere, but which wall was to be determined. The sound itself seemed to shake every inch of the room, like such an immense presence of sound that the moon itself quaked at its magnitude. This room was narrow, a heavy metal gate rolling open as a loud buzzer rang out. I was pushed through this gate, pausing for a moment as it closed behind me and the next one opened. A man was watching me through a window to my right, controlling the gates manually. The further technology progressed, the further it regressed. Things that were automated were easier to override, government facilities began resorting to closed circuit mechanisms like this one to prevent another event like the mass cyber attack that occurred twenty years ago. I knew this room was just one big x-ray, scanning me for anything threatening. They wouldn't find much.

"Tell the warden we have him, and send a message to the IEO, they'll want to interrogate this one personally. We'll be awaiting further instruction in the holding cell. " The Jovian declared to the man behind the glass before guiding me through the gate and into yet another room. There were several tables in this room and a large metal cell in the corner. The Jovian opened the cell door as the Martian emptied my pockets, pulling out a tangle of wires and a small, aluminum device, a tad larger than my index finger.

He turned it over in his hand, running his finger along the machining lines along its edges. "What's this slag?"

"Leave it, I don't trust this one bit," The Jovian said as he took the material and slammed them down on the table. The Martian continued to check every seam and lining of my clothes, taking particular time on my coat as he ran his fingers along the lining between the soft material inside and the rough outside.

"We really ought to take this off him," The Martian suggested.

"You trust him not to make a move without his cuffs on? I don't think so. He's a bounty hunter, you don't want to know what all he's learned. Just put him in the cell, the warden will be here soon."

The Martian dug one thumb into a pressure point on my back as he shoved me into the small cell. He slammed the door behind me, leaving me to sit down on a rickety bench in the corner. The Jovian stood at the table examining the small device that had been in my pocket. The plan was riding on this device, assuming it worked.

⇥ ⇥ ⇥

"Tell me you have an idea, any idea."

"I do," I declared while examining the freight in the ship around me. My eyes locked onto Wendy's bag. I pulled out a thin laptop tucked into the largest pocket and flicked it open, setting it on the lid of a crate as I pulled the communicator from my pocket. "You don't happen to have your knife, do you?"

Wendy pulled a pocket knife from her back pocket, one our father had given her on her tenth birthday. "I never leave without it, but don't break anything."

"No promises." I placed the edge of the blade on the machining lines of the communicator and slammed my palm down on the hilt of the knife. The flimsy metal casing popped open as the glue that once held it together crumbled to dust. A hard breath blew away the excess as I uncovered the mechanics inside. There was a motherboard inside with a small port built into the side.

I held a hand out to Wendy. "Your phone charger."

"So needy," she mumbled while pulling it from her bag and handing it to me. "What are you even doing anyways?"

"This communicator is connected to Sintara's ship. It's designed to be a two way connection, I'm making it three." I jammed the end of the charger into the port and the other end into the computer. The computer attempted to download the files automatically, I allowed it on the assumption it likely wouldn't corrupt any software within. I downloaded the IP of the communicator and uploaded it to an app called "Friend Finder." On the app, I found a connection to an old phone I had long since discarded in a mining colony on Venus.

"Have you been watching me all this time?" I mumbled as I worked.

"Tried to, didn't work for very long."

"You really are just a stalker."

"It's kinda my job."

I disconnected the charger and stuck the casing haphazardly together. Wendy placed duct tape on the lid of the crate next to me. Either we were very equally minded or the coincidence was much to my convenience. Either way, I used it to reseal the communicator, then put the phone charger in my pocket.

Wendy shrugged. "You always said the best thing in an engineer's toolbox is his duct tape. I learn from the best."

"I said that once, as a joke. Well, a half joke anyways."

"Duct tape aside, what is the plan here?"

I pointed at the laptop screen. "Look, this app will show you the active position of this communicator and the location of where it's trying to reach. Sintara's ship was likely seized all the same as mine, and both ships contain critical information about... Mel's people." I whispered the last part in fear of Neeson keeping an ear out for us.

"Wouldn't they just destroy the ships?"

"Too dangerous. Even the most destroyed black box can be reassembled and decoded. They'll keep them somewhere secure, somewhere where they will blend in. Back when... Zivko and I worked together, we'd call in people like Sintara to take away whomever we'd caught. With them, they'd seize their ship as they contained valuable information for court cases. The two are never separated very far."

"So wherever Sintara's ship is, she is?"

"And Mel, and my ship which contains the needed information to find Mel's planet."

Wendy shook her head, mind frazzled by the nonsensical string of connections. "And all this means what exactly?"

"I'll keep this communicator on me as I infiltrate the prison. When I activate it, it will ping Sintara's ship. That's the signal that I've found them."

"And what exactly am I supposed to do then?"

"I'll need you to guide me in the direction of Sintara's ship, and my ship. The moment we arrive there, I'll connect the communicator to Thirteen and he'll upload the files to your computer."

A look of shock sparked on Wendy's face. "Woah, woah, woah, you mean you want to upload the sensitive files the government is trying to keep secret on my work laptop?"

"Yes. Spread them everywhere. You are the media, Wendy. They want to control what people know, but you have to show them the truth."

"And how much more danger could they be in compared to if they don't know?"

"You, Sintara, Henry, Kate, you're all in danger because you're the few people who know. The more people know, the less they can contain it, and the less danger to individuals like you."

"And individuals like you."

I shook my head. "They'll never stop coming after me because they'll know I'm the one who caused this all. I've already done this much damage, I may as well see it to completion."

"No, this is stupid. When you reach your ship, we can decide what to do about the information when you get out of there."

"If I get out of there—"

"When."

"Wendy–"

"No, when you get out, we will figure out a new plan. I'll guide you through the prison to the ships. I'll find a schematic of the floor plan and find the most optimal route through."

I laughed. "Where in the galaxy do you plan on just finding that? Need I remind you this is a secure government facility?"

"I have my ways. The press always knows."

↜ ↜ ↜

The door slid open violently, the announcement of the equally fearsome presence that followed. He was tall, broad shouldered with equally broad arms. He wore a long suit jacket over a white button down t-shirt with slacks. No tie however, perhaps too easy for inmates to grab. He seemed like he belonged in this prison as an inmate, perhaps spent some time here. He was bald with a bushy beard, only a scar across his chin breaking the hairy pattern. He took one look at me then back to the officers standing guard and watching me. What was most surprising to me was that he was most certainly an Earthling. Most Earthlings don't spend too much time on satellite colonies, especially not this far out. Their bodies are sensitive to the lack of sun, making them violently ill for weeks. While this man was certainly ugly, he didn't look unhealthy. Because of that, I guessed he was a part of the military in the past, just like Dad was.

The man had a voice that matched his appearance. Dark, deep, and scratchy like a grave. "You called me for this? Are you simply too incompetent to know how to do your jobs or did he truly face that much of a threat to you?"

The Jovian started. "Sir, this is Apollo Harrison. He is the LCCE's most wanted."

The man halted, eying me closely. "Who brought him in, Zivko?"

The Martian answered this time, beginning with a gulp. "Zivko is dead, sir. He...killed him. His sister brought him in."

"You killed my favorite Shark? I don't appreciate that. Not one bit. You don't look the type anyways. Put him in solitary like the other two and tell IEO that if we don't see some extra cash then the CTA will see some reliable evidence of their failure to protect government secrets." The man rubbed his index and thumb together at the word cash. "And find me a new bounty hunter, someone better than Zivko."

An impossible task. The man turned and exited without another word as both men's shoulders dropped in relief with him gone. The Martian unlocked the cage I sat in after a moment of peace. The second the door slid open, I burst from the bench and slammed my shoulder into him. He was knocked to the floor as I bounced off of him and directly into the table just behind him. My gut slammed into the edge of the table, forcing my face down onto the hard surface with it. Hands seized me in an instant as the taste of blood filled my mouth.

The Jovian spoke directly in my ear, loud enough to make me wince. "Smooth moves. You're dumber than you look."

I bit my lip to keep my mouth sealed as the Martian swiftly raised a fist into my side. "Slaghead."

They led me through the same door the warden had entered and exited through to find a long hallway continuing on my left, right, and directly ahead of me. My left was labeled "Cell Blocks", my right "Solitary and Infirmary", and directly ahead "Hangar and Offices." They dragged me to the hallway on my right, as expected. Each footstep barely seemed to make a scratch on the distance. Something about the perfectly white walls and burningly bright florescent lights seemed to warp the space time around me. Every step seemed to add another two, until we suddenly came upon another heavy gate which led into a shorter hallway with doors evenly spaced across the walls. Most had small lights next to them colored green, but I counted three that were colored red. They came to a door illuminated by green. The Jovian stepped forward and fumbled with a wad of keys on his belt just next to the pistol at his hip. He swung open the thick door on real hinges. The heavy metal made the pins groan as the painfully white cell was revealed. It was a good thing I didn't plan on staying long.

The cuffs came loose from my wrists and before I could make even the slightest move, a hard shove thrust me into the cell. My hands barely caught me in time as I sprawled to the floor. The Martian and Jovian didn't waste time on last words, simply closing the door and sliding the deadbolt into place. Everything here was manual, made to prevent any exploitation a hacker may be able to take advantage of. A gag escaped me. I coughed and sputtered as I spat out the communicator which had only barely managed to fit in my mouth. The coating of saliva and blood on it was less than sanitary. I had fought a war in my mind not to gag during the all-too-long walk to this cell, focusing on taking in details of the prison instead of thinking about the bitter taste of duct tape adhesive against my tongue. I had managed to grab it when I slammed into the table, a pretty smooth move in my opinion, though definitely painful.

The cell was small, though I could hardly expect a five star hotel. It had a single mattress stuck to the floor with threadbare sheets across it. A small sink and toilet sat in the corner. No mirror of course, too easy to make a weapon out of it. I spat into the sink and washed out my mouth, wiping away the blood that had been running from my nose. I finished by washing off the communicator as well. Had the duct tape not held a waterproof seal, I would have been screwed, though it appeared to have survived the arduous journey.

It wouldn't be long before the two guards who escorted me here would notice the missing communicator. As a critical piece of evidence, it would be the first thing to be analyzed. If luck was on my side I could have ten minutes before they realized. I would be worried if I intended to waste time here. Fortunately, I did not. I began by unlacing my shoes and pulling a length of Kevlar string from them. Most shoes were made with Kevlar woven into them as it prevented fraying or snapped laces. Next, I pierced the thin metal wire woven into the collar of my jacket through the leather and pulled it out. The metal wasn't much nicer than a coat hanger, but it would do its job. Making a loop in the metal, I tied the Kevlar string to the end and bent it into an L shape. Crouching up next to the door, my fingers expertly pushed the metal through the door, hooking onto the deadbolt and pulling the string through. I began pushing and pulling the string back and forth across the deadbolt, a whirring sound coming from the building friction between the metal and the thread.

"New kevlar is five times stronger than steel." Zivko's words were a memory soaked in vinegar. It was bitter to the taste at mere remembrance, but the lesson he taught me then was the only reason I could escape from here; he'd done it not very many years before.

He was right though. On a weight basis, kevlar was five times stronger than steel, and wickedly heat resistant. Its tensile strength was off the charts as well, meaning this one string could easily hold my entire weight if necessary. While a string of thread against steel seemed like an impossible battle, the bitter coldness of space which the heating systems fought against couldn't keep the deadbolt to this cell fully warm. The colder and stronger the metal, the more brittle. Rapidly heating it up and the amount of weight pulling on it should snap the deadbolt, in theory.

It took time, likely more time than I had to spare. A panic began to rise in my chest as my arms burned and a sweat broke out on my brow. The whizzing sound of the Kevlar against the metal deadbolt was grating to the ears, but the metallic snap of the metal sent relief soaring through me. I did the same for the bolt of the handle, watching the door swing open on those same groaning hinges. In and out in less than five minutes, though Zivko's record was three. I enjoyed the five seconds of silence before the first alarms went off.

I pulled my belt from my waist and wrapped it around my hand as two heavy footsteps trudged down the hall towards me, the two familiar voices of the Martian and Jovian arguing as they neared my cell. My fingers turned white as I tightened down the belt on my hand, the metal buckle tight to my first two knuckles.

The Martian stepped into the cell first, poor sucker. A meaty smack bounced off the walls of the cell as the metal buckle connected to his jaw. Unconscious or simply stunned, he fell to the floor as the Jovian launched into the battle with a heavy baton. It narrowly missed my head and collided with my shoulder. Pain jolted more adrenaline through my system as he telegraphed another swing. My fingers closed around the heavy metal with another wild zing of pain. It took three punches to render him out of business, still dazed and half consciously pawing at me as I pulled the keys and gun from his waist. The belt fell from my hand as I shook the pins and needles from my fingers. Another lesson learned from Zivko: always wear a belt, even if you don't actually need it. It was their fault for leaving me with one.

My hands patted down the Martian and found another gun on his hip. It was a sleek white gun similar to the one Henry had given me. Through venting gaps in the sides of the barrel I could see the bindings of copper. I drew two extra mags from a pouch on his chest and slipped them into my pocket. I felt like an action movie star with two pistols, but I could hardly use one effectively, let alone two.

I exited the room and into the hallway where blaring sirens continued. Rushing to work, I unlocked the first door which was illuminated red. It swung open, and inside sat a scraggly man with wiry hair and a crazed look in his eyes. I was stunned in horror, caught standing and staring for a second too long.

"Can I help you?" He asked in a calm, kind voice. It only unsettled me further, though I didn't want to judge.

"I uh, don't mean to assume but...you look like you know how to kill someone. Like, way too easily too."

He nodded in a creepily innocent way.

"Could you distract the guards for me?"

"Certainly!" He seemed overjoyed to do what I asked. He rushed from the cell and down the hall in a terrifyingly fast sprint. The first few guards entered the hallway and saw him immediately. Shouting and yelling commenced as the man horrified them just as much as he had scared me. I didn't spend time watching the aftermath, simply moving on with a mumbled "huh, nice guy."

As the door swung open, a blindingly fast punch made my eyes fill with tears and my nose bleed profusely once more. Just as the adrenaline of my previous bout of combat faded, it surged my system again. A headache began immediately, the feeling of my possibly broken nose followed. I crumpled against the wall in an instant as the familiar voice of Sintara yelped. "Apollo! I am so sorry!"

"Good to see you too," I mumbled with a muted voice, pinching my nose shut. She helped me back to my feet as I tried to stop the bleeding with my shirt, handing her the gun with my clean hand. "I probably deserved that. You know how to use this better than I do. We need to get Mel and get to the hangars."

Considering the circumstances for the briefest of moments, she wasted no time getting straight to work. She ejected the mag of the pistol and examined the ammunition inside. It was a coil pistol, firing tiny pins at high speeds using magnets within the barrel. The velocity of the projectiles could be adjusted by a tiny screen in the grip. It could pierce through someone in a short range and do enough pain to silence them at a further range. Quiet and lethal. "Get that door open, I'll watch for guards."

Following her lead of wasting no time, I heaved open the last door to find Mel inside, crouched in the corner. Sat with her knees to her chest like a child, her tall stature still demanded respect and fear. She lifted her head from her knees and looked at me. A dismal expression of worry and fear shifted to a joyful look of relief. While her clothes were singed and dusty, they were still the same ones Wendy loaned. Only a tad oily and matted, her wavy hair still flowed like an ocean's waves. It made the pink of her hair shimmer like crystal. Remnants of past tears still stained her face, and her eyes were tinted pink from excessive rubbing. She seemed exhausted and anxious, but by the grace of God, she was alive.

↵ 13 ↵

Escape

"Apollo?" She couldn't believe her own words.

I wasted no time coming to her side. My hands floated hesitantly above her, analyzing for any wounds or injuries that could possibly put a wrench in our plan. If they had laid a finger on her, there would be hell to pay. "Did they hurt you? Can you stand?"

She took hold of one of my shaking hands and held it tightly. The feeling of another human hand in my own felt alien, but it sent a shock of joy down my spine. I wanted to hug her so tightly, and I was never one for physical affection.

Mel smiled. "Yes, I'm fine. Are you okay? You look...tired."

A quiet laugh escaped me. "I am."

"And you seem...different."

"That makes two of us," I replied.

She nodded with a laugh. "There's a lot to talk about."

"And never enough time, it seems." I found myself smiling like an idiot, and I couldn't explain why. Maybe I missed her more than I thought. "We aren't out of the weeds yet, we gotta go."

"One more thing. How did you get so bloody?"

I side-eyed Sintara for a moment. "I have no idea. Now come on, Wendy is waiting to hear from us."

Mel launched from her position in the corner of the room and rushed to be beside Sintara. Something felt different about standing beside her. Not as though she had changed, though I most certainly had. Like breathing air for the first time after being sucked under the surface of an ocean, something was different between us. More so, it felt as though I had been under that sea my whole life, only for the waves to wash over me once more as I took my first breaths. Reunited with her, my lungs filled with confidence. Though the storm was far from over, it felt more like a thing to be conquered than a thing to be conquered by.

In a fit of desperate rage, that which wanted to conquer us reared its head. As we stepped out into the hall, two guards blocked the way just ahead of us, guns blazing before they even knew what they were shooting at. Sintara dispatched them quickly.

"They'll only keep coming, where are we going?" Sintara asked.

I held the communicator to my mouth, pressing a button on its side. "Wendy, do you hear me?"

Her voice buzzed from a tiny speaker within it. "I heard way too much. Did you swallow the dang thing?"

I sighed. "It's a long story. We need directions, I swear all the punches to the head made me lose my sense of direction."

She obliged my request. "Down the hall, through the gate, further down, to the right. That's where the hangars are."

"And the offices, where the most guards will be. You're absolutely certain?" Sintara asked.

I nodded. "Thirteen is just as much a part of this team as any of us are, I'm not leaving him."

When I had first programmed him, it didn't take long for 'it' to become 'him'. To say that Thirteen wasn't human would be to say I failed the intent of his programming. His designed purpose was to seem as human as possible, though deep down I could never know whether it was a facade. When an AI convinces itself of something, it can quickly become a reality, even sentience.

I nodded harder."Besides, he's literally our only way out."

Sinatra sighed. "Lead the way."

I rushed down the hall with the others in tow, pausing several times to listen for incoming guards that never seemed to show up. As we came up to the first gate with no way through, I realized a gap in my planning. Before I could even consider our options, Mel stepped forward and took hold of the bars. They twisted and groaned as she pulled them apart. With a bit of work, a gap was made in the bars just large enough for Mel to pass through, and consequently, Sintara and I. Her height had some disadvantages, but her inhuman strength had none at all.

Mel waved us through with an impatient look. "Come on, it's clear over here."

Sintara couldn't help but give an entertained laugh at the display. "Glad to see I was worried about nothing when sending you off with this slaghead."

Ignoring her harsh comment, I slipped through the bars last. In a sense, I felt deeply out of place as the smallest of this group. There was no time for such worries however. Making our way further into the jail, the odd lack of guards became abundantly clear. Something was distracting them, all of them. Whatever that something was, it was nearby. A rumble began below our feet, the rumble of a crowd. Shouts and screams and stomping feet of excitement and enjoyment. Just as we rounded the right turn towards the hangars, straight ahead of us was a sight to behold. A crowd of prisoners in white jumpsuits ranging all sizes, heights, and races came charging down the hallway coming from the cell blocks. Sintara raised her gun immediately, but I swatted her hands down as they came to a stop just before us.

The same scraggly man with wiry hair I had released from solitary confinement led the charge, putting all of them to a silent stop as we came face to face. This man clearly had a plan in mind, for in the few minutes we had spent in confinement he appeared to have released the entire prison's worth of prisoners.

The man stuck his bony finger at me with the claw-like nail covered in a substance vaguely like blood. "You, blue haired fellow! He's who let me out of my cell!"

The crowd erupted in cheers, many of them calling out compliments or thanks. Maybe these guys weren't so bad. They were murderers, thieves, and criminals, but then again, so was I.

Sintara punched me hard on the shoulder. "Apollo, what the hell did you do?!"

My whole body reacted to the harsh attack, rubbing at the bruise already existing across the left side of my body. "I had to guess which cells you were in. I guessed...and I was wrong the first time. But all's well that ends well, right?"

A new rumble arose beneath us, like a great tidal wave of clattering gear and guns. I stepped forward to take a look down the hall coming from the offices and hangars. An army of guards in full gear with batons raised came charging towards us all. Sintara didn't have nearly enough bullets for all of them, but we had enough men.

I cupped my hands around the sides of my mouth, shouting out to the crowd. "If you wanna show your thanks, get us to the hangars!"

A mere second of silence passed before the first voice arose. "For Apollo!" Everyone joined in them, each man shouting in unison as the unstoppable force met the immovable object. The battle was vicious, neither side ever truly seemed to be winning. Part of me wanted to look away, the other refused to. Sintara watched with her jaw slack and confusion framing every inch of her posture. Mel's brow was furrowed, equally confused but impressed by the shared agreement between equally-minded people.

"Make way boys!" One voice cried out over the chaos. The waves of men split like a sea. Armed guards still stood between us and the hangars, staring down the lane through the chaos and locking eyes with us. If there was any debate about my status as a criminal before, the suggested collusion of breaking so many prisoners out of jail was enough to solidify me in history. The leading man smacked his baton down on his palm and took the first steps toward us with eyes burning like fire through the visor of his helmet.

Sintara led the charge, raising the gun and sending several bullets colliding with the plates of his ballistic uniform. Punches or kicks to a uniform like that would break your hands or feet before it would hurt them, and it would take more bullets than we had to break through the plates protecting them.

"Any ideas?" I asked.

"Hit them before they hit you." Mel's feet shook the ground like a mighty earthquake. Even the men locked in brawls all across this room took a moment to see what had made the sound. She crashed into the first man and sent him careening backwards into the guards behind him. She shook her hands with a grunt of pain and readied them for more fighting.

Sintara slipped past her and into the path of another guard rushing in. He swung his baton in a high arc, bringing it down in a sloppy swing that Sintara took hold of. With a twist of her hips she threw him onto the ground and stomped down on his neck. Both hands became critically occupied with relieving the pressure on his windpipe; the action practically handed Sintara the baton as she cracked it across his helmet in a devastatingly loud swing that knocked the man out cold.

The crowd of fighters surged forward, breaking through the waves of guards and out into a room big enough to hold even the largest of ships I worked on. Dozens upon dozens of ships filled this room, neatly lined up across the hangar. A large circular opening sat on the ceiling of this room, an airlock that led to the outside. Our small army of convicts was dwarfed by the size of this room. My eyes fought through the chaos to seek out Thirteen, but something broke my focus. A sound like an empty can being tossed clattered amongst our feet, particularly just near my own. I looked down to see a small tube pulsing with blue energy. The pulse quickened, and I suddenly recognized this object.

"Everybody get down!" My voice was harsh against my throat as I pushed Mel to the ground and sought to cover her head. A few others followed the suggestion, including Sintara, but not all. A fuzzy explosion threw small discs of metal into the air with electricity arcing between them and the origin of the explosion. Several of the small discs stuck to the convicts, six of them wreathed in arcing electricity. Every muscle in their body contracted as they flopped to the ground. More electric pulses bounced off the walls of the room as even more tiny discs of metal whizzed past us. They didn't want to kill us, but they wanted to stop us.

"Keep your head down and stay close to me!" I scooped an arm under Mel's arm and pulled her up. We slipped into the first row of ships as more metal clattered against the wall of the ship just beside us. Mel stopped for a moment, looking back into the madness.

"Where is Sintara?"

I stopped now, looking back to see her nowhere, neither in the crowd or in the continuing skirmish against the guards of the prison. One step forward proved to be my downfall as I sought to catch sight of her. A guard rushed around the corner and pulled the trigger in an instant. The metal disc tore through the fabric of my sleeve and shredded the skin of my right arm. I flopped against the wall of the ship beside me in a knee jerk reaction, careening out of the trajectory of furthering projectiles. A burst of blind confidence carried me in a blind rush at the man, taking hold of his collar and slamming him against the wall of the ship now. I pivoted on one foot and shoved him towards Mel who held an arm out beside her, clotheslining the man into the immovable object that was her strength.

He was out cold, part of me wanted to spit on him for the pain he caused me. I rummaged through the man's possessions, taking his gun and ammunition while glancing behind us. "She'll catch up with us, I trust her."

"I didn't leave you on Zion, I expect you would do the same for her."

"We're not leaving her. It's Sintara, we're doing these poor men a mercy getting her out of here before she escapes on her own terms." Any sensible man would fear Sintara, and though I was hardly a sensible man, even fools held respect for her.

Mel took a step towards me, hands floating towards the blood that ran down my sleeve. "Your arm—"

"--will be fine." I finished her sentence for her. Rude, yes, but I blamed the adrenaline. "We need to go, any sight of Thirteen?"

An electronic beep came from my pocket as an answer to my question. My hand pulled the communicator out in an instant, urgent to contact Wendy. At least, that's what I had intended.

"Thirteen is two rows down to your left. Get flying, I'll provide cover fire." Sintara's voice was powerful, even through such a small speaker.

The engines of a ship roared to life somewhere in the room, overtaking the sound of the skirmish and explosion of stun grenades. Matte black and tinted windows. The Wasp, Sintara's ship, hovered just overhead, like an angel of death. Guns blazed, tearing through ships and striking true fear into every man in that room.

A laugh escaped me as I watched the hauntingly beautiful beast. "I told you! A lack of her presence is a mercy on all men!"

Mel shoved my head down as more guards came around the corner. She led me by the wrist to the next row over, then to the right, then to the left. The directions seemed random at best, chaotic at worst. Her feet hit the ground in a halt as she pressed up next to the ship just beside us. She bent her knees and got low to the ground, pressing her back into the wall of the ship in a strained battle. The plan had dawned on me, and though I was no help, I too pressed hard against the ship. It was a freight ship, similar to The Toad. Top heavy in nature, and an all too weak base. It groaned on the metal holding it off the ground, then crossed the tipping point.

Shouts came from the other side of the ship as guards screamed in a panic, diving out of the way of the massive thing. It crashed heavily against the ship beside it, knocking it over into the ship past it, and beyond. A domino of ships and freighters, all to cut off the guards from our position. It was nearly perfect, if one guard hadn't made his way past it. More projectiles whizzed in our direction as we rushed for Thirteen. He was in sight, but out of reach. Mel screamed as one of the metal discs tore into her leg, embedding itself into the flesh of her calf. They weren't seeking to disable anymore, they were seeking to kill.

I dropped to the ground beside Mel, flopping onto my back and drawing the gun from my belt. I took aim and fired several shots. One buried itself in the man's neck. His hand came up to meet it in an instant, blood gurgling from his mouth and seeping through his gloved fingers. His gun clattered to the floor, and an eerie silence filled the room. It wasn't quiet, by all means it was still loud, but that silence that filled my ears was newly and horrifyingly familiar. The kind of silence that was louder than anything else; that which followed the final breath as life left the body. I squeezed my eyes hard, the silence would not overtake me this time.

Mel hooked her arm around my neck as I lifted her off the ground as best I could. She leaned heavily against me. Admittedly, I could barely carry her. On Zion, I had my full strength, now my wounds were taking effect. Any further distance and I might have collapsed with her. We came up to Thirteen, finding ourselves stuck on the outside. My body felt lighter than ever as Mel slumped against the side of the ship on her good leg.

"How do we get in?"

I looked up at the side of the ship and drew a deep breath. The ship looked taller than before. "There's a porthole up top, as soon as I can get inside and get the power on, we'll be out of here."

"How long will that take?"

I thought about it for a second, taking the gun from my belt and placing it in her hand. "If anyone finds you, you aim this at them and-"

"I know how these work." She took it and checked the ammunition. "Start climbing, I'll cover you."

Though I had intentionally installed a series of notches and steps for this exact surface, the blood on my hands made the climb slicker than an iced over pond. I held close to the wall as I ascended and picked up the pace as I looked over my shoulder to see even more guards approaching us. Scrambling onto the roof of the ship like a fish out of water, my hands took hold of the lever attached to the porthole. It hadn't been open since I built the ship, I'd hardly known if it would move at all. My teeth gritted in my mouth as I cranked it open. I laughed briefly to myself, knowing Mel would make it look easy.

My fingers slipped at the last moment as I swung myself down into the dusty, dark abyss. I crashed to the ground on my side, grabbing at my ribs as I lurched to my feet and patted along the walls of the ship. I knew this place like the back of my hand, but I didn't care to get any more bloody noses by running into a closed door. A light poured through the windshield as I came to the bridge. I flicked a series of switches along the dash, then reached up over my head and flicked two more. A dull whir came from the ship, yet no power seemed to reach the bridge.

"I didn't come this far for her to die!" I slapped my hands down on the screens hard. Blood was smeared across the smooth surface, but in a miraculous instant, the screens flickered to life.

Light flooded the ship, the engines whirring to life for real this time. The flood lights flickered on, illuminating Mel as she ran past the front of the ship, arm outstretched behind her in a blind fire at the people who followed her. My fingers swiped across the screens smoothly and I took hold of the joystick to the right of the captain's chair, thumb pressing hard to the button atop it. The guns fired in three massive bursts, tearing holes through the ship in front of us. The pursuing guards dove for cover as shrapnel tore into the ground and was flung through the air.

"Thirteen, can you hear me?"

"Loud and clear, sir." I didn't think I'd miss that voice so much.

"I need the port side door open, now."

"Right away, sir."

My feet carried me out of the bridge and across the ship as the port side door swung open with a hiss. It was a small, narrow door that I didn't use often, but I was very glad I installed it. I braced myself against the wall and held a hand out to Mel. She stepped up onto the landing gear of the ship and took hold of my hand as I did my best to pull her into the ship. Her strength did half the work, both of us collapsing onto the ground as I slapped a hand hard on the pad just right of the door and sealed it shut.

"Thirteen, get us out of here," I said breathlessly.

"That is a cause I can get behind. Engines are hot."

The ship lifted off the ground in a jittery liftoff. I dragged myself onto the deck and into my chair as we rose towards the airlock in the ceiling. The communications system buzzed as Sintara tuned in.

"Don't tell me you intend to blow your way through there." Her voice had been half joking, we both knew there was no easy way to get us out of here.

"It's not the worst idea I've had all day," I mumbled.

The ship tilted back as the guns took fire at the airlock door. The pressure in the hangar dropped in an instant. A few more shots blew the door open entirely. Alarms filled the room further with red floodlights overtaking everything. A secondary door began sliding into place.

"If you want out, now's your chance, Sintara."

I heaved the throttle forwards and the thrusters burned the air. Mel and I were forced back into our chairs as the ship made way for the rapidly narrowing gap. Admittedly, I squeezed my eyes shut for just a moment, opening them to find us breaking out into open space and away from the surface. The screen showed a camera attached to the back of the ship, a perfect view of seeing Sintara take flight out of the prison with mere inches to spare. Relief overtook me, I leaned back in my chair and sighed. My eyes grew heavy as I looked down at my arm once again.

"That's a lot of blood." That was the last thing I could remember saying before the world faded to black once again.

↩ ↩ ↩

"What do you mean I 'damaged the asset'?!" I screamed into the glass as I wrangled the writhing mass of fat and muscle bound beside me. We were both sticky with blood, fresh bruises developing on my face. He was far worse off, a broken nose swelling his eyes closed as he gurgled profanities and sprayed blood through his blood-covered lips.

"An excess of injuries sustained by a bounty is a deduction to the overall reward." Her voice was painfully monotone, her lack of care was aggravating. She pushed the glasses up the bridge of her nose and looked away from the screen built into the table. "The payout will be five thousand units, final offer."

"That's half the original payout! I demand to speak to whoever is in charge here."

She rolled her eyes. "It's an automated system, sir. If you want to speak to a supervisor you can take It to the CTA office on Mars."

"Well...can I turn him in now and argue my payout?"

"When the bounty is turned in, the payout is finalized. If you wanna argue the payout you'll have to wait until the case is settled."

"But the law says I can only keep him for forty eight hours!"

She shrugged. "Best make it quick."

The man was aghast. "You can't leave me with this little psycho for 48 hours, I have rights!"

I took him by the collar and pulled him close to my face. He flinched wildly as I growled. "You're right, they'd best not leave you with me for forty eight hours. Dead or alive, was it?"

"Alive, sir. You will not get your payout if he is killed, and you will be charged for murder."

The threat felt a whole lot less like a threat after that, only a bad idea. We'd seem to reach an impasse, one that ended with myself drawing the short end of the stick no matter what the solution might be. In this moment of tensity, I felt a cold hand press against my shoulder. I glanced to see a taller man in a dark uniform standing beside me. He had a permanent smirk pulling at his lips, one that was instantly recognizable. Zivko, the Star Shark. Any bounty hunter worth his salt knew him.

"If I may, I can't help but say I witnessed this man break his own nose on the way in for the sake of cutting the payout." His voice didn't convey someone trying to tell a convincing lie, rather someone who didn't need to try. Whether it be his reputation or otherwise, it was easy to believe him. He tapped me on the shoulder with the back of his hand. "Tell her, kid."

I hesitated for a moment, still unsure whether or not all this was truly happening. I swallowed my pride and nodded. "Uh, yeah. He's right."

The woman looked to Zivko, then back to me with eyes just a little bit softer. She didn't believe him of course. Perhaps she just wanted to move on with her day. Perhaps she was a friend of his, though I found it hard to believe anyone could be friends to such a grumpy disposition. "He has still sustained significant damage."

"Yet you have no proof that it was caused by this poor chap. Let's be honest, it's a miracle he ever subdued this man in the first place." He scanned me up and down for a moment with a jeering smirk. "He couldn't have hurt him that bad."

The woman sighed and shook her head. "Fine, the original payout of ten thousand. Just leave already, you're getting blood on the floor."

She pressed a small button that opened a door just to the right of the small window she sat inside. Two men in LCCE uniforms stepped through the door and took hold of the man. They led him through the door and into some kind of cell that would keep him until an officer would be available to take him back to Mars. I wiped my hands hard on my jumpsuit. It was already horrifically stained, how much worse could blood be on the fabric?

"Name's Zivko." The man held a hand out to me and introduced himself as if I wasn't very much aware of who he was. "That'll be two thousand five hundred for my services."

"What?!"

"I'm kidding, I'm kidding." He shrugged hard. "I have bigger fish to fry than tax evaders."

I shook his hand now, making sure to leave just enough blood on his hands to be inconvenient. He seemed unshaken, as I should have expected. If half the stories about him were true, I was certainly shaking hands with death. He knew how to wash blood off his hands.

"If I may, you seem new to the trade," he said.

My eyes narrowed on him. Wherever this confidence had come from, I enjoyed it. "What gives that impression?"

"Mostly the rope as handcuffs, secondly the amount of damage you did to that poor lad." He ended the sentence with a whisper as he stepped away from the window. "You look like you need help."

"I'm doing just fine on my own."

"Well I can't have bounty hunters walking around using ropes. We aren't Neanderthals." He dug into his pocket and pulled out a set of cuffs and tossed them to me. They were nice, really nice. Collapsible so they could fit in your pocket, made of real steel. The kind of stuff the pros used. "In other news, I hear you're good with ships."

"From whom exactly did you hear this?"

"The eight other people on this spaceport who paid you to repair their ship, and for a cheap price at that. You must be really desperate." He checked his watch for a moment. "I can pay you better than they can, and help you get paid better."

I pocketed the cuffs before he had the chance to second guess the gift. "What exactly are you proposing?"

"A partnership. I think our skills could work well together. Money to be made, for both of us. What do you say?"

Infectiously charismatic. To ignore him was like ignoring a celebrity. He had helped me, and I was desperate. It would be a fool's error to pass up this opportunity. I swallowed my pride. I couldn't keep fighting for scraps like this. "Where do we start?"

He rolled his shoulders back with a smile, one with a crooked smirk still peaking through the lines of his face. "Food court. I'm starving."

I followed him. I played along. He was a shepherd and I was a desperate sheep. I set aside my moral standards, the ethics that I held at my heart. It was dirty work, but boy did it pay well. They were criminals after all. I was doing the right thing. At least, that's what I convinced myself.

He was funny, and seemed to have an infinite amount of stories to tell. He never showed fear, never thought twice about anything. He was always so sure of himself, and it inspired me. He wasn't the first friend I had ever had, but he was surely the closest. I helped build him the fastest ship in the galaxy, he gave me lessons in fighting, strategy, and negotiation. I was plenty "smart", but he made me street smart...or space smart.

One day, lounging in the bridge of the Dark Matter, we were swapping stories about scars. He had much more to tell, but I thought I would one up him as I rolled up my sleeve and showed the line where my old and new flesh met. He laughed the second he saw it.

"Flash clone replacement? You'll get a kick out of this."

He rolled up his sleeves, and his pant legs, revealing that every one of his limbs had been replaced, old and new ending and beginning in different places. His left arm changed just below his elbow, his right arm at the top of his shoulder, his left leg at the thigh, his right at the ankle. He had been torn apart and put back together like a ragdoll.

"You think I got this good at fighting without a few scrapes?"

"Those are more than...scrapes."

"Sometimes bullets are the best teacher."

That motto was too true for him. I could suspend my guilt when we took down child laborers, murderers, arsonists, gang members, and worse. For every evil we removed from the world, I felt a little bit more like a hero. But the feeling slowly died when Zivko got bored. The big things got too dangerous, I was too sloppy to get things done effectively. He handled the dirty work, I merely stood there and took a piece of the cashout. He always said to not worry about it, that my work on his ship was all I needed to earn my cut. But I couldn't stomach it as he started punching down. Tax evaders, speeders, debtors. I couldn't handle taking down normal people, everyday folk I saw myself in more than I saw myself in Zivko.

It all tore as I stood there, holding back a mother and child as Zivko traded punches with a young man late on his loan payments. The man had no chance against Zivko, but Zivko let him believe he did. He was toying with the man, with his wife and child watching. A hard blow to the man's nose opened a river of blood from it. Zivko laughed as the man stumbled back, hardly able to breathe or see. The wife screamed in agony, his child smacked at my legs in anger.

"Let my daddy go! I hate you!"

My stomach turned as Zivko threw the man to the ground, tightening cuffs around his hands. The woman punched me in the side of the head and leaped onto Zivko, clawing at his face with her nails. She barely had a chance to hurt him before he had broken her hand and shoved her aside.

"Apollo! The hell is wrong with you??" He held his face with blood running down his cheek.

The child ran past me and dashed to his mother, crying over her as she cowered.

"This is stupid. This man didn't do anything, he's just another victim of the system and you're toying with him!" I shouted harshly.

He grabbed hold of my collar, staring at me through the scratches over his eyes. "He's a criminal just like the rest of them, dimwit! If you weren't such a coward, you might actually work off your own debt before you die. And here I am dragging around a deadweight moron like you!"

"I won't be so needlessly cruel to people like this, especially not in front of their family!"

Zivko shoved me away and pulled the man to his feet, leading him to 'our' ship. "Well grow up, damn it. For once in your miserable life, man up and make yourself more useful than just making me ships."

I was left standing there beside a crying wife and child, whose lives I had a hand in ruining. Instead of helping, instead of freeing the man, I left. I didn't follow Zivko, I left without even saying goodbye. It was better to start from scratch than try to reconcile with a monster. I couldn't live like this anymore, I couldn't live with myself. I didn't think I could be any worse than I was that day. I tried to find that wife and child a few weeks later, but they were nowhere to be found.

Every day I thought about those people, people whose lives were ruined by the system. The same system that ruined my own life. I became a part of the system to save myself, but at the cost of others. I wouldn't do it again. I would only take bounties to rescue people, fix other ships, transport people or things from one system to another. None of it eased my conscience, and every day I lived in paranoia, thinking Zivko would come back and take his revenge. I never did forgive myself for doing that, nor for ever being friends with that monster. For a brief moment, I saw myself in him, and he showed the worst of humanity. I could only hope I wouldn't turn out like him.

⤳ 14 ⤳

Space

Weightless. Empty. Cold. It was as if the mere idea of space permeated anything existing within it. Any creature born on a planet with enough drive to leave it knows the feeling. Every muscle and tendon feels it. Every cell in your body knows that you are no longer bound to any single celestial body. Rather, the vague pull of every celestial body in the universe calls to you, a nagging feeling that draws you towards every terrestrial, gas, and ice planet within the observable universe. It was as if the stars were some being which whispers to each of us who call ourselves explorers, beckoning us to be the first human to see one of the billions of stars. But all that space in between was what interested me most. The emptiness, the loneliness, the quiet. The call of the void. Freedom.

And yet I was bound. I knew the feeling, I knew exactly where I was. Held to a firm cushion by a blanket. A blanket that attaches to hooks in the side of the couch that sits in the "living space" of the Thirteen. A pillow sat behind my head, also attached to the couch using hook and loop. I was home, back with Thirteen. I'd wished I'd open my eyes to find nothingness; empty space with stars surrounding me. The void I glimpsed into during the explosion on Zion. The deep, rich, blackness of the trip to the prison.

Instead I saw the warm yellow light of Thirteen. The gray and blue painted walls. The mismatched, shoddily patched gash in the wall. The lockers holding the small assortment of junk I called valuables, most of which had been soaked through with salt water and destroyed. The familiar hum of the engines, the hypercore I built with my own two hands, the nearly inaudible buzz of the electromagnetic floors.

As I expected, my body ached. My arm still stung and the smell of disinfectant clung to the wound. A tight bandage was wrapped around my bicep. My ribs and shoulders were tender, my knuckles buzzing with bruises and fingers swollen from punches. Worst of all, every bruised and swollen inch of my body itched. The kind of dull itch that is just enough to piss you off. A body's way of saying it was healing, but in an utterly infuriating manner. Above all, pins and needles danced along the surface of my right arm. That was normal. It was nothing out of the ordinary really, only another thing to add to the pile of ailments.

My head flopped to one side to find Mel sitting beside me. She sat on the floor with her head craned back, resting on the cushion where my feet rested. Her pink hair was greasy and matted. Her eyes held dark circles though they were closed. Her skin held a light sheen of oil and sweat. She was asleep, and she seemed more beautiful than ever. More radiant than any star I'd seen in this galaxy.

"You saved my life." The words trickled off my tongue like a mist, barely a sound at all.

Footsteps approached, two sets of them. Along with it, dull chatter between Sintara and Wendy as they entered the living area from the bridge. Sintara had ditched her uniform and retreated to a jumpsuit, Wendy still wore the mag-gravs she "borrowed" from Neeson. The moment they entered, they both made an equal glance at me, checking to see if I was still breathing and relieved to see I was awake.

"What happened, where are we?" My throat was like sandpaper as I croaked out the words, pain washing over me as I attempted to sit up. The attempt was in vain as my body made equal parts to keep myself reclined as Wendy did, stepping forward with anger in her eyes at the very idea of me trying to stand.

Wendy rubbed at her eyes as she whispered worry-filled words. "It's a miracle you lived long enough for us to reach you, don't push your luck."

"We need to get moving before they find us. It won't be long-"

Sintara raised a hand and interrupted. "I took care of it for now. We have at least a day, maybe longer."

Wendy wiped her hands on her pants and sighed. "Not that we have the resources for any longer than a day. We'll need supplies for what comes next."

I still wasn't properly awake. My ears took in the information, but my brain failed to put any of it together. Like a toddler trying to put the square peg through the round hole. "Slow it down and fill me in. How long have I been asleep?"

Sintara thought for a moment. "About twelve hours. We put you under so we might actually get something done without your opinion getting in the way."

I ignored the harsh comment and groaned out a pair of coarse words. "Twelve hours?"

Sintara made a gesture for me to lower my voice before continuing in a low tone. "You needed it. Mel told us you had barely slept in days."

I sighed, accepting how tired I had been, and still was. I struggled to release myself from the hooked blanket. "Explains why I can barely move."

"That is partially why, but let's consider the fact that you've been putting your body through absolute hell for days on end. Bar fights, fighting Zivko—twice, and breaking in and out of a jail? Are you trying to get yourself killed or trying to kill me with worry?" Wendy's whisper raised to a sharp hiss, folding her arms and pacing the room. "Thanks so much for 'filling me in' back on Mars by the way. Sintara and Mel helped make it real clear just how well you've been taking care of yourself the past week. I can hardly take my eyes off you for half a second without having to come pick you up off the ground or save your sorry ass!"

"You think I don't want you to stop saving me? You've been doing it since I was a child, I'm a grown man now. Now when I stand up for myself, you get mad at me for putting myself on the line!"

"What is with all the yelling?" Mel awoke at the commotion, yawning and rubbing at her eyes. She glanced around the room, then at me, eyes widening immediately. She reached out and grabbed my hand with both of her own. "Apollo, thank the titans you're okay! You made me worried sick."

I made a move to sit up now, making moderate progress by slouching against the armrest of the couch. "You made me worried too."

A weight dropped off my shoulders in the moment, a weight that had held me to the couch and pulled me down. I hadn't been myself since I'd faced Zivko, but even less so been myself without her. In only a few short days, she'd come to complete me. Not in a sappy romantic way, but in which she'd become my sole purpose in life. A true mission to replace the miserable life I had lived only a week prior, and yet our first meeting and the beginning of our journey felt like an eternity ago. We felt so close to the end now, but what might I do then? The idea gripped me like a vice.

Mel raised a questioning eyebrow. "Why do you look so angry at him? Hasn't he been through enough?"

Wendy shook her head. "He's been irresponsible, selfish, and unruly. You're going to get yourself killed with this ego."

Mel's brow furrowed in confusion. "Selfish means to be focused on oneself, correct?"

Wendy nodded now. "Yeah?"

"Apollo has spent the last week sacrificing everything in his life to protect and guide me. Even when he has failed, he has continued to redeem his mistakes and make right where he has been wronged. There's nothing selfish about anything he's done. In fact, I believe it's the least selfish thing I've ever seen him do." Mel looked at Wendy with a look of curiosity. "Perhaps the most dangerous thing we might do to ourselves is to be selfless, for it leads us to forget our own needs for the sake of another's. To be selfless is not a bad thing of course, so long as we are selfless to those who are selfless for us."

Mel looked at me now, her eyes agreeing with the whispers of my mind. We'd come to rely on each other in everything, two halves of a whole. She continued. "I like to think I've done the same for him, and once we'd become separated there was nobody to care for our own needs. With all due respect, I find it more selfish for you to wish for him to stop being selfless for your own sake."

The ship was silent as Mel finished her thought. My lips pursed, then curved to a bunched smile. I tried as hard as I could to contain the smile, but I didn't even know why I was smiling. Whether pride for the person Mel was or simply the feeling of having someone stand up for you, I was unsure. Regardless, my heart fluttered, and I refused to like it.

Wendy's face was as red as her hair, closing her eyes tightly and shaking her head again. "You wouldn't get it, Mel."

"I think I might. When I first met Apollo, he'd been the most cruel and ignorant man I'd ever met. He's far from the same person he was then, all in the span of just a few days. Just how much more might he have changed since you were both children? Might you need to treat him differently after all that?" Mel tilted her head over to one side and sighed as her now sorrowful eyes glanced at me. "I've changed since we first met too. I suppose I should expect you to treat me differently as well."

A light bulb flicked on in my head. "Your memories?"

"They have returned to me...and there is much to discuss."

There it was again, that determined but concerned look. Her shoulders sagged as the stone words collapsed on her. Heroic, yet defeated. The situation was dire, but it was about to get far more dire. Nobody knew what to say, but Mel's stomach spoke for her as it growled loudly.

Mel raised a polite hand with a now embarrassed expression. "Might I explain over some food? I am starving. Your prisons don't feed convicts very well."

Wendy face palmed for a brief second. "How could I have forgotten, of course you're all starving. Everyone sit down, I'll bring us something to eat."

I pulled myself into a sitting position as Wendy shuffled off, making room for Mel and Sintara on the couch. Mel sat next to me immediately. I would have made the time to be flattered had I not been in so much pain. We sat in peace for a moment, taking a near unified breath of relief. After all this, I could use a vacation or two, not that there are many vacation homes available to wanted men. I shook my head and brushed the thought away. There was no time to waste on useless thoughts.

I cleared my throat before speaking. "I remember what you did for me in Zion, after the explosion."

She folded her hands in her lap, hiding her thumbs inside her closed palms. "So you do."

"I didn't even know it was humanly possible to...do any of that."

Mel laughed lightly. "Well, I am not human."

The realization hit me quickly, about as hard as my own palm hit my face. "Right. I also recall something when you were handing me over. You whispered something, but I couldn't hear you. What did you—"

"Foods up!" Wendy declared as she waltzed into the room, carrying an armful of foil packets that radiated heat.

Our meal was spent mostly in silence. I'd have been lying to say I didn't miss a meal like this. Before finding Mel, I'd been surviving on freeze dried calorie bars and sparkling water. Money had never been easy to come by since I'd gotten out of the game of hunting people for cash.

I shook my head hard. Bad memories, nothing I cared to remember at least. The food was good, some kind of pasta and chicken dish. My surprise at the quality was quickly subdued when I realized Wendy had pulled these from Sintara's ship. Not sure what I had expected, there was very little food to be found on my ship. Food worth eating, anyways.

Sintara and Wendy both dug deeply into their food, Mel ate hers slowly, yet I could tell how desperate she was to do the same. I watched her for a long moment until she glanced at me through the strands of her wavy pink hair hanging in front of her ears. The look forced my eyes away, blinking away the sight.

"I have a question," Mel said after a moment of quiet.

"We might have an answer," Sintara mumbled as respectfully as possible through a mouthful of food.

"Why does Apollo's face turn blue when he looks at me?"

Wendy doubled over to the side, holding an arm over her face as she fought to keep both her food in her mouth and her laughter suppressed. I could feel my face flush, a heat filling my ears and cheeks as I looked further away and stuffed more food into my mouth.

Sintara seemed unperturbed, politely finishing her bite before speaking. "Martians have blue blood due to a higher presence of cobalt within their body. The first cities on Mars were built on craters that had blue sand. Turns out that mysterious blue sand on the red planet was cobalt. Cobalt is toxic to humans, but they adapted a resistance to it as it had a higher presence in their food, and it turned their hair, eyes, and blood blue. That's why Apollo has some blue qualities, including his blood."

"So it's like, blushing?"

"Exactly like blushing," Sintara nodded before returning to her food.

Mel's face was bunched with curiosity and confusion, then her eyes slowly widened, then narrowed again on me, then wide again as she looked down at her food and blushed herself, a pinkish color.

"Let's change the subject, shall we?" I grumbled.

Thirteen buzzed through the speakers. "I have a subject to speak on."

"See? The robot can make better conversations than you." I leaned back into my seat, proud of my programming. "Let's hear it, Thirteen."

"I have good news and bad news, which shall I start with?"

Thirteen had no way of understanding what news was good and what news was bad. To him, news is just news, matters of fact and nothing more. For him to ask such a question meant that the news was so horrible that even he could recognize it as bad. Nobody knew this but me, but their eyes read my face and quickly realized there was good reason to worry.

"Let's start with bad news."

"The bounty has been raised. Apollo is being charged for kidnapping, harboring a dangerous fugitive, aggravated assault, conspiracy, resisting arrest, breaking and entering, three charges of unauthorized removal and retention of classified documents, prison escape, and two accounts of second degree murder. All of this for a grand total of a ten million dollar bounty. Along with this, a new bounty had been placed on Sintara Clarke for desertion, collusion with a known criminal, theft of government property, aggravated assault, prison escape, several accounts of homicide, conspiracy, and vandalism. That bounty is currently listed at four million."

A heavy moment of silence. A long, palpable, painful bout with the quiet of open space. The blood flowing through the veins in my head made a deafeningly loud roar as my heart picked up pace. That was bad news. Very, very, very bad news.

"The good news?" I deadpanned.

"The three most wanted people in the galaxy are on this ship, making this the most valuable ship in the galaxy."

I bit my lip and nodded several times. The type of response I should expect from a robot I designed, but woefully out of place in the situation "I really need to program appropriate timing for you."

"This is...not good," Mel mumbled.

Sintara shook her head. "Nope."

We'd exhausted seemingly every option, and every step forward was two steps back. With every step closer to getting Mel home, more people got hurt, more people were put in danger. Now nearly every person here was under threat of life, and the next person would be Wendy if I didn't do something about it.

I crumpled up the empty container of my food and tossed it to the side, picking myself off the ground and taking my toolbox off the shelf. I launched its sling over my head and stomped off to where Sintara's ship was connected to mine.

Wendy shot up from her chair to follow me. "Where do you think you're going? We need a plan."

"I'm going to remove the tracker on Sintara's ship before it draws half a galaxy worth of officers to our location looking for a big payout. Let me clear my head and I'll think of something." I began the descent down the hatch and ladder into Sintara's ship. In this sea of stars, it was sink or swim now, and I had to get everyone to somewhere safe.

⇀ ⇀ ⇀

It never got any less relaxing to be surrounded by pieces and parts. The world was a messy, weird, confusing place, but machines had laws, rules, and guidelines to follow. A machine would always do what it was designed to do, so long as it was designed well. Even the most well trained, obedient human can still do incredibly stupid things, machines wouldn't. Besides, I relished every opportunity to tear apart LCCE equipment.

I whipped open a panel on the floor next to the table that doubled as a computer. Slipping into the gaps in the pipes, my toolbox popped open and revealed the mechanical marvels inside. My mind recalled the pieces and parts of LCCE ships I had worked on before, including Sintara's. This type of work always was easier than anything on a hypercore. At the very least, you could trust your memory here.

My gloved fingers ran across pipes and tubes lining the space around me, seeking through the darkness for one thing in particular. Through a gap in the pipes, I could see a blinking rhythmical light. Yellow brilliance lit up the space around it, barely enough for me to fit a single arm through. A flashlight from my toolbox flickered on as I attached it to a magnetic strip on the shoulder of my jumpsuit, giving me a bright yet shaky view of the system inside. It was a thin metal tube connected on either side by a spaghetti of wires. The navigation and communication systems of a ship were hosted on its own internal servers, but a tracker like this was placed inside government starcraft to observe and monitor a ship's vitals and positioning when necessary. They were designed to be difficult to reach for good reason, and it wasn't just the placement that made them hard to remove.

There were twelve wires connecting the tracker to the ship, and all twelve would have to be removed in a particular order to prevent an emergency signal being broadcast to all Spaceports and LCCE ships within range. This would assure that only engineers with the knowledge of the code of removal could do so, and while I was most certainly not a certified mechanic on a ship like this, it was one of the few things Zivko had taught me that I knew might be handy some day. I'd left the code scratched into the inside of my toolbox. I never thought too deeply about why he had it, or what he had to do to get it, but I let myself be convinced he was simply very good at making friends with engineers.

If nobody had found us yet, it meant that they had yet to realize Sintara's ship was missing from the prison, as it was one of the dozens of LCCE ships docked in that hangar. It wouldn't be long now, and I couldn't know when it might send out its next signal. I'd have to work swiftly, with focus and precision, nothing to distract me or get in my way.

"Apollo?"

I looked up to see Mel staring down at me from the floor of the ship, her eyes just barely peeking over at me as I sat in this dark, cramped space.

"Can we talk?" Mel asked.

I sighed. "Can it wait? This is direly important."

"Everything is around here, isn't it?" She took a deep breath between her sentences. "It's about my home…my memories."

I hesitated for a moment before running a finger over the code etched into my toolbox. Start with even numbers descending, twelve, ten, eight. "This seems like something to bring up around Wendy and Sintara."

"They can't know. I can't be certain what it will mean for them if they do."

My fingers felt along the array of wires along the bottom of the tracker, feeling a series of bumps along the metal that numbered each wire. I yanked the twelfth wire, then the tenth. I spoke with a bland tone, the kind you muster when focusing on something a bit too much. "You're starting to scare me."

The eighth wire popped out with a beep from the tracker as Mel began. "Back on Zion, my memories returned to me after the explosion. Many things came to light in my mind, including that look you and Sintara shared before we went to retrieve my home's coordinates."

In truth, even we were unsure of what we knew. Her guess was as good as mine, likely better. Odd numbers ascending now, one, three, five. My fingers ran along the top side of the tracker now. "So you know our little theory?"

"You believe that I was sent backwards in time when the ship crashed, a feat that I am led to assume has never been achieved."

One and three yanked now. "Not to my knowledge, but it's a big universe. You never know really."

"You believe it to be the reason nobody from my planet has come looking for me, but there is more to it than that."

"I'm all ears." Fifth wire out now, another beep.

Mel took another deep breath. "My people have never left our planet, at least, not to the extent I have now. Long ago, we placed satellites in our sky to search the stars for other life and to protect ourselves. Our scientists believed they had found nothing. My people believe that our planet is a heaven of sorts, that we are perfect so we have no reason to leave. Looking into the stars was purely curiosity, though now I am led to believe it was for other reasons. Something worse than being alone in the stars."

This was odd, to say the least. To think we'd been looking for each other all these centuries and never finding each other was near impossible, unless we had found each other and chose ignorance. Even numbers of the first half descending now. Six, four, two. "Any low powered satellite should be able to detect something human, even that far out."

Six pulled. "As would your satellites." Four pulled. "I believe...our people knew of each other, have known for centuries, perhaps." Two pulled, another beep. "You don't need me to convince you that your government has been hiding something from you."

"It's basically all they do. But if we'd chosen to stay separate, why would you have come here?" I scratched my chin for a moment, thinking about it as if Mel didn't intend to tell me. Odd numbers of the second half ascending now. Seven, nine, eleven.

"It wasn't my choice," Mel said.

She stopped, as did I. I pulled the last few wires and a loud beep could be heard. I slipped the device through the small crack and tossed it onto the ground outside the hatch, packing up my tools quickly and sitting on the edge of the opening in the ground. Mel looked frightened, her eyes just barely glazed over with tears and face vaguely pink. But she wasn't scared for her own sake, she was scared of something else, someone else.

"There's people on my planet much like you, and Henry, and Kate. But they're not as passive as you are. They want to see the destruction of those who sought to keep those secrets hidden. The secrets are slipping through the cracks like sand through one's fingers, and an insurrection is building. Destruction is approaching."

My eyes narrowed at the words as I struggled to make sense of it all. "And you're one of the insurrectionists?"

Mel shook her head and breathed again, this one shaky. "My home is ruled by Queen Kore and the royal family, descendants of ancient holy beings who landed on our planet from the stars long ago. They rule every city and town across our entire planet, and they work in close ties with the church to keep a holy and righteous people. They've done terrible things to keep the insurrection quiet, but they couldn't have predicted what the rebels would do to get attention. They kidnapped the crown princess and tried to find their way to the stars on their own."

"It wasn't your choice…" I mumbled.

Mel nodded, saddened and afraid. "I am her. Princess Melinoe of Elysia, daughter of Queen Kore. My family has done horrible things to innocent people, the same way your rulers have done unto you."

A quick laugh escaped my lungs, heat constricting my chest and the air slipped free. "Talk about the most important person in the galaxy."

Fear and horror seemed to grip her heart. Her face went pale as she spoke levelly, saying nothing but the truth. "My people will come looking for me, and when they do, I can hardly imagine a peaceful resolution to it all. You cannot win against them, your people will fall. We are stronger, we're smarter, more advanced. It won't be a fair fight."

A sigh of relief escaped me. "Good thing you'll be home in no time."

"There will be no refuge for you," Mel said. A few tears ran over her white cheeks. "If they don't kill you, they'll toss you in a cell and let you rot, the same way your world has sought to do unto me. You're wanted here and you're not welcome there. There's not a single place left in this galaxy safe for you...I'm sorry."

My head bobbed up and down in a repetitive nod. A fear arose in me, something deep and primal. I didn't want to die, I wanted safety. A purely human reaction, an experience that would make a valuable reminder that I was still very much alive, had my life not seemed so short from here forward. Despite my heart's desire to reject this reality, to deny it all, to run, my mind knew the truth. My life for every human life in the solar system, and it would have to be soon. It would have to be now. "I understand."

Mel squeezed her eyes tight, tears running free now. She didn't sob, she didn't cry, but empathy flowed from her as it always had. "I can't ask this of you, Apollo. It's not right to have to ask this of anyone."

"But it has to be done. Someone has to take you home."

Mel nodded. "I've thought hard on every possibility, every solution. There is no easy way out of this."

Something odd sparked inside me. A light feeling, like helium welling within my lungs. A foolish, naive, and careless idea floated into my mind, an idea that tumbled off my tongue in a manner just as ridiculous as it was. "Maybe there's a chance it will all work out, you know?"

"This is no time for blind optimism, Apollo."

I shrugged. "I've seen a lot of impossible things in this past week, things I can only call miracles. But in the face of certain death, maybe there is another miracle or two awaiting me."

A pain filled laugh escaped her, breath wracking as she drew it back into her. "That's just what us humans do, right? Tell yourselves pretty little lies until the truth swallows you whole?"

Eating my own words. "Sometimes it works out."

Mel sniffed. "Not always."

Her shoulders hung low. She truly had given up on it all. It was as if I was a dead man sitting in front of her, and she felt my blood was on her hands. "I can't bear to see you die, Apollo. Not after everything you've done for me. You've already sacrificed everything for me, you shouldn't have to sacrifice this too."

"That makes two of us," I mumbled before a tiny smirk pulled at me. "I didn't know you cared about me so much."

The tiniest giggle escaped her at this, not out of comedy, out of pain. Laughing through tears. "I could say the same about you."

"We'll figure something out, like we always do."

"Let me guess, that's what humans do?"

I corrected her. "That's what engineers do. We see a problem and we solve it. We can't help it, it's like a bad habit."

In an instant, Mel reached for me, taking my hand inside her own and holding it close to her chin. I felt a rush of blood into my face in the instant. Her hands seemed infinitely soft, starkly contrasting my own calloused and grease-smeared hands. "Why don't we just give up? We could find some moon colony somewhere, change our names, hide away. Nobody would bother you, my people would never find me. I'll be as good as dead to my people, and you'll be as good as gone to your own. We can live peacefully. No war, no pain, no death, no imprisonment."

A cold hand closed around my heart, icing over my soul and freezing my mind in place. As cold as the very vacuum of space, I understood my place in this all. She was everything, crown princess of the most powerful people in our solar system, the most important person in the world. I was nothing, a being whose life surmounted to a dollar amount paid out by a government that wanted only my demise. But at the same time, I too was also everything. I was the lynchpin of this chaotic, messy situation. She was the wheel that kept the universe spinning, but I had to bring her home. My life, completing this journey, held the universe together. As if I was gravity itself. After that, I would go back to being nobody, and death was inevitable. She would live forever in history, I would be a footnote.

But she didn't want to go home. It wasn't because she loved it here so much, or because this world loved her more than her own did, though both could also be true. She wanted to stay because she wouldn't have to carry the burden, the responsibility of knowing our world and who was in it. She would be one of the monsters keeping our world hidden, a cog in the machine. She didn't want that. As sure as the collapse of a dying star, she didn't want me, she only wanted company.

My fingers slipped free of hers, bringing it back to my own heart. "That's not what you truly want."

Her brow furrowed. "It's exactly what I want."

"We could never live in peace knowing we've doomed millions and millions to death because of our inaction. Their blood would be on our hands because of our cowardice." The last word was like poison on my tongue, I despised it.

I had never expected to become so familiar with silence after living such a loud life for so long, but now the grip of silence felt less like a suffocating ocean and rather the return of a dear friend. I breathed it in, letting it empty my mind.

As it always was, the silence was disrupted. This time not by words but by a sound and a feeling. An explosion, one that rocked the floor beneath us and rattled the metal between us and an unpleasant death in space. Scrambling to my feet, I leaped into the tube connecting Sintara's ship to Thirteen, soaring weightlessly with Mel close behind me.

As I quickly neared the exit into my ship, Sintara's hand shot out and grabbed my own, pulling me up onto my feet as the magnets in the floor quickly held me down. Sintara and Wendy tried to share words with me but my concern for my ship overwhelmed their voices as I rushed for the bridge. Dropping into the captain's chair, the screens around me came to life with yellow and red.

"Thirteen, what just hit us?"

"Some type of electromagnetic explosion. My sensors detected a blast much like that on Zion, only far more condensed. The left engine is offline, attempting to restart it now."

I leaned in my chair with eyes darting around the dark vacuum surrounding us. Searching for the assailant. "Where is it?"

"It's right in front of us, sir."

With squinted eyes, I sought harder. "Now is not the time for jokes, Thirteen."

Mel was at my side, staring out into the stars with eyes wide. "He's right, it is in front of us."

Nothing but darkness to my eye, I felt as though I was crazy.

"I'm not picking up any transponder, nor any communications between it and any nearby spaceports. It didn't come from the direction of any nearby populace, rather from somewhere out in deep space. I can only see it through my electromagnetic sensors. It's like a ghost."

Mel's voice shuddered. "It's worse. It's Elysian."

15

Pluto

Staring in the face of death, yet seeing nothing. I squeezed my eyes shut, hard, pouring every ounce of energy into thinking of a plan. A plan that wouldn't get anyone killed, a plan that would result in all of our safety, a plan for the greater good. We were at an intellectual disadvantage, a technological disadvantage, a physiological disadvantage. We had nowhere to run and nowhere to hide. There was no plan, no right answer.

"What do we do?" I mumbled.

"I don't know," Mel replied. "Even if we surrender...no, we can't do that."

"You're right, we aren't doing that." Sintara came to my left, squinting out into space and glancing back and forth between the screen and the invisible ship. I turned to see Wendy standing in the doorway to the bridge, unable to comprehend exactly what she was looking at, which was nothing at all.

Sintara continued. "Wendy, you're with me. I'll lay down some cover fire while you get your engine back online. I'll need some time to disconnect, and get my own engines hot."

Thirteen spoke now. "That won't be hard. You're getting an incoming signal, sir. I'm unsure how, but the frequency is compatible with my OS. Presuming this ship is extraterrestrial, that shouldn't be possible."

Had the moment not been as horrifying as it was, his words would have supplied enough shock to restart my rapidly beating heart. The more I knew, the less I understood. How could their signals match our own frequencies? Beyond that, how could the very ship that brought Mel here have a hypercore so similar to our own? I shook away the questions, there were no answers to be found here.

I nodded. "Get to your ship, but do not go weapons hot. We try diplomacy, violence is the last resort."

"They'll be on standby. I'm not talking with aliens without some insurance." Sintara said before leaving the room.

The disapproval in Wendy's voice was palpable. "This is a terrible plan—"

Mel cut her off, an action that took even me by surprise. "It's the only plan, Wendy. Now go with Sintara and stay safe."

With one last grunt of disapproval, Wendy disappeared to follow Sintara. I turned back to my system and began opening the incoming transmission.

"Whatever you do, don't speak." Mel said with that familiar edge I saw in her on Zion. Power, respect, determination. Like a hero from mythology, she was ready for whatever came her way.

I swallowed the fear lumped in my own throat, daring not to expose it. My fingers continued to spider across the screens as I finally came to the button that would establish our connection. To my astonishment, the signal showed a video component, as well as an attached note in English.

Show The Princess alive or be glassed.

My trembling hands tapped the button as a screen was projected upon the glass between us and the ship invisibly before us. What I saw made any scrap of hope left in me drop. Had it been what I expected, the bridge of a light cruiser with a pilot and copilot, part of me might still believe there was a chance. Instead, the camera showed the bridge of a ship far bigger than our own. There were at least six soldiers manning the mass of systems, all clad in dark clothing with masks over their mouths and noses. Three sat at computer screens on either sides of the center focus of the video, all glued to their stations. In the center of the screen was a tall captain's chair with, presumably, the captain residing within.

Even sitting, he was terrifyingly tall. A length of pink hair lay close to his head, combed back and laying over the closely shaved sides and back of his head. He had a sharp jawline with the scraps of pink facial hair dotting his face and neck. His eyes were a light gray, and like the steel they resembled, they bore into me like knives. The only relent from his glare was a glance to Mel, then back to me, staring me down like a beast stares down his prey. He didn't question his ability to destroy me, he only contemplated how to do so.

"Uncle Ermis, nice of you to finally come looking for me."

His brow cinched for a moment. "How impatient. You certainly are my sister's daughter." A smile that seemed to pain him formed on his face, as if he was allergic to the idea of happiness and joy. "I suppose you can hardly stand to be in this unknown place any longer."

Mel winced at the sight, it clearly pained her to see it as much as it pained him to force the smile. "There is much to discuss. As crown princess, I find the lies and deception to be not far from treason against the royal family."

"I think you'll come to find your mother quite involved with this all," he said. His eyebrow raised, showing he expected her to have known about the hidden world of our solar system. He took the information graciously.

Mel's shoulders rolled back and her hands clasped behind her. She seemed to grow ten feet taller with the change in posture, as if I could not feel any smaller observing this conversation between giants. "That is quite the problem. I expect you to escort us to her."

Like chum in the water, the words sparked a fire in the man. The idea appalled him, and entertained him. Sharks in the water, circling, eyeing me. Invisible beasts ready to strike. He seemed to like the idea, only for the sake of playing with his food.

"We both know full well what needs to happen to...it," he said with lips curled into a grin that showed the sharp points of his teeth.

Mel's head swayed, slowly and seriously. "You are a strategist, are you not? Why get rid of such a valuable asset? He has knowledge of human civilization, a vast knowledge including the depths of their technology. More so, we share a common enemy. He is wanted by his own people, I would not find it difficult to turn him against the humans."

The insult was almost too much to bear. If she wasn't the crown princess, we'd almost certainly been decimated for the comment. The beast rose as the cutting words slashed at his ego. He towered over the camera even more, his head just low enough not to hit the ceiling. He had to have been a foot taller than Mel, likely more. I could see why he of all people would be sent to find Mel, and he was not something humans could ever stand a chance against, technology aside.

"Human? Is that what they are called? Our technology is vastly superior to theirs, our people are vastly more intelligent to theirs. All he is good for is a test tube, a cell, or a cage to be displayed in. I know how persuasive you can be, and I know that he is not the one who is being persuaded at this moment. The only thing I don't know is why; why would you work so hard to protect this inferior race? The sun is setting on their worlds, niece, and the sun is rising on ours. Why delay the inevitable?" Of the many things he knew, this was truly the only question on his mind. Knowing Mel, she wouldn't give that up so easily.

"You have always said the best way to destroy your enemies is to know them. If there is one thing I have learned in my time amongst the humans, it is that they do not give up easily. We cannot rely only on our own technology to defeat them, their willpower outweighs their sense." Mel looked at me with a hint of respect.

If all that was known about the human race was based upon me, it'd be a disrespect to the many far better than I. Yet Mel had seen the truth at the center of every human in the solar system, a spark so deeply rooted into our genetics that we could live without it as much as we could live without food or air. The determination to not just survive but to live, the dedication to continue. The indomitable will of man was the basis of our survival, the very essence of what it means to be human.

Ermis leaned deeper into his seat, sinking into the cushioned throne he sat upon. He scratched at the scruff of pink hair around his chin, considering Mel's words. He had no respect for me, but he did respect his niece, even if only because he had to. Though ignoring her words and wishes would be treason, she clearly carried a reputation that gave her words weight. Being princess was one thing, but she held respect far beyond her last name.

"I suppose they'd put up just as much of a fight as any other pest, they will be stubborn to remove, like a cancer on our new world." Ermis agreed more quickly than I expected.

"Only you would not find contentment in our home, it is heresy to want to leave. I need a vow of your word that no harm will come to him without my explicit say so," Mel demanded.

"You have my word, niece. If you are not concerned about him as a threat, he means less than nothing to me. Do as you wish, surrender the controls of that ship to us and we will be on our-"

The somewhat peaceful negotiations for my life were cut off in a highly unpeaceful explosion wreathing the invisible ship in a fire that showed its true force and magnitude. The ship didn't budge an inch in the blast, and not a scratch was to be found upon its hull. The shape in the smoke showed that the ship was like a largely winged bird, massive wings stretching out wide that dwarfed my own ship. The body of the ship alone was far larger than the wingspan of Thirteen, the guns along the front big enough to eviscerate us in a single shot.

Sintara's ship curved wide around the hull of the invisible ship, the lasting smoke revealing a clear target for her guns to dig into. The raining lead made no effect on the target, harmlessly slapping against the vague material without so much as a scratch. She rolled hard to dodge out of the blast of a large beam of light that burned the air around her ship.

"Sir, I'm detecting massive amounts of radiation nearly identical to that of the hypercore, and it's growing."

A curse escaped me while I rolled hard, sending Mel reeling for some hold on gravity as a blast of light arced off the edges of the ship. A wave of confusion prodded at my mind, a wave I sloughed off like a wet winter's coat as we escaped the edges of the light. We boosted hard as we arced under the bottom of the ship, seeing an array of guns all aiming towards us. They all lit up in an instant as we zipped from side to side, dodging just enough to stop ourselves from being shredded in an instant.

I pulled hard as we arched around towards the top of the ship once more. Through the lasting smoke radiating off the hull of the ship, I saw a massive gun take aim at us. It had no barrel, instead two long prongs with electricity arcing between each other. The crackling energy lit up the bridge through the glass, in the reflection I could see Mel's horrified face. Surely they wouldn't kill us, but they would do enough to stop us, and there was no escaping this. A direct energy weapon at this range would fry Thirteen in an instant, including life support. I'd suffocate as they board the ship, and Mel would watch me.

A beam of light burned the space between us as I braced for what may very well fry me at impact. The light was blinding, even through my eyelids, yet for a moment it seemed the light stopped. I opened my eyes to see Sintara's ship soaring between us and the beam, taking a blow on her right wing and spinning uncontrollably as the ship absorbed the energy.

The blood drained from my face in an instant, a harsh scream tearing at my tongue as I chased after them. Bullets rattled against Thirteen as we tailed the spiraling ship, one engine still burning hot and pushing them further and faster. No other electrical signals were showing on board.

"Sintara? Sintara, do you hear me? Sintara!" My voice broke as I shouted.

"Where are you going? We need to face Ermis! He'll glass us if we run!" Mel grabbed at the controls. I smacked her hands away, evidently with enough strength for her to wince back.

Anger boiled over inside me and singed my insides. "My sister is on that ship!"

Sintara's ship careened through space with no sign of stopping, except for the planet it made a clear trajectory for. Pluto was rapidly approaching, and its gravity, albeit weak, was pulling Sintara's ship nearer. They would strike the planet's surface dead on at this rate, and that would mean certain death.

We soared up near their ship, still spinning rapidly. I angled the ship so that they were right above us. I looked up at the burning, black body as it spun. Gritting my teeth, I pulled hard on the controls. The top of Thirteen slammed into their own top, stopping the spin in an instant. Metal scraped against itself as Pluto neared closer. I pulled harder on the controls as we entered the weak atmosphere. A fire broke out over both our ships. The harder I pulled, the heavier the controls became. The nose of the ship pulled up, but it wouldn't be fast enough.

Mel's hands closed over my own and pulled back on the controls with me, the nose rising to the horizon of Pluto as the stone below came horrifyingly close. The ship struggled to stay stable as we fought hard to stay level, the ground scraping at the bottom of the ship.

"Brace!" I shouted as we made first impact, bouncing once and launching Sintara's ship off our own.

The two ships followed a similar trajectory, but drifted apart slowly. We made a second impact, this time our nose digging into the rocks and sand below us. My seatbelt dug into my chest as we scraped along the ground, Mel holding onto me with no buckle to keep her from flying if she had not. Clinging to myself and my seat, we bounced hard in seemingly every direction. The ship groaned to a halt, and for a moment, I enjoyed the quiet. All there was to be heard was Mel and I breathing in sync, and all there was to be said was Thirteen breaking the quiet with a damage report.

"Landing gear and hull are both marginally damaged, life support and artificial gravity still intact. It may not feel like it now, but we're actually having quite a lucky day, sir-"

"Not now, Thirteen." I groaned as I unbuckled myself from my seat and slipped free of it. With our nose buried in the sand, I collapsed into the center console and laid on the sheet metal for a moment, trying to find where on my body I hurt the most.

Mel slipped from the chair and fell beside me. I could see now that she had wrapped her arms around my seat so tightly it made a dent where she had held for dear life. It was a good thing that wasn't me.

"Are you okay?" I asked, pulling myself up into a seated position.

"I should be asking you that," she replied.

I pulled at the collar of my shirt, wincing as my fingertips brushed across my collar bone. My already bruised and battered body couldn't take much more of this, all I could hope was that whatever fracture had formed wouldn't be the straw that broke the camel's back.

"We need to get to Sintara's ship." A groan escaped me as I pulled myself to my feet. I stood shakily for a moment. I needed a plan. Mel alone couldn't defend us from all of them, and would she defend us at all? Even the most fit human in the world couldn't stand against a single Elysian, let alone a broken, weak human like myself against an indeterminable amount of them. Wendy was right, I needed a plan, and I might just have one.

As I started to hike up the steep floor of the ship, a plan began formulating in my head. Every creature had a weakness, even Elysians, and I just so happened to know exactly what that was. I glanced over at the light burns that still lasted on Mel's clothes and skin from our time on Zion, the only thing that made her wince and she still hadn't healed from. She jumped straight into it just to protect me, it felt wrong to use her pain to our advantage. As I slipped on my suit and made way for the hangar, Thirteen announced the terrible news we all knew was coming.

"The Elysian ship is landing now, sir."

There was no time to waste as I rushed through my parts and tools in the closets and crates scattered all across the hangar until I finally came across the metal container I was looking for. It was about the size of a fire extinguisher with a nozzle for liquid sticking out of the top end. It was cool to the touch, but when used, what was inside was very not cold. Nitro methanol, a personal mixture designed for my hybrid motorbike in case of battery failure on a low atmosphere planet.

"We gotta move fast," I said as I opened the hangar door, the air in the ship being sucked out into the thin atmosphere in an instant. Even extended, the door was practically level with the horizon. We leaped from the pad of metal onto the icy surface of Pluto, Mel nearly slipping instantly without the non-slip boots of a suit on. Running normally was hardly possible here, each step carrying us fifty feet or more. It was fast, but hard on the knees.

"The air here tastes weird," she said as we ran towards Sintara's ship which laid on its side atop a large hill.

"The atmosphere here is mostly nitrogen and methane, it's far richer in heavy chemicals than most other planets," I informed breathlessly as we continued our long strides across the landscape.

"It hurts," Mel said again.

"The haze here is an even richer consistency of these chemicals. Even Elysians can't aspirate very long here. That's exactly why we need to move fast."

As we reached the base of the hill, the haze broke as the Elysian ship began setting down. Its invisible form created a perfect print in the haze, showing every corner and edge to the complex machine. We were running out of time. I dug my heels into the ice and kicked hard, launching myself an easy twenty feet in the air and forward at least a hundred feet. I landed at the base of Sintara's ship, beaten and bruised but still intact. I jumped up onto the "top" of it, which was truly its left side.

"We need a way in."

"On it," Mel said as she landed beside me. She knelt down to the sliding doors I stood beside and took hold of the tiny gap between them. Even she struggled to pull it apart, but no air rushed from the break in the air seal as I expected. The main of the ship had depressurized, creating a pit in my stomach as we dove inside.

Naturally, the inside was a mess. Cracks and gashes covered the walls from crates rattling around. Sintara's collection of old Earth weaponry was piled at our feet, bullets scattered across the "floor", which was actually the wall of the ship. I knelt down and picked one up, a small handgun with a loaded mag inside. This one hadn't been a part of her armory, it was attached to the underside of her table for emergencies. I noticed it last time I was here, I thought it might be of good use eventually. It was narrow here, only one way in and out. We'd be cornered in an instant, which left me very little time for my trap.

"The bridge is sealed, it must be pressurized." Mel's voice echoed from further into the ship. I had no doubt that such measures had been taken, but it let me breathe easier.

I opened the lid of the metal container at my side and began splashing its contents across the floor in wild arcs. A mist came off the liquid from the temperature, but it didn't freeze in an instant. The life support systems were still online and attempting to flood the ship with oxygen. The cold was creeping in fast, but it would not be fast enough

The first boots hit the surface above me. Every step was like the impact of a meteorite, crashing and slamming with each footfall. I splashed the last of the liquid onto the ground as I backed up into Mel whose ear was pressed against the door.

"They're alive, I can hear them in there," she said.

"We have bigger problems than that right now."

The first soldier dropped down into the ship, a flashlight illuminating the direction of the weapon he carried. Compared to a human rifle, the thing was massive. Its caliber was enough to be an anti-vehicle round by our standards, I didn't want to imagine what their anti-air weaponry was like. His armor contained segmented, sleek, black panels that covered every inch of his body. They seemed moderately flexible, presumably bullet proof. It likely had some life support when contrasting his relaxed breathing to Mel's hard, deep breaths. His form was clearly well built, though shorter than Mel. He was either the most experienced of all or the rookie, considering they sent him in first.

His light came upon us, he became stiff in an instant as he shouted a brief word in an unfamiliar tongue. There were many languages to be spoken across the galaxies, this one sounded only vaguely familiar. I'd heard many, yet only ever spoken English. It was the most common in the systems, unfortunately.

Mel stepped between the man and I with hands raised, speaking back in the same tongue. I stood behind her with one hand at my side, trying to hide the firearm I held in a subtle manner. Two more soldiers dropped down into the ship and came to the first's side, and behind them came Ermis. Naturally, he was even more menacing in person. He wore similar armor from his neck down, yet even sharper and bolder than his grunts and made from a matte material. It seemed impossible for any sentient creature to be that tall, and yet there he stood.

"For a moment, I thought we were reaching an agreement," he said.

"They're other humans, friends of his. They only wanted to protect him. You must understand that they were considerably afraid of you." Mel seemed to be attempting to flatter him, but it didn't seem to work.

"If they were afraid, they would have run. We must put them in their place." He waved a hand and the three men began stepping forward.

The instant the first took a step into the liquid on the ground, I took a shot at the floor near to us. As the bang echoed through the ship, so did a white-gray flame erupt from the liquid coating the ground. It wasn't easy to see, but it burned incredibly hot. Mel took a step back in the heat, and flames crept up the soldiers' legs in an instant. They shouted and flailed backwards, attempting to pat the flames away. Once nitromethane was ignited, it was not easy to extinguish.

"You insolent brat!" Ermis shouted. His voice shook the ground.

The heat rising from the flames made ripples in the air between us. He and I locked eyes in a deadly stare down. It was like he was trying to kill me with a look alone, I thought he might even succeed. I couldn't keep my hands from shaking, though if you had asked me, I would've blamed it on the cold.

"A negotiation goes both ways, Ermis. I will come peacefully, if you let these other humans go," I offered.

"Apollo, I said to let me speak!" Mel shouted, still wary of the flames.

"Let the man have his word," Ermis said. "You are quite bold to be negotiating with me, and to attack my men. Who are you to speak for mankind?"

"I am Apollo Harrison. Amongst men, I am nobody. They won't even notice my disappearance. But I know everything about man's technology, it is what I have dedicated my life to. However I, like yourself, have a family to protect. Now I offer that I come peacefully in exchange for these humans' lives. They're my family, their lives come before my own, and I won't sit idly and watch you kill them for protecting me."

Ermis gave a small laugh to himself about this, his massive arms folding in a look of almost respect. "I admire your courage, Apollo Harrison. But how can I assure that your human friends will not bring your armies against us? I'd care to not waste my time on you."

"For all they know, you are just pirates like any others. They know not of your origins, I swear by it." Speaking like this felt weird on my tongue, but I had been speaking with more grandiose since Mel told me she was a princess, not even on purpose really.

Ermis stared deep into my eyes, now searching for something within me. "In your eyes, I see an honest man. Honesty can make men weak."

"All I hope is that my honesty assures their survival."

Ermis held a long pause as the fire began to die down. Time was running out, the oxygen in the ship was either burning or leaking. I could only hope I had persuaded him.

"You've happened upon a good man, Princess Melinoe. I think he makes a better prisoner." Ermis pulled a set of metal cuffs from his belt and tossed them across the burning mass between us. "It seems we have reached an agreement, peaceful surrender in exchange for your human friends' safety."

I dropped the firearm in my hand and grabbed the cuffs. "Lastly, I ask that I might say goodbye. They will attack again if I do not inform them of our deal."

Ermis waved a hand dismissively. "Make it quick."

Ermis spoke briefly to his men in their tongue as the last of the fire died away. He spoke directly to Mel, then turned away and leaped effortlessly out of the ship.

Mel's voice was low and laden with fear. "His men will watch you as you say goodbye. I must have a serious conversation with him now."

She began stepping through the dwindling flames with her head hung low, giving me one last mournful glance as she walked away, as if I was a dead man walking.

↪ 16 ↩

Hades

As Mel vanished from view, I was left with only the silence and the three soldiers standing before me. They had managed to put the fire out, and their hands still held tightly on their weapons. I would be more offended if I hadn't been the one who set them on fire.

"No hard feelings?" I said, trying to break the awkward silence. Nothing came back from them. "You...don't speak English, right."

The door behind me hissed open and out rushed Wendy and Sintara, both in suits and with weapons at hand. In an instant, the soldiers snapped their rifles into place, only I between the two livid parties.

"Guns down! We aren't fighting!" I pushed their guns towards the ground and shoved them backwards. The soldiers hadn't flinched, keeping their guns level and traced on each of our heads.

"The hell are you talking about?" Sintara growled, eager for a fight she couldn't win.

"I made a deal with them."

Wendy was in utter disbelief. "You. Made a deal. With the evil aliens who tried to kill us."

"They aren't evil, and we tried to kill them first! Sorry about that by the way." I spoke that last part over my shoulder towards the soldiers, disregarding their lack of understanding.

"Get explaining right now or I will shoot you and them," Sintara said and truly meant it.

"I surrendered, in exchange for your lives."

I expected for them to scream at me, hit me, react in some way. Instead, it was quiet. Wendy's gun fell from her hand, and Sintara's shoulders slumped. After a short while, Wendy spoke.

"Why would you do that?" Her voice wobbled, a heart broken by my words, by my actions.

"It was one life or two. It was...the logical choice."

"You selfish brat!" Sintara shoved me back. I stumbled on my own feet, hitting the ground hard. This was the reaction I was expecting. "I told you we weren't gonna surrender. I told you if the negotiation didn't work we'd fight our way out! Why the hell would you make such a decision without us? You never even gave us a say!"

Wendy stepped forward. "Sintara, stop-"

"You stop, Wendy." Sintara pushed her back and continued towering over me. "I've bent over backwards for you again, and again, and again. I've risked my career more times than you know to keep you safe. And now I've thrown it all away, all for you! And you...you didn't even give us the chance to speak, or even a chance to fight! We don't trade lives, Apollo. Now isn't the time to be pulling this cowboy crap and thinking we can live with ourselves knowing you'd still be alive if it weren't for us!"

Her voice had broken, hard. Through the glass of her helmet, I could see tears running down her face in long streaks. Her shoulders bunched now, and her weapon lay at her side.

"I never had a family to speak of, Apollo. I never had a little brother to care for, or parents to look up to. But for a brief moment in my life, I had convinced myself you were something like a brother to me. And now you've thrown it all away, and for what?! For a world that never cared about you? For the safety of two worlds that both want you dead? What kind of a moron sacrifices himself for a world that hates him!" She basically screamed the last part. "And if I feel all this, imagine how Wendy feels. Imagine how she'll feel having to tell your parents that you died protecting the person who was meant to protect you. And atop all of this, we'll never get to see Mel again. Of all the selfish things you've done…"

Her emotion overtook her. She stepped aside with hands in fists. She tried, but couldn't hold back the racking sobs in her chest.

Laying on the cold metal of her ship, I thought I had finally come to my senses and sacrificed the only thing left for the only people who mattered to me anymore. And yet it was a choice they'd never want me to make. In truth, many men will sacrifice their life, but very few have the courage to let someone else sacrifice themselves for him.

Sintara spoke again as she calmed her nerves. "Wendy, tell him to change his mind. Make him change his mind!"

"I can't."

"The hell you mean you 'can't'?"

Wendy went to wipe the tears from her own eyes, stopping when she found the glass around her head stopping her from holding back those emotions. "You're all brains, I've been trying to talk some common sense into you all my life. I told you I couldn't protect you forever. I knew you were gonna do big things, help a lot of people. I just never thought..."

She stepped forward, holding out a shaking hand to me. "Who am I kidding? I know you too well. You've already got a plan cooking in that big brain of yours. You've always got an angle, some idea bouncing around."

I took her hand and pulled myself up. "I don't plan on dying, but if it happens, so be it. I haven't given up on myself, or you, or Mel. I'm going there to protect you. I won't go down without a fight."

"I know you are." Wendy nodded, blinking hard to wash away the tears. She took a deep, shaky breath before taking hold of my shoulders. "I'm giving you one week to come back. Do whatever you have to, make your time count, but come back. And if you don't, we'll fight off a thousand of those ships just to find you or die trying. And when we do find you, I will kick your ass so hard for scaring me the way you are right now, you got that?"

Tears welled in my own eyes. "I got that."

"They need you, Apollo. She needs you. Be there for them." Wendy pulled me into a deep, deep hug. The kind that wraps around you and constricts like a snake. As if she was trying to take a piece of me to remember me by. Part of me wanted to take some of her with me too, her courage maybe. The kind I only wished I had when I was a kid, the kind I always tried to have as an adult. I hoped maybe a hug this tight would share some of it with me.

"You can't tell anyone where I've gone."

"I know, and I trust you." Wendy stepped back and began digging into a bag over her shoulder. "You'll need these though. After I heard about the surgery, I've always kept some on me in case of emergencies."

Her gloved hand held out a small, well-sealed bottle of medicine. Immunosuppressants. A small laugh escaped me, she had really thought of everything. She really was the best journalist alive.

Wendy sniffed up the last of her emotions and bolstered herself. "Now go. One week, starting right now."

"Thank you for trusting me-"

"I said go, before I change my mind...one last hug." She grabbed a tight hold of me again, squeezing with all her might. She stepped back after a few moments and elbowed Sintara.

"I...Stay safe. Come back." She held out a hand to me.

"Yes ma'am," I said and shook her hand firmly.

Stepping away from the two of them were the hardest steps I'd ever taken in my life. As I looked at the handcuffs in my hands, I began my final words. "Thirteen is your responsibility n-"

"No need sir, I'm coming with you." Thirteen buzzed on my wrist.

"What?" I sputtered.

"The Toad is en route to pick up Ms. Wendy and Officer Sintara. It will be here in approximately...one hour. I contacted its captain and sent an SOS in Wendy's name. They will be safe."

"But you're not coming with me."

"They've already confiscated my mainframe. I am currently inside the Elysian's ship's port."

I drew a deep breath and sighed. I would've facepalmed myself if my suit didn't get in the way. "I can't get away from this damn AI."

"I'm with you till the end, sir."

I clasped the handcuffs tightly over my own wrists and turned towards the soldiers. They'd lowered their weapons now, hanging loosely at their sides. Evidently, our display had made some impact on them. I walked up to the tall men and held my wrists out. The leader took hold of my wrists and assured the cuffs were tight, nodding to the others. I looked back one last time at Wendy and Sintara.

"I love you guys."

As we shuffled across the dusted ice of Pluto, I already felt dwarfed in a great big world. The stature of their ship from the ground made it seem near impossible for it to fly. Though I could only see its shape in the mist, it towered over me like a mountain with wings. If I had not worked on ships this large myself, it'd seem utterly impossible for something this large to take flight. A long ramp had extended from the front of the ship, it seemed like a portal to another world. Where the invisible walls of the ship ended, the door into the ship opened into a vast hangar. At the top of the long ramp stood Ermis and Mel, looking down at me.

Mel had taken a million steps into uncharted territory, daring into our land with the reckless ambition to follow a fool like me. Now, I followed her into an unknown fate, though all signs pointed to death. I would not give up so easily, I would not bend or break. Not after all the strength she had shown me. The first step onto that ramp put a pit in my stomach, the second a pain in my heart. I was leaving my family and my home behind, and for what? That much was to be seen.

I continued my walk of shame closer and closer to the waiting giants at the top. Mel had changed out of the human clothes Wendy had spared and back into that same material I had first found her in. The clothes she wore were a sleek, white material, a thick line running across the seams in long patterns down her sides, arms, and legs. The clothes clung close to the body, yet seemed breathable and stretchy. They seemed very comfortable, I was almost jealous. I wondered how I could get some.

Once more, her mannerisms had changed back to that same regal confidence. That edge to her eyes, the cut of her voice. Like a sharpened blade, without an ounce of fear. The way she could change in an instant was almost frightening, I wondered what face she had been wearing all that time. Not cowardly, only confused and alone. I was the coward now. Small, frightened, afraid. Mel and I seemed to never break eye contact, but it wasn't the same. She looked down at me with her chin up. I looked up at her through my brow.

"I'm glad we've cleared the air between us, for a moment there I'd almost thought you had gone AWOL," Ermis said. AWOL? Human words. Surely that must be a coincidence.

"As offended as I am by such thoughts, frankly, it does not matter to me. Now, we must leave. My mother must be worried sick." Mel waved a commanding hand. "Take him to the brig, I'll be in my quarters. I've spent long enough around these loud, wretched creatures."

"Of course, your highness." Ermis also spoke with a different voice now, a voice that showed only a hint of hesitation to listen. On his ship, he wanted to make the demands, but Mel held rank over him. Now she was in charge, within reason.

Ermis turned to the men who had led me to the ship and spoke in their native tongue, orders that they did not hesitate to listen to. One of them saluted in an odd way, the first to enter back on Sintara's ship. Definitely the rookie, leaving him to do the dirty work. Every one of them kept a distance away from me, not like I was some dangerous criminal, but like I was some pest. It was as if I carried some disease, and nobody wanted to get close. They kept their distance out of disgust, not fear.

I was shoved forward by the soldier behind me. As I passed Mel, I couldn't tell if this was the facade or the real thing. She was a good actor and I couldn't tell what she was faking, our friendship or her loyalties. If everything we'd gone through had been a lie, it might just break my heart. Something in me believed her loyalties must be the lie, I couldn't imagine the pain of the latter.

We finally broke eye contact as I took my first step into the ship and was greeted with an old friend in chains. Thirteen indeed did reside within the hangar of the ship, reminding me just how massive it truly was. The gray walls stretched at least two hundred feet high, the ceiling a dull pink color with catwalks and lights stretching across it. Across the top of the back wall, a broad window looked into what I assumed to be the bridge. Two small ships were mounted against the wall, jagged, black things that were sharp and menacing. Soldiers stood at seemingly random points around the room bound in that sleek black armor, others in dirty clothes and wearing cloth masks I had to assume were engineers. I even noticed a few soldiers with pipes coming from their helmets, as well as sleek flight suits on, pilots for sure. It was an honest to goodness battleship, and Ermis controlled it all. At the center of all the organized chaos, Thirteen sat.

His wings were folded in, a few panels torn off, and large binds held him tight to the floor of the hangar. I wondered how they had brought him in, had he come willingly? As I looked around, I realized the entire side of the battleship was able to open, on both sides. Opened to its fullest extent, you could likely stare right through it like a vulture, and a vulture it was. They could only harm the precious cargo so much, it and all the things aboard were still important evidence. They could only go so deep, but they would most certainly still test. Like cutting open a thing while it still squirmed just to see what would happen. Anger bubbled inside me, seeing my friend cut open like that. Deep down, I knew he didn't care.

We had reached the other side of the hangar and were approaching a series of doors. Two different hallways led deeper into the ship, on opposite sides of what must have been an elevator to the upper levels. Naturally, the brig was always in the deepest parts of the ship. Scum belonged at the bottom of the barrel. The soldier pushed me forwards into the right hallway. As the sounds of Thirteen's torture faded, the quiet I thought I might appreciate was only a reminder of just how lonely I felt.

Our footsteps echoed in an ominous rhythm. I kept thinking there was another pair of footsteps following us, looking back to only see that same soldier leading me on. In the bright light of the ship, I could see through the dark tinted glass of his smooth helmet. He had light eyes, pink hair, and ashy white skin. He stared deep into me, not taking a moment to break his sight. I could feel his eyes burning into my back as I looked forward once again.

A firm hand grabbed my shoulder and jerked me to a stop suddenly. I turned to see the soldier step up to one of the cells and place his fingers into three holes on a panel and twist. Through the glass door, I could see three short steps down into a dark containment area. It couldn't have been bigger than ten feet on any side, with a slab for a bed in one corner and a toilet in the other. The door hissed open as he turned to me, taking the cuffs off my hands and slipping my watch off my wrist in a smooth motion. I nearly fell down the steps as he shoved me into the tiny enclosure. The second I had entered the cell, a beep rang off. His eyes scanned the panel for a moment before entering the cell himself, eyes angry.

I raised my hands in the air and stepped back until I was against the wall. "Whatever happened, I didn't mean to do it man."

He brushed the back of his hands down my sides swiftly, stopping at my pockets and reaching in to pull out the same gun

I had picked up on the floor of Sintara's ship. I laughed nervously.

"Worth a shot, right?"

He stared at me, and for a brief moment, it almost seemed like a smile. He wasn't opposed to taking me to my cell at all, he wasn't even opposed to patting me down and removing my weapon. Compared to the intensity of the other guards, he was completely relaxed. Above all that, the tiniest of smirks on his face at my joke was the most terrifying. I didn't know Elysians could even be happy. He stood up and backed up out of the cell, keeping his eyes on me. As he stepped up the steps, he reached for the panel, but hesitated. After a pause, his eyes dashed to either direction down the hall, then back to me.

"I...hear-ed what you say. To your friends. I am...sorry. Not fair to you." He spoke slowly, piecing each word together part by part. He blinked hard on the pauses, gathering his thoughts before vocalizing them.

"You can speak English?"

"Not all of we can. Be careful with your words. The Queen, the princess, the royalty, the advisers, they speak it. Most us, not so."

"How do you know English?" I forced myself to speak slower, in hopes to make my words easier to understand.

"It is...long story. I explain later." He slid his fingers into the panel once more, sliding the door shut. He shifted in a movement that suggested he intended to walk away, but paused once more. "You want to protect family. I want to protect family. I want peace...for our people. You are better alive. I will try to protect you, but I cannot promise."

I couldn't help but smile. Making friends already, it seemed. "I am very thankful for that."

"I help you get home safe, if I can. You are brave. I hope you are as smart as you are brave."

"That makes two of us."

He looked at me, confused for a long moment. He nodded slowly and squinted vaguely at me. "Welcome to the Hades."

⇁ ⇁ ⇁

It was official, I was sick and tired of being locked up in cells. Nothing could make the time pass, or everything could. Without my watch or the sun, I had no idea how long it had been. It could've been five minutes or two hours for all I knew, but the boredom gnawing at my brain suggested the former. Most cells I spent any time in, I spent trying to get out of. This was the first I had ever intended to stay in, and as I quickly discovered, it was very boring.

Every once in a while, I'd hear footsteps coming down the hallway, and every time I had hoped to see Mel appear at my doorway. I was never so lucky, only ever seeing a soldier or two passing by. I truly felt like an animal in a cage by the way they all stared at me in both awe and disgust. I had already memorized their patterns, and spent a good portion of time counting and waiting to hear those footsteps again. But when I came to the end of my count and no footsteps began, I knew something was up.

Before long, I heard that familiar hum. A hypercore, one that sounded just like our own no less. It was comforting, like an old friend. The only thing left that I felt I truly understood. No politics, no relationships, no risking my life. Just rocket science, elementary astrophysics. To me, it'd always be simpler than anything else.

Those same red lights flooded the ship, and those same creeping shadows began once again, pouring into my cell and pooling at my feet like ink. As it reached my shoulders, I took a deep breath and closed my eyes. I could see the red glow through my eyelids fade as the darkness overtook me, filling the room, the hallway, and the entire ship. All would be subject to the same feeling, the listlessness of the mind. Conscious unconsciousness. All except for me.

I laid flat on the slab of a bed within the cell, feeling the knots of my back and shoulders press against the hard stone. How long had my shoulders been bunched? How long had I held my stress in the muscles of my back? I couldn't say, but a series of deep breaths relaxed that stress. My jaw unclenched. My eyelids began to droop. In the deep abyss of the speed of light, I found peace. For this time, for this short while, I would be safe. No cares. No worries.

Eyes opened or closed, it didn't matter, yet the lids of my eyes still drooped at the weight of exhaustion all the same. The fuzziness of sleep began to overtake me, losing my perception of time in the only natural way possible. Sleep, however brief, was so relaxing.

That was until the peace of dozing off, the safety of the darkness, the silence of the ship, were all broken by a sound. Some sort of movement was echoing down the halls. Was it the tap of shoes, or some kind of shuffling? Whatever it was, it was trying to be quiet, and it was failing. But it was also getting nearer.

"Apollo." A tiny, impossibly quiet whisper rattled down the hall.

At the word, I nearly leaped out of my skin. I slid from the slab with a dizzy head, patting the ground carefully as I crawled on my hands and knees towards the door. I felt the edge of the stairs hit my hand and crawled into the corner beside it. I pulled myself into a tight ball and held my breath, just in case whatever it was could see or hear me. It had felt against the laws of the universe to be conscious before, perhaps this was my punishment for breaking such laws.

"Apollo, it's Mel."

All of the fear in my system snapped into confusion. I thought I had been the only person affected in the blast, the only person breaking the rules. I heard her hands patting the wall as she came closer and closer.

"Mel? You're...awake too?" I whispered back, being quiet for very little reason.

"Apollo? Apollo!" She whispered louder this time as I heard her hands tap on the glass to my cell.

I crawled up onto the steps and placed my hands on the glass. "I'm here. I'm right here."

"Are you hurt? Are you safe?" I could hear her clothes ruffle as she got near to the ground.

"No, no. I'm okay."

"Thank the stars. I was promised your safety, but—the point is, I'm glad you're safe."

"I'm just glad to hear your voice."

She gave a small laugh to that, full of pain and spite for herself. "Most people aren't. Not in my home."

"They seem like they love you."

"Of course they love me, they have to. I'm the princess after all. They don't care who I am in any aspect other than that." Her voice was soft, muffled by the glass. Regardless, I could tell she spoke near to the material between us. Our faces were near to one another, separated by a thin pane and hidden by an endless shadow. I was glad she couldn't see the rush of blood to my face at the thought.

"How are you...here?"

"I could ask you the same question, and I have no idea." She ended with a soft sigh.

"I guess I am relieved to not be alone in the matter, I suppose."

"That makes two of us."

I could hear her breathing on the other side of the glass, soft and slow. "I would've come to see you sooner. You know I didn't mean what I said back there, right?"

Thank the stars. "Just playing the part, I understand."

Silence, for a few moments. "Can I ask an odd question?" She said the words quickly, like trying to spit them out before they poisoned her.

"Sure?"

"Do you believe in god?"

My eyes went wide, though no light came to them. I blinked hard a few times, laughing in spite of myself. I had hardly even thought of the idea in years, not since I last visited my parents for Christmas and listened to my dad say grace over the food. "I was kinda hoping the most advanced society in the galaxy had the answer to that one."

She sighed deeply this time, clearly hoping that I knew the answer. "Unfortunately not. It has been a topic of much debate amongst my people. Some think there is one out there and it has spoken directly to us, some think there is one out there yet it has never spoken to us. Some think there isn't any at all, some think there are many, and some think we are all our own gods."

"Sounds a lot like us humans. What do you think?"

"I think...if there is one out there, which seems very possible, I have lived a life too privileged to know what it's like to need a god. I only ever believed as much as I needed to, which was very little. But now...I think I know a bit more of what it is like to pray for help. What about you?"

I thought hard for a moment, gathering my words like papers lost to the wind. I had to dust off the very idea to even consider it. I never had anything against religion, until I learned about the Angel Lights. I didn't hate everyone who believed in a god because of them, in most part because of my dad. He always did despise everything they've done, including the expectations they forced the world to place on other religious people. "Vengeance is The Lord's," he would always say.

"When I was a kid, I was bullied. A lot. Kids would do things that put my life on the line, for the sole reason that I was half Earthling and half Martian. I came pretty close to death a couple times, I don't even think they realized how close I was. But every time, without fail, someone would show up to save me. Whether it be Wendy, Dad, or Mom, someone would show up just in the nick of time. I never thought of it as divine intervention of any sort, but the coincidence—well, if it were up to those kids, I'd be at the bottom of a lake or decomposing in a forest somewhere. My dad believes. Every time he'd scoop me up into his arms and thank God for his provision, his protection. I always thought if I was really protected He'd never let that happen to me, but it did make me who I am today. Though maybe it would be better if I were anyone else." I leaned my back against the glass now, resting my head against the hard material. "If there is a god out there, I'm listening now. I always thought I could do anything on my own, but not so much anymore. Maybe He will protect me now like He did when I was a kid."

I could feel the glass being warmed by the heat of her body as I leaned heavily into it. Tears stung at my eyes, but I couldn't understand why. Was it so cathartic to whisper a prayer to a god you didn't know was listening? But now, it felt like He was listening, maybe He always had been. Maybe if I made it out of this mess, I'd ask Dad what he's meant all these years. Maybe I could atone for the sins that sat heavy on my heart. Maybe He could wash away the blood on my hands.

"Give thanks to the Lord, for He is good; His love endures forever." My father's words echoed in my mind. He used to say that in every prayer, the least I could do is thank The Lord for bringing me Mel, for keeping us safe, for protecting me this far.

Mel spoke softly. "If it means anything, I'm glad you are who you are, and that I got to meet you."

I suddenly became very happy that nobody could see me or my tears. "Thanks."

"If it weren't for you, who knows what would have happened to me? Now I'm finally going home, and it's all thanks to you."

I sniffed hard, rubbing at my eyes. It wasn't really me doing anything, it didn't feel like it at least. I was a mess, still am, and it still worked out. I felt like I couldn't take credit. "It's nothing."

"Not to me it isn't."

For the rest of our time, we simply sat there in each other's presence. We both knew what was to come, and yet we knew so little of what the future might hold. I wanted to give her a hug. Though a thin pane of glass separated us, I had never felt so connected to another person. A mystery from the stars, and a mess from Earth.

↳ 17 ↰

Elysia

I awoke with a jolt. I had fallen asleep, slumped against the glass of the cell door, with Mel nowhere in sight. Her voice had lulled me into a sleep that wasn't interrupted with violent nightmares, but rather a peaceful one with her. I could see her on the beach of Oregon, looking out over the waves. Her hair danced in the wind, the sunset silhouetted her frame. I was standing in the treeline, I tried to call out to her.

Rather, I was jolted awake by a knock. The guard who had spoken to me previously was tapping at the glass with the toe of his boot. He crouched down low, knocking on the glass just near my head. I snapped from my half-awake state for certain at that.

He spoke in a hushed tone, the same broken English as before. "We are near home. Be prepared."

"What should I be prepared for?"

"The Queen. Have good behavior near her."

"Then what?"

"I have none idea."

He stood up from his crouched position and tapped at the small panel beside the door. He placed his index and thumb into the panel this time, turning it slowly. A hiss filled the room as a white mist poured all over me. It had a strong scent, painfully sterile and stung the nose. I gagged at the cloud of mist before it vanished as fast as it came. I had truly snapped awake after that. Not a single trace of sweat or grime was left on my body, leaving my skin feeling dry and cracked.

"Little warning next time?"

"No more germs, so we no sick."

"What about the germs on you that will get me sick?"

"Good luck." He twisted the panel once again and the doors slid open. He pulled a set of cuffs off his wrists and threw them into the cell. I knew the routine by now, slipping them on just tight enough to pass but not tight enough to hurt.

I climbed the steps out of the cell as the soldier turned and started down the hall. He wore his sleek black mask, but his weapon was magnetized to his armor on his back. Clearly he thought I wouldn't attack him, which he was right in assuming. Regardless, firing that weapon would likely send me flying farther than it would send him, considering the size of the massive thing.

"Where are we going?"

"The bridge, princess orders."

We continued further, nearing the door at the end of the hallway. As we walked, I noticed that his posture was stiff and tight. His shoulders were bunched, elbows slightly hinged, and fingers twitching in irregular intervals. He was nervous about something, and it made me nervous.

"What's your name?" I asked.

"My name?" He hesitated for a moment, as if speaking his name would place a curse on him. "Theseus."

"I'm Apollo."

"I know."

Theseus led me out of the hallway and back into the hangar where Thirteen was still on display. Most of his panels had been removed now, and the pulsing blue glow of his hypercore shone through the cracks and gaps between the pipes that made up the insides of the ship, like a still beating heart exposed and out on display. It pained me to see him like this. Not only had I built Thirteen from the bare frame of an impounded scrambler, I programmed his AI from the ground up. I had done as much to keep him alive as he had done for me.

I felt a firm hand pull on my shoulder, spinning me and leading me through the doors of the elevator that extended upwards through the ship. I felt like a child standing by an adult's side in this elevator, the ceiling vaulted at least ten feet from the ground to fit the size of the massive Elysians. Theseus spun a panel on the wall and the doors sealed. My balance swayed as we began moving upward, sealed in the painfully quiet metal box.

I cleared my throat before speaking. "I asked you before how you knew English, but I'm just now realizing, how do any of you speak English anyways?"

Theseus' head shifted towards me for a moment, then back at attention ahead of him. He spoke with an impressive clarity on this topic, his words coming to being like he had recited this a thousand times. "You speak an ancient language. It was the language spoken by our first ancestors, the founders of Elysia. Only the royals are meant to know the ancient tongue."

Mel's words from back on Sintara's ship echoed in my head. "Ancient holy beings who descended from the stars, that's who the royalty is descended from, right? Aren't all of you descendants of them? Shouldn't you all know?"

"The harsh conditions of our planet have had changes on us, the royal family have been the least impacted. They bear the strongest likeness to the...we call them Aggeloi. In your tongue, you call them angels."

"But why can't the rest of you speak it then?"

"It is a holy language, sacred. Speaking it of dirty blood is blasphemy."

"But you speak it."

His shoulders bunched, ever so slightly. "My father was a linguist, and a historian. He work closely to the royal family. He taught himself your tongue so that he might access older documents. He teach me when I was a child. He discovered something in the ancient texts. Then he was..."

"Silenced?"

"Yes."

The silence was palpable now. "I'm sorry for your loss."

"I practice in his honor. I suppose it makes me a blasphemer…but I hear everything the royals don't want me to hear."

"And what have you heard?"

The door hissed and slid open, revealing the bridge of the ship I had seen in the transmission from before. Computers lined the walls with six men stationed throughout the bridge. In the center of the room sat the massive captain's chair atop a raised platform. Sharp stairs led to the top of such, and at the top sat Ermis, beside him stood Mel. She was clad in that same white clothing from before and her hair was tied up in an ornate hairstyle with a silver pin through the bundle of pink coils. Strands of hair ran down the side of her face, framing her sharp gaze. This had not been the same Mel I knew, and every new glance only made her more foreign, and more beautiful.

"Enter," Ermis said.

Theseus led the way, taking the first step before I dared to do so. We walked until my toes touched the first step leading up to the royals. The titan who sat in the captain's chair rose and towered over both of us, my neck hurt just by trying to look up and match his gaze. I looked past him for only a moment. A planet was approaching, one of deep blues and grays. There were far less ocean than land, unless much of the white I saw were frozen over lakes and seas. It was as if the planet was frozen solid, yet along the equator I could see spots of life beginning to peek through the freeze. The whole planet seemed to be a single biome, an icy tundra.

"It's beautiful, isn't it. It's cold, uninviting, and dangerous. Stone and rock make up most of our planet, the few forests are brutal and expansive. She'll see that you are dead if you are weak, and I have reason to believe you wouldn't last a day. She's harsh, but that is the beauty of her."

"You speak of it as if it is a person," I said.

Theseus tensed further at my audacity. A prisoner brought upon a foreign ship and was brought to see the captain speaking out of turn. Had Mel not been standing there, I may not have the same confidence, but I had dealt with bullies my whole life.

Ermis nodded. "And like a person, she is changing. Prophecy is coming true, the light is returning. Do you know what that means?"

"I've read case studies on your planet, though they were only theory. It orbits our sun every ten thousand years, has a mass ten times that of Earth, and orbits twenty times further from our sun than Neptune. If I had to guess, for the past five thousand years, you've been in the dark."

"Your theory is impressive, though not exact." Ermis turned towards me. "Religion and science do not pair well together."

I rolled my shoulders back. Though I thoroughly disagreed, I had no time for debate. "Why have you brought me here?"

"To Elysia? Ask my niece." He glanced at Mel, she stood unshaken. "But here at the bridge, I thought I might reward your boldness. Besides, a proper introduction is needed. You are the first human to ever enter our planet. How did you find your accommodations?"

"Terrible on the back. You speak to me like some kind of guest, but you treat me like a prisoner. Why?"

"In a way, you are one. You are…" he paused to collect his words, choosing them carefully from a wide selection, skipping over the insulting ones he wished to say most. "A herald, a courier, a diplomat. Choose your title, however you like it. Do not be mistaken, I am in control here, and you will treat me with respect as your captor. You are my prisoner."

"No, he is mine." Mel stepped forward. "If it weren't for me, his blood would be iced on that planet. As the highest ranking member of the royal family present, I will take charge of him."

Ermis drew in a growled breath. "With all due respect, this decision will be The Queen's, and so long as either of you are passengers on my ship, I am the captain of what happens to either of you."

Mel squared her shoulders up with Ermis, tilting her nose up at him. "This miserable journey on your ship is soon to be over, and the second our boots hit the ice of Elysia, control over the human will be transferred to me. You have more important things to attend to, do you not? I see you making no haste to track the men who kidnapped me and broke the sacred law of abandoning our planet. I see you making no haste to stop the insurrectionists who plague our cities. I see you making no haste to silence the rumors that those very criminals are spreading. It took you all this time only to find me, what exactly are you doing to solve the rest of your laundry list? You made this mess, now clean it up."

A vein in Ermis' neck rose with his blood pressure. His lips pulled tight against his clenched teeth, and he spoke through them. "You test my patience, princess. Had I not done all this work to find you, you would still be stuck amongst the humans."

Mel pointed a finger to me. "That man was transporting me with coordinates discovered on the wreckage of the insurrectionists' ship to bring me home. Had you not come, I would still have found my own way back to Elysia faster than you could even find me."

"You would have been vaporized in an instant, just as the last ship tried!" Ermis shouted in her face. He drew a deep breath and turned away from us, collecting himself. Many seconds later, he spoke again without turning back. "When we land, the prisoner will be transferred into Princess Melinoe's control. He will be processed in accordance with the sacred law and all orders of The Queen will be followed in an exact manner."

"And what will you do?" Mel asked.

Ermis truly growled in his words now. "What I do best. Hunt."

"Good. Now land this miserable piece of scrap, I've had enough space travel for a lifetime."

Ermis waved a dismissive hand and took his seat shamefully. The crew began speaking loudly to one another, presumably performing preparations to land the ship. The planet had come closer now, more of its glory was shown. A swirl of clouds wrapped around the poles of the planet, and a band of blue stretched along the equator. Though we neared her home, Mel didn't turn to revel in its glory. In fact, her expression was near that of grief and disgust. After all the work we did to bring her back home, perhaps we had made a mistake.

"What will you have of us?" I asked.

Mel looked to Theseus and began speaking quickly in Elysian. She spoke clearly, yet sternly. A sharp edge to match her gaze. She was clearly giving instructions, I only wished I knew what they might be. Theseus spoke a single fast word back to her before turning away and walking for the elevator. At first, I didn't move. Mel and I held our gaze for a brief moment. Her gaze softened and the smallest of smiles cracked in her face, an echo of who I remembered. It was painful to break eye contact with her.

↩ ↩ ↩

Theseus and I stood by the door that we had entered the ship by. The ground rocked and rattled more than it ever had before, telling me that we were nearing the planet rapidly. We stood side by side, both looking up at Thirteen. The many people who had been working on him before had all stopped their work of pulling him apart. Most of them had vanished, but a small gathering of soldiers had made a circle under one of his wings, talking and laughing loudly. Their helmets had been removed, revealing a variety of shades of pale skin and pink hair. Some were more tan than others, some so pale they were ghostly white. Some had a light shade of pink closer to white, others a rich pink closer to red. They were all very tall, and though there were both men and women in the group, height didn't seem to prefer one or the other. Both the tallest and the shortest in the circle were women, the three men a variety in between.

Though they reveled in their chance to relax, my presence seemed to put them on edge. Each of them would take turns glancing at me between jokes and bouts of laughter. Some looked with curiosity and wonder, others with disgust or fear. It appeared all species could appreciate a good laugh and needed a break from work. I could barely contain my own laughter when a small argument started between two of them, both being backhanded by the tallest of the group and scolded for their childish behavior.

"Keti!" Theseus called.

The room went quiet as the tallest of them raised her head. She looked around the room for a moment before jogging over to us, eyes locked on Theseus. As she approached, she spoke a single word I was able to catch.

"Nai?"

Theseus replied with a long spout of words, gesturing to me briefly midway through the sentence. She got tense after the gesture, glaring at me for a brief moment. She replied with more words, a tone of concern. Theseus replied again, this time a hint of frustration. The woman sighed and threw her hands up in the air as she turned away.

"Oti, oti!" she said with exasperation before speaking to the group as she passed them. She jogged to the back of the ship, into the hallway I had not entered before. After a short stint of time, she returned with two sloshing metal canisters, handing both to Theseus.

"S'agapo," Theseus said with a grin.

"Oti," she said once more, walking away.

Theseus handed me one of the containers, opening his own and taking a long sip. Water, I assumed, yet part of me wondered if something in it might just kill me.

"Water. Your arm." Theseus said between sips, gesturing to my pockets.

I couldn't help but raise a confused brow as I pieced together his words. "My arm? Oh, my medicine. You remembered?"

My medicine, the medicine Wendy had given me before leaving. Though flash clone transplants solved some problems, it didn't solve all problems. It was explained only vaguely what might happen if I didn't take the medicine that suppressed my immune system from believing the replacement arm to be an invader, but I could only imagine it would not be pretty. My arm rotting off my living body would not be a good first impression amongst the Elysians.

"You didn't answer my question earlier." The words were harsh on my tongue as I swallowed the medicine with a swig of water, fighting not to cough the bitter taste. I couldn't tell if it was the medicine or the water that was bitter, but I was too thirsty to care.

"I have heard many things. Many things I wish I did not. Things that get me in big trouble."

"You think they'd silence you too if they knew?"

"I know they will."

I nodded. "Well let's try not to let them know then, shall we?"

"Sounds like a deal."

"Tell me, how bad of a situation am I in here? On a scale of one to ten."

"You are still alive, for now. But The Queen has yet decided what to do with you. If you survive meeting her...about an eight and a half."

My stomach churned. "That's if I survive?"

"If," Theseus repeated.

I sighed. "Great."

I finished the water and fiddled with the now empty container. I could hear heavy footsteps echo across the massive room as Theseus snatched the container from my hand and held it behind his back.

My back stiffened as Ermis and Mel, backed by half a dozen guards, were approaching. Theseus stood at attention, arms tight behind his back and shoulders back. Ermis spoke loudly to the soldiers loitering around the room, they all saluted with a nod, speaking a loud single word in unison.

"Ciru!"

In an instant, all of them filed off quickly, disappearing into the ship in an instant. I was left standing where Theseus once was, dwarfed ever more by the height of Ermis and Mel. The soldiers were shorter than either of the two, by half a foot or more, but the presence of the royals made me shrink in on myself. My height was half the feeling, but the ever pressing fear tightening around my heart was the other.

"We're entering the atmosphere. The gravity on our planet is stronger than that on your planet. Try to stay on your feet when you're presented to The Queen, and do not pass out," Mel spoke plainly, despite the fear rising in my heart.

"And if I do?" I stuttered.

"Don't. Trust me, don't." Her voice was sharp now.

I cleared my throat, "I'll do my best."

The ship around us began to shake. The groaning sounds coming from the walls, ceiling, and floor were familiar to me, the sounds of a ship entering the atmosphere. The molecules colliding into one another against the blunt walls of the ship creating so much heat a fire would break out over its surface. The lurch of the floor beneath you as your ship was forced to slow at the drag of the air. I'd seen it for myself all too many times, I could only imagine the spectacle of a ship this large entering the atmosphere.

My stomach began to turn, had my fear started to overwhelm me? I was just getting started, but my gut screamed for me to turn and run. There was no going back now, there hadn't been since Pluto. This was it, this could be one of the most important moments in human history. The first human to step onto a planet inhabited by alien intelligence. The first human to die there.

My head began to pound. It suddenly dawned on me, it was not fear turning my stomach and tightening my heart. It was the gravity. It was indeed heavier here than at home. Even if not by much, it was enough to make my eyes blur from the force. I fought to bring the air into my lungs, keep my head above my toes. I blinked hard, focusing on it would not make it better. But it hurt.

"You look pale," Ermis smirked.

"I wasn't made to be here," I said breathlessly.

"I think we all know that quite well," he replied.

A loud clanging sound echoed through the ship, it shook the ground, and my head. Two soldiers took position in front of us as the door hissed open. I had expected for light to flood into the ship, instead, the light from within poured out. The two soldiers cast great shadows down the ramp like towering beasts. A force hit my back and pushed me out onto the ramp. As the first breath of Elysian air hit my lungs, it became evident just how harsh these conditions were. The air was bitterly cold, even more bitterly thin. Elysia, the people and the planet itself, wanted me dead.

When we reached the bottom of the ramp, the two soldiers in front of me stepped away, allowing me to see past them and observe the audience waiting for us, for me. Half a dozen Elysians in white clothing similar to that which Mel wore all stood watching me. Some looked disgusted, others intrigued, but all confused.

"Its hair is blue."

"It's smaller than I expected."

"This is what we were so worried about?"

I deduced that these must be the royal advisers and officials. It seemed they all wanted a closer look, but dared not get any nearer.

"Move."

The crowd split to make way for who I knew in an instant was The Queen. She was taller than all the rest, though just shy of Ermis. She wore a long dress of matte white fabric with pleats all throughout. It came all the way up her neck to just below her chin. The sleeves were long, all the way down to the palm of her hand. Her thumb was looped through a hole in the sleeve, keeping it tight to her arms. A large bundle of silky white furs had been wrapped around her shoulders like a heavy cloak. Her skin was ghostly pale, her hair a pink so light it appeared almost white. She and Mel shared nearly the same face, though The Queen's eyes were framed by crow's feet and her skin showed signs of age. She was, by all accounts, regal. She didn't even glance at me, her eyes were locked behind me.

"Melinoo," she sighed with a widening smile.

Mel rushed past me and into her arms. Without a word, she leaned heavily into her mother. She was home, safe once again, but a guilt rose in the part of me that desired to claim responsibility for it. The two stood together for a moment, enjoying the peace of the reunion. Mel stepped back, but her mother kept her hands tight on her shoulders.

"Were you hurt?"

"No, Mother."

"You poor thing, you must've been so frightened."

"I was, for a time. But not always." Mel looked at me with glassy eyes. "He saved me. He protected me. He brought me home."

The Queen gave me a glance so brief I almost missed it. "And now we can forget about all of this and go back to how things were."

"No," Mel said seriously. "No, we can't."

The Queen sighed, releasing Mel. She turned to me, squaring her shoulders and tilting her head back. A hand pushed me to the ground, the ground being particularly inviting. I was kneeling, trying to catch my breath. Though I didn't particularly enjoy the idea of bowing, I did enjoy the moment to catch my breath. My legs, my back, my neck, they were all stiff from the weight already. No matter how deep a breath I took in, it always felt too shallow.

"You are bowing before Kore Ouranos, Queen of Elysia. Do you understand that?"

"I understand," I said breathlessly.

"Do you understand that your efforts have returned that which is most precious to me back to safety?"

"I...yes." I nodded. "I didn't know who she was, I only sought to do what I thought was right."

"He sacrificed everything for me. He has no safety left in the whole galaxy, solely to see that I might return home," Mel said.

The Queen looked at Mel, then back to me. "You mean to tell me that you sacrificed everything for a person you didn't know?"

I nodded again. "I saw someone in trouble. I only wished for her to be safe, to be back home again."

"Rise."

My legs struggled to pick myself back up, straining under the weight of my own body. As I looked up to meet Mel's eyes, I found her kneeling before me. Her head hung low, her hair shrouding her face.

"I owe you my life," she said.

The Queen and all her advisers were appalled, faces painted with shock so clear it frightened me. A princess bowing down to something with no worth at all. It was a sight for the ages. Mel lifted her head, her eyes meeting my own. There, hidden between the locks of her hair, was the Mel I had known. Innocent, pure, caring. Mel rose to her feet, her mother at her side in shock.

"We do not bow to...whatever he is." She said harshly in her ear.

"His name is Apollo Harrison, and he is a hero," Mel declared loudly. "We will welcome him as a herald of his people."

Discourse roared amongst the group, immediately descending the air that was once quiet into chaos. Advisers argued amongst each other, Ermis declared something loudly in Elysian, and The Queen sighed heavily, pinching the bridge of her nose. Every loud word was like a hammer against my skull as my heart pounded in my chest. My head tilted backwards, eyes tracing past the faces of the giants around me, up into the sky. I could see the Milky Way stretching high above us, the smattering of stars and galaxies all around this planet, and the brightest light in the sky, the sun. It was distant, dim from here, but it was there. This world was trapped in perpetual twilight, but dawn was approaching.

"Silence."

The Queen did not shout, she did not raise her voice, but spoke with clarity and dignity. Her single word silenced the crowd. She looked down at me with pity in her eyes. It seemed no person could read her, not with any ounce of ease at least, but I saw something in her. In her eyes, I saw the spark of the same look she gave Mel, a look of motherly care.

"We will welcome him, quietly. Nobody outside of the castle can know of his presence. He and the princess will give an account for what has happened, after that, a vote will be held to decide his fate."

A smile of relief smeared across my face, my breath flowing out of me in clouds of fog in the cold air. "Thank you, Your Majesty."

"He will stay in the visitor's suite," The Queen continued, gesturing at one of the guards standing nearby. My stomach turned harder than ever. "And he will be his private guard to ensure no foul play takes place."

The Queen turned and eyed her advisers.

"Allow me to make myself perfectly clear. The human is not to be injured, tortured, or interrogated without my explicit say so. Any foul play will be counted as treason, and your life will be forfeit to pay for your crimes." She turned again to meet Ermis' gaze, which I could only imagine was that of pure rage. "That goes for you as well, Brother."

A few whispers were exchanged.

"This reception is adjourned. Now leave my daughter and I alone, we have much to discuss." The Queen declared.

She placed a hand on Mel's shoulder and turned to guide her away, but Mel didn't move. Her eyes were locked on me, turning more pale than she already was. I gave Mel a breathless thumbs up with a smile as one last breath left me. I tried to draw in another, but no air came.

"Call a doctor!" She exclaimed as my body became weightless. The ground came up to meet me, and the void of darkness above welcomed me with open arms.

⤙ 18 ⤚

Castle

My lungs burned as I came to. My eyes flung open and my arms thrashed outward; I was upside down, and my head was pounding. I was strapped to a table with a thin cloth laid atop me. A mask was strapped to my face, white plastic rubbing against the skin around my nose and mouth. The table I laid upon was tilted just slightly backwards, causing the blood to pool in my head. It felt as though a vice was bound around my head, squeezing ever tighter. All of it was becoming a maddeningly familiar feeling. If I was strapped to one more table in my lifetime, I might lose it.

"Hello?" I said exasperatedly.

I could hear the hiss of a door somewhere in the room, then footsteps leading in. "Ah, you're finally awake."

The table I laid upon slowly became flat again, the pressure in my head easing almost instantly. An Elysian stood over me, his hair barely pink, mostly gray. A rubber mask with two vents on either cheek was strapped to his face. He wore scrubs made of an odd material.

He pulled a thin flashlight from the pocket on his chest and shined it in my eyes. "It's actually quite the miracle you survived the night. Whomever you pray to, keep it up. Clearly it's working."

"Who…where's Mel?"

The man raised his eyebrows. "I think you mean Princess Melinoe, and for your knowledge, she's fine. Look this way for me?"

"I need to leave."

"You'll leave when I discharge you, now look here please." He waggled a finger on the right side of my face, then my left. "Eyes are still a bit bloodshot."

His cold hands clasped around my left hand, lifting it up to the light. An IV was buried in my wrist, and the edges of my fingers looked vaguely blue. "Skin is less blue. It was far worse on your other arm. Are you feeling confused? Do you have a headache? Anxiety? Rapid heart rate? Sweating? Wheezing? You seem restless so I'll write that down."

I pulled my hand away. "I'm fine, I need to leave, please."

"You suffered a bad case of hypoxia, son. I should keep you bed-bound for days. Fortunately for you, I have orders from The Queen to release you, after a thorough examination."

He began unbinding the restraints across my chest and legs. After unbinding me from the table, he slowly removed the IV in my hand and taped a ball of fluffy white material atop it. He helped me sit up and swing my legs over the side of the table. I looked down to find myself wearing similar clothing to what I saw Mel wearing on the Hades. The lines along the seams of this pair were a light blue, and at closer examination, a tiny triangular pattern of only barely different shades of white was woven throughout the clothes. The pants were the most comfortable things I had ever worn.

"So tell me son, how do you feel?" He leaned against the table beside me, flipping through the clipboard.

"Stiff," I said with a groan while rubbing at the tense muscles around my neck.

He nodded, running his finger along a line chart on the page of a clipboard. "Sounds right, muscles need oxygen to function, something you direly lacked upon first arrival."

I tugged at the mask tight around my face. "I'm guessing I won't be taking this off anytime soon."

The man set aside his clipboard for a moment and grabbed a box from atop a counter in the corner of the room. "To your luck, some eggheads from down below brought something for you. Orders from the princess, according to them."

He opened it to reveal a small, white mechanism not much bigger than a smart phone with clear tubes running from it. He clipped the machine to a loop on my pants and unwound the tubes, revealing it to be the sort of device doctors place on a patient's nose to provide oxygen. "Specifically made just for you. We use these on our elderly sometimes, but we had to get the sizing right for you. We usually use ones this small on teenagers, but even those are a bit big on you."

I took the mask off my face and began placing the new one into place. "A portable oxygen concentrator. How did you make it so small? We haven't managed that yet."

"Not sure, but I heard they had to make this one special to produce the amount you need." He took up his clipboard again, thumbing through the pages once more. "Tell me son, how is it that we can be so alike if our species have never met before?"

I thought about that, hard. Too many questions to weigh at one time. There was a mystery at play here, and I couldn't connect any of the dots. "Not sure...why is it that you saved me?"

A smile pulled at the man's eyes. "I swore an oath to protect all who came into my care, and it was The Queen's orders. I am the royal family's personal care provider; it seems you're getting the royal treatment."

I couldn't help but laugh at that. I had expected my arrival to be much different. Considering how dire Theseus seemed to make my situation, I had expected far more violence. I would believe torches and pitchforks before I believed innocent kindness. Something about all this felt off, really off. "Thank you."

"Well, you're free to go. You come back if you're ever feeling ill, I'm not sure how your body will adjust to our environment." He patted me on the back and opened the door, gesturing for me to exit. My legs still felt weak under me as I came to my feet. Head foggy and slightly dazed, I took my first step to leave, then paused.

"Wait, how could it be that I ran out of oxygen here, but not on the Hades?" I asked.

"Ah, a question I also asked. The answer is your ship. The engineers tore it open, trying to find what made it tick. It was pumping out oxygen at alarming rates, so much so it had begun to make the crew sick." A mischievous smile arose when he mentioned that. "No matter what they did, it wouldn't stop. All to keep you alive, it seems. Whatever you did to that ship, it makes for a good guard dog." I hadn't considered that their lesser need for oxygen might make them sick when exposed to too much of it. I wondered how Mel might have felt in her first days amongst humans.

The man guided me out of the room, pressing a gentle hand against my back. "Now, I do have other patients to attend to, and you have a trial to prepare for. Bye now, take care."

"Thank you, Dr..."

"Petrellis, Dr. Petrellis, and you're very welcome."

He pushed me out into the hallway and closed the door behind me. I jumped at the sight of a soldier standing beside the door, hand laid loosely on the hilt of a blade on his belt.

"Stars alive you scared me," I mumbled.

"Better scared than dead," a familiar voice replied.

My brows bunched together. "Theseus?"

He turned and began making his way down the hall. It was long, with white walls and black floors and ceilings. Many doors lined the walls, all labeled in an odd text. "You did not listen to Princess Melinoe. She said not to pass out."

"I did my best," I grumbled.

We stepped out into what looked like a lobby for the doctor's office, but every seat was empty. An Elysian woman sat behind a counter in the corner, her head down. I couldn't catch a glimpse of her face, not that I cared much. In this room, there was a deep blue carpet, harsh and coarse. I quickly realized that my sneakers were missing. I suddenly felt naked without them, feet completely bare on a foreign planet. As we stepped out of the lobby, I was faced with an astonishing view.

A pane of glass revealed a massive city below us. We were at least half a mile off the ground, with more building above us. Dozens of skyscrapers peppered the city, tall buildings lining the streets below. Most buildings were made of a sleek white material of some sort, giving off a sheen like quartz. The glass of each building shimmered with a deep green, and the streetlights throughout the city gleamed with a light blue shine. A million twinkling lights dotted the edges and surfaces of every part of the city, each tiny shine another piece to an army fighting against the eternal night. Together, they created a soft blue glow to everything. Long raised tracks were woven throughout and even through some of the structures, tunnels and stations installed straight into the buildings. Far down below, I could see streets filled with people and vehicles. From this distance, I could hardly extrapolate anything about the "cars" they drove. All I could tell is that they did not touch the ground.

This was life for them, and they knew nothing different. How scared they might be when the sun finally approached? A world of people never near enough to the sun to even call it that, suddenly thrust into a world of night and day instead of just dark and darker. And yet they live on, normal lives like normal people.

"It is beautiful," I said.

"It's home," Theseus nodded.

I pressed a hand against the cold window, watching a few flakes of snow tumble from the sky in a dust that covered the rooftops and windows. The snow covered roofs went on for miles, I was unsure of where the city ended and something else began. Had the lights been all I could see, I would think the horizon ended where the city did. But far on the horizon, I saw mountains. Like a wall of rock circling the city, they stood in frost and snow covered majesty. I could tell there was something between us and them, a deep dark void that consumed all light that entered it, like a black hole.

Whether a forest or something else, an oppressive darkness surrounded the city like a moat of emptiness. I wondered if the darkness made the people feel protected or surrounded. Like walls between them and the wilderness or an army standing just outside, waiting to invade. Above us, an aurora arced across the sky. Thin ribbons of pink, blue, and green dancing across the stars. They weren't bright enough to illuminate the city, but they were bright enough to be beautiful. Of all the planets, of all the systems, this was the most beautiful sight I had ever seen.

"I've never seen anything like it," I murmured.

"One of a kind," Theseus agreed.

I pulled my hand back, leaving the fogged outline of my fingers and palm on the window. I turned to follow Theseus, but I couldn't help but look back to that window. It stretched down the entire length of the hallway, all the way down and around the corner. Every floor of this building had a perfect view of the city, looking down at its inhabitants. Ruling from above. An ivory tower.

Theseus opened the door to an elevator. "In."

I didn't want to break my view of the city, and it pained me to watch the doors hiss shut. The whir of the elevator and the buzz of the machine on my hip were all that accompanied us here. We'd already shared so many words, but I knew the risk Theseus was facing by speaking to me. The Queen said nobody outside of the castle could know of my presence, which likely meant the castle was locked down. Everyone inside this building was stuck here, because of me. Claustrophobia began tightening around me, likely as it was for everyone here.

"Do you...have any other family?" I asked. It was a dumb question, and I knew it was the second I said it.

Theseus pulled at the fingers of his gloves. "My little sister and my mother. They live on the edge of the city."

"Are they well?"

He nodded, pulling off his gloves entirely and clipping them to his belt. "My sister in school, my mother a plant scientist."

"A botanist, interesting," I mumbled.

"Your family?" Theseus asked, wiping his palms on his pants.

"My big sister is a reporter, my dad works in marketing, and my mom used to do photography." Emotion welled in my throat remembering them, I shook my head and rubbed at my eyes. "Are you nervous about something?"

"No," Theseus lied.

"Your hands are sweaty, and you're breathing fast. What's wrong?"

"I fine," he said sternly now. "The princess is waiting for you."

The door swooshed open, we were even higher now. We had to be nearing the top of the building; it was hard to believe we could even get any higher. I followed Theseus out and to the right. He walked stiffly, and quickly. Something was bothering him, and it was beginning to make me nervous. We walked for what felt like forever, though my shorter legs carried me slower than his. He came to stop at a massive door, ornately designed and labeled in large, broad text. He placed his fingers on the panel beside it and twisted. Like the elevator, the door here slid open with a soft swish.

The room inside was massive, a short walkway leading into a large living room. The floor was sunken in the middle, a square of couches embedded in the floor around a large table. There were massive windows on the left wall, opening up into the city. The ceilings were high, and a raised walkway encircled the room above us. A staircase staggered up onto the raised area, with short hallways leading further into the building on the top and bottom floor. To my right was a small bar with stools placed around it, behind it a large window revealing an unmanned kitchen inside, large enough for half a dozen cooks. The walls were white, the floors made of what seemed to be a black stained wood, and the ceilings a deep blue. The room was illuminated by chandeliers of whitish blue light hanging from above, hanging perfectly still in this silent room.

I felt my jaw drop open. "This is..."

"Pretentious," Theseus grumbled. "Your room will be on the second floor, a bathroom across from it. The clothes you came here in are in your closet, as well as clothes for you to wear during the trial."

I shivered at the word. I hated all the tension. "Again with the trial stuff, you guys are scaring me."

A door hissed open somewhere in the space, sending a chill down my spine. Mel stepped out from the hall above, practically running down the steps when she saw us.

She exclaimed something in Elysian, rushing down to meet us. "Thank all that is good you're okay! You scared me half to death."

Before I could say anything, she pulled me into a tight hug, pulling me up onto the tips of my toes. She drew in a deep breath before letting me go, holding her hands tight on my shoulders and analyzing my face. She ran a finger along the tube stretching across my cheek and behind my ear.

"This world hasn't treated you well already," she said solemnly.

"I've seen worse," I replied. "My body feels…heavier than I'm used to, but I'll get used to it."

She sighed. "Well, I'm glad you're alright." Had you told me when I first met her how comforted I would be to see her smile, I would've laughed in your face. Now, her smile was all that I had to remind me of Earth, of home. She was my safety, my oasis. "There's so much I want to tell you, so much I want to show you…"

I laughed nervously. "If only we could leave, right?"

Mel turned to Theseus and spoke to him in Elysian, placing a hand on her chest and nodding at the end of her sentence. He shifted beneath his gear and nodded.

"Do forgive the soldiers around here, they're quite stiff necked. It must be lonely being stuck around people who don't speak the same language as you," Mel said. Her face was painted with what must be nostalgia, thinking back on a distant memory.

"He's alright, once you get to know him," I said.

Mel laughed hard at the joke, likely not realizing I wasn't joking. She spoke to Theseus again, his breath hitched. He nodded again, looking all around us for a moment.

Mel spoke to me now. "I'm allowing him to take a break for a time, I imagine it must get stuffy under those helmets."

His hands shook as he placed two fingers on the back of his helmet. It unlatched with a snap, splitting down the middle and hinging apart from the top. He took it off and snapped the helmet closed for a moment, holding it to his side and looking down at Mel's shoes. Her face, once happy, faded to confusion.

"You...I know you," she said with a look of confusion. "Why can't I remember your name?"

"You know Theseus?" I raised an eyebrow, looking at him.

"You know his name? How can you know his name?" Mel looked at me, confused further.

"We grew up together, Your Highness." Theseus said, ashamed. "My father was the librarian of the castle."

"You can speak...English?" She looked back and forth at us.

He nodded. "Whenever my father needed help in the library, he would bring me. We used to play together, read each other's books."

Realization had begun on her face. "I...I do remember that. You're that boy? I thought you just vanished one day. The librarian, he's..." Mel placed a hand over her mouth, eyes wide. "Oh stars alive."

The air was so thick it was as if it wanted to push me out of this room and into somewhere I could breathe better. It wasn't hatred or contempt that floated between the two Elysians, only sorrow. Mel had not done anything, and it was not because of

Theseus, yet his father was dead and her mother allowed it. There was no atonement, only mourning for the dead.

I cleared my throat. "If I may, I think we're all tired. Maybe it's time we all get some rest."

Theseus and Mel looked at each other once more before looking at me. Their eyes were heavy on me, conceding that there was no answer to this problem. We couldn't bring his father back from the dead, we couldn't hold The Queen accountable. The best we could do was make this a motivation to succeed.

"Yes, we must be well rested for the trial." Mel folded her hands and held her head low. "Theseus, please understand that I am not the person I was when I left. My time amongst humans has taught me many things. I hope you understand that I desire to change Elysia for the better. Change is coming whether we like it or not, I'd like that change to be to our benefit and not our destruction. I can't do it alone, and if you allow it, I'm relying on both of you to help me."

Mel and I both looked to Theseus now, fidgeting in place. I could see pondering in his eyes, dashing back and forth between the carpet and walls as he thought hard. He drew a deep breath and nodded.

"I must protect my family, I won't let us be destroyed any further." He said, face steeled with determination. "I'll help in any way that I can."

A weak smile arose on Mel's face. "I owe both of you everything, and yet I still have the audacity to ask for more. I don't deserve your grace, but I thank you with the whole of my heart."

I fought for a smile through the heavy emotions, and Theseus smiled back. He was a good, honest man. Ermis said that honesty makes men weak. I could only pray that it wasn't true, for his sake. The thought escaped me with a sigh.

"Let's all get some sleep, we've earned it." I placed a hand on Mel's shoulder, making myself feel awkward for how high I had to reach to do so. "Everything is going to be fine, just take a deep breath."

She obliged, her chest rising with an air of hope. "Sometimes things just work out, right?"

"We'll figure something out, we always do."

She smirked. "Does that mean I'm an engineer now?"

"Nope!" My head tilted down, looking up at her through my brow jokingly. "Don't push your luck."

She couldn't stop herself from laughing at this, smiling once more before heading for the door. She looked back as the door hissed open. "I'll see you two tomorrow. Sleep well."

It hissed shut, leaving Theseus and I alone. Her contagious smile still stuck to my face. I looked down at my hands for a moment, realizing just how much we had shared together. Connections with people always were odd to me. One day you're strangers, and before you know it, you can't imagine life without them.

"We can't help it, it's like a bad habit," I mumbled, echoing my own words with wonder.

"You share a connection," Theseus said. "It is clear to see."

"Let's hope The Queen can see it too," I replied.

"She does see it, that is why she hates you."

I thought on his words for a moment, a jolt of adrenaline rushing through me. I imagined a world in which we reached this point without an ounce of connection, with the same hatred and vitriol we shared when we first met. I wondered if it would be easier, for both of us. If I were to die, she would feel nothing. If I were to leave, I'd have no desire to come back. Because she cares for me, my death could define the rest of her life. Because I care for her, I could not keep myself from coming back to see her, if even just one more time.

All of this because of a connection, some invisible force drawing two things together. Celestial bodies, once separate, now in an orbit that would mean the destruction of both if it were broken. Binary stars, soaring through space blindly, with nothing to trust but the other. Our connection saw the union of two worlds, a star system with lives in the balance. We were intertwined, and if that connection broke, it would destroy both worlds forever, and ourselves. I saw the truth, if that force hadn't bound us, we would never have made it here alive.

After Theseus had led me to my room, which was just as luscious as the living room had been, I changed into a pair of soft clothes which hung loosely around my body. Before I crawled into the bed, which was large for an Elysian and massive for me, I looked around the room one last time with an eerie chill crawling up my spine. The large desk and chair in the corner was accounted for, the tall closet containing my few sets of clothes neat and tidy, and the mirror on the wall as spotless as it was before. It was installed in the wall to the left of the bed, giving me a view of the door no matter which side I laid on.

I crawled into the sheets which seemed to swallow me whole and surrounded myself with the half a dozen pillows which lay on the bed. It was the most comfortable bed I'd ever slept in, though the bar was low. Warmth wrapped around me in a tight hug as the lights faded to dim and I breathed in the most welcome rest, praying for a night without a nightmare of Zivko, and his blood on my hands.

To my despair, the sleep was fitful. I dreamed of Wendy and Sintara coming to find me, eviscerated as they attempted to enter Elysia's atmosphere. I could hear their screams as the plasma burned their bodies to ash. I could see Elysians on the streets of Arcadia. Their blades cut down the Martians with ease, their guns shredding through their bodies like a dying star shreds atoms. The city collapsed in flames, burned to the ground in mere moments. My parents couldn't make it out in time. At last, I saw Henry on Earth, coming to respond to a knock on his door. He pulled open the hardwood to find an Elysian at his door. His eyes were filled with wonder, until a blade found a home in his gut. As the light faded from his eyes, I knew it was my fault. All of this was my fault.

I awoke from this dream to find the room still dark, the flickers of aurora gleaming through the blinds. I'd placed a pillow on my head to make myself feel smaller, cozier in this massive space. The curtains swayed for a moment. There was no fan in this room, no vent I'd noticed. The air shouldn't be moving, not like that.

A creak made my skin crawl. Then another noise, a slow, drawn out sound like fabric rubbing fabric. It continued until I stirred in my bed for a moment, coming to a stop instantly. I brought a hand to my face, using my index and middle finger to lift the pillow off my face just barely. I continued to draw in long, deep breaths, yet my heart pounded in my chest. Through the gap in the pillow, my eyes adjusted to the light of the room. My head was tilted towards the mirror, and in the corner of the room, I saw it. A soldier, clad in black armor and a sleek black helmet covering his head.

I feared they could hear my heart pounding the way it drummed in my ears like a symphony of percussion. I opened my mouth to speak, but fear gripped me. They began moving, stepping closer to me, slowly, carefully. It felt as though time came to a standstill as they neared my bed, and before I could believe it, they stood mere inches from the bed. A hand rose to their chest, slowly and carefully. I could see the hilt of the knife on their vest, tucked between two pockets across their abs. Their fingers wrapped around it like serpents and pulled the gleaming metal from its scabbard.

Aurora light shone off the blade as they lifted it. My muscles tensed as I pulled my head down into my sheets as slow as I could, slipping from underneath the pillow atop my head in careful precision. My eyes slipped beneath the covers, and I could no longer see my doom approaching. My only hope was that the soldier could see just as poorly as I, and the pillow that was once on my head disguised my escape. My breath shook.

An impact shook the bed just above my head. The knife was driven deep into the pillow and into my mattress. A light gasp came from the assailant, attempting to pull the blade out, but bringing the pillow with them.

An impact could be heard, an unstoppable force meeting an immovable object, then a loud slam. A curse was shouted, and I scrambled to pull the covers off my head. The assailant had been thrown against the wall, struggling under the constricting hands of a man in tight gray clothing with pink hair. It was Theseus, barreling punches down on the assailant. The enemy's helmet cracked, but he returned with a hard shove and a kick to the chest.

Theseus tumbled backward as the man rose to his feet, lunging at me with his still-pillow-covered blade. I shouted in fear as I scrambled backwards, falling off the bed backwards as the tip of the blade met the mattress again. The man crawled across the mattress, but something grabbed his leg and drew him back. His knife shredded through the mattress as Theseus rained more punches down on the helmet. The helmet hissed and Theseus dug his fingers into one of the cracks. He ripped the helmet off the man and began beating him with the broken defensive wear. The man's eyes were in a daze.

Theseus was flung off of the man. Another soldier had appeared in the fray, wrapping his massive arms around Theseus's neck and pulling him back. Theseus's teeth grit as his fingers scratched at the soldier's arms. Fist made impact against helmet, a wild elbow was thrown, but the soldier was strong.

"The closet," Theseus sputtered through grit teeth, struggling to breathe. I rushed to the closet without a second question, rifling through the clothes quickly. I found my shoes lined neatly beside my jacket, and inside of one lay the gun I had picked up off the floor of Sintara's ship.

My fingers closed around the weapon. I couldn't kill them, I wouldn't. My arms leveled, taking aim for the soldier holding Theseus. It was the soldier or Theseus, and it was an easy choice. Theseus jerked sideways, revealing the broad back of the soldier binding him. I took a few shots, bullets pinging off the armor of the soldier until one buried itself in a gap on the shoulder. The bullet shredded their flesh and they screamed in pain as Theseus took action. He broke the grip and threw another elbow. The soldier stumbled back. Theseus pulled the knife from the soldier's vest and turned it on him.

Theseus lunged for the man, the two of them tumbled out of the door and into the hallway. The soldier on the bed began to rise. I took aim at him now. The moment he saw the weapon, he raised his arms to his face. I took a few shots, two bouncing off his chest and one off the armor on his forearm. He tucked his head down and charged at me, I leaped to my side and he slammed into the wall. He turned to me once more, I rolled to my back and took a shot. Red sprayed across the wall, his arms rising to his neck as he fell forward. His heavy frame held my legs to the ground as he grabbed at my clothing with one hand, the other holding at the hole in his neck. The tight ball of his fist tore my shirt, then gave way. Blood poured from his mouth and the light faded from his eyes.

I crawled out from under the man in horror, grabbing at the carpet to scramble away from the corpse. I rose to my feet and ran from the body like a child knocking over a lamp. I had taken another man's life. It was so easy, but there was no unconsciousness to allow me escape from this reality. I felt sick to my stomach. My feet carried me out the door to find Theseus driving the knife into the other soldier's chest, throwing another punch across their helmet before taking hold of their collar. He slammed their head down on the railing of the balcony, one, two, three times. Rage overflowed from him in a battle cry before heaving the limp body over the railing. A crunching thud was heard below, followed by no sound at all.

Theseus heaved in deep breaths, the muscles in his arms tense like ropes pulled taut under his skin. His shoulders rose and fell with his breath, hunched over just slightly like an animal on the hunt. He turned to me with harsh breaths, blood staining his lip and a gash across his cheek. He glared at me through the thin hairs that hung in front of his eyes, analyzing me for a moment like sizing up an opponent, then slowing as he recognized who I was. I held still, frightened, afraid any movement might prompt him to attack. For a moment, I thought he'd kill me. His eyes alone could do it. His breath picked up as his shoulders rolled back. His hand pushed the hair from his face as he looked around confused, then shook his head and blinked hard. He went from a savage animal to the calm, peaceful man I had known him as. He was no ordinary soldier.

"Are you alright?" He asked, still heaving.

"Yeah…you?" I asked in return, frightened by the sight.

"I'm fine." He wiped some of the blood from his lip, then tapped at the wound on his face. He rubbed it off on the gray of his clothes that was now spattered with blood. He grunted with annoyance. He gave me one last glance before turning away, eyes devoid of emotion. "Welcome to Castle Ouranos."

↳ 19 ↵

Court

I pulled Dad's jacket tight around my shoulders, but the cold still gripped me. Theseus stomped down the stairs and threw the weight off his shoulder, the body he carried slumping beside its companion. One was soaked through with blood, the other had a knife poking out of his back. The poor soul had landed on his chest when he fell, meaning the knife Theseus left in his ribs had found its way all the way through him. Theseus had torn the helmet off each of them, revealing two Elysians with darker skin than others and hair a pink so dark it was almost scarlet in the dim light. Their helmets lay beside their heads, all of the above cracked and barely held together. The bodies were stiff as boards now, faces taught with anguish in death. They died painfully.

Theseus grabbed one by the face, struggling to turn the head to either side, checking their ears. He began rummaging their gear, turning their pockets inside out. He drew another knife from the soldier's boot, then a sidearm from his hip. He started creating a pile of their weaponry.

He spoke gruffly, clearly uncomfortable dealing with the bodies. "Where are your clothes for the trial?"

"I feel more comfortable in this," I said, tugging at my human clothes. They smelled fresh, like they'd been washed. I certainly hadn't done it, had a servant been stuck with such menial duty? I shouldn't be surprised, but I still felt bad.

"Perhaps it will make you seem more defenseless," he mumbled.

Footsteps entered the room behind me with a swish. I turned to see the soldier who brought us water on the Hades. She looked exhausted, armor slightly askew from being put on too quickly, helmet hanging at her side. She carried something under her arm, something I couldn't make out. She stopped in her tracks as she walked in, looking warily at the bodies.

"Eto astera," she mumbled.

Theseus looked up at her and nodded a greeting while speaking in a placid tone. She hesitated before nodding, gesturing at the thing under her arm. He gestured at me, she hesitated further.

"Your firearm, it's not enough. You need something that get through armor, at the weak points anyways." He spoke as if he could see straight through my shirt and the handle of the weapon sticking from my waistband, perhaps he could.

The soldier spoke again, speaking a retort to Theseus. He glared at her and she submitted. She took the thing from under her arm and shoved it into my arms, saying a brief word while watching me nervously. It was a bundle of hard fabric and straps. It was a holster, and inside lay a heavy firearm that made my hands seem tiny in comparison. It was a matte gray with black lines running down the barrel. Two magazines for the gun lay in pouches on the outside of the holster. I began loosening the straps, and something fell loose. It was a knife in a tight scabbard, clips to hook onto my belt attached.

Theseus nodded. "Keep them hidden, and keep them always."

I lifted my shirt and flung my previous gun into the pile. I strapped the holster around my waist and kept it on my back, placing the knife on my right side. Between this and my oxygen concentrator, I was beginning to feel cluttered by the amount of things I had to carry. The soldier beside me looked sick to her stomach as I dropped my shirt over the weapons.

Theseus didn't look away from his work as he spoke. She didn't make any trouble at him speaking English to me, it led me to assume the two were close. "Apollo, this is Atalanta. Call her Ata."

"Nice to meet you, Ata." I held a hand out to her. She looked at my hand hesitantly, eventually taking hold of it and shaking it firmly.

"Kala mora," she said quietly.

"It means hello," Theseus said as he drew a small piece of paper from the pocket of the bigger soldier. It wasn't much bigger than a playing card, inscribed with an odd text. He turned it over to find a hexagonal symbol with a star inside. He scoffed, handing it to Ata.

He brushed his hands off and stood up. "As I expected, the royal of the deep south."

Ata read the card, turned it over, and pursed her lips. She spoke plainly to Theseus, he nodded at her words. "She said he made the biggest fuss about you staying in the castle. These two were part of his private guard."

"Will he be punished for this?" I asked.

A loud bark escaped Theseus, telling Ata what I had said between bouts of laughter. She snickered and shook her head, mumbling something in Elysian that made Theseus laugh harder. I sighed with a roll of my eyes, clearly I was out of my depth here.

"She says that he would have been punished if he had not tried to kill you," Theseus said while wiping a tear from his eye. "Royals do not look at us. They do not care about us. This is good. It means you are important. It is a strength for you, a weakness for him. Inconvenient though."

I raised an eyebrow. "You expected me to be assassinated?"

"I was ready to fight, wasn't I?" Theseus shrugged. "I had hoped they would try. It will help us later."

"You were that confident you could protect me?" Frustration built in my chest, it clearly showed in my voice.

Theseus's face dropped, falling plain as my words jabbed at his pride. He mumbled what I said to Ata, she pursed her lips and raised her eyebrows, mumbling something back with a nod.

"She said you have not seen what I can really do. She would trust me with her life, and I would trust her with mine. We have not survived this long for nothing." He walked closer to me, making me shrink into myself as he looked down the bridge of his nose and into my eyes. "Trust is the only valuable currency here. Allies and enemies, strength and weakness, that is all there is on Elysia."

"Mechri thanatou,"Ata said, arms folded.

Theseus closed his eyes and nodded. "It means unto death. If we want to survive, we need to trust each other, unto death." He opened his eyes now. "Is this understood?"

"Understood," I said.

There was something in his eyes, something I hadn't seen before. It was as if he was possessed, his gray eyes darkened by ghosts. Whatever he had seen, whatever he had faced on this planet, his kindness had only barely survived. He wanted me to know that. I didn't trust him, and I took his trust for granted. I wouldn't do that again. His face eased, and he took a step back, drawing a deep breath with his eyes closed. Ata placed a hand on his shoulder, saying a calming word to him. Last night, I had seen part of what Theseus was capable of. I would trust him wholly from now on, and hopefully his trust in me would not be shaken.

"S'agapo." Theseus breathed easy now, hands steady as he looked down at the bodies below. An air of unease had settled in my mind. Standing beside bodies was not a common experience amongst humans, yet the soldiers looked at them like trash to be removed.

"Can I...ask a question?" My voice warbled as I looked away from the bodies, unable to stomach it a moment longer.

"Sure," Theseus nodded.

I looked up at the ceiling and thought carefully. "When you were attacking them, it seems you focused on removing their helmets. Why?"

"Our helmets are similar to that machine." He pointed to my waist. "It provides more air to us. The more air we have, the stronger we are. It is in limited supply on our planet, so our helmets make us stronger, faster, and smarter."

That must be why Mel always seemed so strong on Earth and in human atmospheres but was weaker in places without as much oxygen. I wondered why not everyone wore helmets all the time, but keeping your soldiers stronger than the average person was a smart choice, I suppose. "So you removed them so it would be a fair fight?"

Theseus smirked. "It was not a fair fight to begin, not with me there."

The floor squeaked behind me, and in a blink, Theseus and Ata had both half drawn their weapons. In a glimpse of realization, they returned their weapons to their holster and saluted. I turned to see Mel standing in the doorway, one hand over her mouth in shock.

"Are you hurt?" She spoke calmly, walking near to me while scanning up and down my body. I shook my head. She drew me in for a hug, one I hesitated to lean into for a moment. The warmth of her arms began melting away the chill that still gripped me.

"I'm okay, they didn't even lay a finger on me. Theseus did very well at protecting me," I said.

"I can not take all the credit, Apollo defended himself well, Your Majesty." Theseus bowed.

"I'm sorry this has happened, I should have warned you of the possibility." She backed slightly and placed a hand on my cheek, looking carefully at me. Her eyes slid down to the bodies beside us, then up at the broken railing.

"Don't worry, the bed is even more ruined." I laughed in spite of myself.

Mel frowned. "This won't do. You'll stay with me in my quarters tonight. It's much safer there."

Mel whirled on her heels and marched for the door, waving for us to follow. I hesitated for a moment, but Theseus and Ata walked past me without a second thought. Ata placed a finger against her throat as she walked away, speaking aloud to some unseen being. Before I knew it, I was alone with the bodies, and I didn't like it. I rushed after the group, struggling to keep up with their long legs. A trio of soldiers in all white clothing marched past us as we followed Mel down the hallway, heading for what was my room.

"Medics, they also double as morticians," Theseus said under his breath to me. I shivered at the words, pushing past them to catch up to Mel.

"So, I keep hearing about this...trial," I said.

"You should be hearing about it, it's happening in only a few hours," she nodded, head held high.

"Is it...for me?" Another highly stupid question, I wanted to smack myself for asking it.

"We are both the subjects of discussion, which is why we're going to get our story straight."

My face tightened in confusion. "But there's only one story, we both lived it. You make it sound like we're fabricating some lie."

Mel pursed her lips. "Your first lesson in politics; every word counts. If you do not choose your words perfectly, it could be the difference between peace and war."

↩ ↩ ↩

Mel had led us to her domain, of sorts. We'd taken an elevator up several floors, leading us down the hall to a pink door with bold lettering atop it. An ornate carving was etched into the door, that of a large rose with thorny vines all around it. Two soldiers stood on either side of the door, the only thing different about them to other soldiers being the bright pink buttons that held the collar of the flak vests they wore. One opened the door for Mel as she walked up.

"S'agapo," she nodded with a smile as we marched inside. The soldier who opened the door looked to their partner on the opposite side. Though their face was masked, I could see their shock in how their back straightened and their shoulders rolled back. Just one word changed the soldiers' whole mood.

We marched inside to find a room even more lavish than the one I had found in my own suite. On the wall across from the door, a massive wall of windows displayed the glory of the city below. Staircases rose to a walkway above similar to my own room, but the ceiling was vaulted even higher. A long crystal chandelier hung down from the ceiling, the prisms casting rainbows across the room. The floor and ceiling was white here, but the walls were a light pink that matched Mel's hair. She had an array of couches and bean bags scattered across her main room, and the walls were covered in shelves filled with books. Other knick knacks were scattered throughout the shelves all around, I stopped beside one and picked up a small picture frame.

When I picked it up, the image came to life. It was a little girl with pink hair wrestling a grizzled, broad shouldered man with graying pink hair and beard. They both wore a smile that warmed my heart, and the echo of laughter came from the image. I set it down and the video faded.

"My father," Mel said, silently appearing beside me.

"He seems wonderful," I replied.

Mel smiled tenderly, pain held behind joy. "He was wonderful. Come, I have a place for us to speak."

She led us through a door on the first floor, into a square room with a large table in the center. Papers and files were scattered across the table, and about half a dozen chairs were scattered around it. I was glad to see that even advanced cultures can appreciate a clean piece of stationery. The walls here were covered in more shelves, as well as filing cabinets, except for the wall across from the door which also held a floor-to-ceiling window that let the aurora pour in.

"I once spent hours in this room as a girl. Drawing, writing stories, reading books. Now I call it my war room. Every battle I've ever waged has been through these papers. I find it quite boring that my call has always been through words." Mel marched around to the opposite end of the table and swept the papers off to the side. Her palms pressed against the table as she leaned heavy on it. I could feel the weight of this room. She pulled at a drawer and slid a small, white box across the tabled towards me.

"It's best we don't lose anything through translation," she said.

I opened it to find a small triangular device, not much bigger than a ring for one's finger, about as thick too. It was weighty in my palm, but one side seemed to stick to my skin without leaving any residue.

"Place it behind your ear," she explained. I did so, sticking the device behind my ear. A small buzz filled my head for a moment, then the feedback settled.

"What does it do?" I asked. A buzz came from the device, playing words louder than my own voice spoke. It sounded like Elysian, but it also sounded like me. It carried a different accent than I had heard others speak, something closer to my own. The buzz felt like the words were playing from the device, but also from my own mouth at the same time. It was a bizarre feeling, and made my tongue feel odd.

"It's a translator." Mel spoke with a different accent, her words more swooping and ornate, similar to how the Elysians spoke in their own language. Yet it was still distinctly Mel.

Ata's eyes widened. "I didn't know such a thing even existed."

The inflection of her voice was the same as it had been when she spoke Elysian, but somehow it translated her words to English without losing an ounce of her personality. She leaned close to me, analyzing the device and speaking into it loudly.

"Is it working? Can you understand me?" Her voice boomed into my head painfully.

"Yes, I can understand you!" I leaned away from her face with a wince. "You have a wonderful voice."

She waved a dismissive hand with a smirk, clicking her tongue and shaking her head. "That thing can't hardly convey the majesty of me."

Mel cleared her throat, covering a flustered look with a fist over her mouth. What had flustered her in the first place? "Can we focus please?"

Her tone seemed to be entirely business, but I could hear the melodies beneath her breath. Jealousy of my attention elsewhere, I realized. I didn't know whether to be offended, honored, or uncomfortable.

"Yes, please. I'm all ears."

The Elysians all looked at me oddly.

"It's an expression," I mumbled awkwardly.

Mel waved a hand at the three of us. "Look, I don't mean to be hurtful, but you three are...not the diplomatic type. You two are trained soldiers only ever taught to say 'yes sir', and you look for any reason to punch someone or give them a reason to punch you."

I pursed my lips. "See you say you don't mean to be hurtful but..."

"The point is, this isn't a fight, not by fists anyways. We're battling through words, facts, and logic. Like any court, there are people to be convinced, but instead of a selection of the people like you humans do, we're appealing to the most powerful people on that planet with the most to lose. They're royals, but they're all about business. They don't take unnecessary risks, they don't lose something unless it makes a profit, and they most certainly are not charitable. If I'm being completely honest, there isn't exactly much reason to keep the humans alive at all." Mel winced at her own words. "In their eyes, I mean."

"You are making this sound impossible," Theseus said.

Mel's hands smacked down hard on the table. "We need to be…realistic here. These people don't bend to emotion, they aren't convinced by wiles and whimsy. They won't see the beauty in human life, the way each person lives individual, powerful, important lives. The way every person carries passion and love for something in their hearts, for good or bad. They bend only to what profits them, and that is war."

"How can we know if we don't try?" Ata asked.

"Because I'm one of them " Mel's hands were fists against the table now, head hung low, hair in front of her face. She looked up at me through her brow, through the locks of her hair. I could see the shine of tears upon her eyes. "They can't see those things about our own people, how are they to see that about humans? Elysians and humans aren't hardly different at all. We're all full of love and passion and care. We all fight to become the best version of ourselves, even when the world tries to break us.

"Kindness persists, it finds a way. But they don't see that. They see pawns ready to follow orders, to be sacrificed at the drop of the hat if it meant their benefit. I know this because I thought this way once…I was this way once. Maybe that part of me still lives, and maybe I'll never atone for all those who I've wronged…but my family has done terrible, awful, horrible things. If they hate me, it means I'm doing something right. Now I'm either going to try to save even the few lives I can or die trying, and damn it I'm going to try."

Her voice cracked on the final word. Emotions strained her, physically and mentally, and it showed in her voice. The taps of tears running off Mel's nose was all that could be heard, followed by the sniff of her choking back her emotions. She ran a hand through her hair, her brow furrowed in utter anguish.

"Saying I'm sorry will never be enough, and nothing I do can replace the lives myself and my parents and my parents' parents have ruined. I deserve all the punishment in the world, but all I can do is try."

I reached a hand across the table, placing it on Mel's tense fist. Her muscles softened at the touch, melting into my palm like a glacier rejoining the sea. Her gaze softened as she met my gaze. I could see a lifetime of pain in her eyes, as if she had opened her eyes to find blood on her hands.

"I forgive you," I said. "For what it's worth."

Theseus's hand landed atop my own. "I forgive you too."

Our eyes slid to Ata, who stood with shoulders bunched. Her face was bunched like a brutal pain had come to meet her. She shook her head, hard. "My sister was assassinated by that southern warlord bastard." Her hand smacked down atop of ours. "But I forgive you. All of you."

Something between a sob and a laugh escaped Mel, squeezing her eyes so tight that more tears ran down her face. "I don't deserve you all."

"It's not about what we deserve, it's about grace. We're giving you our forgiveness, that's all that matters." I squeezed her fingers tightly. She weakly squeezed back. "Now let's do this. You only have a few hours to turn me into a diplomat, we can't waste a second."

～ ～ ～

Engineering, thermodynamics, astrophysics, and quantum theory look like child's play when compared to understanding people. In the lesson I had hoped would ease my nerves and give me confidence, I gained only a newfound hatred for politics and the realization that I simply do not understand people. My head buzzed like a toy with dying batteries as we made way for the door. Ata tried to speak to me, but her words went into one ear and out the other. Hazy minded, I followed Theseus and Mel out the door, but Ata stopped me. I turned to see her handing me a glass of cold water, which I gratefully took a long swig of.

"Thank you." I gasped as the cold liquid woke me up from my diplomacy induced stupor.

"I won't have you floundering now, not after all that jabbering," Ata mumbled.

"Helmet on," Theseus said, gesturing for the door. Ata complied, not before making a mocking face and snickering to herself. The helmet hissed as it sealed shut around her head. I could see my own face in the dark reflection, I thought of the soldiers who had tried to kill me just hours before. Seeing it made me sick to my stomach.

"Oh, Apollo, wait." Mel walked up to me and began messing with my hair. She squinted hard as she tried to make some semblance of sense with my unruly curls. Her frustration was quick and evident.

"Now you see why I don't bother," I shrugged. She sighed, admitting defeat and running a finger along my eyebrows to straighten them out. I suddenly became very self conscious about my eyebrows.

"We must hurry, it will start soon," Theseus said.

"One last thing, I swear." Mel stepped towards Ata, fumbling with her collar for a moment at Ata's confusion. She stepped away then moved to Theseus. I could see that she had changed the clasp on Ata's collar from black to pink. Mel did the same with Theseus. "I'm sorry it isn't more regal but…you are officially a part of my guard, even if just for today. If you wish to stay, I can make it so. But at least for today, you will be one of my personal guardians."

Theseus touched the clasp on his collar, hand slightly trembling. I could hear the smile creeping into his voice. Like a childhood dream coming true. "T-Thank you."

We followed him out, past the guards outside, and into the elevator, rising upwards. When the door opened, I could see that we were at the top of the castle, likely the highest floor of the tallest building in all of Elysia from what I could tell. Of course the shallow royals would want to be high above all the people. We all stepped out, making quick turns to the right and walking past the elevators, stomping into a large waiting room. A massive set of ornate doors stood on the far wall, carved benches lining the walls to our sides. Upon the large door, the constellations were carved. Almost the same as on Earth. All those stars are so many light years out, even the thousands of miles between Elysia and Earth only make the slightest difference compared to the pictures in our skies.

My stomach knotted as the doors began sliding open, slowly. As the gap widened between us and fate, I could see the court we were to face. The room was massive, tall and long. The walls were carved with depictions of Elysians, likely ancient kings and queens. They all wore ornate cloaks or dresses, all of their hands holding a scepter and orb. The walkway down the center of the room was raised above lowered sections on either side, the stairs beside the entrance suggesting them to be standing room for crowds to witness tradition. There was no audience for this, so my death would be quiet if necessary.

We marched down the long walkway, approaching the far end of the room. Stairs lead up to a raised platform. Atop it was a tall throne, the back of the seat at least ten feet tall at its apex. Long hexagonal pillars jutted from the ground in a variety of heights to create the odd design. Naturally, The Queen sat atop the throne, a majestic dress draped down its steps. The geometric pattern of her dress crawled from below her feet to the top of her collar, head tilted sideways as she looked down at me. Behind her and her throne, box seating jutted from the wall high above us; pillars sticking out from the wall to hold up the hexagonal platforms which held many different people. I counted six total, adding up to the seven sovereigns of Elysia. Six rulers of six continents, one queen who ruled them all, that's what Mel taught me. Three men, three women, all dressed in black and pink. One of them was Ermis, staring down at me with murderous eyes and with arms folded.

Their poisonous gazes bore into my chest as I stood helplessly at the steps of the throne, hands folded in front of me as if chained together. It felt appropriate somehow, as if being chained was better than freedom in the presence of authority. I bowed my head along with the others, saluting in the way they taught me. I tapped my heart with two fingers, then my forehead, then held my hand out towards them. Same way I had watched many Elysians salute.

The Queen sat up straight and rolled back her shoulders. "This court is now in session, in the presence of all seven sovereigns of Elysia. The princess shall step away and await her testimony and questioning, along with her guard."

Mel, Theseus, and Ata stepped away from me, leaving me alone at the foot of the almighty. I bowed a head once more and drew a deep breath. Confidence is a pivotal piece of diplomacy, as Mel had taught me. Whether genuine or not, I would hold my head high when possible and humble myself when necessary.

"May the Titans will be upon me, and let the conclusion of this court see to their great justice." The Queen spoke with eyes closed, reciting something written on the slate of her heart.

The Titans, those ancient ancestors of the Elysians who are believed to have come from the stars and settled on Elysia. They're seen as both founders of Elysia as a whole, but also deities of sorts. Speaking ill of their name is considered blasphemy, and the main religion present in Elysian culture revolved entirely about those mysterious ancient beings whose will is believed to still be echoed through the royal line. The royals are the closest blood relatives to the Grand Titan Dias, first king of Elysia, who led the many children of the Titans into an era of prosperity and glory. Queen Kore was one of those many kings and queens, the purest in blood of all Elysians, seen as a goddess of sorts who is praised and worshiped in temples all throughout Elysia. Whether she liked it or not, Mel was too, a child goddess who was destined to rule the planet one day. In this way, religion and state were one in the same, and by the will of the Titan's, all justice and injustice was performed.

The Queen began the formalities. I could not tell whether she held distaste for these menial questions or for me; the answer was likely both. "Please state your name, family name, age, and place of birth."

"Apollo Harrison, twenty five, born in New Seattle, Washington on Earth, Your Majesty." I spoke clearly, confidently, and decisively. Mel had warned me of this preamble question, so I was prepared.

"Elaborate on that. Earth." Queen Kore said.

"Earth is...the third planet from the star of the Sol system. New Seattle is a city, in the state of Washington, on the continent of North America, Your Majesty."

The Queen raised an eyebrow at me. I felt myself shrinking back into myself, but I refused to do so. I cleared my throat, rolled my shoulders back, and nodded.

"Tell me, do all humans look like you?" Her brow was bunched in a look of vague disgust.

"N-No, Your Majesty. My father was an Earthling, my mother a Martian. I inherited her hair and his skin, if you will...Your Majesty." So much for confidence and decisiveness. The question of my lineage was likely to come up, but not supportive of my case. Bloodline is very important to Elysians, according to Mel.

"Tell me, son of Harris, why is it that your hair is blue?" A woman's voice echoed from one of the stands behind The Queen. I winced at what they called me, almost needing to fight back a laugh.

"The first settlers on Mars were exposed to the high levels of cobalt in the sands. It turned their hair and eyes blue, Your Sovereignty." A murmur of confusion came from them.

"The first settlers on Mars, who were they?" Another voice came from the wall, a man this time.

"Humans, from Earth. It was the first planet we colonized, Your Sovereignty." Amongst humans, which planet you came from was very important. Both a source of identity and social credit. Here, it seemed all humans were simply humans, all equally easy to crush.

"When did you begin to colonize the system?" The Queen asked now.

"About four hundred years ago now, Your Majesty. We've expanded to other systems now, successfully planting in four different systems." A gasp came from the sovereigns, murmurs of discontent echoing around me. I wished I could swallow my words down again.

"You have conquered four systems now?" The Queen continued, leaning forward in her chair.

"I wouldn't say conquered." I placed my hands behind my back and weaved my fingers together. "The planets we've colonized have all been uninhabited. Aside from the occasional virus, no life has been found on any planet we've discovered...until now. Your Majesty." I regretted my words again, more murmurs rising.

"I will have silence in my court or else." The Queen pinched the bridge of her nose and sighed, the murmurs dying immediately. "Tell me, do your people know about us?"

I thought about it for a moment. "Not for certain. Your planet has been...a theory, for many years, hundreds of years. Some people are...led to believe you exist, after seeing Mel, but nobody can know for sure. Aside from me, Your Majesty." I laughed nervously at my own joke at the end. The court did not find it entertaining.

"Start from the beginning, how did you find my daughter?" The Queen pressed the tips of her fingers together, leaning closer to hear my story.

"From the beginning, right." Fear welled in my throat. I gulped it down, cleared my throat, and nodded. "I was orbiting around Jupiter one day when I received a distress signal from out of system. I made a jump to the system Proxima Centauri where I found a shipwreck on a planet we call Zion. I didn't find anyone else alive but her, stranded in a pod that had depressurized. I assumed she was dead, but to my surprise, she woke up. I brought her to my ship and went to cash out on answering the distress call when..."

The Queen squinted, concentrating her deathly glare sharper into my chest. "Don't bother lying, I'll know. Continue."

"She didn't remember her name. At least, not her family name. She didn't have any identification, no record anywhere, a complete ghost. I didn't get my pay because of it so I might have been a bit...rude." The very words shot pain down my spine, like The Queen might snap my neck for that alone. "I was childish, and immature, but then some men tried to hurt her. They thought she was half-blood, someone with parents from two different planets, someone like me. They don't particularly like us. I protected her to the best of my ability, with the help of a friend, Officer Sintara. She's a peacekeeper amongst humans, at least she used to be. Sinatra was the second person to meet Mel, followed by my older sister, Wendy. We tried to help Mel together but ran into some...trouble."

"You will address her as the princess." The Queen declared.

"Right, I apologize. For whatever reason, the government wanted the princess, and they wanted to capture me for helping her. We ran, but they assigned the best assassin in our galaxy. He shot us down, we landed on Earth, and sought refuge with another human. To our luck, he was a scientist, one who studied the theory of your planet. He believed he knew where the princess had come from. He helped us, we escaped the assassin, and went back to the crash site. We tried to find more information, find a way to bring her back here, but there was an explosion. We were attacked, and I..." My eyes closed on their own, trying to blink away the visions of what I have done. "I killed the assassin, to protect her. But we were separated, the humans imprisoned the princess. The humans tried to make a deal with me, that they would forgive my crimes if I'd renounce any knowledge of the princess and Elysia. I refused. With my sister's help, we broke her out. We were going to bring her back here when we were intercepted by the Hades. I think you know the rest after that."

A quiet had settled over the court, though I felt tension. I could feel the sovereigns holding back their questions, waiting for The Queen to allow them. The Queen only watched me, analyzing me with wizened eyes.

"Tell me, why exactly would you do all this for my daughter? It's clear you humans aren't the benevolent kind, you wouldn't have saved her in the first place if you didn't know it meant money for you. But even after you were not repaid for your work, you continued to protect. After you lost everything, after you were hunted, you protected her. Even when you failed to protect, you still sacrificed everything to see her safely home. Why?"

Why? How am I to explain why I would do something so illogical through reason? How am I to explain that I would give up my life just to hear her laugh, to see her smile, just one more time? How am I to explain that knowing she is safe makes my whole life feel like it has meaning? How am I to explain that being with her feels like I can breathe again?

"Honestly, your honor...I don't have a good answer for that."

"Try." Her voice was sharp. It cut the air, bore into my stomach. If words could make someone bleed, I'd be drowning in red where I stand.

"I—Well...I did it because she's my...friend. I did it because she had nobody else to protect her. I did it because she needed somebody, anybody, and nobody else was going to do it. I did it because she needed me, and maybe I needed her. More than riches or status or safety, she has always been more important to me."

The Queen's curiosity was piqued. "So you would sacrifice anything, even your own life, for her?"

I nodded. "I could not die without knowing for absolute certain that she would be safe forever. If my death meant her protection, I would welcome it with open arms."

Her sharp words were softened now. "You love her?"

"I do. So much that I would do anything if I knew it meant her happiness, even if it meant a lack of my presence in her life, I would watch from a distance with a smile."

There is no logic to love, to care, to kindness. There is no reason behind sacrificing yourself for another. There is no benefit to losing oneself to gain another. This was poetry, it was philosophy, thousands of years of human hearts connected, united in pain. Love is agony, love is sacrifice, but love is worth it. Love from the heart is blind, but love from the heart, mind, and soul is reckless and powerful.

The Queen leaned her head on her hand. "I have one last question for you: do you think humans are worth protecting? You've been wronged by them, hunted by them, what makes them worth protecting to you?"

Evil bubbled in my mind. Every instance of bullying, prejudice, and hatred. The vitriol they hold for me, the bounty they put on my head, pitchfork and torch raised against me, against my sister, against my family. An evil part of me wanted to watch it all burn, to warm my hands on the flames of their destruction. With a simple word, I could make it happen. A mere glimpse of power already corrupted my heart.

"Yes, Your Majesty. I believe humans are worth protecting. Humans make mistakes, humans can be driven by hate, by jealousy, by envy, but they're also driven by love. Humans nearly destroyed the planet they came from, more than once, and yet their determination kept it alive. Their willpower, their devotion, humans simply refuse to die. Our history is lined with war and destruction, but generations are remembered for the beauty of what they created. Grand societies, beautiful cities, masterful works of art. Music, poetry, novel, cinema, humans have an intrinsic desire to create that which holds beauty. They seek to create homes, start families, and raise children. Being human means to face darkness and respond with beauty, those who fail to do so have…lost their way."

"Humans refuse to die?" The Queen reiterated.

"The human spirit is powerful." I couldn't help the faintest of smiles that pulled at my lip. "Our will to survive is unparalleled. We most certainly won't go quietly, Your Majesty."

"Hm." The Queen thought on my words, turning them over in her mind. "I've heard enough. Step away, Princess Melinoe is to be a witness."

I bowed deeply, head hung low. My feet carried me to Theseus, keeping my eyes low as I came to his side. Mel stepped forward now, coming to the foot of the stairs. Theseus elbowed me and whispered.

"What happened to facts and logic?"

"How can anyone get that existential and not be abstract?" I whispered back.

"Princess Melinoe Ouranos, you stand not at trial, but as a witness to the human called Apollo Harrison. You are not accused of any crime, nor under threat of any punishment, but here to assure that all which has been said about humans is true. Do you understand?" The Queen seemed pained to do this, as if forcing her daughter to relive the horror would cause her more pain than ever.

Mel replied with a nod, fingers intertwined behind her back. "I understand."

"Is it true that Apollo Harrison saved your life on the planet Zion?"

"Yes."

"Is it true that Apollo Harrison treated you disrespectfully?"

She hesitated. "Yes, though he did not know my status."

"One might hope he'd pay everyone with equal respect." The Queen scoffed, then waved a dismissive hand. Mel's hands tightened in a ball at The Queen's words. "Is it true that he defended you from an assailant?"

"Yes, two of them."

"Is it true that he sought to assist you in recovering your memories?"

"Yes. He gave me safety, gave me food, gave me clothes."

"Is it true that he murdered someone?"

Silence, for a moment. Mel's teeth were half gritted now. "It is true that he defended his own life with equal force that threatened him."

"More force, considering he still lives."

"He did what was necessary to protect me."

"And yet it was not enough. Is it true that you were imprisoned by the humans for a time?"

Mel didn't want to say it, she wished she didn't have to, I could see it in her eyes. "Yes."

"Did the humans abuse you during this time?"

"Absolutely not." Her voice rose for a moment, anger threatening to boil over. She stopped, drew herself back. "They treated me fairly. I was left alone in my cell, except by one man who came to speak with me. A reporter and diplomat of sorts. He came to speak to me only hours before Apollo saved me."

The Queen's curiosity arose. So did my own. Mel had not mentioned anyone speaking to her at the prison, and I knew who it must be: David Marshall. The Queen leaned forward once more, eyes analyzing for information. "What did this man say to you?"

"He seemed to know I was from another planet, said he'd spoken to…the scientist we spoke to on Earth. He said he would offer communication between our people and the leaders of the humans if I accepted his terms."

"Those terms were?"

"To...forget I'd ever met Apollo. To never speak to him or any other human I'd met again. He said if I did so, they would all be kept safe. But I could hear it in his voice, the threat against them was him. He meant to promise not to hurt them if I accepted. I...believed I could protect them better myself, so I refused."

"Why?"

"I had a bad feeling about it."

"You made that decision off of instinct?"

"There were not enough facts available to make a logical choice, so I had to act decisively. All I had was my gut. That is what you taught me."

The Queen rolled her eyes. "Is it true that Apollo Harrison rescued you from this prison?"

"Yes, at the risk of life and limb. He was severely wounded in the process, it was a miracle he survived."

"Perhaps he shouldn't have," The Queen mumbled under her breath. "I have only one question left for you, daughter. Do you believe human lives are worth protecting?"

"Yes. I believe that humans have something unique to them, different from Elysians. Something that makes them a force to be reckoned with."

"And that is?"

"The ability to grow, to adapt, to overcome difficulty. We have only ever followed tradition, for thousands and thousands of years. Humans live only by the desire to know more, to do more, to see more, to expand, to improve their lives. They aren't limited by tradition or rules or even laws of the universe. No matter what, humans find a way...and I think that makes them a danger to us, because we may very well lose." Mel brought her hands in front of her, staring deep into the space between her hands with brow furrowed. "Never in my life have I seen someone so...determined. That no matter what he encountered it could not stop the force of his passion, his strength, his ability. The humans terrify me, for they bear an indomitable will, and an unbreakable spirit. Wherever a human exists, hope thrives. They may bleed rivers, break like glass, or fall like a mighty tower, and yet they always get back up. It's as if they are immortal..." Mel's eyes met my own. "At least, he may be."

Murmurs arose, the court began to dissolve at the idea. Mel's conviction had convinced them, what she claimed to have seen terrified them. I could not see such a thing in myself, and yet that look in her eyes told me she believed it. That what she had seen from me was supernatural in some way. It was awe, wonder, and love.

"I propose a final verdict," Mel spoke over the murmuring court. "We must ally with the humans. There is much to gain in a partnership with them. We need not share every aspect of our lives, but to establish political agreements that we might prevent a galactic war. We must communicate with the humans, to make a peace treaty with them."

Murmurs arose again, but The Queen raised her hand for only a moment. It fell silent again. The Queen sighed, staring deep into her daughter's eyes with that which can only be described as disappointment. Mel shriveled at the sight, hanging her head low.

"A vote will now be cast, majority rules. If the vote passes, the humans will be protected, and we will decide the best way of negotiating with them." Her voice was flat as a stone.

The light flickored off. Darkncoo owallowcd us whole in an instant. Tense, deep, palpable silence. I could feel Theseus's hand on my shoulder. A light switched on, illuminating one of the six platforms on the wall. An older woman with frightened eyes stood there. Moments passed, another light, this one over a younger woman. More seconds passed at a snail's pace, then a third light, a thin man with large glasses. Finally, another light, illuminating a tall woman with broad shoulders. Ermis's platform did not illuminate, nor the one beside him. Nor did the Queen's.

"The court has ruled in favor of the humans."

The lights turned back on now.

"This meeting is now adjourned. More negotiations amongst the sovereigns will be held to ensure a proper course of action." The Queen's tired, disappointed eyes met my own. "Your kind gets to live another day. Celebrate that, and pray we do not change our minds."

↵ 20 ↵

Styx

Our bodies felt weightless as we crashed down into the soft plush of the seating in Mel's living space. However uncertain, we were relieved to have survived the court. Throwing my jacket off, I slipped my arms free from the sleeves of my jumpsuit. I tied them around my waist and concealed my rattling belt, covered in its assortment of devices. I had practically sweat through the shirt underneath, not to my surprise. My arms felt like noodles as I laid deep into the cushions, laying my head back exhaustedly. Mel landed beside me, sitting stiff as a board. I thought she'd be more relaxed to have that said and done. Ata stretched out over a couch opposite of me, leaning her head over to one side with a long sigh.

"All your talking made even me stressed, glad that's over," she said.

"You were not even the one whose life was at stake." Theseus added before crashing down next to her, leaning forward on his legs while rubbing at his head.

I couldn't help the smile that pulled at my tired face. "You were worried about me? I'm flattered."

"I always cheer on the little guy, that's why I stick by Theseus's side." She patted him on the back, to which he swatted at her hand with a grumpy look.

"For the record, I had no doubt in you," Theseus said.

"Liar, you were jabbing me about my lack of facts and logic the second I stepped out of the spotlight!" My voice was louder than I had intended it to be.

Ata threw up her hands with a shrug. "Hey, none of us had perfect hope after you started prattling about love and stuff."

My cheeks warmed at the words, to which Ata laughed and Theseus gave a chuckle. Ata leaped to her feet and began rummaging around the room. She found four small glasses sitting on a tray beside an ottoman and pulled a flask from a pocket on her side.

"Seriously?" Theseus said at the sight of the shiny metal.

"Thought I might pour one out for the little guy if it didn't go well, or celebrate if it did go well." She proceeded to fill the cups with an opaque brown liquid with a distinct smell. She filled the last cup, notably less, and handed it to me.

I raised an eyebrow at the glass. "Really? That's hardly half a shot."

She smirked. "This is fine Elysian liquor, a full shot would knock you out for a week. It's probably double as strong as what you humans can make, or more."

I grumbled and pondered her words looking at the murky glass and giving it a whiff. It burned my nose just to smell, my head pulled away by mere instinct. Perhaps she was right, but I still wanted the challenge. My eyes slid to Mel, who swirled the glass in her hand and pondered her reflection in it.

Ata raised her glass high as she handed the other to Theseus. "Here's to the hero of the hour, Apollo. Unto death!"

"Unto death," Theseus raised his own.

Mel and I repeated, then downed the drink. It burned the whole way down, it tasted like cinnamon, toasted nuts, and smoke. I couldn't suppress a cough that arose from me. Ata smacked me on the back and took my glass before I had the chance to drop it. My head spun as I tried to swallow away the burn

"Okay, you were right," I rasped.

Ata shrugged. "Always am, you'll learn that soon enough."

The fog in my head made it easy to shake away the comment. I leaned back and looked over to Mel. "So, what do we do now?"

"We wait for orders," she said softly.

I nodded slowly. "Alright. Are you, uh…okay?"

"Just tired from the trial," she mumbled.

She stood up instantly, walking away with a quickened pace. Everyone was silent as she disappeared down the hall and into a room, presumably her own. My gut twisted with guilt as we all sat there, quietly. A sigh escaped me before Ata cleared her throat.

"Well?" Ata said plainly.

"Well what?" I replied.

"Aren't you gonna go to her?"

"I…I want to, but she wants quiet, doesn't she?"

Ata sighed, grumbling a few words too quiet for my translator to hear. "You men, I'll never understand your denseness. Her heart is heavy because of what you said, you need to go to her."

"She's right," Theseus said with a nod.

"How do you know?"

Ata smirked. "I told you, I'm always right. Now go, she needs you."

My legs wobbled beneath me as I shot to my feet. The room spun around me as I made my way down the hall and to the door I had watched her enter. I looked down at the white floor beneath me, trying to gather my words. But how could I know what to say if I didn't even know what I had said to make her upset? I fiddled with my nails, trying to think of something, anything. Nothing. I simply knocked.

"Who is it." She spoke in monotone, not in the question of expecting nor wanting a visitor.

"It's me," I said. It was a stupid way of saying it, but she knew my voice, at least I hoped she would. Seconds passed before the door slid open.

Her whole room was pink; or some shade of light red. There was carpet on the floor here, it looked soft, fluffy, and perfectly clean. I kicked off my shoes before stepping inside, the plush comfy against my tired feet. There was a desk in a corner to my left, beside a large bookshelf. On the back corner to my left, the entrance to a bathroom. Beside that, a thin door was left open with a walk-in closet inside. Her fancy clothes had been abandoned on the floor, boots sitting beside the door.

On the right wall, two large windows framed space for a bed, but the bed had been pushed to the side so that it sat parallel to the cold glass. I could tell by the lack of imprints in the carpet that she had always liked it like this. The bed was larger than my own, a veil draped around it on tall poles. Its pink fabrics contrasted the dark window behind it, and through the veil I could see the outline of Mel, bundled in the messy blankets of the bed and looking out the window. Snow trickled down from the sky and landed peacefully against the window, melting into long drops of water running streaks down the glass. My feet came to the foot of the bed, pulling the veil aside only an inch or so.

"May I?" I asked.

She nodded. I climbed atop the bed and sat down beside her. The blankets were warm, but the window was cold. I could see the city far below, the brightest star in the sky beginning its descent towards the horizon. Its light was only barely enough to distinguish night from day, an eternal twilight of sorts.

"Are you okay?"

"I am now." She pulled the blankets tighter. I could see through the gap that she was wearing her human clothes, the ones Wendy gave her. Perhaps they gave her as much comfort as my own did. "Do you really love me?"

A nervous laugh escaped me. "Well, I wouldn't exactly lie to your mother, she could kill me with a look."

"I'm serious, Apollo."

I sighed. "Yes, of course I do. I don't know how anyone can go through everything we have without falling in love."

Mel gave a small laugh at my bluntness, sniffing as her joy faded to sorrow again. "You don't even know me."

"How so?"

"You don't know the things I've done. All the people I hurt, the people I took advantage of, the people who suffered at my hand."

"Then tell me so I can love you anyways."

Mel glanced at me with glassy eyes, a moment of quiet before she spoke. "My mother rules the planet, but I was given this city to rule. It was a show of my ability to lead, to rule with dignity and assurance. This castle, this city, it was all mine to rule, so that I might learn how to govern the whole planet. I made many terrible mistakes."

"Like what?"

"I made a decision about controlling the weapons in the city, and crime skyrocketed. More people died from firearms than ever before. It took me months to rid the illegal arms trade from the city. In the end, the same amount of people were hurt as was before, only by different means. I tried to limit alcohol within city boundaries, but it only made people desire it more. I gave up after only a year. I tried to cut back on gambling, the people rioted. Tried increasing law enforcement in low income areas, it just led to more arrests."

"It sounds like you had good intentions," I said.

"I didn't. I just wanted to show I could rule them, that I could impose anything upon my subjects without remorse. People were hurt, I failed, and I never felt regret."

"You don't sound like you don't regret it."

She sunk into her blankets further. "I didn't, until I met you. Until I saw how the lowest of society were treated. The way they're treated by the law, by the people, by their friends and family. For once, I wasn't in my ivory tower. I was one of the people, and I was suffering. All because of people like me, because of the person I didn't know I was."

"You've changed, for the better. It will take some work to fix things, but that doesn't mean it will be in vain."

She shook her head, unsure of any of this. Her voice warbled, she had truly lost hope. "How can I convince the people I've changed?"

I drew in a deep breath, and shrugged. "Go talk to them. Be amongst the people. Shake their hands, learn their stories. Listen to them. Be one of them. Maybe make a few of them your friends, people who have lived in the pain. Learn from the people, not the statistics."

Mel gave a laugh at my suggestion, I didn't think it was all that ridiculous. "Why would they want to help me?"

"Because their love for their home far outweighs their hatred for your mistakes. And when they get close to you, they'll see you're not the same."

Mel's head hung lower. "How could you know? You only love who you think I am. You never knew the person I was."

"Maybe not...but I don't care."

"How can you not care?! How can you not care how horrible I was?" Her voice shot through me like a bullet. Her sharp gaze met my own, but it was not anger inside her eyes, it was remorse.

"Because you saw how horrible I was, and you still saved me."

Her face softened at the pain in my own eyes. "It was...the least I could do for all the trouble you put yourself through for me."

"It meant more to me than you'll ever know. In the last few years, I've never had someone to watch my back. I was only ever on my own until you came along, and you brought me closer to my sister, to my parents, to my friend again. I was in pieces, you helped put me back together again."

"You threw your life away for me..."

"And I'd do it again, so long as it meant you were safe." My lips curled into a smile at the thought, Mel safe. It was all I wanted now. "If after all this, we part ways and I never get to see you again, knowing you for even a brief moment will have been worth the pain of saying goodbye, so long as it meant you were safe."

It was silent for a moment, then a punch to my shoulder made me jump. I fell back in surprise, looking up to see Mel throwing off the blankets and towering over me on her knees, anger painting her face.

"That's exactly my point! I hate hearing you say that, it isn't fair! You offer to throw away your life, to sacrifice yourself, but you never offer to do what I actually want you to do!"

I was hopelessly confused. "And what's that?"

"Stay with me. Help me. I can't do this alone, Apollo!" She threw a wild hand towards the window, gesturing at the whole city, the whole planet. "I need someone to help me figure it all out. I need someone to help me through the pain of learning. I need...I need you. I don't need you to throw your life away and sacrifice yourself, I need YOU!"

Her body was tense as she fell back into her bundle of blankets. Tears, like snow melting down the window, ran down her face. She sniffed hard, rubbing at her eyes with the back of her hands.

"I didn't put up with you for all that time just for you to leave after I fell in love with you," she said.

A pain shot through my heart as realization hit me. My promises of sacrifice, my oaths of giving it all for her, they didn't comfort her, they pained her. Who would want the person they love to promise they'd die for them? If it meant to live the rest of their life without the person they loved, it was no promise of comfort, it was a promise of torture.

"I'm sorry, Mel, I was just-"

Her face bunched again as one last tear ran down her face. She pushed her wild hair out of her face, looking down at me with pained eyes. A frustrated blush arose on her cheeks, eyes tinted pink from crying. Her hair billowed around her like a halo of pink. Even through her tears, she was beautiful."Promise me you'll stay. Promise me we'll stay by each other's side just like we have all the time we've known each other. Say it."

"I promise. Mechri thanatou. Until death, I will be by your side." I held out my little finger to her, which she looked at with curiosity. I took her hand and intertwined our fingers. "Pinky promise."

A half laugh, half sob escaped her. "Pinky promise?"

I smiled. "It's the greatest form of a human promise."

I bobbed our hands up and down a few times, Mel laughed. My fingers closed around hers, I had never noticed her hands were bigger than my own. But my hands were rough from years of working on machines, and hers soft from years of reading books. Her lip still quivered as a smile arose on her face as she looked at our hands, then a curious look at me.

"So, what does that mean exactly? 'Pinky promise.'"

"I think it means if I break the promise you get to cut off my finger," I said plainly, half certain of my understanding.

"What?!" Her face switched in an instant, shocked and horrified by the prospect.

"I'm kidding! Mostly..." I couldn't help a laugh, turning myself back towards the window. The star in the sky was lower now, casting a slanted light over the city that forced large shadows over the streets below. I could barely see the streets now. "It's beautiful."

Mel came to rest beside me again. "It's more beautiful now that I can see everyone who lives in it."

"And for now, it's safe. Because of you, I might add."

She scoffed. "For now."

She wrapped the blanket around both of our shoulders, leaning into me heavily. I could feel her breath rising and falling, her head on my shoulder. Her hair smelled of flowers. Her eyes peered at me through the strands of her hair, a gentle look of anticipation. My hand rose to her face, by some force unknown to me. My fingers melded to the curve of her cheek. My heart raced. I leaned closer to her.

A rumble shook the room. Both of our stomachs dropped. A flash of light could be seen on the streets below. Hasty knocks rapped at the door, we both scrambled to escape the confines of the blanket. The door opened just as our feet hit the ground, heads still dizzy from the alcohol and the intimacy. Theseus stood at the door, Ata behind him with her weapon prepared at her side. Both were ready for action.

"We have a problem," he said.

"Explosions not common around here?" I asked.

He spoke in Elysian now, speaking faster and clearer than he could with English. "There's been some kind of explosion down below, they're calling for all soldiers to respond to...something on the south side. They're calling it a riot."

"I suspect an attack," Ata mumbled. "I spotted a fleet of cruisers outside, circling the castle. They aren't responding to any radio calls; they've been hijacked."

Mel raised a hand. "Wait, do you hear that?"

Everyone silenced themselves, listening closely. Theseus closed his eyes and turned his head ever so slightly, Ata furrowed her brow and let her weapon slouch for a moment. I tried to force myself to hear something, anything, but I couldn't. Theseus snapped.

"Ata, the front door."

"On it," she said, ducking out of the room while raising the weapon to her shoulder.

Theseus looked up, listening close and taking careful steps around the room. "Both of you, backs against the wall by the door. If we need to run, be ready."

We obliged, and I pulled the weapon from my waistband. Theseus came to rest beside the window opposite of the bed, back pressed against the pink wall. His weapon hung at his side, ready to be raised in an instant. My body tensed as a head poked down from the top of the window. The helmeted head peered around the room, stopping as it locked onto us.

A shadow eclipsed the window as glass poured into the room. A soldier had rappelled through the window, landing on the floor with a slam. Theseus stepped forward and kicked out the knee of the soldier. A shout of pain was heard as he crumpled down, firing a few shots wildly past Theseus. Another smaller soldier dropped in, but Theseus was prepared. He dropped a hard kick into the chest of the soldier, sending him flying back out of the window with a terrified scream. The rope yanked taut and a crack could be heard. I hoped it was the glass below, rather than his bones.

The first soldier took hold of the rope he rappelled in on and wrapped it around Theseus's neck. The rope groaned under the weight, my feet pushed for me to save him, but in a swift move, the rope around his neck was cut, and his body lurched forward. The soldier was thrown over his head, tumbling out of the shattered window and falling with a long scream, ending as his breath ran out before the ground came to meet him. The following crack was surely his bones.

"Let's go," Theseus growled. We made a push for the door, but a soldier lunged from the opening. Theseus was tackled to the ground in an instant. The heavy body held him down to the ground, but I couldn't take time to observe it. Another soldier was already on us.

The soldier rushed me with a knife, but I pushed against Mel and fell back into her room. His knife scraped against the frame of the door, sparks glinting off the sheen of his armor; like villainous eyes scattered across his face. His knife took aim at us again, I kept myself in front of Mel. If he was going to get her, he would go through me. I raised my knife, he hesitated. For a moment, I thought he'd resign. Surely.

He flipped his knife in his hand, holding it by the tip of the blade. It shone in the light as he reached his arm high above his head. He was going to throw it, and moving meant it would bury itself in Melinoe's flesh. The knife was pulled from his fingers and ran across his throat. Blood poured onto the carpet at our feet as a gurgle bubbled from him. Theseus stood over him, staring angrily at me.

"You hesitated," he growled.

"I thought he…"

Theseus wiped a smear of blood from his lip with an angry grunt, speaking in Elysian. "You thought he'd give up? Resign? All because you also had a blade? Don't be stupid. It was your life or his; make the choice, and don't hesitate next time."

"I understand," I mumbled.

Ata stumbled in the room, her helmet on now. She was beaten, battered, and sliced, but she was still standing. I couldn't know how many she had fought off, but I was impressed regardless. "If they're here, they're other places in the castle. We need to move."

Mel spoke now, voice shaky. "My mother, is she okay?"

Ata held a hand to the side of her neck. "I haven't heard much from her guard, we need to find her."

I shook my head. The Queen wouldn't die so easily. "No, we'll get her. I need you two to go release Thirteen. If they're attacking the castle, they want to take it down. The lower we go the more enemies we'll find. We need to go up, it's safer there, for now. The elevators will stop working eventually, we're too high up, we'll never make it down in time without a ship. Mel and I will go find The Queen."

"That's great...what's a Thirteen?" Ata asked.

"My ship," I restated. "After the Hades, where did it end up?"

"The lab is a few floors down. The ship is still functioning, only its shell is stripped." Theseus knelt down next to the body in front of us, I gagged as my nose caught the overwhelming smell of blood. Theseus pulled off the helmet and turned the head to the side. "Look familiar?"

Ata's head drew back. "Timor? I thought he was stationed on The Hades. He's one of the insurrectionists?"

"Did he seem like one to you?" Theseus asked with a squint. The question concerned me, but I pushed it out of my head.

"There's no time for forensics, we need to move. Get to Thirteen, open the doors, and get in. You'll pick us up on the roof." I turned away from the body and raised my wrist to my mouth. "Thirteen, you're having visitors. Get the engines hot."

"The Queen's quarters are three floors up, the roof is three floors above that. Get moving, we'll meet you up there." Theseus stripped magazines off the body and slotted them into his vest, gesturing for us to follow. We stumbled through Mel's room, past half a dozen bodies that Ata had left behind. It sickened me, I'd never get used to it. We moved as a group towards the elevator as Theseus twisted the panel beside it in an odd way. Instead of the door of the elevator opening, it was a door that was flush with the wall beside it. Inside was a flight of stairs leading both up and down.

"Be safe," Mel said to Ata and Theseus, who nodded in reply. They began rushing down the steps, Theseus stopped just before exiting sight.

"Don't hesitate next time," he said seriously.

I nodded, but couldn't help a grimace. I didn't want to take another life, never again. But Theseus was right, I couldn't hesitate next time. Mel and I met eyes, a nod to one another before beginning our hike up the stairs. I felt confident after the first flight, then the second, then I realized that each floor was actually two flights of stairs tall. Three floors was actually six, and the stairs were made for people far taller than I. My breath heaved, my legs dragged.

"Keep moving, we're almost there," Mel said without any breath lost.

"Easy for you to say." I gasped for air.

We broke onto the landing of the stairs. My hands slapped hard onto my knees gasping for air. Mel took my wrist and pulled me through the doorway into the hallway.

"No time for rest!" She shouted.

As we rushed down the hall, we came to a massive doorway, the largest I had seen for one's quarters, with the door slid open. I took the lead, stepping forward into the room. A fist collided with my mouth and a foot kicked me over. I collapsed atop a body sticky with blood, gagging as I shoved myself off of it. The blood covered my hand, and the pain in my jaw disappeared as I fought the urge to faint. The assailant was over me now, but Mel took hold of their shoulders.

Her voice was harsh against my ears. "Mother, it's just Apollo!"

The Queen stopped, towering over me menacingly as she squinted. Her once perfectly white dress was now stained with a spray of red, a tear running down the gown that allowed her to move more freely. She was like a goddess of war, blood thirsty and ready to take mortal lives. If intimidation was her goal, it was surely working. "So it is."

"We came to save you, though it seems like you don't need it." I couldn't help but mumble from the pain in my jaw. I rubbed the side of my face with my clean hand, rubbing off my other on the carpet. "You punch very well, Your Majesty."

The Queen held a hand down towards me, I took it and she pulled me to my feet with ease. She dusted off my shirt and adjusted my collar, handing me a handkerchief for my still half-bloody hand. Her words were hesitant. "Thank you for coming to help me. It seems my guards traded their lives with the last of the attackers."

I pushed aside her lack of grief. "We need to get to the roof, my ship will pick us up there."

Her face tightened, her crow's feet accentuated by her disgust. "You want me to ride in a human ship?"

Mel's lips pursed. "Mother, might I remind you that we're being attacked? There is no other option."

"Fine, lead the way, daughter."

We left the lavish but bloodied room, back towards the stairs. My head fell back as I realized what I was in for again. The Queen and Mel moved faster than I ever could, even at the peak of my energy. In my exhaustion, I was falling behind faster than I should have.

A rumble shook the stairwell, some pulse rushing through the air that turned my stomach in a familiar way. The Queen stumbled from the feeling, Mel turning back to catch her mother.

"Are you alright?"

"What was that?" The Queen said with a hand over her likely nauseous stomach.

A terrifying thought sparked a fire in me, my energy returned in a flash. "I'm not sure...but I have a hypothesis."

I rushed past them and to the top floor, twisting the panel and opening the door to the roof. A cold wind surged over me, chilling me in an instant. I stepped out onto the hard concrete of the roof, a coating of snow over everything. The elevator and staircase were built into the base of a tall spire that continued high into the sky, a spike of glass that reached high into the air.

The roof was already massive, at least five hundred feet on each side, but a long landing pad stretched out from the building on the north side. The Queen and Mel began making their way for the landing pad, when another pulse ran up the building and over us. I was prepared for it this time, but The Queen fell hard.

Curiosity demanded I satiated my theory. I rushed to the south side of the building. My hands smacked against the cold of the railing, leaning over the edge and peering down at the city below. It was a horrifyingly far way down, my head spun at the sight. There was a ship crashed at the base of the castle, cracked open like a geode. The snap of gunfire and the screams of terror and warfare echoed through the city, and a bright blue light bled from the ship. A hypercore, it was overloading, and it was intentional. The ship was a bomb that the soldiers were protecting.

I turned and ran back to the north side, rushing up to Mel and the Queen. "We need to get out of here immediately!"

The Queen was leaning against one of the large floodlights that illuminated the landing pad, leaving us in a bright, obvious light. Mel stood beside her, a worried hand on her shoulder.

"What's going on down there?" Mel asked, failing to split her worry for her mother and the current situation equally.

"It's a ship." I panted for air. "It's...the hypercore."

"Just like on Zion," Mel mumbled. It felt like déjà vu.

I nodded. "We need to leave immediately."

The Queen pointed to the sky. "There, is that your ship?"

My eyes lifted high, tracking a ship soaring through the night sky. The lights on all sides were too bright for me to see the ship properly, but it was alight with flame. Massive gunshots cracked through the air, making the fire surge harder. Flames arced from its hull and lit the night sky. It began spiraling, careening down, down towards us.

It slammed down hard on the landing pad, shaking the floor beneath us. The landing pad shifted with a groan, and it tilted. The floor fell to an angle, taking The Queen off her feet immediately, sliding down the harsh angle. I didn't hesitate this time. I pulled the cable from the waist of my jumpsuit and clipped it onto Mel's belt, pushing her to the opposite side of the pole of the floodlight from me. Her feet fell out from under her and she was pulled against the pole harshly as I leaned into the ever growing slant of the collapsing landing pad. The Queen grasped for any way of slowing herself, her speed picking up quickly. I leaned into the slide, feeling the heat of the friction growing between my clothes and the concrete. The spool of my cable ran out and snapped tight, swinging me into The Queen violently. I grabbed onto her with all my might, my knuckles scraping against the stone as I wrapped around her. She screamed in terror as all came to a slow stop, leaving us swinging back and forth across the stone. She held onto the lapel of my jacket with an iron grip as my hand stickied with blood.

"Are you okay?!" I said louder than intended.

"Do I look okay to you?!" She shouted in my face.

"Just don't look down!" I recommended it, but she didn't listen to me and pulled herself closer.

"Get me down immediately!" She shouted into my chest.

The roar of a ship filled the air as floodlights poured over us. I looked up to find Thirteen hovering just above, a cable stretching down towards me. I held The Queen tight with one arm, hooking the cable to my belt. It began tightening, lifting me up to the open bay doors of the ship.

Theseus and Ata were at the ready, taking hold of my jacket and pulling both of us up with immense strength. We flopped onto the floor of the ship, but Mel's weight was already trying to pull me back out. Theseus and Ata pulled at the cable until Mel's hands took hold of the edge of the ship. They pulled her onto the floor of the ship and the bay door hissed as it lifted to close.

We sat in breathless quiet for a brief moment, The Queen trying to take herself to her feet, but her legs wobbled as she attempted. She pushed her loose hair out of her face and backed away from me. She spoke between shaky breaths. "You humans...are utterly...insane."

"How in the starry hells did that even work," Ata said.

My hands shook as I analyzed the damage, my knuckles torn up and bleeding. "I refuse to ever do anything like that ever again."

Mel wrapped her arms around me in a hug. "You saved us though."

"Welcome back, sir." Thirteen echoed through the ship. "Just like old times?"

"Just in the nick of time." An exhausted laugh escaped me, leaning heavy into Mel's hug. "I hate to say it, but I've never been more glad to see you, stupid robot."

↳ 21 ↲

Asphodel

It felt as though fire had sprung from my hand as Mel poured a waterfall of clear liquid over my fingers. My leg bounced in pain as I struggled to keep my hands from shaking. She slowly wrapped bandaged around my hands, intertwined between my fingers and anchored with a tight wrap on my wrist. She whispered something comforting, I couldn't tell if it was meant for me or herself. I wouldn't know, the words never fully reached my ears. My hands still shook as she finished, tying them off and holding them tight in the warmth of her grasp.

"I know it hurts," she mumbled into my hands, breathing a warm breath over them.

"I'll be okay," I nodded, pulling myself to my feet. The Queen sat on the couch to my right, watching us closely. Mel's face was only inches from mine; a warmth rose on the back of my neck. Mel pursed her lips, eyes darting to her mother for a moment before a laugh bubbled up. I nodded with a laugh of my own.

We walked carefully over the ever shifting floor and stood quietly beside Theseus who leaned heavily on a panel just beside an open hole in the side of the ship. He'd been taking and making radio calls for minutes at a time, constantly mentioning evacuation, fire, and assault. He was listening carefully to something, giving a nod when it finished.

I cleared my throat before I spoke, gazing out the window at the city passing by. "How's it looking out there?"

"It's getting worse. The castle is only half evacuated, a fire has broken out halfway up. Everyone above the medical wing is trapped."

Only the wind soaring past the ship could be heard for a moment, before a massive pulse rushed through the city and through us. Theseus steadied himself from the feeling, The Queen gave a groan, yet I hardly felt a thing. When I looked at Mel, she seemed unaffected as well.

"Then there's the elephant in the room." Theseus huffed a breath through his nose. "Whatever that ship is doing, it's making people sick. Some of the men suspect a chemical weapon, I don't."

I shook my head. "I know what it is. It's a hypercore. It's used to travel beyond the speed of light. It's overloading, and it's going to explode. They're trying to take the castle down."

"How so?"

I closed my eyes hard, a headache rising in me already. My class spent an entire year just understanding and studying the fine mechanics of the device, trying to explain how it functions in a few mere words was a near impossible task. "I'm an engineer, I've worked with them for years, and believe me when I say that it is going to be catastrophic."

Mel shuddered, her face looking haunted by the memories of Zion. "I've seen impossible things caused by a device like that."

"This one will be worse." I scratched at the scruff of my jaw. "What we saw was moving away from us in time. It was trying to move backwards, back to when it exploded somewhere in space. The light we saw was red because it was moving away from us, backwards in time. This light is blue because it's moving towards us, past us. Am I making any sense at all?"

Both of them held a look of utter confusion, wide eyes and shaking their heads slowly. I groaned, it was all too difficult to explain.

"The point is, that thing has a ton of energy. Enough to warp space and time, and it's getting stronger. Every one of those pulses means it's gathering more and more energy, until it can't handle the energy it's producing. Then it's going to...explode." I said the last word quietly so that The Queen might not hear.

"How bad would the damage be?" Theseus leaned towards me with a side eye on The Queen.

I spoke in nearly a whisper. "It's hard to say...but considering all of the skyscrapers here to knock down, the city won't be left standing."

Theseus and Mel mumbled a curse in Elysian that my translator refused to translate. Theseus held a hand over his mouth. "There's thirty million souls in this city."

That wasn't all there was to it, not to Theseus. I could see it in his eyes, he was terrified. I had seen the ruthlessness in him, I could see a new thought bubbling to the surface. His family still lived in the city, and he wanted to go save them. He caught my look, seeing that I knew his thoughts. I shook my head. He drew in a deep breath and nodded with pursed lips, he knew he couldn't leave thirty million souls to die. I couldn't even imagine a number that large, even less so imagine the weight of each life with every digit.

I cleared my throat. "We can stop it. Rather, I can stop it. But I need to be inside that ship, and as soon as possible."

"We don't have the manpower..." Part of him still wanted to run to his family. He shook his head. "We'll find a way. We can drop in behind a building southwest of the castle, it's about a block away. The streets will be in complete chaos."

"And my mother?" Mel asked.

"You and The Queen-"

Mel interrupted. "No. Just my mother. Not me."

Theseus nodded. "Ata will stay here with her, this ship can take her to the safe house in the north mountain range."

Mel and I turned to Ata, who was just behind us listening for who knows how long. Ata leaned heavily against the side of the ship, bleeding and bruised from her battle in the castle. She nodded at Theseus's order, not raising any rebuttal. At first, I thought she'd want to be in the fight, but protecting The Queen was an honor.

"With only three of us, we should be able to slip through the chaos and get inside, titans willing." Theseus turned back to the hole in the ship, watching as we circled the castle. Billows of smoke poured from holes in the smooth surface and an orange glow filled the entirety of the middle floors. "With any luck we might not even need a miracle."

A voice cut the air and sent chills down my spine. "My daughter is not going to fight insurrectionists like some...soldier." The Queen was righted on her feet now, but still wobbly. Whether from the sickness of the hypercore or her lack of flying experience, I couldn't tell.

"With all due respect, Mother, I am. I've done terrible things to this city, I owe it to them to try to save what's left of it."

Her face was screwed up in disgust. "Owe it to them? You owe them nothing. You are royalty, daughter of the titans, they are...chaff. We must look at the big picture, who will be left to rebuild if we are all dead?"

Mel scoffed. "The people would, and they would rebuild a world better than that which we've made."

The Queen's now frizzy hair shook with her head. "It would be chaos, disorder. We are all that keeps this world running, our justice, our benevolence. Don't tell me you've lost sight of that."

Anger radiated off Mel like heat from a flame. She stepped in front of me with head raised high, looking down at The Queen over the bridge of her nose. "I've opened my eyes, now you can either wish me well or think down upon me as I face the fate your arrogance has made for me."

For the first time, I realized that Mel was taller than The Queen. Mel didn't cower anymore, she stood above the pressure of the past generations, shaking it off like dead weight. Without the weight of tradition on her shoulders, her strength doubled.

The Queen tried to raise herself higher than Mel, but she realized she could not. "What has happened to you, my daughter?"

"I see my fate, they have opened my eyes to it. It's time you open your eyes to your own and correct your mistakes, lest they eat you whole like this rebellion has tried to do with me."

The Queen's face morphed from anger to anguish. She folded her hands together and her head fell low. Her words were quiet. "You blame me for your father's death."

"It seems you blame yourself."

The Queen drew in a raspy breath. If it was anyone else, The Queen would call it treason, heresy, and the words would vanish as quickly as the person would. But this was her daughter, her words weighed more on her heart than anyone else's. "The pain…it blinds me, I swear it."

Mel nodded, tears welling in her own eyes. "I know, and I didn't understand before, but now I think I know what it would be like to lose the love of your life. I'm sorry that this is what fate has dealt you, but we must learn to grow from it, not destroy ourselves and others over it. Your pain has a purpose, but you must look through your tears to see it."

The Queen sighed, a harrowed yet motherly smile rising on her face. Her eyes were strained, looking up at her daughter. "You always want your child to become better than you, but it's so hard to accept the moment they don't need you anymore. I see a queen in your eyes, better than I ever could be. It seems I only need to stop standing in your way."

Mel stepped forward and took her mother's hands, holding them close to her chest. "I will never stop needing you, Mother. But we need to change. For the sake of our people, and for ourselves."

The two looked deep into each other's faces, one scared of the future and one embracing it. The Queen looked at me now, that same motherly smile. "How dare you change my daughter for the better. Protect her, I beg of you."

I nodded deeply. "I promise, Your Majesty."

Her eyes steeled now, looking not at her daughter and some human from Earth, but at heroes. Normal people given supernatural destinies. "Go save our people."

↩ ↩ ↩

The engines burned hot as we soared over the city. The bay door hissed open. I checked the weapons on my belt and pulled tight the strap of my toolbox over my chest, adjusting the oxygen tube under my nose. Theseus drew back the bolt on his weapon, checking his gun up and down. Our hair whipped in the wind as Mel tied her own back into a tight ponytail. The destruction below was horrifying, the smell of smoke and metal filling our lungs. The ship that had crashed at the base of the tower was leaning over on one wing, its other sticking out into the sky. A massive hole had been ripped open on the first few floors of the castle, gunshots and bullets being traded between the insurrectionists surrounding the ship and the soldiers inside the castle.

Theseus elbowed me. "Do me a favor, don't get shot. I don't want to see what our guns do to a human."

I shuddered. "We have a word for it; red mist. There won't be much of me left if that happens. Believe me when I say I don't want that."

He pulled his helmet on as the destruction disappeared behind a passing building. Thirteen lurched in a circle and expertly landed in an empty lot, some kind of construction zone. The bay door hit the ground, and we stepped off. I could see Mel gazing back, waving to her mother. She racked the slide on Ata's pistol, nodding to the two of us.

We followed Theseus past piles of metal and white panels, slipping to the edge of the dusty lot where fences held thick white tarps over them. He found a gap in the fence and cut through the fabric, stepping out onto the street. We followed him through, immediately finding ourselves in the shine of a streetlight. We ducked behind one of the dozens of abandoned vehicles that sat in rows on the street. They didn't have wheels, only long metal rails underneath them. Magnets? I didn't have time to consider it.

Theseus pushed for the next vehicle, sliding down beside it. We rushed over to him, pressing our backs against the door and looking up through the glass of the window. It shattered into a spray of shards as Theseus shoved my head down. He leaned around the edge of the car and took a shot, the explosion in the chamber so loud my hearing cut for a moment, a ring persisting. He took another shot, then another. Across the street from us, I could see two soldiers flanking us on the right. I took aim, they scrambled for cover as my shots pinged off the heavy armor on their chest and shoulders. One lifted up to fire, my bullet grazed the side of his neck. He shouted and fell flat as his partner rose to suppress fire. Theseus took notice, and a shot. The man's hand was gone in an instant, his weapon clattering to the ground. My missing hearing protected me from the sound of his scream.

A pulse rushed through our bodies and the gunshots ceased for a moment. Theseus steadied himself on the vehicle in front of him for a moment, but realized his opportunity. We followed Theseus to the next car, bullets whizzing overhead. Mel rose up to fire with Theseus as the two of them fired at an enemy I couldn't even see through the layer of smoke coating everything. Another soldier came from the side, rushing to the aid of his comrades. I fired at him, my bullet plinking off his armor again, and one off the large handgun he held. The gun was sent flying. I went to fire again, but I was empty. He noticed.

He rushed towards me as I scrambled to unload the magazine from my gun. I felt through my jacket to find my extra mags, but there was no time. Instead, I pulled the pipe wrench from my toolbox, a huge hunk of half-rusted metal that Cratus gave me. I ducked under a haymaker from the assailant and cracked the tool over his helmet, cracking the plating of his mask as he fell flat to the ground. Cratus did always say a good pipe wrench would save my life one day, I just didn't think this is what he meant. Theseus ducked down and ejected the clip from his rifle, seeing the unconscious body. I could tell he was exasperated even under his mask.

"Really? A wrench?"

"I know right? Who knew?"

More bullets whizzed over us as I pressed against the car again, I could have sworn there was less shooting just a second ago. Theseus jammed another clip into his gun and went to continue firing, but a bullet pinged off his helmet the second he went to rise. He ducked back down, looking around for something, anything to distract or stop the firing for even a moment. Our answer came surprisingly.

A ship soared over us, not Thirteen, but a sleek white ship with sharp angles and swept delta wings. The massive guns attached just under its nose revved, spraying a rain of fire on our enemies. It pulled back and hovered in place, a large panel opening on its underside, and half a dozen coils of rope fell from it. Soldiers began sliding down the ropes as the massive gun continued its fire. These soldiers didn't wear black like Theseus or Ata, they wore sleek white armor with light gray flak jackets underneath. Their boots hit the ground and they immediately took a position of offense, slinging the weapons off their backs and following the ship's example of raining lead on the enemy.

The last soldier to hit the ground came over to us, undisturbed by the chaos around us He knelt down beside us and pulled off his helmet, revealing darker pink hair with skin almost as pale as his white armor. His eyes were pale gray, his face was young, and a scar ran over the bridge of his nose, slightly crooked from a past injury.

"You know, I always thought you were more into diplomacy." He spoke in perfect English.

"Brother?" Mel gasped, a smile lining her face. She threw her arms around him and pulled him tight, both of them ducking down as the firing from the enemy resumed. The ship had torn off into the sky again, fighting with the fleet that had been hijacked.

A laugh of relief came from Theseus. "You're the miracle we've been praying for, Prince Zagreus."

"I could've made it a bit sooner, but you don't look too worse for wear, friend. How's your family?" He gave Theseus a playful smack on the shoulder. His ashen eyes came to me now, widening at the sight. "Is this the human I've heard so much about? You're making quite a stir! People say my sister is quite smitten by you."

Mel whacked him on the shoulder with a blush, he gave a brief laugh before ducking at an all-too-close bullet. His smile dropped to a look of annoyance. He pulled his helmet on and swung the rifle off his back, this one with a longer barrel and wider body.

"Small talk later, I guess. No need to fill me in on the mission, just stay close." His voice was the essence of pure confidence. Calm, cool, collected, but on target. His words gave me chills, like I could fight the whole army on my own if he only said the word.

Theseus nodded. "On you, General Zagreus."

"Just call me Zag," he said before rising to his feet, firing a series of shots that dropped men left and right. Theseus stood up after him and followed as he walked around the edge of the car. Neither flinched at the bullets whizzing by, only focusing on each shot they took.

We followed them to the next line of cars, slowly nearing the ship. The wing of the ship was nearly directly above us now, casting a shadow over us as the aurora was blocked from view. It wasn't that far, on a planet with lighter gravity I could easily reach it. Not here though; it was simply too far away. Another pulse ran over us, this one stronger than ever. Even I had begun to feel it in my gut, that twisting pain in my head, but I pressed on. The firing stopped as soldiers reeled in pain, but Mel made a move. My hand whiffed as I reached for her shoulder, but she was already running. She skidded to the ground and slammed her back into the next line of cars, holding her hands below her with fingers intertwined.

"Up and over!" She shouted. "Trust me!"

Not an ounce of me doubted her. I leaped over the hood of the car I hid behind and ran towards her with all my might. The bullets whizzed past me, but I kept my eyes on her. My boot landed into her hands and kicked hard as she lifted with all her might. My stomach fell into my shoes as I was launched high into the air, high enough to know better than to look down. My chest slammed into the edge of the wing, my hands struggling to find a handhold on its smooth surface. My fingers found a gap in the ailerons of the wing and I heaved myself over the edge.

I took hold of the cable on my belt again, unwinding it and throwing it down towards her. I felt it pull taut as my boots slipped on the wet surface of the wing. I fell to my hands and feet, crawling away from the ledge with all my might. The line went slack and I looked back to find Mel clinging to the edge of the ship. I dove to grab her and yanked her over the side as bullets tore through the panels below us. We slid down the angled wing of the plane and crashed into the back rudder.

"I did not think that was going to work honestly," Mel sighed as she pulled herself to her feet.

"You seemed so confident though!" I replied and took the hand she offered me. I righted myself and dusted the snow off of me. "What about Theseus and Zag?"

"They've never lost before, I don't think they intend to lose now." I couldn't argue with that.

"I dunno, it seems like they're allergic to actually hitting us or something." I smirked, maybe getting a bit too cocky.

"They're just not used to shooting at something so small." She elbowed me with a cheesy grin. "We need to get inside."

I followed her across the cobalt blue surface of the ship, slick with rain and snow. Neither of us could make out any panels lining the top of the ship, no secret entrances or anything of the sort. Mel waved for me to follow as she crouched down at the furthest part of the ship, the bridge. She took a shot at the glass protecting the sensitive console inside and slipped in. At the sound, bullets began pouring in my direction. The sharp edge of glass scratched at my jumpsuit as I slid into the warm air of the bridge.

The ship was dark inside, an ominous black void of a hallway leading out of the bridge and further into the ship. The air was warm and still inside, but a chill ran down my spine as cold air flooded in through the hole we had just entered through. Her hand scooped under my arm and pulled me to my feet. My hands itched as I dusted the glass off my coat and pants, scratches so small they were practically invisible covering my hands.

"We make a good team," I said.

"If we didn't we'd have died by now. Either that or beginner's luck. Do you know where the core is?"

I squeezed my eyes shut. "In theory. I should be able to-"

A shout rang out, Mel shoved me aside and blasted at a figure entering the bridge. The figure fell to his face as blood pooled on the ground. I was sickened by how little I reacted to the smell. I thought familiarity breeds contempt, I guess not. Loud footsteps echoed down the halls, someone massive was coming our way.

"Be swift but be quiet," Mel whispered in my ear.

We stepped over the body and further into the ship. The hallway split in two directions, one on either side of us. They went for a short distance before turning again, leading in the direction of the back of the ship. My feet began carrying me down one hallway, but Mel grabbed my shoulder.

"Wait, I know this ship, this is the same model the insurrectionists kidnapped me on." She jerked a thumb over her shoulder. "It's slower this way, but listen."

The footsteps were getting closer, in the direction of the hallway I had picked. I thought hard, and she was right. This was the same ship that was on Zion. I wasn't used to seeing it in one piece, suddenly the layout began to piece together in my head.

"I can't hardly see anything anyways. Following you," I nodded.

We walked carefully through the darkness of the ship. As I squinted hard to see, Mel seemed to navigate perfectly fine in the dark. I held to the back of her shirt like a child, allowing her to lead me through the dark. She stopped abruptly, my eyes watered and my nose ached as I slammed into her back, stumbling backwards. She twisted a panel to her right, a door opened into a broom closet. Brooms, mops, and cleaning chemicals lined this tiny room, not bigger than three feet on any side.

"This is where they kept me," Mel mumbled.

"Stars…that's awful."

"It's not all bad." Mel stepped into the closet and pushed the brooms away, lifting at a handle hidden in the wall. A secret door unlatched and swung open, revealing a corridor pulsing with a deep blue light. "I wouldn't have known that was there if I wasn't."

She ducked into the passageway, myself after her. The walls here were hardly walls at all, but layers of pipes and wires all connecting to the beating heart of the ship. Most of the pipes ran along the ground with a mesh of metal laid over top to make a floor of sorts, rising up in the center of the circular room, others ran along the roof and attached at the top of the core. Its blue glow pulsed and swirled with a menacing growl, like a sickened beast laying down to take its last breath. A last breath that would kill millions.

Mel was mesmerized by the thing, taking a step towards its glow. She went to press a hand against the glowing porthole into the center of the core, inches of glass with thick layered filters keeping her from losing her vision with a single glance. Her hand lurched back as she felt the heat even from a foot away, and a shine of sweat built on her forehead.

"It's beautiful," she whispered.

Waves of light like an aurora fluttered off the edge of the core, then a pulse that shook me to my bones. The beast groaned in pain, it wanted to die so badly, but it had been sent into motion of a brutal death. I dropped my toolbox down at my side and slipped over to the computer screen I had become so familiar with on Zion. At least it wasn't backwards. I fumbled with the keys and tried to remember what Mel had said on Zion.

Much to my luck, I was able to access a diagnostic screen, bar graphs with things I assumed were numbers surrounding a digitized image of the hypercore. Though the numbers meant nothing to me, the bar graphs proved that everything was high, far too high.

"Mel, I need to access a console menu. I need to access the computer inside the core."

"Right." Mel pulled herself away from the core and stepped towards me, chin resting on my shoulder while she examined the screen. She tapped a few buttons, then pointed towards a menu option on the screen. "There."

I used the arrow keys and clicked on the tab. A deluge of Elysian code poured over the screen, writing and rewriting itself over and over again. It was erratic and random, no sense to be made anywhere.

"What's the Elysian word for 'abort'?" I asked.

"Apovalli," Mel said as she typed into the keyboard. She hit the enter key and her text entered in red. A buzz rang out, and the command was swept away in the flood. "That's weird."

"Did you type it wrong? I need it to stop doing whatever…this is."

"Of course I didn't type it wrong. It's not responding." Mel tried again, and again. The same red flash, swept away into the storm.

"It's a virus," I mumbled.

A click echoed through the chamber. A chill ran down my spine. Mel and I spun, and froze. On the far side of the core chamber from us, with a massive pistol in hand, Ermis stood. He wore that same black armor, that same glare, that same smug face. His gun was locked onto me, I could see right down the barrel.

"Time to back away, children," he said. "Show me your hands."

"What in the Titans' names are you doing?" Mel asked as she slowly raised her hands.

"Something I regret not doing sooner." He took a hard step towards me. "Show me your damn hands!"

His voice boomed, and I launched my hands upwards, the pistol I was reaching for flinging from my belt and clattering to the ground. Ermis boomed a laugh.

"So you are dumber than you look! For a second there, I really thought you humans might be more clever than I gave you credit for. I told my soldiers you were smart, they aren't compelled by easy fights."

"You did all this? All to kill me?" I asked.

"You think too highly of yourself. No, the assassins were meant to kill you. But that damn bodyguard of yours stopped it. Should have known he'd win, I taught him how to fight myself. I thought the strike team might do it, but..." The gun shook in his hand, not by fear, but by the iron grip he held on the gun. His rage boiled over, he wanted to kill me so bad, but he wanted me to know just how badly I'd gotten played first.

I scoffed. "This is pathetic. You're throwing a fit because you didn't get your way in the vote?"

"It's more than the vote. The fact that I ever entertained the idea of bringing you back was the biggest mistake I'll ever make. The biggest mistake our royals ever made was giving you a chance at peace. Disgraceful." His teeth grit and he shook his head. "I spent all this time creating the riots, orchestrating the attacks, trying to show that humans were such a dire problem. I knew our lies were cracking, I knew the people knew. I just wanted a head start on the war, then little miss Melinoe just had to survive the abduction."

Mel stepped back in fear. "You were the one who abducted me?"

"How else could insurrectionists pluck a princess from her own bed? I rigged the ship to destroy itself, everyone was supposed to believe the humans did it. Then the ship you're on vanishes without a trace, and who shows up? Some damn hero saving the princess." He took another step forward. Mel and I both backed up against the wall. "I thought I could convince The Queen, but it seems my sister is just as stubborn as her daughter. The only answer was that I had to take the throne, lead the war myself. Now here you are, ruining all of my plans, again."

Melinoe's voice shook. "All those people, innocent Elysian lives, just so you could kill humans?"

"Stop playing stupid, Melinoe! We all know what's coming. Our planet is nearing the star again, the humans were going to find out eventually. We need their materials before the years of darkness come again. We won't survive a second time!" Spit flew from Ermis' mouth as he barked his words like a dog. "This planet, these people, they're all fools. I take pity on them, on their arrogance. Someone has to fix this broken, miserable trash heap. As the only sane person left, I knew they'd follow me like the good sheep they are."

"You traitorous, lying, bastard! I knew I'd never trust you, you've never had a heart." Melinoe spit on him and dared a step forward. He stomped forward, pressing the gun into my chest and nearing her face as she cowered back again.

"I fulfill the will of the Titan's." He growled like a beast, murder was in his eyes.

He was a monster, and the cruel laugh that clawed its way from his viscous tongue proved him to be truly heartless. To imagine anyone sitting on a throne in hell and laughing at the screams of the damned seemed like nonsense until I saw the cruelty in Ermis' eyes. He was not a monster, he was the devil himself. I froze, I felt hopeless against him.

His hand closed around Mel's neck as he took a lurching step backward. He lifted her off the ground with ease, the tips of her shoes reaching helplessly for the ground which was all too far away. My feet started for him, but the barrel of his gun pushed into my chest. An animal's growl came from me as I watched Mel choke for air. His powerful arm pulled her close to his face once more. A horrific smile curled his lips, revealing his fang-like teeth. His face was no longer human, he was nothing more than an animal. He didn't just want to kill us, he wanted to make it slow, make it hurt.

"Ever since you were a child, I sought to see the light fade from your eyes. Now I will relish the opportunity. It's about time I take the pound of flesh I've longed for."

A gunshot pierced my ears and Mel dropped to the floor. Blood ran down Ermis' leg as a hole poured red from his side. He stumbled back and pulled his helmet on, protecting him from any lucky shots. Mel hit the ground and gasped for air. My arms dug under hers and I dragged her behind the hypercore, pulling her head into my chest tightly. A bullet bounced off the glass of the hypercore as we hid from the beast we called Ermis. He came around the side of the machine and took aim.

A blur of motion and a crack of impact struck the air. Theseus slammed into the beast's side and made Ermis stumble, dropping his knife into the gap between Ermis's armored glove and forearm. The knife glinted straight through his arm and his gun hit the floor. Ermis threw a punch into Theseus's side, Theseus responded with a kick to the bullet hole in Ermis' side. Ermis grabbed Theseus by the shoulders and cracked their heads together. Their helmets splintered as Theseus was dazed. With a massive hand, Ermis tore Theseus' helmet off.

"There he is! My star pupil, second only to Zagreus. The one soldier I never could turn on the humans, but always needed to." A crunch came from Theseus as the vice grips of hands squeezed his shoulders together. "You should have listened."

Mel tried to make a move to help Theseus, but I held her back, terrified of Ermis getting his hands on her again. He threw Theseus to the side, cracking off the shell of the hypercore with a viscous crunch. Theseus collapsed to the ground, unmoving. I crawled towards him quickly, cradling his unmoving head in my lap. The side of his face was burned.

"Hey! Talk to me buddy, you're gonna be alright." I shouted near directly in his ear, smacking his face gently.

He weakly opened his eyes, pupils searching around for something, anything. The skin on the left side of his face was red and cracked. Blood poured between his brow and down his nose, a long gash running up his forehead and into his hair.

"Apollo." His words were weaker than I ever wanted to hear. "It hurts...I can't see."

My head shook. "You're gonna be okay, I promise. We'll get you fixed up in no time."

A sickening sound echoed as Ermis drew the knife from the bones of his wrist, the metal clattering to the floor. The steel of Ermis's gun scraped against the ground as he knelt down to pick it up. "Poor Apollo, wanting everything in the world, never having anything. Don't you understand? You can't save everyone. Someone has to die."

My head rose to find the barrel of his gun pressing against my forehead now. I could barely see him through the tears in my eyes, only a mottled mix of blues and pinks.

"You bastard!" My scream shredded my throat.

A pulse pounded through my body, making Ermis hesitate. From the shadows behind him, Mel latched onto his back and bore a knife into his shoulder. Blood sprayed across her face as the blade ripped through his flesh slowly. Mel's battle cry mixed with Ermis's scream of pain as they stumbled backwards against the wall. She was crushed between the weight of Ermis and the steel of pipes, the wind sucked from her once again. She held onto the knife for a moment, twisting it with a nauseating squelch. The blood made her fingers slick as she fell onto her back, squirming to crawl away. Ermis yanked the knife from his shoulder and analyzed it carefully. He was bleeding profusely now, I could see his body struggling to keep itself upright. He swayed in place, shoulders beginning to slouch.

"Not bad for a little girl," he said.

He stood over her with the knife in hand, sticky red shining in the blue light. She screamed in terror, kicking at him wildly from the ground. He took hold of one of her legs, twisting it hard in a direction it was never meant to go. Her scream sparked some well of energy deep within me, something purely animal rising to the surface that spoke only one word: rage. Her leg twisted in a petrifying way with a crack like a green branch, a sound etched into my ears I would never forget. He bore the knife into her leg, straight through the flesh of her twisted calf. A scream shredded my throat. I tasted blood. I thirsted for more.

"MELINOE!"

Something lifted me to my feet, something pulled the knife from my sheath. I kicked off the ground and took hold of his collar, burying the knife into his cracked helmet. Only its tip emerged the other side, but I pulled it harshly down the length of his face. The helmet was ripped off of him with the sickening tear of flesh. A long, curved line ran from his forehead, over his brow, through his eye, and down his cheek.

"You BASTARD! I'll make you know more pain than you could ever IMAGINE! You'll PA-"

Something struck me, struck into me. A roar raised from him as he dragged the knife through the flesh of Mel's leg and dug it into my side. All air within me left in an instant. All I could feel was that blade, buried deep into my flesh. I felt it in my lungs as I tried to breathe. My body slammed onto the floor beside the core. A horrible sense of déjà vu overwhelmed me as my oxygen mask fell from my face. The mangled Ermis was barely recognizable as angry anymore, only a beast seeking revenge. Something in me still raged, but the child in my heart was afraid. The child took control, wishing to duck under the covers, to run to mom. The flame of that indomitable spirit still raged, but fear of dying reared its head. I dared not kick at him as he walked towards me, instead crawling towards Theseus. Ermis flipped me over and pulled the knife from my side. His massive hand closed around my shoulder, crushing the bones in my arm, pinning me to the metal below.

"You humans are resilient, I'll give you that. Just how much can you take before you crack?"

He leaned over me, bloodied face dripping red onto my own. A gnarled smile rose on his face, his lips split from the tearing of my knife. Blood lined his teeth, and his breath smelled of copper. Pain wreathed my neck like a vice binding my bones together. I couldn't help a groan of pain, half sobbing from its relentless torment. Through ragged gasps, I spoke.

"So long as I live, I will make you know pain."

With my free hand, I reached up and took hold of his ear, tearing at it with the might of my whole hand. It began to tear free when my grip loosened under his blood. His scream shredded the air as he leaped back in pain. Something had broken in my shoulder. I felt no breath left in me to be used, but I had to rise. He hurt her, and I would hurt him so much more.

"Mark my words, this is your final day alive." My feet demanded ground, my body demanded revenge. No amount of pain could stop me anymore. "I would have killed you for even thinking about hurting her."

Ermis rose to his full stature. My sight broke through the red I saw, and I realized just how truly large he was. He looked down at me, seething through growled breaths. Blood poured down his face, only one eye was left to dig into my soul.

No matter how shredded, he still smirked. "You think you're big? You think you know what strength is? Take your best shot."

My breath sped, my heart raced. I wouldn't cower any more, I wouldn't back down. I had to make him pay, he hurt her.

I dug in, pushed forward, closing that small gap quickly. The toe of my shoe dug in, shooting me off the ground and up in the air. My arm was locked with the whole of its potential waiting for the perfect moment. I reached the top of my leap and heaved my fist. His head snapped to the side with a crack, stumbling back slowly. I fell to one knee, then rose to meet his eye again. A devilish laugh rose in me, until I realized the crack I had heard was not his bones but my own. I swallowed hard as tears filled my eyes in the pain. He wiped away the blood on the once clean side of his face, giving a laugh as he realized it was not his own blood but mine.

"Weak."

In a flash of movement, he threw a punch. It cracked against my temple and launched me into the metal of the wall. My skull cracked across the pipes and my world spun. I collapsed against the wall, eyes still dazed. A fog wreathed around my head immediately, I couldn't think straight. He took a step towards me, a gurgling groan escaped me as I prepared for another attack.

A bullet tore the air between us, colliding with a pipe just beside Ermis and unleashing a torrent of steam at an unfathomable temperature into his face. He retreated with another roar.

"That's enough!" Zag stood in the passageway with his rifle leveled. "In the name of the royals of Elysia, I command you to stop."

A sinister look raised on Ermis's mangled, blistering face. "Thank the Titans, General Zagreus! You friends, they are insurrectionists, I came here to stop the attack and they turned on me."

Zagreus's eyes lowered to Mel for only a moment. His face didn't change, but something did behind his eyes. His cool look was melted away by fire. "I always knew you were a liar."

Ermis raised an arm as Zagreus took a shot, the bullet bouncing off the armor of his forearm. Ermis charged at Zagreus, but the prince was clever. Where Ermis tried to crush him against the wall, he found the barrel of Zagreus's gun burying into his gut. Zagreus fired, and a bullet tore through the stomach of Ermis. Yet, he still fought. His hand closed around Zag's neck, lifting him up against the wall. Fear filled the prince's eyes, clawing at the massive hand around his throat as panic arose within him.

"I'll kill every royal in the city before I spend a day bowing down to human pigs." Spit flew on his last word. It mixed with blood and sprayed on Zag's face. "All humans must die."

My toolbox sat just beside me, kicked over and popped open in the chaos. Cratus's pipe wrench sat atop the pile of tools. My fingers closed around it. It felt powerful in my hand. My eyes met Mel's curled, shivering body, the pool of her blood near her leg. The child within my heart let go, rage took the wheel. My hand burned against the pipes of the core as I steadied myself. My body lurched between Ermis and Zag, and my wrench cracked against his knee with a crunch. He collapsed to one knee, almost as if he was bowing. I grabbed a fistful of his hair and held his head up to meet my eyes. One of his eyes was gone now, the other barely open from the swelling of his burns.

"Burn in hell."

I cracked the metal of the wrench across his jaw and he collapsed backwards. His hand shook as he tried to rise. His breath was a ragged groan as he tried to speak, but his broken jaw suppressed his devilish words. I stepped over him, looking down at his pitiful, broken face. Rage. It was all I could feel. My wrench lifted high above my head.

"You deserve so much worse than this, you BASTARD."

I dropped it down on his face, hard. Then once more. A shout tore from me the third time before I realized how little breath was left in me. I screamed with the last of my air, throwing my wrench hard against the wall of the ship. I wanted to make him hurt more, I wanted to strangle every last bit of life from his body, but that opportunity was gone.

He lay still, broken, and unbreathing. He was dead, just as I wanted him to be. I had wanted to kill him, and I gave into that. Just as he wanted to do to me. It was me or him, Wendy would say. But I chose him, I relished the choice. Now he was dead, and not an ounce of my anger was gone. I was left with it, festering in my chest like some disease. Nothing was left to satiate my rage. The end justifies the means, right? I wished it to be true. Yet I still raged, it felt as if it would never end.

A shrill scream escaped me once more, trying to release some of my anger by any means necessary. I sputtered into a coughing fit, finding blood on my sleeve as I fell to my knees. My lung had been pierced. But I couldn't give up. Rage would not fix what he had broken.

A pulse ran through the ship, flooring me completely as well. I was slow to rise as I stumbled over to Mel and knelt down next to her, pulling her into my lap with tears running down my face. Her breath was so fast, I thought she might hyperventilate. Her head trembled as she tried to look down at her horribly broken leg. I grabbed her by the chin and forced her to meet my eyes. Adrenaline hit my system at her look, she was so scared. Her face was smeared with the blood from her hands as she tried to wipe away tears. I swallowed the emotion in my voice.

"You're going to be okay, look at me."

She nodded hard, squeezing her eyes shut.

"Don't go to sleep, okay? No matter how tired you feel, you fight back. Understand?"

"I...understand." She spoke between her rapid breaths, eyes glinting down at her leg for a moment. She gagged. "That's a lot of blood."

Zag came to my side, taking a hold of his sister's hand. He held it to his chest as he assessed the damage. "H-He's right. You'll be fine! Fit as a fiddle in..." He swallowed hard. "No time at all."

I nodded to Theseus. "Get him, we need to get out of here."

"What about the core?" Mel asked weakly. "The city...they'll all die."

I shook my head. "To hell with the core, to hell with it all. We're getting off this godforsaken planet."

"Apollo...please–"

I threw Mel's arm over my shoulder, trying to lift her to her feet. She was heavy, and her leg hung loosely beneath her, barely keeping herself up on her one good leg. She sobbed in my ear at the pain.

"I know, I know it hurts," I whispered. She could only whimper a response. Zagreus listened for Theseus's heart, then lifted him up onto his shoulders. He was out cold, but he was alive.

"Come on, let's go!" He shouted and squeezed through the corridor.

Mel and I shuffled and stumbled out into the hallway. Mel screamed in pain as she tried to catch herself on her bad leg out of instinct. She cried in my ear as I struggled to keep up with Zagreus. We limped down the hallway towards the back of the ship, feeling the heat of the core on our backs as we went. A hole had been blown open in the ship's side, gunfire still rang through it. I lifted my watch to my mouth.

"Thirteen, I need emergency evacuation immediately!" Speaking so loudly left me completely breathless, I felt I might collapse. It was hard enough to breathe with the air so thin, I wasn't sure how long I could hold onto consciousness.

"Already nearby," Thirteen replied.

Mel stumbled, falling to her good knee. I dragged her along for a few steps before she regained the strength to hop over the mangled metal of the hole in the wall. We stumbled out into open air and were met with gunfire. We barely made it fifteen feet from the ship before collapsing behind a car. I leaned Mel against it and looked for a weapon; I had left everything on the ship. I peeked up to see Thirteen tearing through the sky towards us. The pain in my chest rose again, I wasn't sure if it were tears or the stab wound. I pressed a hand hard into the hole in my ribs, pain wracked my body.

"Hey, Thirteen's almost here, we'll be alright," I said in the calmest tone I could. My adrenaline was fading. Mel's eyes drooped through her pained expression. She couldn't handle a second longer of pain. "Apollo, I...I'm so tired. I don't know if-"

I shook my head hard, snapping in her face to wake her up. Her dreary eyes snapped open and met my own, eyelids still heavy. "Don't talk like that! He's right there, just give him one second, please."

"Apollo, you have to go stop the core," Mel said seriously.

"I already told you, to hell with it. We're leaving, getting you help."

"No! My people need to be saved, Apollo, and you're the only one who can do it. We could never live with ourselves...not with their blood on our hands. Millions of lives..." She clung to my collar, pulling me close. She was desperate. She'd lost hope for herself, but not for her people.

I pursed my lips and shook my head again. "They're all worth nothing to me if you're not there."

"Please, Apollo. Don't let them die just for me to bleed out–"

"You won't!"

"Please–!"

"I can't! I can't fix it! There's no time. The final collapse has already begun. It's already over. We...I failed."

A sob took the last of my strength as I slouched, it hurt to cry. My head hung low as the crackle of energy ignited the air. I lifted my eyes to see a beam of blue light tearing through the roof of the ship, melting away the metal. Pulses rushed from the ship in rapid succession, one every few seconds, and the gap was ever slowing.

A tear ran down my face. "I'm sorry Mel, we're out of options."

"Hardly, sir."

Thirteen tore the air above us, above the beam rising from the crashed ship. He hovered in the air above the ship, lowering himself down over the cobalt blue heap of metal.

"Thirteen, what are you doing?! I told you to pick us up!"

"I am programmed to protect organic life. I've done the calculations, nobody else must die today, sir."

His landing gear jutted from his sides, not just touching the ship, but closing in on it. They clamped down on the ship like massive spikes, burying into the metal of the ship and binding the two together. The heat of the core was melting through his underside, welding the two ships together.

"Thirteen, what the hell are y–"

His engines burned hot, hotter than I'd ever seen. The ship beneath lurched as its wings leveled, pulling from the rubble of the castle. Insurrectionists screamed and shouted, shooting at Thirteen to take it down. They climbed up the sides, firing at the landing gear and clambering into the ship, trying to find a solution. Thirteen burned the air for one last flight, sailing for the aurora.

The ships soared over our heads as he raced through the city. The conglomeration of metal seared the air with a roar of engines I'd never heard before. A trail of smoke and blue energy lined his trajectory as he pulled high into the sky. A curved tail of smoke followed him, like a shooting star. The orange fire of his engines didn't glow as bright as the blue he bore. He was a star in the night sky, a star of my making.

"It has been an honor to serve you, sir. Thank you for all the adventures. I'm glad you built me."

"Damn robot," I choked. "Thank you, old friend."

The light vanished for a moment, then it returned in a radiance I never thought I'd ever see. The ships had been forced into a hyperjump, and the energy from the explosion had painted the sky. Like a stroke from a massive brush, the blue hue of ionized air met the streaks of green and purple of aurora. It was like a crack in the sky, a glimpse of the blue skies of Earth on a foreign planet. A boom so loud it shook my bones, and a deep whine like a synth instrument losing power. It was beautiful, like a melody. A dying song from Thirteen, a final farewell from my greatest creation.

My eyes fell away from the sight as my head hung low. The city was saved, and it only cost an AI, yet a loss panged my heart. He had been a friend to me, whether I designed him or not. I felt as though a piece of me was missing, like I had given him a part of my soul to make him alive, and now that part was dead. The light had begun to fade, but it would never leave my mind. As the eternal twilight began yet again, I felt colder than ever. A tear pulled itself from my face and frosted on my cheek, I could only imagine the parts and pieces of Thirteen scattered about the stars. Now, Thirteen was just another piece of space junk scattered across the galaxies, yet every sparkling dot in that deep ebony sky was simply another part of him to remind me of every memory.

Mel's arms wrapped around me, pulling me into her as a sob wracked my weak body. I could hear her heartbeat, slow and weak. I leaned into her, feeling the warmth of her blood on my skin. My sobs stole the little breath I had, my own life pouring from my side and onto her still. We'd shared only a brief moment in our lives, and now I believed we might share our deaths. Her breaths were shallow, but with the little breath she had, she spoke.

"I'm sorry," she whispered.

"Don't go, Mel. Please. You're all I have left."

"I know...I won't...I'm here...with you. Always."

↳ 22 ↲

Olympus

It was morning, not long after starrise. Under the twisted shadow of a radio tower I modified, we waited. The red lights pulsed their ominous glow high in the eternal night air. The tower was barely taller than the trees around it, but the lights set it far apart. The clouds poured a faint mist over everything, the kind of rain that soaks everything in an instant. I breathed in the familiar smell of damp soil, of the forest breeze filling my lungs. I gave my hood no mind, trusting my poncho to keep me dry. My hair soaked in rain, curls sagging heavy under the droplets clinging to the strands, but my clothes were perfectly dry and warm. I squinted as I stared past the floodlights above and into the pitch black sky, wondering, waiting.

My eyes wandered to The Queen beside me, huddled under a poncho of her own, eyes shining under the shroud of her hood as she examined all that was above us. A soldier stood behind her, holding an umbrella over her head, but she looked past it in wait. She glanced at me and gave me a nod. I nodded back.

On my other side, Zagreus lazily stood, leaning heavy on one side while rolling his head back and stretching out his neck. He wore his white armor with rain running down its waterproof surface with ease. The sprinkle ran down the smooth surface of his helmet in long streaks, like tears from invisible eyes. I'd feel sympathy if I didn't know he was as lax as ever, feeling not even an ounce of stress. Beside him stood Ata, at attention and head straight forward. She had adopted his white armor as well, being brought into his platoon after a position had opened up. She still wore Mel's pink button at her collar, sparkling in the fluorescent light.

What we were waiting for finally arrived. Engines burned the air as something descended through the clouds. I saw its thrusters first, then its deep blue and orange body. It was long and rectangular with thrusters like feet on each corner, descending from the heavens and onto the vast landing pad before us. The trees around us swayed and groaned under the gale of the ship, rain whipped too and fro in the sudden chaos. It all burned away as the ship set down with a groan, its back end facing us. The ship's end was slanted, stretching out further at the top than at the bottom. The whole of the back of the ship opened on long pistons, lowering a large platform and revealing a large cargo bay full of boxes. The crew within feigned work and craned to see the world outside, to see someone or something from this odd new world. They knew they weren't the first human to see the surface of Elysia, that honor belonged to me, but being one of the first few still made quite the story to tell back home.

Three figures walked down the platform. Two soldiers in gear identical to that which Sintara used to wear, before she was made wanted and hunted. Strapped to their faces were oxygen masks, silicone and rubber connected to oxygen tanks strapped on their back. I had warned them to bring them, I was glad they listened. In front of the soldiers stood a figure I dreaded seeing. When I had sent a signal to IEO, the voice that answered was the last one I had ever wanted to hear. David Marshall, the man who wanted me to feign my death to cover his tracks and make Mel forget me to save her own life.

He wore a long polyester coat that swished as he walked and a heavy wool jacket beneath, black slacks and dress shoes that clacked as he stepped off the metal and onto the concrete. His hair was split down the middle and immediately soaked in water, face bearing that same smile and glasses nearly instantly coated in a mist of rain.

"You must be The Queen," he said with a brief bow. An awkward lack of response made me cringe. He nodded and turned to me, holding a hand out. "And you, Apollo. Thank you for doing the right thing and reaching out to us."

I didn't shake his hand. Zagreus snickered under his helmet, I fought hard not to give a smile myself. I felt like I was back in school again, trying not to laugh in the middle of class after my friend had whispered a killer joke. He drew back his hand and placed it into one of his jacket pockets.

"If I may ask, where is the princess? I expected she would join us."

"The Princess will not be joining us today." The Queen spoke in monotone. She squinted at David. "You're the one the humans sent? I expected you to be taller."

In my fear of what he might be capable of, the height difference I was blind to became obvious. The Queen looked down on him, in both stature and confidence, and it drowned his own in an instant. I fought harder to suppress a grin at that realization. He nodded and cleared his throat.

"The human delegations are eager and willing to begin communication. Seeking peace is a unanimous goal for all of human leadership. About the same in the people too." David said the last part was quieter than the other parts.

"Then we have one common ground, which is just enough to begin building something," The Queen said. "However, allow me to make myself clear. Our skies are not open for any foolish human to fly in and out of on a whim. Our skies are closed for travel indefinitely, unless approved. Don't consider this invitation to be an eternal promise."

David nodded. "Understood."

"That would be 'understood, Your Majesty' to you," Zagreus folded his arms.

David repeated himself. "Understood, Your Majesty."

"Don't take me for a fool, young man. I know the direness of our situation. Within the decade, our planet will be in the midst of your well traveled solar system. I intend to defend my planet as we pass you in our orbits, and prepare our people for the age of twilight to come after that. I do not seek to unite our societies into one, I do not seek to be a part of your human world. We will be separate, but united in the cause of survival for both our peoples." The Queen's head shifted to me, eying me in the corner of her eye. "And I believe the people should deserve the choice of which world to live in. I can hardly fathom how many humans would like to live here, but my people will be...fascinated by the prospect of space travel. I'm done hiding things from my people, all knowledge should be available to those who seek it."

David winced at the words. "And if the people take offense to you, their leadership, hiding such things from them?"

"I am mature enough to admit my mistakes and apologize, are you?"

"It's not that simple in human leadership, see-"

"Maybe you need a real leader. A single leader for all to unite under. Someone who sees the people, knows them. Someone like him." The Queen nodded in my direction. An anger lit behind David's eyes as he glared at me, forcing a softened gaze as The Queen met his eyes again.

"Maybe, but until then, I am still subject to the council's commands." David turned and gestured up towards the ship behind him. "This is all the radio equipment you will need to communicate with us most effectively. The council has requested we exchange a manifesto of sorts. Someone to be a spokesperson for this...merging of societies. You'll receive a script of sorts for what we'd like you to relay to your people, and we expect some sort of transmission back in the same spirit. Something to start common understanding with, if you will."

"I understand," The Queen spoke sternly. She looked at me again, a smile so small I nearly thought I imagined it at first. "We will write our declaration, and he will be the herald."

David choked down a laugh and nodded. "Are you certain there isn't an...Elysian you want to do this job? I'm certain the people would like to see what our new allies are like."

"He seems to understand the human condition well enough, and he knows the Elysian people well. In a few short days he's become nearly native, only lacking in the language." The Queen tilted her head and narrowed her eyes. "There won't be a problem with the herald I have chosen, will there?"

"No, Your Majesty. It's only that...well, public opinion hasn't treated him well amongst our people and I'm not sure if it will convey the message the way you intend." David locked eyes with me as he spoke to The Queen.

The Queen nodded long and slow. "Ah, yes, the bounty you placed on him and my daughter. Surely that injustice will be wavered, no more than an accident really."

David swallowed hard. He wanted to make a fuss, make excuses, but how could he? Not to The Queen. "Yes. Merely a miscommunication."

"Good. In that case, I ask that you leave." The Queen made movement to exit the conversation, but paused, speaking over her shoulder. "Oh, but first, take a list of requests from my herald, as to ensure he will complete the task at hand quickly and effectively. I expect you to fulfill them in full, and perform whatever is necessary to complete them. I will continue negotiations with your superiors. Good day, sir..."

Anger boiled within him again. "David Marshall, Your Majesty."

Without another word, The Queen exited, her guard in tow as she made way for the nearby vehicle awaiting to deliver her back to the safe house a mere half mile away. My eyes followed her, watching the trees sway, and through the gaps in branches shone the sparkling lights surrounding the safe house. My heart ached as I looked back, but danger was in front of me. I turned back to meet David's ire.

"You make friends quickly, I admire that," he said with a smile. I could hear the curses he wanted to speak in the fire in his eyes. "Alright, Herald. I'm listening."

"Just give me a moment, I really want to savor this." I drew in a deep breath, battled the pain in my side, and sighed. "Man, this really makes it all worth it."

"You're hilarious, but there's a job to be done here bigger than either of us. Tell me if you need something and let's both move on." He cut the act faster than I expected.

"Sintara, is she pardoned?"

"She will be, along with you and the princess."

"Good. Bring her here. And Wendy."

David laughed at this. "It's hilarious you think she'll even pick up my messages. Believe me, I've tried."

"She'll listen, trust me. Oh, one more thing." I held out a small box wrapped in white plastic, a hefty thing that rattled. "Go to Earth. A small town called Monmouth in Oregon. There's a bar there called Angel's. Give this to the owner."

David scoffed harder at this. "I'm not your errand boy."

"That's not what The Queen said," I mumbled.

He frowned and took the box, handing it off to one of his soldiers. "For the record, I hate you."

I nodded. "The feeling is mutual."

He turned back and whistled to the crew on the ship, unloading procedures beginning immediately. The crew worked fast, whether intimidated by the soldiers all around the landing pad or desperate to get out of the rain.

"Did I distract him long enough?"

"Yep," Zag replied.

"Clear?"

"Yep."

"Did you really think they'd have a bomb up there?"

Zag shrugged. "I don't know what to expect from you humans yet. But I'd like to find out."

"Don't make me your case study." I grumbled.

"Nono, nothing like that." He held a hand out to Ata, who handed him black box barely big enough to hold in one hand, too big to hold in my own smaller hands. It was dented, ashy, and charred, but I recognized it in an instant.

"How..."

"One of my men found it close to where Thirteen landed when he brought Ata and The Queen here. It's a mystery how it got outside the ship." He shrugged again. "With Ermis gone and myself promoted to Admiral of Homeland Security and Sovereign of the Northern Front, I need good people to help us move into this new age. Space travel isn't exactly perfected here, but it needs to be, and soon. But we also need to protect ourselves, and frankly, our ships aren't going to cut it out there. I need someone who knows his way around a ship to help us stay with the game. If you want, I have a position for head engineer open in my regiment. I'd love to have you by my side, and with the spare parts you can work on rebuilding this."

He tapped the box with a strong hand. A laugh of joy escaped me, looking at the box and back to him. "I...I'll think about it."

"I understand it's a big commitment. But do understand, I have no doubt that you are worthy for the position, I only wonder if you are willing. Take all the time you need. You and Ata have somewhere to be?"

"Yeah, we do." I looked at Ata. "Ready?"

"Ready."

Ata walked past me, and as I went to follow, I looked back again. My eyes couldn't be drawn from the box in my hands. I ran my thumb across a small groove in one corner, the rain helping wash away the ash and char built up on the surface. Printed in small letters, it read "Thirteen."

"Thank you, so much. For everything."

"Anything for a friend." He nodded.

↩ ↩ ↩

Under the dancing branches of trees above, Ata and I sat and waited. The trees were deep, rich colors of green and blue, and their bark was like ash and soot from a fire yet hard as stone. An ash moth danced around us before landing on my hand. I could hardly focus on it and the story at the same time. These little guys were my favorite of the fauna of Elysia I had met so far. Ata told me they were fireproof, but I wasn't confident enough to test the theory. I couldn't risk killing one of the poor things. The rain made a gentle noise on the glass covering of the train stop, illuminated by blue lights lining the tracks.

"When I told Theseus and Neus this story, they tried to act tough, but I could tell they were scared."

"Wait, go back. You were telling them a scary story about...witches?"

"Yes, witches. They live in these woods, you know. I've seen them, on a witch's sabbath they gather and feast on the fallen animals."

"Only on a witch's sabbath? Sounds like confirmation bias."

"Always a witch's sabbath, that's when bad luck is strongest."

It hurt to laugh. "I didn't take you for the superstitious type."

Ata was appalled at my words. She was cocky before, seemingly unaffected by the scary story, but now true fear showed in her eyes. "I am not! I've seen it with my own eyes. An old friend from my village was bewitched by one after he hit a ball through her window. He was coughing up pins and needles, talking manic, and howling at things for weeks. It's a miracle he survived."

The idea of spitting out pins and needles did make me squirm. The train rattled as it rounded the corner through the woods and slowed to a stop before us. Its magnets weakened and it set down on the tracks, doors opening and welcoming us in with heated air to cool our iced bones. The train was quiet today. We walked past a mother and her child and sat in the row behind them, myself at the window looking out into the woods.

"Okay, fine, I believe you. What happened then?"

"We returned to our tents, but I could've sworn the two shared one tent out of pure fear. In the night, I heard footsteps and cracking branches entering our camp. I slipped from my bedroll and found my knife and-"

"Saw a witch?"

"Almost worse, an earth shark."

A harsh laugh escaped me, my tears welling in my eyes from the pain of doing so. "Pause, my translator must be busted cause it just told me that you said 'earth shark.'"

"That's what they're called!"

I shook my head, realizing she must not know what a shark was. "On Earth, sharks are big fish with fins and rows of teeth. They're prehistoric, older than trees...though I doubt it."

Ata nodded in agreement. "Gray skin, massive teeth, narrow eyes, but with four legs. They're born in the water but walk onto land when they get hungry enough for game bigger than fish. They're earth sharks!"

My brow furrowed with a mix of humor and confusion. "There's no way we're talking about the same thing."

Ata shivered at the thought of these earth sharks. "The things are terrifying, they'll eat anything and anyone. We fought it with only our knives and took some of its teeth to prove it really happened, and I have the scars to match."

The child in the seat in front of us peered at me between the seats. His red-pink hair was soaked through with rain, stuck to his forehead and framing his round eyes filled with both wonder and hesitation. His eyes were locked on the curls of my hair, and the blue of my lashes and brow. When he noticed my eyes looking back at him, he slipped behind the seat and out of view.

"You said the same thing about that bar fight and showed me the same scar from your training exercises," I said.

"Well I mean it this time." Ata unbuttoned the collar of her jacket and pulled at it, revealing a half circle scar over the whole of her shoulder. It was three circles of serrated teeth marks layered just like a sharks. Maybe we did mean the same thing. "Theseus saved my life that day, as he has many times."

My eyes snapped away from the gnarled scar as Ata fixed her uniform. Her face had fallen dismal, running a finger across the smooth surface of her helmet. I knew why she was so upset. As optimistic as she was, it tormented her inside.

I put a hand on her shoulder, squeezing it tightly. "Everything's gonna be okay, you know."

Her head bobbed, but she was as downcast as the weather outside. "It's just…if I had been there, maybe-"

"I told you to stop thinking like that."

"I know, but if I was, maybe Theseus would've been just fine. Maybe you wouldn't have been injured. Maybe the princess…"

My breath left me in sorrow, agony twisting in my stomach. It was obvious she blamed herself, and I couldn't stop her until I could prove everything would be alright. I looked up to see that we were nearing our stop, gliding over the tracks in the outer part of the city. "I understand, but try not to let it eat you up. We have work to do, and this is our stop."

The doors opened and the crowd flooded in. It wasn't hard to push through however, Ata's white armor and my blue hair made most people uninterested in getting in our way. The crowds eyed me as they always had, but less today than they had yesterday. I recognized some people from days past, average people going about their average routine. The spark and interest of being among Elysian's had nearly worn off, in a few short days I almost felt like one of them. An older woman bumped into me hard, the sharp edge of her bony shoulder digging into my arm. I whirled on her, unsure whether to glare or accept an oncoming apology. She looked at me with terrified eyes, her voice was like gravel.

"Gios'Haus," she growled. I shuddered at the word which my translator seemed to ignore, turning away from her.

We broke free of the crowds around the train stop and down the streets of the outer neighborhoods. Our destination wasn't far, stopping at the gate of a tall and narrow building. It was all white, a simple house with windows sporadically assorted along the sleek surface. It had a gabled roof so flat it hardly looked like a slant at all, long pillars stretching down to the ground in each corner. At the base of each pillar was a simple spiral design, as well as shallow fluting running upwards. Ata told me it was to help keep the rain off of the building.

We crossed the small yard between the street and the front door, knocking hard to be heard over the rain. I looked down at the tiled porch just outside, a mat laid out with a word in Elysian; 'Kala irtheis', meaning 'welcome'. The door opened to an older woman with wrinkles around her eyes and gray-pink hair, Theseus's mother.

"Kala mora, kiria," I smiled as her arms wrapped around us.

"Kala mora, gios ka kori!" She exclaimed before stepping back and drawing us into the house. I didn't need translation for this saying, Ata had taught me. "Good day, son and daughter."

In the Thalassa household, we were welcomed as family. We removed our boots and dripping coats and laid them on hooks over a blazing heater, steam rising from the fabric instantly. The whole house smelled of clove and cinnamon, far more tenderly cared for inside than the brutal minimalism of the castle or safe house. Instead of being solely practical, this house aimed to be cozy. With deep green walls and gray carpets, cozy couches with blankets strewn over the top and covered with soft pillows. Candles were alight everywhere, illuminating with warmth instead of blinding fluorescence. As I turned to enter the living room, Theseus's sister welcomed me with overwhelming enthusiasm.

"Kala mora, Mr. Apollo!" Thekla, sister of Theseus, threw her arms over me with a brutally tight hug, which shot pain through my shoulder like no other, taking a hurried step back from me as Ata entered the room and gave her a narrow look. "And you as well, Lieutenant Atalanta."

Ata smirked. "You're spirited today. Something make your day?"

"I'm always glad when you come to visit," she smiled, only ever looking away from me to speak to Ata. At all other times, she traced the curls of my hair with her eyes, the line of my jaw, the curve of my face. It made me squirm.

She was a kind girl, hair often in a braid or left in wide waves around her head. Her face was a permanent smile, ever soft and kind. She always wore thick sweaters and loved to tell me all about the books she liked to read, most of them relating to the apocalypse. The idea of romanticizing tragedy with zombies transcended cultures, it seemed. She was 28 flickers old, the Elysian form of years, each about 300 days long, their days being about 30 hours. Only a little younger than I, according to my math. If she hadn't made it painfully obvious, I had gathered that she was infatuated with me. I had made it obvious that I didn't reciprocate. It didn't stop her from trying regardless.

I turned to Aethra, mother of Theseus. "How is he today?"

She gave me a smile to ease my worry, but her own anxiety was hidden behind squinted eyes. "He was up this morning, wandering the house. He was scrounging through old things before I sent him back to rest. He's been working on something in there all day."

"May I talk to him?" I asked.

"Of course."

Ata gave me the nod before I even asked, mouthing words to me. "I'll keep her distracted, you go."

My feet patted along the soft carpet of the stairs leading upwards. I could see the light through the crack of Theseus's door before I even neared to hear the sound within. He was mumbling something to himself with the glide of pen on paper. I knocked and the noises stopped.

"It's Apollo," I said.

The door opened to reveal Theseus's cozy childhood bedroom. The walls were a deep blue, illuminated by a warm lamp beside the desk just below the window. Rain pattered on the glass as he rose from his chair, walking through the papers covering the floor.

"How did the meeting go?" He asked. A few days speaking English consistently did wonders for his ability to do so. He was speaking much clearer than he had before, especially after hearing me ramble for so long.

"The Queen seems to have taken a liking to me, she was more than willing to insult the fool they sent. On my behalf, of course. I hate that guy. We're establishing contact with the human council now, we'll be broadcasting a manifesto to both worlds soon." I picked up one of the papers off the floor and analyzed the marks on it. It was Elysian text, messy and unaligned, but legible. I could recognize the letters I had been taught, but the words made no sense to me, aside from Ata and Mel's names, along with my own. "Did you make these?"

He ignored me. "Who will be reading the manifesto?"

"To everyone's surprise, me. The Queen ordained me to do so. It would be Mel if..." I picked up another paper, this one torn and scratched with a pen. The writing was hardly legible here. "How's your vision?"

"It's…better. About fifty percent. Dr. Petrellis said it could return once I'm healed, or it won't. Everything is still dim, like looking through fog just to see my hand." He waved a hand in front of his face exasperatedly. He was healing quickly, but he wanted to help already.

"That's better than it was yesterday." I sat the papers down on his desk, looking at the freshest ink there. It was nearly perfect, impressive for someone with half their original vision. Beside it lay a small plastic tool with the shapes of each letter carved into it, large enough for a pen to pass through.

Theseus dropped onto the edge of his bed and rubbed the side of his head. "My grandma used to use it to write letters, I thought it might help me. It did."

"You'll be alright, I know you will. Before you know it, you'll be back to full strength and can join Zag and Ata."

He scoffed. I turned to see tears welling in his hazy and unfocused eyes. He did so much to protect his family, and he sacrificed it all to protect me. Now he felt helpless. I knew the feeling well. I walked over and placed a hand on his shoulder.

"Everything's going to be okay."

He nodded hard, sniffing his emotions away and rubbing his eyes. He spoke with a dry smile. "Thanks for coming to…see me."

I couldn't help the smallest of a laugh. "Hilarious."

"They say tragedy plus time equals comedy."

Ata entered the room in a rush, one hand to the side of her head as she nodded at the words spoken to her. She replied to whomever was communicating before speaking to us. "Hate to cut things short but they have the manifesto. They need us back at the safe house now."

I looked to Theseus, not wanting to abandon him in his darkest hour. He could feel my eyes on him and shook his head. "Go, I'll be fine."

"We'll be back tomorrow, I promise."

"Don't worry, my sister will scare you off eventually." He lifted himself from his bed uneasily, wobbling on his feet for a moment. "I expect a more thorough report tomorrow."

A leader as always, from the looks of him, he didn't look injured at all. He may be half blind to the world around him, but he still saw more than those with good eyes. He sniffed again, the last of his agony fading.

"I'll be listening. Say it well."

━ ━ ━

When Ata and I stepped into the war room of the safe house, all went quiet. A dozen soldiers were scattered about the room, protecting the many royals who filled the room. Six of the sovereigns were present, Zagreus in Ermis's place and the southern warlord not present. They were discussing something, and the silence as we walked in meant I was likely the topic of conversation.

"Glad you joined us," Zagreus said with a half sharp cut of his word.

"We got here as fast as we could," I said while walking up to the table in the center of this room, a map of Elysia underneath the layer of glass over top. "Did the humans send anything good?"

"That's up for debate, but there's nothing to be done about it now." The Queen leaned on the table, eyes scrolling lazily over the paper in front of her. She seemed dissatisfied, but accepted it regardless.

Zagreus stepped forward and placed a hand on her shoulder. "There's always something we can do, Mother."

"Not this time." She took the stack of papers and walked around the table, everyone who was once in her way stepping aside like she had the plague. Her presence had lost none of its edge. She placed the papers in my hands and met my eyes. "I want this message out as soon as possible so we can move on, I don't want a real rebellion starting with all this confusion."

"Yes, Your Majesty."

"Take your time, make yourself comfortable with the words. I don't want you stuttering and stumbling on the most important broadcast of either of our histories." The crowd split again as she returned to her place at the head of the table once more. "The first page is the humans' address, the second is ours."

I hesitated to speak, fearing she would take offense to the clear blunder in my hands. "There's three pages here, ma'am."

"I imagine you have some words you'd like to say, no? Write them down, don't improvise it on the fly. Though, I intend to look over them and make sure they aren't stupid."

Much to my surprise, I felt very seen by The Queen. Clearly the events that occurred had changed her, I only wondered how deep the change ran. She seemed genuine, but looks can be deceiving. I took the thoughts captive; she was my ally, not an enemy to be studied.

"I wish the princess was here to do this," I said.

If possible, the room felt even more quiet. The Queen nodded and sniffed. "I do too. But you're the best we have, Apollo. Frankly, you're not fit for the job, but you're the only one who can."

A small laugh escaped me. "I know that feeling well. I'll do my best, Your Majesty."

I read over the text half a dozen times, memorizing difficult sentences and long stretches of speech. Quiet conversation carried in the room, The Queen snapping at the royals who got too loud for her liking.

"It's okay, the background noise helps me focus," I mumbled.

I drew a pen from my coat and began writing on the last paper in the stack. I didn't want to go on long winded, but I also couldn't help myself. When I fell into a sentence entirely about

Mel, I scratched it out. No need to embarrass myself in front of the entire galaxy, more than I already was.

Zag put a hand on my shoulder as I finished the last sentence. "I don't mean to rush you but..."

"I'm ready."

"Oh, good. Follow me."

We followed him out of the war room and into the communications room. The walls were lined with consoles similar to those I saw on the Hades, soldiers in black uniforms with headphones over their heads and microphones at their mouths sitting before them. Elysia had televisions, but they were exclusively used for news broadcasts, so most citizens didn't keep them in their homes. Radio was the way to go on Elysia, some broadcasts being only moderately entertaining.

The center of the room had been cleared out, equipment from the boxes on David's ship set up to a semi-haphazard degree. One of these pieces of equipment was a camera on a tripod and microphone, a black curtain hung over the window where they were pointing. The stage of sorts was set, now it needed its performer.

Ata spoke at my side. "I know I'm not Mel but...I believe in you. Just take a deep breath and say what needs to be said."

I was grateful to have her with me, it was far better than being alone. "Thank you."

"We'll have a translator relay your message to the Elysians. Don't try whatever ounce of our language you know, you'll just embarrass yourself." The Queen gestured to where the camera was pointing. "If you would please."

I stepped before the lens and stared deep into the glass. It was like looking down the barrel of a gun, at least the turn in my stomach felt that way. I cleared my throat and looked down at my papers, the letters mixing around the page in an instant.

"We're not live yet, just breathe," Ata whispered from behind the soldier manning the camera.

"Right, right." I drew a deep breath. Who knew of all the dangerous, psychotic things I had done in the past two weeks that this would be the thing that makes me faint from fear. "I'm ready."

"Broadcasting now, Your Majesty."

The room fell deathly silent, like the air itself had stopped to listen. I drew another breath, this one shaky. I couldn't take my eyes off the camera, I knew the whole galaxy was watching. Movement in my peripheral vision drew my eyes to The Queen. Her face was softened, looking at me like a frightened child and not an enemy to be crushed. She nodded, I could see my own mother in her eyes. My eyes clenched and my breath escaped me in a sigh. I looked down at the paper and cleared my throat.

"Citizens of the galaxy, I come to you on this day bearing news of a uniting galaxy. For many years, both our worlds have shared rumors of the existence of the other, and it is time for our leaders to come clean about the truth. To the humans, there is a ninth planet in the Sol System. Planet Nine is real. It is the planet

Elysia. And to the Elysians, you are not alone in this galaxy. Humans live as far as their inventions have managed to take them, and yet your world is hidden from them.

"To Elysia, the humans seek only to build unity and trust amongst our societies, to expand trade and commerce, exchange knowledge and information, and do all that is necessary and possible to improve the lives of our citizens. We seek not to harm, nor start war, but to make an alliance and friendship with the people we have left in the dark for so long. The humans promise life, liberty, and freedom to all Elysians who might seek to enter our society. In times where tensions arise, we believe it necessary to seek the peaceful union of two worlds instead of the destruction of either.

"To the humans, Elysia seeks to protect the social, political, and religious structure of its society. They desire not to compromise the sanctity and sovereignty of their world for the sake of convenience or even to prevent war, were it necessary. The Queen's sovereign decrees are to be respected so far as her jurisdiction reaches, whether it affects human or Elysian. Our world will have closed borders, being careful in who is welcomed and how they are welcomed. Should these restrictions be lessened or lowered, further discussion will occur. For now, Elysia is protected by its armies from any foreign invaders or unwarranted guests until a safe and stable system of trade, commerce, and travel is established. And to all people, knowledge in regards to language and history of the humans or

Elysians will not be restricted by any, whether by civil or martial law, or even royal decree. Humans and Elysians will be allowed to communicate with no limitations to language, so that a proper culture of peace, tolerance, and friendship might be established."

I looked at the last paper, eyes glazing over the words. I hadn't looked at the camera in a fair moment now, simply reading the text for what it said. My hands fell to my sides, the papers bunched in my fist.

"But you're probably wondering who am I to say all this anyways. To the humans, I'm probably that person you saw on TV with a bounty on his head. To the Elysians, I'm just some weird guy with blue hair you've seen on the train or walking down the street, maybe heard rumors about me. In truth, I'm just a normal person like all of you. I went to school, worked a few jobs, and have a kind family. I had dreams, I made mistakes, I fell in love. I think all of you have experienced that too.

"In the short time I've been in contact with the Elysians, I can tell you…we're one in the same. We're all just people trying our best, playing the best game we can with the hand we have. Life hits us hard, and sometimes life hits the people around us hard. We need to remember as our worlds collide that deep down, we're all just people. At the end of the day, our planets will keep orbiting, but together, we can write a hopeful future together. Be kind, be hopeful. When we make a mistake, apologize, and forgive those who wrong us. Welcome new opportunities, make new friends, learn new things. We're all just trying our best to survive, so be kind and forgive one another. Please, it's all I ask of you. Thank you."

The camera clicked as it shut off. A breath of relief filled the room. I nearly fell over as the burden fell off my back. I was only glad it was over, now we wait. The worlds would meld together in peace, or they would fall apart. It was up to the people now, it was out of my hands. I gave a quick prayer, one of thankfulness for carrying me through this and peace upon the people. If all had gone well this far, I believed we wouldn't fall apart now. It was the only hope I held onto.

"How did I do?" I asked The Queen.

"You've done well, Apollo Harrison." She walked forward and took one of my hands, half bowing as she did so. "All of Elysia owes you for your efforts."

The room was astonished by the sight, sovereigns with faces painted in shock and horror. Ata took a knee and bowed as well, Zagreus following with a smug smile at the sight of the sovereigns. Other soldiers in the room bowed, then some of the sovereigns. Not all did, not all would accept me or any of the humans, but no society would ever accept anything completely.

I felt unworthy, but maybe that was the point. I didn't deserve this destiny, but it was given to me. I didn't deserve the tragedy, but I would face it with strength. I didn't deserve the praise, but I would accept it with humility. Something guiding me through the storm, all I had to do was trust whomever it was.

A soldier burst into the room.

"Your Majesty, urgent news."

All rose in an instant. Half expecting the humans to be taking their revenge and half expecting him to say it would rain tomorrow.

"The human ship has returned with two others, they claim they know Apollo, Son of Harris."

The Queen looked at me with questioning in her eyes, I nodded back with a smile that rose. Wendy and Sintara were here. I had much to tell them. We all breathed relief, the tension leaving the room instantly.

"I have more news. The princess, she's awake."

↳ 23 ↵

The Fields

When my eyes opened, it felt as though it was a dream. I thought it was so, just as I had experienced so many times. I'd open my eyes to see him, so close, but when my hand passed through the mist of my mind, I'd be left standing in a field of sun soaked flowers. I'd seen others too; my mother and brother, Wendy and Sintara. No matter how far I reached or how fast I ran, they were always out of my grasp.

Worse than that familiar illusion was the absence of it. My eyes fluttered at the light that burned my eyes. I saw not him but a soldier passing. As a groan passed through my lips, his head turned in a moment.

"She's awake." He'd whispered the words before making a mad dash from the room, shouting. "She's awake! The princess is awake!"

I wasn't in my room, not beside the lovely sight of the city. I was in a room with a low ceiling, cozy blue carpet and gray walls. The furniture was purely functional, and the blankets over me were heavy and thick. My clothes were soft against my skin, but my leg tingled. I could feel my hair pulled up into a bun, and my eyes ached from being closed for so long.

I tried to move myself from where I lay but stopped at the sound of a voice. Just beside me was a radio, once playing the quiet symphony I had heard repeated in my dreams, now echoing a familiar, comforting voice.

"-had dreams, I made mistakes, I fell in love. I think all of you have experienced that too."

"Apollo?" The words left my lips weakly. I reached for the radio, my hand meeting its cold metal softly. Last I saw him, he was bleeding from a hole in his side, but he was alive, we were alive. "Apollo?"

The once still world around me became a whirlwind within a moment's notice. Dr. Petrellis had appeared within the blink of an eye, shouting happily with hard to hear words, vague through the fog of my mind. Part of me didn't want to hear him, I only wanted Apollo here so he could know I was alright.

He poked at my face, flashing a painful light in my eyes, looking in my ears. He wrapped a band around my arm, inflating it and reading a gauge. He listened to my heart, to my breathing. He spoke all throughout, but the words wouldn't reach my ears. I listened only for Apollo, to hear the comfort of his words, the warmth of his touch, the familiarity of his scent. My head spun, but my eyes lay heavy on the door, waiting for his presence. Surely he was nearby, he had to be. He had to know I was okay. He must've been worried sick. The cold metal of a stethoscope touched my ribs and shocked me into lucidity.

"Where is Apollo?" My words hardly reached my own ears still.

The doctor's words had begun to take form in my mind. My head ached from it all. "I need to run some tests first."

"He needs to know I'm alright," I said.

My ears twitched, footsteps approaching. I could hear him, somewhere. His voice boomed through the door, but unlike other noises which twisted me with nausea, I welcomed it. Anxiety twisted my stomach, I would have been eased by the sound of anyone at all, but at his voice I was relieved.

"Let me through damn it! I want to see her!"

The muffled sounds of excuses and pleading fought through the door, the soldiers outside arguing with Apollo loudly. In his words, the panic and fear poured through. He was terrified, putting on that gruff, angry voice he always did when he was uncertain. If they wouldn't let him through, what could that mean for me? What could he assume had happened? What would the people think? What had happened to me?

"I don't give a damn what you've been told, I am going through!"

The arguing continued until the door opened, shouting pouring in with an ache to my head. My mother walked through the door, Apollo shouting as two soldiers fought to keep him from barging in. I felt like a little girl again, ill from the cold I never protected myself from. My heart was so focused on Apollo that I had forgotten just how much I wished for my mother to hold me. I wanted her to bind me in her warm arms and remind me all was well, and I wished that I could say for certain that all was indeed well. But from the worry in her eye seeing the state of her daughter, I knew it was not so.

My mother made no sound as she approached me, rushing to my bedside and wrapping her arms around me. I leaned into the warmth of her hair, the fire of her love melting the ice of my days of loneliness. She was one of the few who could understand my anxiety, and one of the fewer who could ease it. I held her with all the strength left in me, which was admittedly very little. I had spent days whirling through an uncertain dreamworld, she was the rock that proved I truly was awake again.

"Mother, what's happened to me?"

"You've been asleep for nearly a week, my dear." She held close, but leaned to meet my eyes. Tears glazed her irises. Her voice broke at her own words. "I was so worried."

"I'm okay, Mother." I squeezed her arms tightly. "Only bad dreams."

Mother spoke to the doctor, exchanging words my mind was still too foggy to hear. I tried to pull myself up, but Mother pressed me back down.

"Rest, daughter. You need to rest."

"I've been resting for a week, I need to see Apollo, I need to care for my people." My rigid response may have been rude, but I no longer needed to dream. Everything important to me was here, in the waking world. I wouldn't live in my head a second longer.

"Just stay with me, daughter. For just a moment, let me be with you."

I relented to rest, squirming under the sheets as my body began to feel itchy and restless. A breath of ease left her, perhaps she expected me to fight back harder than I had. "What did I miss? What has happened with Apollo and the humans?"

"Your friend has taken to our world quite easily. He's already begun learning our language, and has spent every day the past week working. These days, he helps us communicate with the humans. In the evenings, he visits your friend in the city. He and Ata have been inseparable."

I winced at the words, envy writhed under my skin like a jealous serpent. Apollo would not forget me so easily, would he? Mother recognized the concern covering my face, it seemed. The littlest of laughter escaped her, she found my distress just slightly amusing.

"The two are like siblings, constantly bickering and fighting amongst each other. They can't seem to get along about anything without arguing first, only to find an uneasy mutual agreement at best."

I breathed easy at the words, muscles I had not noticed being tense beginning to relax. Mother smiled at the reaction, taking my hand and squeezing it tightly. Her sadness had been sifted from grief to gladness, she didn't seem to hate Apollo anymore, at least not to any visible extent. Perhaps she only cared because I cared.

"You worry too much, my love. He's been worried ill about you, starting each of his days and ending each of his nights by checking on you. He only managed to see you once, snuck past the guards late at night. He claimed he couldn't sleep out of worry, said he couldn't sleep even further after seeing the state you were in."

"Was I that bad?" I shivered. The doctor brought me a tall glass of water, placing it in my weak hands. Mother helped me rise for a moment, bringing the glass to my lips as she spoke again.

"The doctor assured us you would be fine, he had triple checked. But the human was worried regardless, it seemed he had some personal concern about the procedure."

"The procedure?"

Mother's lip trembled, swallowing down pain in her throat and fighting away tears. She lifted herself off the bed and pulled at the blankets gently, revealing my left leg slowly. The difference was clear as day. My left leg, the one which had been mangled by my monster of an uncle on that ship, was not the same. It was even more pale than my skin already was, nearly as white as a sheet of paper. The blue veins beneath were so clear, it was terrifying. I lifted the edge of my gown slowly, running a finger along the line just above my knee where the skin shifted in shade.

"There was no way of saving your leg, it was simply too broken. We knew we'd have to amputate, but the human claimed to have an answer. We rushed you off to a human hospital, it pained me to watch you be wheeled off into that operation room. They spared me the details of how exactly they did it...it took them hours of operation. Eventually, they brought you out. Cold, pale, comatose." Her shoulders bunched, and her hands balled into fists. I recognized that rage, a mother bear feeling that she's failed to protect her cub. It was terrifying, the anger radiated off her in waves. Her eyes told the story, that she should have never let me follow Apollo into that battle. Vengeance had bound her heart, a vengeance she could never fulfill. All because Ermis was dead. No justice could be served, no pain would mend that desire. "If that good for nothing bastard I called a brother was still alive, I'd kill him myself for what he's done to my...my poor girl. My dear Melinoe...I'm sorry."

Mother had broken into full tears now, crying into her own hands. I drew her into my shoulder, allowing her to cry into my neck as tears rolled down my own face. I looked down at the leg, my leg, but different. It felt similar, but it wasn't perfect. Somehow, someway, I knew it wasn't my own, but it was still me. Just like Apollo's hands, the tone of his skin never matched. It was my own, another me at least.

"It's okay, I'm okay." A shock of laughter escaped me as I considered the joke in my head. "Better to have one foot in the grave than all of me."

"Don't make such jokes!" Mother gasped.

"Only making light of bad times, that's all!" A laugh escaped me again, Mother rolled her eyes, fighting to laugh at my terrible humor. "Blame the humans, they're a terrible influence on me."

Mother wiped tears from her eyes. "Better this than death, I suppose. It isn't fair to you, though."

I took her hands and forced her eyes to meet my own. "Mother, may I please see him now? He did all that work protecting me and bringing me home, he deserves to know I'm well."

She sighed. She did like him, deep down, but the idea of some human being close to her little girl still made her squirm. Were it any other Elysian girl, she wouldn't mind. Matter of fact, she might encourage such kindness between the peoples, as it would help inspire peace. But her little girl beside a human she knew was dangerous, dangerous enough to be the person to put the final blow on Ermis, it didn't sit right with her. Not yet at least. "I suppose I should, before someone ends up with a black eye or broken nose out there…eat first, then I will allow him in."

I nodded. "Deal."

She presented me with a platter of my favorite foods, pastas and deep fried sweet breads. My appetite was lacking regardless, I tried a few bites of the food, but I managed only the toast on the edge of the plate. I could see it in my hands, the bareness of them. I was deeply malnourished, but my stomach twisted in need of something else. Mother placed the plate aside and brushed herself off, wiping at the tears that had started again merely by watching me.

"I'm happy to see you well again, daughter." She sighed and spoke three more words before taking a step away from me. "I love you."

I grabbed her hand before she could leave though, making sure she saw my eyes to her own before speaking. "I love you too."

She smiled, something I had not seen her do so genuinely in years. Not since my father had passed. As she exited, the doors slid open to reveal Apollo sitting against the wall across the hallway. His curls were frizzed and face tinted blue with one eye half swollen, along with a cut on his lip. How hard had he fought the guards to be let in? His brow raised and his face lit instantly, rushing to his feet so quickly he practically tripped through the door.

"Mel!" He shouted in joy, sneakers squeaking as he rushed for my bed. He gave no courtesy for my injury or his own, nor worry for my weakened state, and I didn't want him to. I leaned forward, reaching out for him as he tackled me back into my bed, arms around me tighter than I had ever felt him before.

"I was so worried, I didn't know what to do, and I don't know anything about politics, and I needed you s-" His words were like a flurry, desperate to tell me everything.

I laughed and ran my fingers through his soft hair. "It's okay Apollo! It's okay, I'm here now."

He held my face in his hands, looking at me closely, eyes both filled with pain and relief to see me awake again. Though my eyes were sullen and cheeks weak, I was awake. I could see my own face in the reflection of the deep blue sea of his eyes. Before, they seemed dark and dim. Like a raging storm had swallowed the surface of that ocean whole. I could hardly tell his eyes were blue through his squinting and frowning. Now, his eyes were clear, bright, and shining. The storm was gone, the light had returned.

"I thought I lost you," he whispered, tears rushing down his face in a long river. A sob escaped him. "You said we'd stay by each other's sides. I thought you'd broken our promise."

"Never. I could never. I would never." My own hands met the warmth of his face, the scratchiness of the scruff around his jaw. He choked down his tears. "We're okay, we're gonna be okay."

He nodded with eyes closed tight. "Yeah, you're right—"

I could taste the blood on his lip as I drew him close. He drew a sharp breath in surprise before electricity leaped between us as our lips met. His fingers sifted through the waves of my hair, I felt his curls in my palm. I didn't want to let go, I never wanted to let go again. It could've been for a moment, or for hours, it was all the same to me, but we fell apart from one another as footsteps approached.

Apollo fell back onto the bed, face flush with blue blood hot under his skin, he looked terrified as he eyed the door, praying quietly that my mother would not enter. The footsteps came to the door, then passed. He sighed in relief. A laugh escaped both of us.

"How long have you wanted to do that?" He asked.

"Since you were the only thing I could think of in that prison," I replied with a blush.

His eyes landed on the pale white skin of my leg, placing his hand on it. Our skin was nearly identical in color, even the veins beneath shining the same blue. His face shifted from elation to anguish as he ran a finger along the line where the new and old met.

"We're the same now," he whispered.

"It tingles," I said.

"You get used to it," he said with a nod. "You'll probably struggle to walk for a while, you might not ever walk the same again."

"Better than not walking at all," I added.

He sighed with a look up at me. "When did you become so optimistic?"

"Things sucked, but they got better. If we can survive all this, is there anything we can't survive together?" I placed my hand atop his own. "We did it, Apollo. Can't we celebrate that?"

He nodded yet again, a shy smile covering his face. "You're right."

"Mechri Thanatou," I said.

"Mechri Thanatou," he echoed. I took hold of his chin and drew him near for another kiss, but we jumped apart from one another as a different voice broke the air.

"Are we interrupting something?"

Our eyes snapped to the door as two familiar figures entered the room. Sinatra and Wendy both wore oxygen masks, though Apollo's looked far more comfortable, sitting just under his nose instead of over his whole mouth like theirs did.

"Wendy!" Apollo yelped while tumbling off the bed entirely. I stifled a laugh as he shot back to his feet, fixing his shirt. "I...She uh—"

Wendy ran into him with a tight hug, binding around his ribs so tightly the air was squeezed from his lungs. He heaved for breath in pain as she berated him with her words. She took a half step back and grabbed him by the shoulders tightly, Apollo wincing at the pinched skin beneath and sleeves of his Elysian-made clothing.

"You said you'd talk again when it was safe, and who shows up at my door? David freaking Marshall saying he has a message from you!"

"I know, I'm sorry!" He groaned under Wendy's iron grip. "Did you punch him?"

Wendy slugged him across his sleeve, Apollo producing a shout of pain and stumbling back. "Of course I did! Harder than that, about as hard as YOU deserve for scaring me with your idiocy!"

I felt a warm hand on my shoulder and shifted on the sheets. Sintara stood behind me with a smile that could mend a broken heart, so warm and comforting. Though the smile was through the foggy plastic of an oxygen mask, it was still that same comforting smile which told me all would be well on the spaceport. An embarrassing squeal of excitement escaped me as I threw my arms around her neck.

"Sintara! I missed you so much!"

"I missed you too princess!"

I frowned, leaning into her more. "Don't call me that, everyone calls me that. Please, call me Mel."

"As you wish, Mel."

My weight forced her to take a step back, pulling me away from the edge of the bed I was precariously balanced on. My foot went to catch me, but my new leg had no strength. I tumbled to the ground with a loud thud. I tried to leap back to my feet as Apollo did, but my leg gave way again and I fell back down to the ground.

"Are you alright?" Sintara had come down on one knee, to my level on the ground. Her eyes fell upon my ghastly pale form, weakly pushing against the floor as if I could will myself to walk. Wendy peeked over her shoulder and both of their faces fell dismal. "Ah, I see."

Wendy spoke through the hand over her mouth. "When—How did that happen?"

"About a week ago, I only just woke up." Sintara took my hands and helped me up, balancing on my good leg and placed on the bed like a precious doll. I hated the feeling. "It'll take me some time to get used to it."

"You were supposed to protect her!" Wendy hissed and slapped Apollo's arm again.

"Hey, I got literally stabbed, so don't act like I would have chosen this path for us."

"You WHAT?!" Wendy swatted at him again, but he swiftly stepped out of this one. "What asinine plan of yours led to that result?!"

"It wasn't his fault," I said sternly. "We weren't the only people injured in the battle, we all lost something that day."

Apollo's face joined the chorus of sorrow, his head bobbing in a nod. We both mourned for our friend. "He's alright, by the way. His vision has yet to return to its full strength though."

Wendy and Sintara didn't know who we spoke of, but they relinquished themselves to grief regardless, Sintara speaking her apologies. "I'm sorry for what has happened to all of you."

"It was worth it." The words poured from me before I even gave a second thought to them. I looked at Apollo, to the gentle look in his eyes, the eyes I'd do anything to look into forever. "And I would do it again."

He nodded at me, his eyes speaking for him. He'd do the same for me, but above all, we'd do what was necessary to protect one another, not needless sacrifice. We've both moved on from being heroes, we just wanted to be people again. We wanted to start from scratch, begin again, without the threat of death constantly looming. Wendy cleared her throat, looking smugly between Apollo and I.

"Seems like we did miss something," Wendy said before getting elbowed by Sintara.

I tried to play the fool. "What...do you mean?"

"Only that you've been staring longingly into each other's eyes for a good five minutes. Should I start wedding prep "

Apollo's face was flush with blue. "Ohhh-kay then! Wendy, you didn't happen to read my note did you?"

"Ugh, that I did. Had to go all the way to Earth for it too."

Apollo clapped his hands together. "Excellent! I'll be right back."

With the words, Apollo vanished from sight. A pang shot through my heart, being away from his presence even for a moment. I drew my legs up onto the bed again and sighed, glancing up at Wendy's smug smile. She glanced at Sintara, who also looked at me with a curve to her lips.

"Don't give me that look!" I frowned.

"What look?" Sintara's eyes rose to the ceiling, forcing her smile down with little effort to hide it. She furrowed her brow, a look of nostalgia pouring over her. "He really has changed, hasn't he?"

"That he has." Wendy dropped onto the bed beside me, kicking off her shoes. "Feels like just yesterday I was pulling him out of lakes and beating up his bullies for him."

"Could've sworn I was arresting him for speeding over Arcadia with an unregistered ship just last week, now he's speaking to the masses like some kind of politician."

"If you asked me two weeks ago that I would be putting my life on the line for the selfish, pigheaded man-child who saved my life for a paycheck, I'd think you were crazy." A sigh escaped me and a smile escalated on my face. "To think I can't imagine life without him now."

Sintara nodded, still suppressing that smile. "So, what now? No more running and hiding, Apollo and I are out of jobs, Wendy's probably dying to write a story about this already."

Wendy gave a shrug. "Can't blame a girl for having work ethic."

"I haven't exactly had time to give it much thought, but..." I frowned. What would happen now? I knew there would be work to do, but to find a way to keep Apollo close...but he was no diplomat. He couldn't help run the city. He wouldn't just sit around and do nothing, that much I was certain of. "I'll find both of you something to do around here."

"No need, Zag offered me a job! He's gonna need a lot of help with homeland defense, I'm sure Sintara could find a way to help there." Apollo's voice sent a rush down my spine as he pulled a heavy cart into the room, hovering off the floor by an inch or so. "In the meantime…"

He began rustling through the boxes atop the cart, as well as the large item atop it. I crawled across the bed and looked over the edge as he ducked behind the cart, fiddling with wires and cable. "Is that…?"

"A TV!" He beamed at me. "Henry sent it, with a whole ton of classic human movies."

Wendy rolled her eyes. "Hey genius, how do you intend to plug it in? This isn't Earth, if that wasn't obvious."

"I made an adapter for it, obviously. I am a genius after all." He dipped back under the cart and fiddled with an outlet on the wall as the TV leaped to life. "Only question is what to watch first."

"Apollo, as much as I appreciate the gesture, there's much work to do. We can't just sit around and watch movies-"

He popped back up to his feet and stared at me with a terrified expression on his face. "I love you, but your mother made it very clear to me that if I don't make sure that you take at least three days to rest, she will personally wring my neck, and I have every reason to believe her. For my sake, and your own, let's just rest. I think we've earned it."

I had no reason to not believe him, as a matter of fact, I'd believe this more than her saying she'd kill me for not resting. She could never really hurt me, but threatening Apollo…she was an evil genius, though really I could tell she was growing fond of him.

I sighed, and fell back into the pillows of my bed, though I missed my window in the castle. I looked at Wendy, she gave a smile and a shrug. I looked at Sintara, she gave me a smile and nod.

"I have no place to judge, last time I got a story on the front page I slept for like a day straight from all the hard work," Wendy said.

"I'm unemployed, so I'm no measurement for work ethic," Sintara added with a shrug.

I dropped my face into my hands to hide the joy on my face. A few days to rest did sound nice, the people probably wouldn't even know I woke up until I made an appearance anyways. What would it hurt?

"I don't like the old stuff..." I grumbled. Beggars couldn't be choosers, I supposed. "Alright, fine. What are the options?"

Apollo arose with a disc case in each hand, analyzing them back and forth. "I found one about two short guys who have to throw a piece of jewelry into a volcano and an animated one about a girl with really, really long hair."

"Both are iconic," Sintara added.

My brow furrowed. "Why are they throwing it into a volcano?"

"Why is her hair so long exactly?" Wendy asked while nabbing the box from his hand and looking at the cover.

"Guess we'll just have to watch both and find out...though one takes like twelve hours to watch the whole thing." Apollo said, pulling the box out of Wendy's hand and sliding the disc into the side of the TV.

Sintara set her shoes nicely by the door, arranging Wendy's beside hers. Apollo flopped into the blankets beside me as the movie began. It was entertaining, but I watched him more than the movie. Before long, he was leaning against my shoulder, half asleep. His eyes rose to my own through the frizzy curls of his hair. The blue of his eyes shined like diamonds in the light of the TV.

"I haven't been this relaxed since Earth," I whispered.

He gave a quiet laugh. "That's a low bar."

"My standards are low, it seems." I shrugged. He looked vaguely hurt. "I'm kidding, by the way."

"You've picked up on human comedy well," he mumbled.

I leaned my head against his. "I've got a thing for humans, I guess."

He drew a deep breath and released all the stress in his body. I could feel his shoulders relax, his jaw unclench. He hadn't been this relaxed in far longer than I had. As crude as he was when we first met, he never stopped caring. Self-centered, but not stupid. I had seen what he kept inside of Thirteen, even the hidden parts. He had read every single one of Wendy's stories, kept a stack of photos of his family in his locker, and wore his father's jacket. He was foolish, but not forsaken. He thought he couldn't be forgiven, especially not by his family. I could tell he wanted to go home, see them once more. He was awake now, and a true hero at heart.

I could feel the bandages underneath his shirt, the sensitive skin beneath that. He flinched as my fingers brushed across the healing wound. He'd endured punches, bullets, and blades for me, all without certainty of his own survival. He didn't heal as fast as an Elysian, he wasn't as strong as an Elysian, he wasn't as quick as an Elysian, but he fought regardless. That was what made him so dangerous, a willingness to face pain with gritted teeth for a greater cause. That knife could have struck his heart, he was somehow lucky to say it pierced his lung, but he took the risks and prevailed. Surely, luck could not exist, for his would have run out by now. It wasn't determination that kept him alive, even that is limited. Something else was watching him, guiding him, protecting him.. Now he could fulfill that purpose without danger, without risk or terror. We were protected.

"Hey Mel, can I ask you a question?" His words were timid.

I nodded. "Of course, anything at all."

He hesitated before he began. "Back on Zion, you whispered something to me, but I couldn't hear you. What did you say?"

Butterflies fluttered in my stomach. I remembered that moment vividly. The words I said scared me more than the circumstances I was in. It took more courage to say those three words than anything else I did that day. "I...I said I love you."

Apollo said nothing for a moment, thinking deep on the words. I was terrified for a moment, I couldn't tell what was going on in his head, not even a little bit. It scared me. His lips drew up into the smallest of smiles. "I love you too."

I squeezed him hard, fighting to keep away any tears. I didn't always love him, but that love had grown into something I couldn't ignore. I could feel his heart as I held him. He was mine, and I was his. He found me on that rock, I found the true him after all else had melted away. We found each other. We found us.

"I could get used to this," I sighed with a smile.

"That makes two of us," he replied, leaning heavier into me.

For a brief moment, I felt true peace. In his presence, surrounded by my friends, I felt nothing could hurt me. Our hard work had paid off, all would be well now. We were safe, we could rest without worry.

I whispered into the warmth of his hair. "You are my safety."

He whispered back with the drawl of sleep. "And you are mine."

Epilogue

The cold lapped at my feet, my heart pounding at the freezing water beneath me. The trickle of rain poured from the gray clouds above, running down my face and flowing down my hair. My curls hung heavy in front of my eyes as I looked deep into the waters below.

I'd have stood there forever, until the waters eroded my bones and washed away my blood. I thought if I'd never moved, nothing would change. Like I could ignore the truth. My skin beamed red in protest of the cold. It was cold, but my feet felt like fire.

These beaches were once land. These beaches were once cities, homes, and people. The dunes behind me littered with the remnants of a not so distant civilization, I thought I could feel the ghosts around me. Like their presence was close enough to touch. The waves pushed a child's toy against my foot, a tiny plastic dinosaur with an eroded smile. I could only imagine the child who once adored such a thing, I could only hope they didn't perish when the first tsunami hit.

"Get out of there, you're gonna catch a cold."

Wendy's hand pulled at my shoulder. I spun in protest, stumbling over the tides as water splashed. Her hair was up with a red bandanna, strands pressing against the hood of her sweatshirt. I shook my head.

She frowned. "Don't be stubborn, Apollo."

"Why are you leaving?"

"You know why! It's a good job in a beautiful city!"

"Why are you leaving me?!"

The waves rose, running over her shoes and placing a shiver over her in an instant. I watched the water lap at the leg of her pants. She frowned at it, mumbling a curse.

"Apollo, I'm not leaving you. You don't need me to pull you out of lakes or fight off your bullies anymore. You're gonna be fine, you and Mom and Dad are going to be fine. Before long, you'll probably join me. You know Mom's always wanted to go back—"

"You can't go. Don't go, please." I couldn't hide that it wasn't only rain running down my face now. "You're my only friend."

Her face was pained as she watched me. "Apollo, you don't need me. You're strong, creative, kind, and clever. You know I love you, and you know I want the best for you. But you can't do all the things you were meant to do by being stuck here, stuck to me. I'm not your crutch, I'm your sister. I'll always be your best friend, no matter where in the galaxy you are. You know that, don't you?"

I shook my head in refusal again, sniffing hard. "You can't go to Mars, not without us."

"I'm sad to leave, you know I am. But I have amazing things I want to do too, things I feel like I'm meant to do."

The waves pushed at my feet, pushing me towards the shore, then pulling me back towards the sea. All this drama, all this emotion over something so trivial. But in my heart, it felt like the world was ending.

"I don't want to be alone, not in such a dangerous world."

"I've spent all these years trying to protect you, not because I wanted to protect you forever, but because I wanted to teach you how to protect yourself. Now you're taller and stronger than me, and you don't need me anymore. I know you're going to do amazing things, I know it."

"How can you know?!"

She threw her hands at me exasperatedly. Her eyes grew exhausted as she looked around as if trying to find some evidence of the conviction in her heart. It wasn't that I didn't believe her, I just couldn't explain why I believed her so much.

"I don't know how I know! I just…I just do. Something in this world, something immeasurable, something immaterial, it tells me that you were made for something. I know it sounds like nonsense, and I know you only ever trust that which you can see and feel, but I need you to believe for just a moment that you are not just a cosmic accident. That you have purpose and meaning. That everything to ever live and breathe and think has something in them that makes them who they are. We may be made of flesh and bone, but that isn't all we are.

"I know you're scared. I've been scared before. I'm scared right now. But I'm not asking you to be fearless, I'm just asking you to trust…me. Trust me that everything will be alright, that you'll find a way. You might not believe it in the way I do, definitely not the reasons I do, but believe me. Have faith, Apollo. You trust gravity to keep your feet on the ground, you trust physics to make a ship fly. I'm just asking you to trust…that bad things happen sometimes, and then good things happen. Call it chance, or fate, or coincidence. I call it God. And I know so many people have used that word to justify so many terrible things, but I'm asking you to let me have faith in Him to protect you, to guide you. I haven't always believed, and there will be times that make that really hard to believe, but I need something immaterial right now, and you do too. I'm terrified to live on a planet I've never been to, to work a job with people I've never met, but I trust that I'm protected. I can't tell you why, but I trust something greater than me. We all do, sometimes. It's what makes us human."

The tide disappeared from my feet. The tide had pulled back, fading back into the ocean ever so gently. Only the smallest depth of water lay in pools around my feet, sunk into the sand below me.

"I have to go, Apollo, my transport leaves in an hour." She grabbed me by the shoulder with an iron grip, demanding I look her in the eyes. Her eyes were the same as my own, that deep blue Dad had. It was genetics which made us so identical in this way, but the soul behind the eyes was something unique. "Trust me in this, Apollo. Please. Of all things for you to trust me, I need it to be this, and for you to never forget that."

"I…"

"Just nod."

I nodded. Her warm arms wrapped around me as I relented myself to tears. I never cried around anyone else, not Mom or Dad or anybody on Earth, but to Wendy I always felt safe. My safety was leaving, and I had to find some new way to be safe.

"Now get out of the cold and come say goodbye. You'll have plenty of time to brood once I'm gone, and I know you will."

"You're not wrong," I said with the croak of sadness in my throat.

Wendy hugged me again, harder than before. "I can't wait for you to join me up there, to see all the amazing things you'll do. I've been dreaming about it ever since Mom and Dad brought you home from the hospital and placed you in my arms."

↵ ↵ ↵

Oil smudged across my nose and my knees cracked as I arose from my crouched posture. My hands, smeared black with grime, ached at the weight of the tools. I hadn't worked this much in a while, bounty life had treated me well enough to keep me out of the blue collar for a while. Between the bounty payouts, supply runs, and transport jobs, I was able to keep my hands clean of anything but blood for a while. Being back to daily work was odd to say the least.

I wiped my fingers on a rag and returned to my drafting desk, taking hold of the blueprints I had sketched out and holding it up to the metal above me. Something about the curve wasn't right, but I had sworn I'd checked thrice. Was the ceiling crooked? Couldn't be.

Somebody had entered my workshop, though the fact that they got in at all assured they were somebody trustworthy. I placed my blueprint back onto the desk, wincing at the smudge of grease on the paper as I tried to wipe it off, only making it worse. I twisted the knob on my radio as the figure came around the side of my project, the quiet piano quieting further so as not to interrupt the conversation that would inevitably begin.

"Burning the midnight oil? It's a miracle you don't fall asleep on the job to music like that." Zag asked, swiping on a tablet while giving a glance at the behemoth standing over him. "Seems like it's coming along."

"Slower than I would've liked," I said while letting go of a breath of exasperation. I drew in my next breath, my oxygen concentrator whirring along with it. "How can I help you this fine evening?"

"New project for you this week, a repair really." He placed the tablet down on my desk and let me analyze it.

I grunted as I swiped through the pictures. "I warned them the airframe would bend if they pulled those maneuvers in the atmosphere."

"Well, you know soldiers, orders are optional when some eggheaded engineer gives them." At least, they are when it's Ata you're ordering around. Zag leaned against the frame and gave an attempt at shaking the hulking thing. "Sturdy already. Can't build these for our ships?"

I shook my head, turning off the tablet Zag had left and placing it in a drawer with several other tablets. No rest for the wicked. Not even on Elysia, it seemed. "It'll be slower than a boat when it's finished. You asked for fast, not sturdy. You can't always have both. My fighting days are behind me, this is purely for business."

Zagreus looked at the blueprints for himself, eyes following the curves I had just been analyzing. He mumbled. "Looks crooked."

I rolled my eyes hard, clear enough for him to see. I leaned heavily on my desk, I was more tired than I cared to admit. There was a reason I didn't sit on the job this late at night. "Did you come all the way out here just to give me something you could have emailed and insult my project or...?"

"You know I can't hardly understand those email things." He shuddered at the idea of using our tech, it was hard enough to teach him as is. He was unappreciative of Wendy's gift to him; a laptop. I've never seen a man so miserable, all to answer the billions of questions from a reporter. "You also know I hate coming this far out into the woods, I wouldn't have come if it wasn't important. Seen any witches lately?"

"No, but when I do see one I'll make sure to send them your way."

"I would gladly put a bullet in one." He tried to speak with all of his courage, but the fear of childhood stories about the witches was still clear in his mind. The corner of his jaw was taut with anxiety, something Mel taught me to look for in him.

I tried to ease the atmosphere, not too much of course. I liked messing with the most dangerous man on Elysia, especially when he's scared out of his mind. "Don't let them spook you too bad, I had one over for tea the other day. Lovely gal, really."

Zag leaped up onto the half-finished floor. The beams of metal reaching up around him in the shape of what would eventually be the body of the new Thirteen. It looked like the ribcage of an ancient beast swallowing him whole. He looked up at the bare outlines that would later be wings. "Your fighting days are behind us for now, but you never know. We might need something more dangerous."

"Don't start sounding like your uncle," I replied. "I have some old designs for faster, stronger ships. Fastest ships in the galaxy at that, just an absolute pain to manufacture, and crazy expensive. Luckily they're behind a bio-scanner that only I can access."

"Humans landed on Elysia the other day." Zag kicked at the floor panels a bit, checking to see if they were sturdy. "They haven't left either."

I could believe him. In the month of connection between humans and Elysians, the progress was slower than even I expected. The humans were antsy to see the new world, Elysians were already roaming free amongst the humans. Elysia was going to be starting travel authorization soon, much faster than they had wanted to due to the incessant begging of the crown princess. I knew this would slow the progress of that. "Couldn't wait another week? Let me guess, new age hippies wanting to meditate on the new planet?"

"Worse, they call themselves Angel Lights. Have you heard of them?"

My own childhood fear arose in my heart. The stories of how they'd drive a stake through my heart, or hang me by my toes off a bridge. Never any explanation of why they'd hate people like me so much, never any reason behind their fear mongering. It was evil under the guise of religious fervor, at least that's what Dad always told me. He drew a clear line in the sand where religion ends and cult began, and never agreed with an ounce of what they believed. He knew real righteous anger, I watched him sock one in the face for giving me a side eye one time. He told me that God loves everyone, but he loves them enough to teach hard lessons sometimes, even if they come in the form of a broken nose. I asked him if I could punch an Angel Light too, he said I could when I was older.

"You should get them off Elysia as fast as possible. They're not here for any good, that's for sure."

"Funny you say that, cause we tried. Landed on the edge of the city, my men intercepted. They followed protocol as per my instruction right up until the shots started." Zagreus dropped from the project and slammed to the ground. "Killed one of my men somehow, a bullet went straight through his helmet. They injured another before they retreated. Ran off and abandoned their ship before we could catch the lot of them. Was nothing left on there but religious text that I sincerely hope the majority of you don't believe. Who are they, Apollo?"

I swallowed the fear welling in my throat as Zag's serious eyes met my own. He might have asked Wendy if she wasn't back on Mars writing news stories, or Sintara if she hadn't been back on Earth trying to bring Henry to Elysia. This was serious, a failure on our hands. "They're a cult, Earthling psychos who hate anything unlike them. They can just barely stand anyone not from Earth, but they hate half-bloods like me. If I had to guess, they're definitely not too fond of something that isn't human at all. They're a tiny portion of our population, a real black sheep when it comes to religion. Real believers hate their guts, understandably. The guy who founded them was a psychotic eugenist billionaire from the old Earth days. Whatever they're here for, we need to find them."

"I have a search party following their trail now. Seems they're heading for the eastern villages." They're heading towards me, towards my safehouse. Zag leaned against the drafting desk and drew in a deep breath. He gently turned the music up and let out a sigh as the relaxing tune eased his posture. He spoke with a peace that didn't match the urgency of his words. "You do understand the implications of these people running rampant on Elysia, don't you? An innocent Elysian was just killed by a trespassing Earthling, this could set us back weeks of progress."

"If I had to guess, that's exactly what they want. If they can prevent Elysia and the humans from uniting, they would be thrilled with the amount of credibility that lends them." I groaned at the thought of it, I didn't want to fight anymore. "I'll go look for them myself if I have too."

"There shouldn't be any need. Unless they intend to unify with the outer villages, they'll never have enough people to shake us. They got the jump on us, but we'll be ready next time. Just wanted you to know that there's crazed killers wandering the woods around here, that's why I came." He said it with such a lack of care, I wondered if he actually did.

"I'll keep my doors locked and my eyes peeled." I mumbled, anxiety tying a knot in my own jaw now.

"I'm not underestimating these people, not this time. I hope you do the same." Zag shrugged with a half smug, half frustrated look. "I'm sure it will be fine though. Pretty music."

I nodded, teeth still gritted out of fear. The urge to check the cameras all around the area was strong. I relented to the distraction. "It's Earth stuff, really old Earth stuff. I'm a fan of the classics."

"You humans know how to make good music, that much is true." Zag made tracks for the door, imparting one last word before he left. "I told Mel about this, by the way. She says she's coming to stay for the weekend, with the whole of her guard, just to assure your safety. Do try to accommodate them well until this all blows over."

"Ugh, you do know I hate prissy royalty in my shop, they never stop asking questions." I groaned teasingly.

"Rude!" A slap ran across my shoulder as Mel appeared at my side. I'd have flinched harder if I hadn't heard her suppress a laugh just a few moments prior. She was wearing human clothes, a few choice favorites of a massive wardrobe Wendy had sent as a gift. "And there go my hopes of startling you."

"My apologies, princess, I didn't know you were listening," I said smugly. Had I not known the royal siblings' desire to mess with me, I might not have seen it coming. Luckily, they were predictable in this sense.

"Don't call me that, anyone but you." She placed a kiss on my forehead, making me flush blue with embarrassment in front of Zagreus. I cleared my throat harshly and turned back to him, swallowing my pride and ignoring Mel's smugness.

"Well, if there's nothing else I can help you with, the night is young. Got any fun plans?"

He stopped at the door and shook his head, back towards me. "Not with these animals running around. I'll rest when they're in cuffs."

I nodded slowly. I agreed, and was grateful he was willing to go on the hunt. I wanted to leave fighting behind me, maybe being a diplomat wasn't so bad, I was starting to get pretty good at it too. But at the bottom of that drawer filled with projects sat a hard drive I wished I could forget. The blueprints for The Dark Matter. I never wanted to see that ship again, especially not to be used to hunt Elysians or humans. "That's uh...valid."

Zagreus shrugged and gave a look over his shoulder. "Regardless, I would not want to stay around here. Can't stand those human movies. They're all so predictable, I don't get how you can watch them over and over again."

"Don't let the witches bite," I said as he left. He gave an Elysian gesture with both hands, one with a very rude meaning. I laughed at it.

"You seem to be getting along well." Mel said while placing her head on the top of my own, reminding me of her height over me as always.

In truth, I very much enjoyed working with Zagreus, he was dry and serious at times, but also knew when to have fun and let loose. But this was different, something pulled at the charisma deep within him. I could see it in his body language, something

Mel continued to teach me how to read better. Tonight, he was stiff. He was worried about what this might mean for him, for us. Nobody could blame him for such a freak incident, but he most certainly blamed himself.

"Hey, you alright?" Mel's voice broke the whirlwind of my mind and made everything stand still.

I nodded. "Yeah, just worried about him."

"He'll be alright. We're all worried, he's just the worst at hiding it."

I half-laughed at that. Were it less true, I'd find it hilarious. In reality, we all shared that same anxiety. Beyond humans roaming on Elysia, especially Angel Lights, we'd all been worried sick. Working hard kept our minds off the stress, but it felt like the whole world was resting on our shoulders. The balance of the world was on a knife's edge, and we were the only people keeping it there. I'd grown sick of being so important, I wanted to go back to being nobody.

Mel ran a hand through my hair, greasy and frizzy as ever. Some of the tangles caught on her nails, making me flinch from the sudden pull. She gave a small laugh and whispered an apology before continuing. Her voice was quiet and tender. Her words made me feel at home, safe. Everything about her presence was calming. My anxiety melted away like honey in warm tea, leaving nothing but sweetness. "You look tired."

"It's been a long week." I drew in a deep breath. I looked up at her through the curls of my hair with a smile. "Nothing some Earth movies won't fix, right?"

A massive smile was pulled across her face. "I like the way you think."

↔ ↔ ↔

My head pounded as I rolled out of bed. My feet carried me across the cold ground and through a door into the bathroom. I steadied myself on the counter as I gagged into the sink. The room spun around me, and my eyes burned with pain no matter how hard I closed them.

The lights began to turn on slowly, starting from the dimmest of light and rising. All lights in Elysia did so, for the sake of saving one's eyes. I could see shadows dancing on the walls behind me through the mirror, my sickly form weak amongst the weight of all that surrounded me. I spat into the sink, a smear of blue running down the side. Had I bit my lip in my sleep? I could taste blood, I just didn't know where it came from.

After my battle with Zivko, dreams like memories were taking hold. Constantly reliving his final moments, constantly feeling the blood on my hands. But after the battle against Ermis, watching that hypercore explode, I'd been haunted by the strangest dreams imaginable. I couldn't tell anyone, not at the sake of being ridiculed or labeled insane. Nobody else had spoken out about weird dreams, surely Mel would have told me. These dreams were simply too bizarre to speak of.

They were always about the same, myself standing atop a mountain looking down over Elysia. I could see a city below me, Castle Ouranos reaching into the sky. A red glow started at the center of it all, growing until it ate up the buildings around it, growing until Castle Ouranos fell, growing until it burned away the forests around me. I'd run, run as fast as I could, stumbling down the mountain, tumbling down hills and off rocks. I could never run fast enough. When the fire reached me, I could feel it climbing up my clothes and melting my skin. Images rushed through my head in a blinding succession.

People bowing, screaming, calling for help, singing with reverence. Fingers pointed at me, figures running in fear, figures pursuing me with war cries. Mel's body in my arms, motionless, breathless. Sintara's tear ridden face, Theseus's disgusted look, Wendy's horror. When I opened my eyes against the flame, I found it had condensed to a point below me. My body was bound to a pyre, and a flame arose. I was surrounded by thousands, faces painted and blades drawn. Uncertainty on their faces, unsure if they'd done right. No matter how much I screamed my apologies, begged for forgiveness, called for my mother, they never moved an inch. I felt the fire crawl up me, burn away my flesh. I felt every moment of it.

When I awoke, it was always the same. A dizzy head, a body still feeling the lingering burn, the taste of blood from my screams. Like it had truly happened, like it would happen again. It happened every other night, at some point I came to expect it. Sometimes I would stop running from the fire, sometimes I would stop begging for forgiveness. I'd run into the fire, scream my curses instead. Like an animal desperate for release, whether release from captivity or from the mortal coil. I'd do anything to make them stop, and thinking I could make it stop was exactly what made it all so maddening.

When did I get so poetic? The lights had risen now. I could see the blood on my lip, the bags under my eyes. I couldn't take another week of these dreams and the restless nights, I'd go crazy, if I hadn't already. I splashed some cold water on my face, hoping to wash away the dreams and the blood. My eyes watched the now-vaguely-blue water swirl down the drain. Something caught my eye. I squinted as I analyzed the swirling water. Something was in there, something thin and metallic. It was sharp and pointed. A needle.

Whatever blood was left in me had run cold. I had no time to ponder the discovery. My ears perked at a noise, almost imperceptible, that made me shudder. It was muffled, pushing through the walls to reach me. A voice, one of a woman. Not speaking, but singing. By all means, the singing was beautiful, but echoing through the trees around my remote home in the woods, it was direly misplaced, especially in the haunting darkness almost identical to day that the Elysians called night. Those woods at night were darker than anything I had ever seen before. Nobody could navigate them at this hour by any natural means. No human or Elysian anyways.

It was a calm, sweet melody. At any other time, I might have even found it relaxing. But in this moment, in this context, the uncanniness overwhelmed the melody. I gave myself a pinch, hoping I was dreaming. I was horrified to find I wasn't.

I left the bathroom with my face still soaking wet, rushing through the dark of my bedroom to my nightstand and throwing open the drawer. I took hold of what was inside. Safety overwhelmed me at the weight of it in my hand. Entering the hallway, my hands held tense on my handgun, as if whatever phantom singer was haunting me might appear out of thin air.

When I entered the hangar, the singing got louder. Its melody became more dissonant, like a warped vinyl croaking out its distorted tune. It was impossible to say whether more voices had joined the chorus, or if the echo off the trees made one voice sound like many. The smell of hot metal hit my nose, making me flinch as the pungent smell assaulted my senses.

"What is that?" Mel asked just behind me, my soul leaving my body in fear. I mumbled a curse and shook my head as she came to my side.

"No idea." My voice was cracked and croaky from the rawness of my bleeding throat. I eyed the human sized door leading out of the hangar. "Damn it, I don't want to find out."

My hand shook as it rose to the panel of the door. I could feel Mel's tension behind me as I twisted the panel. Cold air hit me like a truck, and the song stopped immediately. A sound like wind rustling through the trees and branches swirled around us as we stepped out into the night.

All sound stopped. The air was completely still, nothing to rustle branches or leaves. I could feel something. Something was in the woods, surrounding us. I took a wary step towards the corner of the hangar, towards the large door that opened to the construction of the new Thirteen. With one step, the sounds lit all around us again. A chorus of whispers, dozens of voices saying one word on repeat. My translator refused to tell me the meaning of any of it.

"Gios'Haus. Gios'Haus. Gios'Haus."

That word, I knew that word. I'd heard it whispered to me on the streets, in my dreams. I knew the word without knowing its meaning, yet it felt so personal. I could feel the edge of it, cutting into me. The word was like a knife buried into my chest.

A shadow moved in the corner of my eye. My hands whipped towards it and took a shot. The whispers ceased, my ears rang, I was frozen by fear. In the muzzle flash of the shot, I could have sworn on my life that I saw the reflection of dozens of eyes watching me from the bushes, from behind trees, even up in the branches.

"Gios'Haus, Gios'Astrias. Eleus, eleus!"

I backed up into Mel as my eyes caught a figure lurching around the corner of the hangar. The fur of some animal was bound around her hunched shoulders over a thick, muddy robe. The wrinkled skin of her arms gleaned in the light pouring out from the door, dark geometric tattoos covering her arms and neck. Her dark pink hair reached the ground in gnarled braids, smeared with dirt and twigs caught in the tangle. A wooden mask covered the whole of her face, only the piercing white of her eyes shone through slits in the black wood. It looked heavy, carved with something like runes.

Long antlers reached from her head, I couldn't tell if it was part of the mask or part of her. String stretched between the antlers, sprigs of trees and charms dangling from the thread. Her head twitched as she moved closer, back hunched over like a beast curled in on itself. She moved in stuttered movements, like a doll yanked along on a string. Something in me screamed. A fear I never knew before. I had seen evil in the material, but this was something else. Corruption of the physical, abomination of the design. Supernatural evil. It was vile.

"Gios'Haus, afino, echite eleus!' Her voice was like a creaking door, the legs of a chair scraping the floor. It made me cringe, made my heart race. I gagged. Something poked pain into my throat.

Mel was breathless, grabbing my shoulders with a vice grip. Her voice wavered in fear. "Titans, it's a witch."

The thing hissed at the word, reeling back. She shook it off, clicking her tongue a few times and looking off into the woods at her army which surrounded us. I hoped it was an army of people and not spirits. I could kill one of those options. Her head twitched, then twitched again, like listening close to some whisper from far off. She whispered some words to herself, pointing a bony finger at me.

It felt like a needle punched through my chest, a thread wrapping around my heart. Something rose in my throat, I thought for sure I would throw up out of fear. A sound came from the woods, the sound of someone imitating the call of a bird. The figure's head snapped at the sound, gave a growl, then hobbled back behind the corner of the hangar.

A well of courage opened within me, and I rushed around the corner myself. In the floodlights coating the area just outside the hangar door, the thing had vanished, but something new had appeared. Burned into the metal of the hangar door was text, in both Elysian and English. Words, disjointed and unconnected from any meaning I could understand. Abomination. Apocalypse. Ablaze. But one phrase was repeated several times. The prophecy.

"Titans..." Mel gasped, staring up at the mural of insanity.

"What does it say?" I asked.

"Omen. Immolation. Destruction. False prophet." She squinted at the words hard fear welling within her. "Gios'Haus."

That damn word. "What does it mean?"

"Son of Chaos. That which precedes destruction." She pointed to the longest stretch of words along the bottom, etched in Elysian text. "This is the only part I can make any sense of."

"And that is?"

"It says 'the prophecy is in motion.'" She drew in a quick, shallow breath. "'This is only the beginning.'"

Acknowledgements

Firstly, I'd like to thank The Lord for blessing me with the opportunity to write this book. At the end of it all, I can't do any of this without Him. He's the air I breathe, the rest I find, the dreams in my head. Everything and anything I do, I do through Him. I hope and I pray that this book is used to glorify Him, to show His love and mercy in every story. I believe He gave me the idea for this story for a reason, and I hope He uses it as He sees fit to reach the hearts of people. For all those reading, I hope and I pray that you find God's light in every part of every story you read. He is at the center of it all, remember to look for Him.

Secondly, I'd like to thank my editor-in-chief, my primary beta reader, my brainstormer, my biggest fan, and my wonderful girlfriend, Tabitha Hood. The amount of time and dedication that you've put into this book, all without the promise of getting anything in return, is so much more than I deserve to be given. This book would not have been possible without you, and if it did, it would be a whole lot worse. Every day that you helped, encouraged, critiqued, edited, uplifted, formatted, and inspired me throughout the journey to create this book was a blessing. I feel as though you deserve to be a co-author for this project considering how much of your advice I followed in creating it. I would stand to argue that a fair percentage of this book was your own creation, a dream we shared together as we created and built these characters and world from the ground up. I feel this world is just as much yours as it is mine, and there's no one I would rather share it with. Don't ever stop being you. Until the end of time, and to the moon and back, I love you. Thank you for everything you did to make this possible.

Thirdly, I'd like to thank everyone else who encouraged me, believed in me, supported me, and was curious about this project. This has been a much quieter project compared to my last, but to the few people who did know, your wonder and curiosity of my work was often the thing that encouraged me through the sloughs of writing. My thanks go out particularly to Simone Huynh and Thomas Haskins who so gratefully blessed this work with visual elements I could never have pieced together on my own. Your care for this story means the world to me. To every other family member, friend, and coworker who ever shared even a fraction of interest, thank you. I'm so excited to finally say that this is finally out.

Fourthly, I'd like to thank the media which inspired this book so much. I know it's not likely that anyone associated with these will read this, but on the off chance they do, I'd like to list a few things that inspired this work so greatly. Also, if you're not interested in a long list of media to check out, feel free to skip this paragraph. I won't judge. A few songs that inspired this book include Home's Resonance, Pink Floyd's The Great Gig in the Sky, C418's Ki, Childish Gambino's Me and Your Mama,

Radiohead's Exit Music (For A Film), Glare's Void in Blue, and lastly but most certainly not least, Ark Patrol's Let Go. A lot of emphasis on that last song, it seriously changed my brain chemistry in a way that made me unable to stop imagining this story endlessly. Movies, TV shows, and games that were a big inspiration, even in the first draft made back in 2019, are Netflix's Voltron: Legendary Defender, Netflix's Arcane, Christopher Nolan's Interstellar and Tenet, Adult Swim's Cowboy Bebop, Gareth Edwards' The Creator, Dennis Villeneuve's Dune and Dune: Part Two, Bethesda's Starfield, Bungie's Halo: Reach, Amazon Prime's Invincible, Disney's Percy Jackson show, and Supergiant's Hades and Hades II. That's a long list of many things that probably seem super disjointed and random, but I promise that every single last one of those pieces of media influenced this book in one way or another. Obviously, a lot was inspired by Greek mythology as well, so shout out to Homer and Hesiod I guess. I will admit though, I've learned most of my Greek mythology through Hades and Percy Jackson, as well as greekmythology.com (shout out to you guys by the way, you guys helped me so much). Lastly, but not least, the podcast Haunted Cosmos by Benjamin Garrett and Brian Sauvé. In case one of you guys read this, just know how much your work inspires me.

Finally, I'd like to thank you. Yes, the person reading this. I'm talking to you now, so pay attention if you haven't so far. Thanks for reading my book. I know that's probably pretty simple, but that's all I really want to say. Of course, I'll say it in a much more poetic way. Us writers can't help it, it's a bad habit.

The truth is, none of this is possible without you. All of us creatives know that our work isn't much without an audience. Whether it be a song, a book, a show, a game, a movie, a podcast, or whatever other media you make, it isn't much until someone takes it, loves it, dreams with it. I have a lot of projects that will never see the light of day, and the truth is, they're not very alive because of it. I may build the world, but you're the one keeping it alive. We share something in common now, a world in our head that lives so long as we remember it. In a way, these characters are alive because we share them in our minds. The world of Elysia lives on so long as each of you know it exists. So, on behalf of Apollo, Mel, and all the others, thank you.

To all the dreamers out there, keep dreaming. To the musicians, keep playing. To the writers, keep writing. To the painters, keep painting. To the creators, keep creating. We're all image bearers of the creator, it's in our nature to want to create things just like Our Father, so keep doing it. Do it for His glory, do it to make Him smile. Keep creating, keep dreaming, keep adventuring. God's got something amazing for you to make, so go make it. Don't waste a moment. Keep doing what makes your soul leap with joy. Chase that horizon, make a new trail, climb that mountain. Be the person God designed you to be.

-Your ally, your brother, your friend

Jack Cherry

About the author

Jack Cherry is a Pacific Northwest native, born and raised under the cloud cover and rainfall of Oregon and Washington. After many years of learning storytelling through many different media, he's turned to fiction writing to retell the True Myth of the real world in hopes of bringing glory to Christ.

While building and self-publishing these unique but broken worlds, he also spends his hours pursuing a higher education in hopes of mastering the craft of writing and growing closer to God. He does this in search of learning how to better speak to the human heart and inspire others through characters and story, inspired by the masterful works of C.S. Lewis and J.R.R Tolkien.

Like those titans of storytelling before him, he hopes to show others the light and hope of Christ in a broken world. Not just through our own world, but through the brokenness of every world, fiction and nonfiction, which lives in dire need of a savior. He seeks to show that every person, each just as broken and sinful as his own characters, can be heroes through Christ, while inspiring the saints to pick up their swords and fight back against the darkness which tries to suffocate God's creation.

Made in the USA
Columbia, SC
08 November 2024

21526142-009d-4cf1-9808-bf22a37b8503R01

.